A GIRL
of her
TIME

by the author of
Ring of Clay

'A perfect novel . . . Kaine is great at conveying the
tough times following the Second World War. Beth is an
inspiring heroine, and readers will love her rise from
rags to riches.' *Irish Tatler*

'Kaine has a gift for storytelling.' *Woman's Way*

'A tense and compelling epic.' *U Magazine*

and

Rosemary

'A riveting story, absorbingly told.' *Ireland on Sunday*

'Kaine is a fantastic storyteller and has a knack for
connecting with the reader and making her characters
seem true to life.' *Woman's Way*

About the author

Born and educated in Stoke-on-Trent, Margaret Kaine now lives in Leicester. She began writing ten years ago and her short stories have been published in women's magazines in Great Britain, Ireland, Australia, South Africa and Norway. Her first novel, *Ring of Clay*, won the 2002 Romantic Novelists' Association/Reader's Digest Of Love and Life New Writer's Award and the Society of Authors' Sagittarius Prize for 2003.

A GIRL
of her
TIME

Margaret
KAINE

CORONET BOOKS
Hodder & Stoughton

Copyright © 2004 by Margaret Kaine

First published in 2004 by Poolbeg Press Ltd
First published in Great Britain in 2004 by Hodder and Stoughton
A division of Hodder Headline

The right of Margaret Kaine to be identified as the Author
of the Work has been asserted by her in accordance with the
Copyright, Designs and Patents Act 1988.

A Coronet paperback

3 5 7 9 10 8 6 4 2

A CIP catalogue record for this title is
available from the British Library

ISBN 978 0 340 82827 4

Typeset in Plantin Light by Palimpsest Book Production Limited,
Polmont, Stirlingshire
Printed and bound by CPI Group
(UK) Ltd, Croydon, CR0 4YY

Hodder Headline's policy is to use papers that are natural,
renewable and recyclable products and made from wood
grown in sustainable forests. The logging and manufacturing
processes are expected to conform to the environmental
regulations of the country of origin.

Hodder and Stoughton
A division of Hodder Headline
338 Euston Road
London NW1 3BH

ACKNOWLEDGEMENTS

My special gratitude to Biddy Nelson,
whose interest and perception during the
writing of this novel have been invaluable,
to the Wednesday morning writers' workshop
in Wellington Street, Leicester, for their
friendship and constructive literary
criticism, and, as always, to my
husband, Graham, for his
unfailing support.

For my son, Matthew

"The mind should teach
the heart to feel;
the heart should teach the mind to see."

St Thomas Aquinas

PROLOGUE

In the silent kitchen, Maureen lifted out an egg from the frying-pan and placed it carefully on top of a triangle of fried bread. Already on the warm plate were two rashers of smoked bacon, and two links of pork sausage. Her husband was very fussy about his cooked breakfast. It had to be precisely the same every morning, and she knew that in five minutes he would come downstairs expectantly, wearing the suit she had pressed, the shirt she had ironed.

"I'll say one thing for her," she'd once heard her mother-in-law say. "She turns him out well."

And Maureen did. Just as her own appearance was always neat. Not flamboyant mind, he wouldn't have liked that, any more than he liked her to wear nail varnish. In the two years since he'd returned from doing his National Service in Germany, Maureen had discovered that her husband didn't like a lot of things.

She peered through the net curtain. It was raining; not a heavy downpour, but the sort of misty dampness which clung to your hair and clothes.

For one long moment she remained motionless, then putting on her coat she picked up her handbag, unlocked the back door and stepping out closed it quietly behind her. On tiptoe, she crept down the side of the house and turned into the narrow road. With the sound of her high heels tapping on the pavement, she saw no-one, not even when she turned the corner.

Inside, the table was set in readiness, the brown teapot was snug under its knitted cosy. The note, already beginning to curl over at the top, was propped against a bottle of HP sauce. Just an ordinary piece of lined paper torn out of an old exercise book, it held one line:

Gone for a walk, M

CHAPTER ONE

August, 1956

Maureen had always been deep. It was a trait in her character which even as a child had caused many a muttered dark comment. The Matthews family were suspicious of people who hid their feelings. But Maureen was a watcher, a thinker; as her mother Beryl would say, you never knew what was going on in that head of hers.

By the time she was seventeen, they knew they had a beauty in their midst, although where that hair, black as a raven's wing, had come from, was a mystery. Fortunately, Maureen had also inherited her father's aquiline nose, albeit a more delicate, classical version, which deflected any dubious thoughts about Beryl.

Sandra, who was five years older than Maureen and recently married, had almost wept when she'd first seen her wedding photographs. There she was in all her white finery, and who shone out of the picture? Her younger sister, smiling into the camera, a stunning vision in lilac organza.

"There's no justice in this world," she moaned. "Look at me, I look mousy and fat against her!"

"If you go through life looking for justice, you're going to be sorely disappointed," Beryl snapped. Because of her elder daughter's generous and uncomplicated nature, she knew that any jealousy she felt would be short-lived. Beryl did worry about her younger child, but then Beryl worried about everything.

"If you hadn't got anything to be mithered about, you'd find something," her husband complained, one Saturday morning.

"Well, you wouldn't know, would you? Everything's like water off a duck's back where you're concerned."

But Frank just shrugged and, waiting until Beryl had gone into the kitchen, turned to the racing pages. If he was quick, he could perhaps get a bet on

4

before dinner. A few minutes later, he slipped on his jacket and called, "I'm just going to have a word with Alan!"

"It'll be on the table in half an hour."

"Where's Dad gone?" Maureen had heard him go out as she came down the steep stairs, which led directly into the kitchen, and latched the stair door behind her to keep out the draught.

"Along to see Alan. Probably about his allotment."

Maureen grinned. Everyone knew that Alan, who lived six doors away, acted as a bookie's runner for the local streets. Except her mum, of course. Beryl didn't gossip much with the neighbours.

"I suppose you're off into Stoke this afternoon?"

"Yes. I want to get 'Que Sera, Sera'." She sang the words in perfect pitch, and Beryl smiled. The girl was mad on Doris Day and popular music, and spent all her money on records.

* * *

"Set the table, then come and do the bread and butter, will you." It was an order rather than a question, and Maureen automatically obeyed.

"We always have egg and chips on Saturdays," she grumbled.

"Well, your dad likes it, and it pays to keep him

happy!" Beryl went into the narrow, dark scullery and put slab of lard in a pan ready to heat.

"That's all women do," muttered Maureen, "pander to men."

"Yes, and your turn will come, lady! Are you keeping an eye on that butter?"

Maureen rescued the butter-dish, which she'd placed near the fire, and began to cut a large crusty loaf. Beryl looked on approvingly. Maureen could slice bread wafer-thin, not like Sandra, whose offerings always looked like doorsteps. Fleetingly, she wondered how her elder daughter was getting on. The young couple had put their names down on the waiting-list for a council house. In the meantime they were beginning their married life living with John's parents. Oh, they'd been allocated the front room, as well as a bedroom, but it wasn't an ideal start.

"Mum, you can't lend me a pound, can you?"

"I lent you ten shillings last week."

"Yes, I know, and I'll pay you back, honest," Maureen cajoled. "Go on, Mum, I'm broke!"

Beryl sighed. She was sure she'd be better off if she let Maureen keep her wages, and just pay for her board. But Frank didn't agree with that.

"It's the principle of the thing," he said. "We've

brought her up – it's time she put something back into the household. When I first started to work I got a shilling a week back from my father."

And Beryl hadn't argued. She'd long found it was a waste of time to challenge Frank's opinion about anything. Not openly anyway. But she had become expert at subterfuge. "Just let a bit of water pass under the bridge," she used to advise the girls. "I'll sort it, you'll see."

She looked again at her daughter. Perhaps now was the time – after all, Maureen had been working for two years.

"I'll take you down the Trustees Savings Bank," she said abruptly. "Get an account opened for you, and then when you're eighteen you can just pay your board."

Maureen's face lit up. "Oh, great, Mum!"

"I wouldn't mention it your dad though, not yet."

Maureen immediately began to calculate how much money she'd have each week to spend. Disposable income – that was what it was called. Attracted by a whole page of share prices, she'd read about it in the dentist's waiting-room. There had been pages of them, in a pink newspaper called *The Financial Times*. Maureen loved figures; in fact she loved anything to do with mathematics.

"Why that girl failed her scholarship, I'll never know," Frank was wont to grumble. "Now our Sandra I could understand, she was never one for learning, but Maureen . . ."

And it was true. Maureen had shone at her lessons, and she was a wizard at mental arithmetic. But even now she had nightmares about that dreadful day, when with six other eleven-year-old pupils, she had gone to a strange secondary modern school. There, ushered into a large bare room they were given a test paper that would influence the rest of their lives. Maureen was under no misapprehension about that. The teachers had been on about it for months, not to mention her mum and dad and all her relations.

But as soon as the unsmiling teacher in front gave the instruction, "You can turn your papers over now", Maureen's insides turned to water. Her hands shaking and sweating, she struggled even to write her name. She tried to do the sums first, knowing that the longer she sat there, the worse she would feel, but there was something wrong with her brain. It felt like a piece of knitting-wool in a tangle and she began to panic as it wouldn't reason, wouldn't let her work out even the simplest problem. She stared down at the question, which was about a man digging a ditch and how long it would take. Forcing her sticky hand to pick up her pencil, she made an attempt to work out the figures, only to find the letters and numbers begin to blur and dance before her eyes, and suddenly, to her mortification, she was sick. Not just feeling sick and able to rush out of the room to the toilets, but vomiting a disgusting smelly mess all over the question paper, and down the front of her dress. Everyone was staring at her, and the teacher sitting at the front looked furious. A severe-looking woman, she came to Maureen's desk and, pulling her out of her seat, pushed her out of the classroom and into the corridor. Although another teacher took her to the cloakroom and helped to sponge her down, Maureen, terrified that her whole life was ruined, was inconsolable.

"I don't want to!" She tried to resist but was led back to the examination room, and given a fresh paper. Miserable and almost blinded by tears, she struggled to answer the questions. But she'd known even then that there would be no place for her at the coveted High School.

For days afterwards she'd skulked in the playground, avoided the eyes of her teachers, and borne the disappointment of her parents. When, two years later, top of her class at the secondary modern school, she was offered a second chance, she flatly refused. There was no way she was going through that ordeal again, and who wanted to go to the grammar school anyway, with its navy blue uniform? She looked hideous in navy blue. But beneath all her bravado, Maureen knew that the person she'd let down most was herself.

Beryl and Frank couldn't understand it. The girl wasn't what they would call a nervous child, yet every time she took even a routine test at school, she would get herself in a state.

"She bottles things up too much," Frank said. "Always been the same."

Then when she did leave school, Maureen flatly refused to do a secretarial course. She was adamant.

"Watch my lips," she said. "I am never, for the rest of my life, ever going to take any form of examination."

"What *are* you going to do?" demanded Frank.

"I could see if there's anything going at my place," Beryl offered.

"I'm not working there, either."

That, as Beryl told Frank later, was why she worried about Maureen.

"I mean," she said, "what's wrong with being a machinist? It's good enough for me and our Sandra."

It wasn't that Maureen didn't want to work in a factory – she knew she lacked the necessary co-ordination. Look at her knitting, for instance, it was a disaster, and she loathed any form of needlework.

"No," Maureen declared. "There's only one thing I'm good at and that's maths. I need a job where I can work with figures."

But that wasn't easy, not without qualifications. However, Frank, who worked as an insurance agent, collecting weekly premiums from door to door, had a word with his manager. As a result, Maureen was taken on as office junior and eventually promoted. She now spent her days working as a clerk.

At least she was there physically, her brain automatically totting up columns of figures, keeping precise ledgers, balancing accounts. But her spirit, her soul, was elsewhere, coming to rest contentedly twice a week in a balcony seat at the local cinema. The films she saw there filled her waking moments, and only she knew how much of her life was lived in this fantasy world.

"You're always daydreaming," Beryl would scold, but Maureen knew there was another world far away from the small, grey terraced house in the Potteries. There was a world of sunlight and blue skies, with beautiful houses and furniture, where everyone wore glamorous clothes and had exquisite manners. She adored Cary Grant and Gregory Peck, but her favourite films were musicals, where she was transported into what was the nearest thing to heaven on earth. In utter bliss, she and whichever girlfriend she'd gone to the pictures with, would walk home singing all the songs, their clear young voices causing the few passers-by to smile and think of their own youth.

Beryl would look at her lovely daughter as she came in, her cheeks flushed, her eyes shining, and wonder. Wonder what her future would hold, how she would cope with the harsh reality of life.

"It doesn't do to think too much," was a maxim she'd often heard in her own childhood, and Beryl thought there was a lot of wisdom in the saying, particularly for the working classes. It was better, safer really, just to make the best of what you'd got.

But on that Saturday evening, it was with pleasure and pride that she watched Maureen apply her make-up before the mirror over the tiled fireplace.

"What do you think of this new eyeshadow?" Maureen asked.

"I can't see much difference, it's still green."

"Well, I can hardly wear blue, can I, with my eyes?" Maureen's eyes were green and wide-set, flecked with gold, like a cat's, Frank always said.

"Just don't put too much on, that's all."

"Oh, Mum!" Maureen spat on a block of mascara, then applied the brush to try and lengthen her already dark lashes. Her dress was pink and white candy-striped cotton. With its full skirt flounced by a sugar-starched net waist-slip, and worn with a white waspie belt, it was one of her favourites.

She outlined her lips in pink, removed the steel curlers from the ends of her almost shoulder-length hair, and brushing it out looked at the resulting pageboy style with satisfaction.

"I suppose you're off to Trentham? You know, you're lucky to live almost on the doorstep. Coaches come from all over the Midlands bringing people to dance at Trentham Ballroom," Frank said.

"Yes, I know," Maureen said, putting on her coat. "Right, I'm off – I'll be on the usual last bus. Don't forget to meet me, will you, Dad?"

"I'll be there." Frank was immersed in the *Evening Sentinel*, but Maureen knew he wouldn't let her down, even though it meant him staying up until after midnight.

Pausing at the door to the cosy kitchen, she looked back at her parents. At Frank, enjoying his drink with his pipe waiting in its rack on a shelf beside him, his rimless spectacles perched on the end of his nose. At Beryl, who was darning Frank's socks while she listened to the wireless.

As Maureen stood in the doorway, in a strange way she felt she was on the threshold of a new phase in her life. Then, dismissing the idea as fanciful, she closed the door, the scent of her Evening in Paris perfume wafting behind her. It was Saturday night, the most exciting time of the week, and with keen anticipation she hurried away to meet her friends.

CHAPTER TWO

With the haunting tune of 'It's Almost Tomorrow', filtering through from the ballroom, Maureen pushed her way into the small cloakroom to find a space before the only large mirror. It was crowded with girls checking stocking seams, adjusting suspenders, applying make-up, dabbing perfume, and weighing up the competition. Maureen wanted to experiment with a glitter spray on her hair.

She had come with two friends: Elaine, who worked in Woolworth's, and Carol, who was training to be a hairdresser. All three girls had grown up in the same street, and it was this bond which was the basis of their friendship.

"No, not like that," scolded Carol, seizing the

spray from Maureen.

"I just wish you'd both hurry up!" Elaine tensed to let another girl push past. "All the talent will have been snapped up by the time we get in there."

"That's a point," Maureen said. "Come on then, let's go." She led the way out of the door and the three girls walked self-consciously in their court shoes along to the ballroom. Maureen could feel her flounced petticoat swishing around her legs, and held her head high as they entered the noisy room, where a heaving mass of dancers were now rocking to Bill Haley's number one hit, 'Rock Around The Clock'. The band on the stage blasted out the music and she itched to get on to the dance-floor, her body already responding to the rhythm. But first, they had to find a space where they could stand and, knowing the others would follow, she threaded her way down the side of the room.

Carol, who considered herself the spitting image of Marilyn Monroe, was the first to be asked to dance. Elaine, whose ample proportions were less desirably distributed, sniffed in disdain.

"Rather her than me," she said, as Carol followed the weedy-looking youth on to the floor.

"He's good though," Maureen commented, as she watched the dexterity with which he twirled her friend through a fast routine.

"Wanna dance?" She looked at the gum-chewing youth before her, his bony wrists protruding from his tweed jacket, and hesitated. But she was too late; he'd already diverted his attention to Elaine.

With a quick, appraising glance, Elaine nodded and as she went on to the dance-floor, he slouched after her.

Maureen watched them with amusement, and it was then, as she stood alone tapping her foot to the music, that she first saw him. He was leaning against a pillar watching the dancers, or rather, she suspected, watching the girls' legs as, with full skirts flaring, they twisted and turned. Tall and thin, in blazer and flannels, he seemed apart somehow, like a spectator at a play. Covertly, she watched him, noticing how his fair hair waved neatly back from his forehead. He looked like a younger version of that film star, what was his name? Leslie something – he'd been in *Gone With The Wind*. Leslie Howard, that was it. Suddenly, he glanced her way and she turned her head, affecting an air of nonchalance, pretending she was simply waiting for someone. It wouldn't do for him to think she was a wallflower.

But she needn't have worried, for soon the band stopped playing and the dancers began to stream off the floor, hot and perspiring.

Carol was the first to return, closely followed by Elaine, who complained,

"Didn't you grab a table?"

"There's one," Maureen pointed out, and the three girls quickly laid claim to it, placing their small evening bags on the top.

"Right," Maureen said. "I'll get the drinks."

A few minutes later, she returned with three Fanta Orange soft drinks.

Carol jerked her head in the direction of the pillar. "He's a bit of all right."

"Eyes off," Maureen warned. "I saw him first."

"Hey, he's coming over," Elaine hissed, and all three girls immediately looked the other way, affecting a cool disinterest.

With the band striking up a waltz, he came directly to Maureen, and looking up she gave him her devastating smile – the one she'd spent hours practising in front of the mirror.

"May I have this dance?" His voice was cool, confident.

"Of course," she said airily, and he stood aside as she swept past him, casting a triumphant glance at her friends.

"*Softly, softly,*" the female vocalist crooned in

imitation of Ruby Murray, and Maureen, held firmly in her partner's arms, stepped gracefully backwards.

Trevor told her, when they had exchanged names, that he was studying accountancy.

"What do you do?" he asked.

"I'm an insurance clerk."

"Ah," he murmured in her ear, as he negotiated a space among the crowd of dancers, "so we have something in common."

"What's that then?"

"A logical and ordered mind."

More impressed with every passing second, Maureen smiled up at him, thinking how different he was from anyone she'd met in the past. She tried to guess his age: he was definitely at least twenty-one, possibly more.

The number came to an end and as they drew apart, Maureen glanced uncertainly at him, hoping he wouldn't immediately escort her off the floor, but to her relief Trevor just smiled and as the band began a slow foxtrot, took her once again into his arms.

And that's how it was all evening. She hardly saw Elaine and Carol, as she danced with Trevor, sat out at a side table with him and, mesmerised, hung on his every word. After the last waltz, they walked hand in hand along the tree-lined path to the entrance gate, while her friends tactfully walked ahead. But although she was disappointed, Maureen wasn't surprised when Trevor didn't kiss her good-night before she boarded her bus. It showed respect, she told herself, as wrapped in her own thoughts she sat behind Elaine and Carol.

Oakvale, the area near Stoke where Maureen lived, was actually just a district near the town, rather than a village with an identity of its own. The distance was short and, as she stood by the driver, peering through the front window, she could see Frank at the bus stop.

"You're lucky," muttered Elaine. "I can't see my dad waiting up to walk me home."

Maureen cast her a sympathetic glance, knowing it was true. Elaine's father would have spent the evening in the local pub, and probably staggered home giving an operatic rendering. And, as Beryl said, he was no Mario Lanza. Carol's mother was a widow, as her husband had been killed at Dunkirk.

"Right, girls," Frank said as they got off the bus. "Had a good time, then?"

"Yes, thank you, Mr Matthews."

"Maureen certainly has," Carol said with a sly glance.

20

"Aye, well, I'm sure she'll tell us."

Soon they turned off the main road and began to walk up the steep hill. Then Frank waited to make sure both girls were safely inside their homes, before he and Maureen walked to their own house further up the street.

Beryl was sitting in her armchair, already in her dressing-gown, a plate of sandwiches and pot of tea in readiness.

"I'm off then," Frank said, as he hung up his cap. "I'll leave you two to it."

"Goodnight, Dad. Thanks for meeting me." Maureen reached up and kissed his cheek, then bit into a ham sandwich.

"Well, did you meet anyone?" Beryl asked.

Maureen nodded, saying between mouthfuls, "He's asked me to go to the pictures with him on Monday."

"He? That's not telling me much."

"Okay, his name's Trevor, he comes from Hanford, and he's training to be an accountant."

"Should suit you, then."

Maureen giggled. "That's what he said, well, sort of."

"Hanford's on our bus route, so that wouldn't be a problem." Beryl shot a shrewd glance at her daughter. "How old is he?"

"Honestly, it's like living with the Gestapo in this house. I don't know, do I? Probably about twenty-one."

"Well, find out on Monday. You're only seventeen, you know."

"Oh Mum, I can look after myself!"

"That's what they all say," Beryl muttered, then got up and went to the foot of the stairs. "I'm off to bed. Don't forget to switch the light off when you come up."

But Maureen had other things on her mind apart from the electricity bill. She was thinking of a fair head close to hers, of the faint smell of cigarette smoke on Trevor's jacket, and how she'd felt dancing with him, their two bodies moving in unison. Blushing a little at her own thoughts, she took the tray into the kitchen, and rinsed out her cup, saucer, and plate. Smiling in delicious anticipation of her future date, she emptied the teapot down the sink and, turning on the cold tap, stuck her finger into the soggy heap left in the plug-hole until all the leaves had disappeared.

Then, in eager anticipation of mulling over all that had happened, she climbed the steep stairs to her bedroom. It was still a novelty to have the room to herself and, although she missed Sandra in some ways, it was a luxury to be able to sink into her thoughts and daydreams without her elder sister's distracting chatter.

Only Sunday to get through, she thought as eventually she drifted off to sleep, and then I'll see him again.

* * *

Sundays in the Matthews household followed the same pattern every week. After enjoying his bacon and eggs, accompanied by a couple of hot Staffordshire oatcakes, Frank relaxed in his chair to read the *News of the World*, while Beryl, sitting opposite with a second cup of tea, immersed herself in the *Sunday People*. Maureen, having been dancing the night before, was allowed to have a lie-in.

"Those oatcakes weren't as good as usual," Frank grumbled, as he knocked out his pipe in the fireplace.

"No, that's what I thought. I got them off the market," Beryl said. She looked up. "It's funny, isn't it, how you can't get them anywhere else, only in this area?"

"Aye. The first person to open an oatcake shop in Blackpool would make a fortune."

"They might when the potters were on holiday,

but they'd starve in the winter."

For several minutes they sat in silence reading, then Frank looked up from his newspaper. "You know, there's going to be trouble in Suez afore long."

"You don't mean another war?" Beryl's face paled.

"Could be."

Beryl looked in alarm at her husband's grim face. "You wouldn't have to go, would you?"

"Shouldn't think so, not this time. It'll be the regulars. But I don't want anyone to have to go. This country's lost enough young men." Conscripted into the army during the Second World War, Frank knew he was lucky to have returned safely from active service.

"If women ruled the world, there'd be an end to wars," Beryl declared.

"You all say that. But it's power, do you see? And I reckon women could be just as ruthless as men."

"I doubt whether you'll ever find out. I mean, can you imagine us ever having a woman Prime Minister?" she teased.

Frank grinned. "She'd be declaring war every month – you know what you get like."

"Oh, go on with you!"

* * *

Beryl returned to her paper, but Frank sat staring

into the distance, thinking of the possible implications of President Nasser's nationalisation of the Suez Canal. Then, with a sigh, he mentally shrugged. It was up to the politicians; there was nothing he could do.

Half an hour later, Beryl got up and going into the scullery put the joint of topside into the already hot oven. Then going to the foot of the stairs, she called, "Maureen! If you're going to the eleven o'clock Mass, you'd better get a move on!"

Upstairs, Maureen groaned, and hid her head under the sheet. Nobody else had to go to church on Sundays. One of these days, she'd stand up to her dad, tell him that she didn't want to go to Mass. I mean, what's the point, she thought, I only daydream all through it. It had been different when she was at school; she wouldn't have dared to miss, knowing that her absence would be remarked upon.

"Maureen!" Beryl's voice was louder and more insistent.

"All right, I'm coming!" With reluctance, she swung out her legs and put her bare feet on to the fluffy bedside rug. A Christmas present from Gran, it was the same shade of pink as the frilled skirt on the kidney-shaped dressing-table.

Sundays were boring. She knew exactly what

would happen. After she and her dad got home from church, he would open a bottle of Davenport's beer, and settle down with the paper. Mum would be busy fussing about her Yorkshire pudding, and Maureen would have to do the dusting. She loathed dusting

"I suppose Gran and Auntie Vera are coming for tea?"

"Don't they always?" Beryl replied.

Maureen sighed. It wasn't that she didn't want them to come, she just wished Sundays weren't so predictable. All that sitting about drinking tea and gossiping. And as for eating, they never seemed to stop. First they tucked into an enormous roast dinner, with rice pudding to follow, then Beryl would not only open a tin of salmon for tea, but they'd have cling peaches and evaporated milk as well. On top of all that, Gran always brought round a home-made fruitcake.

But Auntie Vera was always good for a laugh. Well, being Gran's sister, she was her great-aunt really. A spinster, who had lost her only chance of marriage in the Great War, she was the most forthright person Maureen had ever met. Tact, diplomacy, and even good manners seemed to have passed her by.

Her voice, which was stentorian, boomed out the

moment she entered the front door.

"Eeh, I've had a good move this morning, our Beryl. It wasn't half a big 'un."

Frank and Maureen exchanged grins. Not her bowels already!

"That's good, Vera," Beryl said, with a warning look at both of them.

"I feel a lot better for it, I can tell you. Three days I went." She settled herself down on a hard chair at the table. Small and spare, with iron-grey hair scraped back into a tortured bun, Auntie Vera never sat in an easy chair, considering them bad for the spine. And seeing how ramrod-straight her own was, Maureen thought she was probably right.

And what have you been up to, young lady?"

"Nothing, really."

"Yes, she has," Beryl disputed. "She's met a young man, Vera, an accountant."

Vera looked suitably impressed, and Beryl turned to her mother and raised her voice. "Did you hear that, Gran?"

"Eh. What did you say?"

"Switch your hearing-aid on. Honestly," Beryl complained to the others, "I think she does it on purpose."

Maureen had never understood why Beryl called

her own mother "Gran"; it was as though the older woman had lost an identity once she and Sandra were born.

"No, she doesn't, she just forgets, don't you," shouted Vera. She gesticulated at her sister, and there immediately came a crackling sound from the square box hanging on Nellie's ample bosom.

"I was saying, our Maureen's met a young man. He's training to be an accountant!" Beryl shouted.

"There's no need to shout, I can hear you!" Nellie looked across her son-in-law. "Stoke did well then yesterday, Frank. I suppose you went?"

"Naturally. 3-1 against Leicester. Not bad, eh?"

"Well, I hope they have a better season than the last one," she grumbled.

"Don't we all!" He glanced around at the four women. "Right, time I went and had forty winks. Don't forget to call me when tea's ready." He climbed heavily up the stairs.

Vera said, "He's putting a fair bit of weight on. You'd better put him on a diet, Beryl."

"Dad's not fat," defended Maureen.

"He's not thin, either," Vera snapped.

"I think it suits him to carry a bit of weight," Nellie said, and Maureen looked at her gratefully.

"How're you keeping then, Gran?"

"Not so bad, me legs are playing up a bit."

Maureen sat and endured half an hour of chat and then, her duty done, escaped upstairs to her bedroom. She put 'Heartbreak Hotel' on her portable record-player, turning down the volume to avoid disturbing Frank. At first she lay on her bed daydreaming, then she browsed through the latest copy of *Picturegoer*. Later, she'd go downstairs and watch *Sunday Night at the London Palladium*. After that it would almost be time for Monday to come – she couldn't wait to see Trevor again!

CHAPTER THREE

Maureen was early for the date. She stood outside the Majestic cinema in Stoke, wearing a flowered circular skirt with the collar turned up on her white blouse, and waited. The film showing was *The Glenn Miller Story*, with James Stewart, and she peered at the coloured pictures displayed in the showcase near the entrance. There was someone else waiting, a Teddy boy, resplendent in his velvet jacket, black shoestring tie and drainpipe trousers. She looked with distaste at the thick crepe soles on his black suede shoes. Carol and Elaine had both been out with Teddy boys, but Maureen regarded them as common.

Then suddenly she saw Trevor walking towards her. Again he was wearing a blazer and flannels, this time with a pale blue shirt and striped tie. He looked slightly older than he had in the dimmed light of the ballroom, and she felt a little uncertain, until he smiled at her saying with approval, "You're very punctual."

Unlike other boys she'd been to the cinema with, Trevor didn't ask her where she'd like to sit, but simply booked two balcony seats, then with his hand at the small of her back, ushered her up the stairs. Maureen was self-conscious, feeling in a strange way that somehow she'd crossed a line. This wasn't like the few times she'd gone to the pictures with lads she'd met at the youth club. Her feeling was confirmed when Trevor didn't make a beeline for a double seat in the back row, but simply followed the usherette until she flashed her torch along to two seats in the third row from the front.

"I'm a great fan of Glenn Miller, are you?" Trevor asked, once they'd got settled.

"Oh yes," Maureen said, "particularly 'String of Pearls'."

The shrill sound of a cock crowing heralded the *Pathé News*, and it wasn't until it finished and the opening credits of the "B" film began, that Trevor took her hand and clasped it in his own. The film wasn't very good, and Maureen found it difficult to concentrate on the plot, acutely aware of Trevor beside her. The warmth of his thigh occasionally touched her own, and she longed for him to be like her other dates, to casually drape his arm along the back of her seat before kissing her. Hitherto, she'd always found this ploy irritating, particularly if it coincided with a moving love scene on the screen. But it was the accepted rule that if a boy took you to the pictures and paid for you, it entailed a bit of mild snogging in the back row. But as she sat next to Trevor, discreetly holding hands, and he didn't make a move, Maureen could only think yet again that this date was different.

As soon as the film ended and the lights went up Trevor asked, "Would you like an ice cream?

"Yes, please."

"A choc-ice or a tub?"

She thought quickly. She'd really like a choc-ice, but she was bound to drop a messy bit of chocolate down the front of her blouse.

"A tub, please."

She watched him as he went down the steps to the usherette, seeing her smile up at him above her heavy tray. He was *so* attractive.

When the main programme began, Trevor became as immersed in the film as she was. There was no distracting fumbling or silly jokes whispered in her ear. In fact, he was the perfect companion, for in the really exciting bits, she could almost forget he was there. When eventually they stood for the National Anthem, Maureen was bemused, still lost in the sad scenes at the end of the film, her head full of the stirring music.

Trevor too was quiet, simply saying as they followed the crowd down the stairs to the entrance, "Did you enjoy it?"

"It was wonderful."

Although it was dark, the night air was still warm and when Trevor offered to see her home, she said, "We can walk, it's not far."

Hand in hand they strolled along the now quiet main road, then after several minutes Trevor stopped and drew her into the privacy of a shop doorway. "I've been wanting to kiss you all night."

"I'm not stopping you," she smiled, raising her mouth to his.

Trevor's kiss was firm if disappointingly short, but Maureen consoled herself that at least there was no nonsense about him. Other kisses she'd experienced had been those of clumsy youths, often wet as they tried to put their tongues in her mouth. French kissing, they called it, but as far as she was concerned it could stay in France, although Carol told her it was because they weren't doing it properly.

"Would you like to go dancing on Saturday?" he said, after he'd kissed her again at the end of her street.

"I'd love to."

He stood watching until she opened her front door and waved, and then he was gone.

* * *

They went out together regularly after that, twice and even three times a week. Usually it was to the pictures, or dancing, but once Trevor took her to hear the Halle Orchestra. It was the first time Maureen had been to an orchestral concert, and to her surprise she found it an exhilarating experience.

When, her mind still full of *The Dream of Olwen*, she enthused to Trevor, he said in a sharp tone, "Of course you enjoyed it, you'd have to be a moron not to. Surely you know the acoustics in the Victoria Hall are among the best in the country?"

Deflated, Maureen remained silent.

But after she'd known Trevor for six weeks, Frank began to show concern. "It's about time we met him, our Maureen."

"Yes. You'd better ask him for tea on Sunday,"

Beryl promptly agreed, and Maureen knew they'd been discussing the matter.

"Gran and Auntie Vera will be here!"

"So what?"

"I see what she means, love. You know what your Vera's like. She takes a bit of getting used to!" Frank sucked on the stem of his pipe and winked at Maureen.

"Well, I can't help that," Beryl said crossly.

"Just look on it as a baptism of fire," Frank said, grinning at his daughter.

Rather nervously, Maureen broached the subject. Everyone knew that inviting your boyfriend home for Sunday tea held other implications.

But, to her relief, Trevor readily agreed. He'd told her little about his own family, other than that he was an only child. All she knew was that his father was a teacher, and his mother didn't go out to work. But apart from answering her questions, he never mentioned them.

On Sunday afternoon, Maureen lounged on the bed in her parents' room, while Beryl, flushed after a flurry of ironing the best cloth and setting the table, dabbed at her cheeks with Creme Puff. She took a pride in her appearance, insisting on what she called "maintaining standards". Although she didn't have

Maureen's dramatic colouring, she was still an attractive woman despite her middle years.

"I need another home perm," she said, looking critically in the mirror.

"Get one then, and I'll do it for you one day next week." Maureen, sitting behind her on the bed, looked at her mother's light brown hair. "At least you aren't going grey yet. You're lucky, Elaine's mother has to colour hers."

"That husband she's got is enough to turn anyone grey." Beryl twisted round to look at her daughter. "You're pretty keen on this Trevor, aren't you?"

Maureen nodded.

"It's as well we're going to have a look at him, then."

She'd invited Trevor for half past three, reasoning that at least they'd have half an hour before Vera arrived. He was punctual and, although the day was hot, was wearing a jacket, shirt and tie. Beryl, glad that she'd talked Frank into doing the same, held out her hand as Maureen introduced them.

"Hello, Trevor. I've heard a lot about you."

"All of it good, I hope," he smiled.

Beryl could see why Maureen found him attractive. So far as looks went, he was the nearest to a film star she'd ever seen outside the cinema. They now knew he was twenty-three, which was a little older than she'd have liked, but she had to admit that the young couple looked good together.

"Trevor." Frank shook his hand, and looked keenly at the young man before him.

The four of them settled down in the parlour, Maureen sitting next to Trevor on the sofa of the rarely used rust moquette three-piece suite. Beryl and Frank sat opposite each other.

There was a short silence, then Frank said, "I hear your father's a teacher, Trevor."

"Yes, he is."

"Which school would that be, then?"

Maureen sat in discomfort as Frank and Beryl tried to "draw Trevor out", as they would say. Then at four o'clock precisely, the door opened and Auntie Vera marched in, followed by Nellie.

"What's this then?" she barked. "All sitting in the parlour! Has the Queen come for tea, or what?"

Beryl coloured with embarrassment, while Frank intervened, "This is Maureen's young man, Vera. We told you he was coming."

"Aye, you did. Though why Nellie had to struggle into her best corsets, I don't know!" She looked around the cramped room. "And where am I to sit?"

Trevor began to rise to offer his seat, but Maureen

caught at his arm.

"No, it's all right, she likes a hard chair."

Frank went to fetch one from the kitchen, while Beryl vacated her armchair, saying, "You sit there, Gran. I'll go and put the kettle on."

Maureen smiled at her grandmother, who was resplendent in her best pearls, and leaning forward said clearly, "This is Trevor, Gran."

Nellie adjusted her hearing-aid and smiling at him said, "It's nice to meet you, Trevor."

"And this is my Auntie Vera."

Vera, who was wearing a new pair of shoes and already regretting it, gave a short nod, and glared at him. "I hear you're training to be an accountant. Or does that just mean you're a glorified clerk?"

Maureen winced.

"No, it means what it says," Trevor said shortly.

"So you haven't done your National Service yet?"

"I was deferred."

"How long for?" Frank asked.

"Until I qualify. I take my final exams next year."

"Which do you fancy: Army, Navy or Air Force? I was in the North Staffordshire regiment, myself."

"Oh, I think the RAF."

"Aye. More glamorous uniform," said Vera with disdain.

"Oh, take no notice of her," Nellie said. "Now then, Maureen tells me your surname's Mountford. I knew a girl once, called Ida Mountford. She wouldn't be any relation, would she?"

And so it went on. They had tea in style, not only using Beryl's precious Royal Doulton tea set, but even paper serviettes. To Maureen's relief, the conversation gradually turned to more general matters, and then half an hour later Trevor turned to her saying, "It's such a lovely evening – shall we go for a walk?"

Before Maureen could answer, Nellie said, "Yes, you young things go off on your own. You don't want to be cooped up here with us."

Maureen glanced at her mother. "What about the washing-up?"

"Don't worry about that," Beryl said. "Your Auntie Vera will help."

"And I'm not useless, you know," Nellie bristled.

As soon as the front door closed behind them, Frank loosened his collar and tie. "I though I'd choke to death in this heat," he grumbled.

"Never mind that," Beryl said. "What did you think of him?"

"He's nice and polite," Nellie offered. "I liked him."

"Oh, you always see the good in everyone. You'd like Hitler if he sat here and was pleasant to you," snapped Vera.

"Frank?" Beryl looked at her perspiring husband.

"Well, he's certainly a cut above most round here. But he never opened up, not once. And he's a Port Vale supporter, though I suppose I can't hold that against him. Still, I think I'll reserve judgement for a bit."

Beryl frowned. "I can see what she sees in him – he's certainly good-looking."

"Aye well, handsome is as handsome does," Vera said.

"You didn't like him then, Vera?"

"I didn't say that. I agree with Frank, I'll wait and see. There's one thing for sure, our Maureen thinks the sun shines out of him."

"That was very obvious," Beryl said drily.

In Maureen's opinion, the afternoon had gone well, but Trevor was even quieter than usual as they walked down the street.

"Where shall we go?" Maureen said.

"I don't mind. I just wanted to get out of there."

His voice was cold and Maureen looked at him in shock.

"Why? What was the matter?"

"Well, it was nothing but questions."

Maureen stared at him, wondering why he was reacting like this. Surely her family wasn't any different to any other?

"I did warn you about Auntie Vera."

With a glance at her defensive expression, Trevor said hurriedly, "Oh, it wasn't that. It's just me. I hate talking about myself."

"Oh, I see." Maureen wasn't really sure that she did, but then she consoled herself that at least it showed he wasn't the boastful type.

She tucked her hand inside the crook of his arm.

"Never mind. It'll be my turn next for the inquisition, when I meet your parents."

Trevor failed to respond at first, then eventually he said, "Oh, there's plenty of time for that."

They couldn't think of anything else to do, so they went for a drink at a local pub which, as it was Sunday, Maureen knew her mum would have found shocking. Trevor however, had no such inhibitions.

"At least I've been to church this morning," she teased him. "I bet you haven't."

"The Church of England isn't like yours, you know," he said. "We're not brainwashed into thinking we'll go to hell if we don't go to Mass every week!"

41

Taken aback, Maureen tried to make a joke of it. "It's better than being like your lot – Easter, Christmas, weddings and funerals!" She smiled up at him in effort to lighten his mood.

He looked at her and then his features suddenly relaxed, "Don't forget christenings!"

Relieved, she lifted out the cherry in her martini and popped it in her mouth, savouring the slightly bitter taste.

Trevor smiled at her, raising his glass in a toast. "You're quite beautiful, did you know that?"

Maureen blushed. Trevor had a habit of doing that. Just when she was feeling a little uneasy at one of his comments, he would say something really romantic.

"Well, if it isn't the courting couple!"

They both looked up to see Elaine with a tall, thin youth. They made an incongruous pair, as Maureen noted that her friend had put on even more weight over the past few weeks.

"Long time, no see! Mind if we join you?" Elaine said and, without waiting for an answer, pulled out another chair. She looked at her companion as he sat down. "This is Maureen and Trevor, remember me telling you about them?"

"Oh yes," he grinned, his face lighting up.

"Pleased to meet you – I'm Brian."

"Can I get you both a drink?" Trevor asked, although Maureen could sense he wasn't too pleased at the interruption.

"Thanks, mate. I'll come with you. A Babycham for you, Elaine?"

"Lovely."

Once they were on their own, Elaine leaned towards Maureen saying, "Ooh, he sends me, that one! I've been going out with him for three weeks now. What about you and Trevor, is it serious?"

Maureen said cautiously, "It could be."

"Has he met your mum and dad yet?"

"First time today. He came for tea."

"What do you think of Brian?" Elaine asked with a grin.

Maureen glanced across at the bar, where Brian had obviously made a witty remark to the barmaid, who was laughing. She was glancing flirtatiously at Trevor, but his expression was unsmiling as he searched in a purse he kept for small change. The contrast between the two men was marked. One tall and handsome, the other so ordinary you wouldn't remember him if you passed him in the street.

She glanced back at Elaine. "I think he's very nice."

"He is, and he's so uncomplicated. With Brian, what you see is what you get."

And over the next few months, there were several occasions when Maureen couldn't help wishing the same sentiment applied to Trevor.

CHAPTER FOUR

"Married! But you've only known him a year!"

Sandra's reaction was exactly what Maureen had anticipated. She looked at her sister's shocked face and hurriedly explained, "It's because of the money. Trevor says that if we get married before he goes for his National Service, then he'll get the Marriage Allowance. If we save that, we'll have a deposit for a house by the time he comes out."

"But . . . !"

Maureen, seeing an argument coming, said quickly, "Look, you have a think about it, while I have my bath." She picked up the shopping bag she'd brought with her. "You're sure John's parents won't be back?"

Still frowning, Sandra said, "No, I've told you,

they've gone to bingo."

Maureen ran quickly up the stairs. She didn't come over to have a bath too often, feeling guilty about using someone else's hot water. But oh, it was heaven to be able to just turn the taps on, and then soak for as long as she liked. She crumbled a lily of the valley bathcube into the water, and began to undress. At home, she had to manage with a good sponge-down most of the time. They had a tin bath, of course, and Frank would willingly carry it into the kitchen. But it was all such a hassle, not only getting it filled and emptied, but also knowing she had to be quick, as her dad would be impatient to come back in, particularly now they had a television. She took out a striped towel from the bag and hugged its softness. Married! She'd be Maureen Mountford – she'd even keep the same initials!

Then lying back in the soft, scented water, her mind ran ahead, already planning the sort of wedding she wanted. White, of course, and at least she could look everyone in the face, not like poor Elaine, who'd had to get married only weeks before.

"Brian just kept on at me," she wept when, frightened and ashamed, she'd confided in Maureen. "He said it was really bad for a man, being frustrated all the time."

After the first flush of gossip had died down, sympathy had mostly been directed at her mother, for as Beryl said, "The poor woman's got enough problems, without her daughter letting her down."

There'd been no problem with Trevor in that direction! He'd obeyed implicitly her rules of touching only, and above the waist, but she just knew that once they were married, he'd be a wonderful lover. She hooked her toe around the hot-water tap and managed to turn it to let more hot water in. It was quite a nice bathroom, she decided, but when she had her own house, she'd have real tiles on the walls, not these sheets of imitation ones. Perhaps pink, with wallpaper decorated with seashells . . . and she drifted into a pleasurable reverie, imagining how wonderful it would be to have her own home to furnish.

Downstairs, Sandra, trying to take in Maureen's surprise announcement, was thoughtfully making herself a cup of tea.

John had gone out to play darts, so she and Maureen had the house to themselves. For a fleeting moment she felt a pang of jealousy. From what Maureen had implied, Trevor had no intention of ending up in a council house. But then, now he was a qualified chartered accountant, she supposed it was only to be expected. Yet here she and John were, still stuck with his parents. They were trying desperately for a baby, as overcrowding was one sure way to get to the top of the housing-list. Sandra had tentatively suggested trying to buy a house, but even if they saved enough for a small deposit, John wasn't happy about taking on the responsibility of a mortgage. His work could be seasonal and, as he pointed out, if you lived in a council house, you didn't have to worry about maintenance. But although she liked his parents, increasingly Sandra longed for her own home, and tried to satisfy her yearning by buying something each week to build up her "bottom drawer".

"We could be allocated a house at any time," she told John, as she added to the pile of unopened wedding presents in a corner of their bedroom. "Just think how stuck we'd be without the basics."

She sighed as she fished guiltily in the biscuit barrel for a chocolate bourbon, envying Maureen her slim figure. And those legs! Every time she thought of her sister's ankles it caused her to look down at her own with a grimace. But she could never resent Maureen; she'd adored her right from the moment she'd been born. Sandra, only five years old when the new baby was born, still remembered the wonder of first holding her tiny crumpled fist.

And now her little sister was thinking of getting married before she was out of her teens. Sandra wandered into the small lounge and, still munching her biscuit, sat on the sofa and drew her legs beneath her. Although she'd met Trevor several times, she still wasn't sure whether she liked him nor not. But Maureen seemed happy enough, although she didn't talk about him much. But that was her all over; she'd always kept things close to her chest.

When Maureen returned, flushed and rosy and looking lovelier than ever, Sandra's heart sank. If ever anyone lived with her head in the clouds, her young sister did. Did she realise what a momentous decision she was making?

"Have you thought this through?" she demanded. "I mean, where will you live while Trevor's away? And suppose he's posted abroad, he could be away for months, a year even."

"At home, I hope," Maureen said promptly. "God, the thought of living with Mr and Mrs Mountford – I'd go spare!"

"You're not getting on any better, then?"

"Well, it's not a question of that," Maureen tried to explain. "They're not nasty to me or anything – they're just so cold, somehow. They still treat me

49

like a stranger. You know, polite and distant."

"I suppose I'm really lucky with my in-laws," Sandra said. "They've always made me feel welcome."

"They should think themselves lucky to have you," Maureen said loyally. It was true. Sandra was the nicest person she'd ever known. Though, as far as looks went, most people wouldn't give her a second glance. She might have inherited Beryl's curly brown hair, but her complexion was poor and her features unremarkable. This, together with a tendency to put on weight, didn't add up to the conventional idea of beauty. But to Maureen's mind, her sister's beauty came from within, and in John she'd found a husband who appreciated this. The young couple were devoted to each other, and Maureen said impulsively, "I only hope that when I do get married, I'll be as happy as you."

"So do I, poppet."

"So you'll back me up when I tell Mum and Dad?"

Sandra hesitated, "Well, I still think you're a bit young, but I can see the sense in it. That's if you're sure."

"I am," Maureen said with confidence. Of course she was sure. Didn't she think about Trevor every day, miss him when he wasn't there?

"I'll tell them tomorrow," she promised. "And don't let them know I told you first."

"Don't worry, I won't."

Maureen glanced at her watch. "Glory, I'd better go and give you time to get into your dressing-gown."

"Yes, they're bound to notice someone's had a bath. You can tell the minute you open the front door."

Maureen gave Sandra a hug, shoved the damp towel in her bag and, hurriedly leaving, began to wend her way through the estate to the main road. Just one short bus ride, and she'd be back in Oakvale, where she planned to go to bed early and read the latest romantic novel she'd borrowed from the library. As she hurried along in the chill night air, her mind was buzzing with plans. Her next step must be to break the news at home.

Trevor had suggested that they tell their respective parents separately.

"That way, they'll feel free to express an opinion."

Maureen looked at him. "And what if they think it's a bad idea?"

"They won't," he assured her. "Not when it makes economic sense."

But in that he misjudged Frank and Beryl.

Beryl said, "I'm not sure about it, Maureen."

"But why?"

Beryl glanced at her husband. What could she say? It wasn't as though there was anything concrete to dislike about Trevor. He was presentable and had a very good job. In fact, marriage to a chartered accountant would be quite a step up the ladder for a member of the Matthews family. It was just that Trevor didn't seem to fit in, unlike Sandra's husband, John. They'd taken to him right from the start. But with Trevor, you couldn't feel comfortable somehow.

Frank was silent. He was thinking. Thinking of his little girl, his baby, wanting to get married. And what sort of marriage would it be, at first anyway? Trevor would be away in the forces, and Maureen stuck at home with them. As for his approval, well, what could a father do? Maureen would be broken-hearted if he raised objections, for he couldn't substantiate them, and after all it did make sense to qualify for the Marriage Allowance. At least it would offer some security when Trevor was demobbed.

Maureen was looking at Beryl, who still hadn't answered.

"You were only eighteen when you got married," she reminded her.

"Yes, I know I was," Beryl said. Without being disloyal to Frank, she could hardly tell her daughter that many times in those early years she'd wished she had waited. Had felt her young spirit confined, weighed down too soon with responsibilities. But the chance of a couple of rooms to rent had come up and so they'd got married in 1932. It was during the slump and times were hard. It hadn't helped when she almost immediately got pregnant with Sandra, and then Maureen was born just before the Second World War broke out. Frank had enlisted, leaving her with two small children, a struggle to make ends meet, and a profound fear of bombs. Beryl had hoped for a better life for Maureen. But above all, she wanted her to enjoy her youth, those golden carefree years, which once gone would never return.

"And that's worked out all right, hasn't it?" Maureen persisted.

"Yes, of course it has." And it had. Beryl and Frank's relationship was as comfortable as an old shoe, and if Beryl occasionally yearned for wider horizons in her life, then she firmly kept what she termed her "fanciful thoughts" to herself.

Frank, seeing her floundering, helped her out. "I think what it is, love, your mum would have liked you to have had a bit more experience of life. It's the most important decision you'll ever make, you know."

"But we're both sure of our feelings, and it just doesn't make sense to wait. We're not the only ones to think like this – lots of young couples do it, and some of the boys are only eighteen. At least Trevor's older, and will have a good job waiting for him at the end of it."

Beryl looked helplessly at her husband. Maureen had such a persuasive tongue on her when she wanted her own way. And they knew from experience just how stubborn she could be.

"So, what do you think?" Maureen persisted.

Frank glanced at Beryl.

"You've only just sprung it on us," he said. "Give us a few days to think about it."

"But . . ."

Frank quelled Maureen's objection with a look that brooked no discussion, and with that she had to be satisfied.

Although Beryl and Sandra worked in the same department, their sewing-machine stations were in different areas. So, the following day, it wasn't until the tea-break that Beryl had a chance to consult her elder daughter.

"So, what's *your* opinion?" she said.

"Oh, I don't know, Mum. I mean, if her mind's set on it, what can you do? What's worrying you? Is it Trevor? Don't you like him?"

Beryl looked at her. "I don't dislike him," she said guardedly.

"He's very reserved, I'll grant you that. But Maureen seems sure of her feelings, and she's the one who'll be marrying him, not us."

"That's true." Beryl poured herself a cup of tea from her flask. She couldn't explain why she felt so uneasy.

"Is it that you don't want them living with you?"

"No, of course not. They won't be really, because Trevor will be away most of the time. I suppose," she sighed, "I could be being selfish. It'll be the end of an era, you know – my youngest flying the nest, so to speak."

"But she won't be, will she?" Sandra pointed out.

Still anxious, Beryl made a slight detour on the way home, and called in to relay the news to Nellie and Vera.

Nellie, of course, while worrying that Maureen was bit young, thought it all very romantic. "Will he get married in uniform?" she asked. "I do love a man in uniform."

"Don't be daft, Nellie. He won't get his uniform

until he goes in," Vera snapped. However, to Beryl's surprise, Vera supported the idea of the marriage.

"Sound thinking," she pronounced. "It's time someone in this family owned their own home."

Beryl let that pass, knowing it was a dig at Frank. He'd cultivated the art of ignoring Vera's remarks, putting her acid tongue down to her being a spinster. As he often said to Beryl, "She's never had a man – that's her trouble."

"And," Vera continued, "at least they're behaving responsibly, not like that flighty friend of hers, what's her name?"

"Elaine," Beryl said.

"Yes, well, of course our Maureen's got more sense, not to mention morals." Vera drew a deep breath, her narrow chest swelling with righteous indignation, and Beryl suddenly thought, she's right! I could have far worse problems.

So, after another discussion with Frank, approval was given, and as Beryl said afterwards, the joy on her daughter's face was enough to lighten any heart.

CHAPTER FIVE

Trevor didn't consult his parents to seek their approval, he merely acquainted them with his plans.

Henry Mountford was a thin, sour-looking man. He taught science at a local grammar school where, detested for his cutting sarcasm, he inspired few of his pupils. The startling news, reported by a boy who now lived in a neighbouring street, that he was married and had fathered a child, was widely disbelieved. The mystery of sex was a subject that fascinated the lower middle school, but in his case it was decided that he was so cold-blooded the child must have been adopted.

But they were wrong. Between them, in a rare and passionless encounter, Henry and his wife Norah had produced Trevor, whose birth hardly changed their ordered existence at all. A quiet, secretive child, whose good looks were more a cause of embarrassment to them than pride, he'd simply adapted to their way of life. As Norah used to say, "You hardly knew he was there."

But now, they both stared at him in astonishment. Married? They'd met Maureen of course, but they'd never imagined the relationship was serious. As Henry had commented, "She's certainly a looker, but she hasn't had his education, Norah. It won't last, he'll soon find someone on his own level."

And Norah had quietly agreed. But then, he wouldn't have expected anything else. A mousy, permanently tired-looking woman, Trevor's mother had walked in her husband's shadow for so long that it was a rare occasion when her opinion differed from his. Conscious that she hadn't had what Henry would consider a decent education either, she chose not to remind him of the fact.

So, in the aftermath of this momentous news, Henry and Norah faced their son in the sitting-room of their detached house in a quiet tree-lined road. The Wedgwood Room, Henry called it, in view of the proliferation of the distinctive blue and white ornaments adorning every available surface. Powder-boxes, ashtrays, trinket boxes, small and large vases,

they were Norah's pride and joy. Not perfect speci-
mens of course, but her brother worked in the offices
at the Wedgwood factory, and over the years had
managed to buy her "seconds".

Trevor, his face expressionless, sat in the brown
leather armchair opposite, and waited.

"Why in such a hurry?" Henry, his tone sharp and
suspicious, shot the question at him.

Trevor explained the logistics of the decision.

Henry took off his rimless glasses, polished them
with a corner of his handkerchief, and considered.
Then he nodded. "It makes economic sense, I'll
grant you. But is that influencing you? I mean, apart
from that, would you have taken this step so soon?"

Trevor frowned. "Probably not."

"Exactly." Henry pressed the ends of his fingers
together to make an arch and, complacent, leaned
back in his chair.

"But," Trevor continued, "only because we'd have
had to save for a deposit on a house."

"Don't you think she's a bit young?" Norah said.

"She'll be nineteen soon, and Maureen's very
sensible for her age."

"I suppose you're afraid you'll lose her unless you
put a ring on her finger before you go," Henry said.
"I must speak plainly. It might flatter your ego to be

seen with a girl like her, but I expected you to choose someone with a better education."

Trevor said shortly, "You can't always judge people on their qualifications. If you must know, she has a phobia about taking exams."

"A phobia?" Henry dismissed it with a wave of his hand. "Absolute rubbish. Just an excuse people use to get out of things, if you ask me."

"You're entitled to your opinion."

Norah looked uneasily at first one and then the other. It was obvious that her husband wasn't in favour of this match, yet she knew her son. If Trevor had made his mind up, then disapproval from them wouldn't deter him.

Henry must have come to the same conclusion.

"I suppose you're old enough to know what you want," he said grudgingly, then suddenly leant forward, his face suddenly darkening. "I've just remembered something. Didn't you once say she was a Catholic?"

"Yes, but I don't see that as a problem."

"You don't? Then you're a bigger fool than I thought."

There was a sudden silence, and Norah felt a stab of anxiety as she waited for her son to react.

But, although his lips tightened, all he said was,

"Perhaps you could explain that comment."

"Get in their clutches and you never know where it will end. Mark my words, they'll be after your soul. Or if not yours, then those of any children you may have." Henry's voice rose, in growing outrage. "You'll have to make all sorts of promises, and then there's their views on ..." his voice tailed off.

"What? Birth control?" Trevor finished the sentence for him.

Norah blushed to her greying roots, shocked and embarrassed that her son should mention such an intimate subject.

"You've got it in one," Henry snapped. "Have you considered what that could mean?"

"I rather think that's my business," Trevor said. "In any case, you don't need to worry. I think you'll find your fears are unfounded. Mum," he turned to look at Norah, "perhaps you could go down to St John's and arrange an appointment for me with the vicar."

Henry stared at him, his eyes narrowing. "What do you mean? Has Maureen agreed to get married in a Protestant church?"

Trevor flicked a small piece of lint from his trousers and looked at them both, his expression calm and detached. He got up to go to his room, and turned in the doorway.

"We haven't discussed it yet. But she will."

* * *

Maureen, however, was appalled when he made the suggestion.

"What do you mean, get married at St John's?"

"Why not?" Trevor countered. "It's a much nicer church – the photographs would be better."

"I can't deny that. But my dad would have a stroke!"

"Nonsense."

"But why? You hardly ever go to church."

"Neither would you, if you had the choice," he replied.

Maureen fell silent. He was right of course; she found the prospect of a lazy Sunday morning far more tempting than having to sit through a long Mass.

"If your religion meant a lot to you, then of course I wouldn't even suggest it," Trevor's voice was tender and persuasive. They were sitting in the Matthews' barely aired parlour, talking almost in whispers.

"But apart from the photographs, why not get married at my church as it would save upsetting Dad?"

"Because I object to anyone laying down the law about what I can and can't do."

Maureen stared at him with growing apprehension. "You're talking about the Church's teaching on birth control, aren't you?"

"That, and someone telling me how I've got to bring up my children."

"Hang on," Maureen said, frowning. "Are you saying that if we got married in your church, they'd be brought up C of E?"

"That would be something we'd discuss. But it would be our decision, not one foisted on us by some priest."

Put like that, it did sound fair, Maureen reasoned. Shamefacedly, she knew that she'd never really thought that much about some of the teachings of the Church. She'd gone to a Catholic school, and accompanied her father to church every Sunday, but matters of dogma she'd merely accepted without question. Her mind had always been full of other more delightful thoughts and dreams.

"I'm assuming," Trevor persisted, "that you'll want children?"

Flustered, Maureen said, "Every woman does, doesn't she? But not straightaway."

"Quite. But what I don't want is for us to breed

like rabbits."

The coarseness of the remark shocked Maureen. It was so unlike him. With a lurch of her stomach she realised he was deadly serious.

"The Church does accept natural birth control," she tried to explain.

"Russian roulette, you mean. I'll have none of it, Maureen." His face was implacable. "So," he said, "I'm afraid the decision's up to you."

Ignoring Maureen's look of consternation, Trevor rose, picked up his charcoal-grey overcoat, and wound a yellow woollen scarf around his neck.

"It's time I was off. Perhaps you'd better think about it." Opening the front door, he stepped out on to the pavement.

Still stunned, Maureen felt his lips touch hers briefly, and then in bewilderment watched him walk down the street until he disappeared from sight. What did he mean, the decision was up to her? Surely not that . . .

"Has Trevor gone?" Beryl said in surprise, when after a few moments of sheer panic, Maureen went into the warm kitchen. "I was just going to make some cocoa."

"Yes. He said to say goodnight."

Beryl looked at her keenly. "You all right, love?"

"Yes. Perhaps a bit cold."

"I told your dad to put that electric fire on earlier, but you know what he's like about economising."

"It doesn't matter," Maureen said. "Mum . . . how come you only had me and Sandra?"

"It just never happened," she said briefly. "As you know, there's five years between you. I think we were only meant to have two."

Maureen hesitated, wondering whether to broach the subject of birth control, but couldn't pluck up the courage. Beryl had never been one for going into details about intimate subjects. Anything Maureen knew, even about menstruation, she'd gleaned from Sandra.

And that was where she went the following evening.

* * *

John answered the door, and his pleasant face creased in a grin.

"Well, if it isn't the bride-to-be! Come in! Sandra!" he called. "Make another bacon sandwich – it's your Maureen."

Sandra came through into the hall, wiping her hands on her apron.

"Hello, poppet, what brings you here?

"I just . . ."

65

After one swift discerning glance, Sandra said, "Let me just finish this, then we can go up to our bedroom."

Half an hour later, in the chilly room, they huddled under the eiderdown, leaning on pillows propped against the wall.

"I'm going to have one of those quilted headboards when I get my own place," Sandra said in apology. "Now then, what's the problem?"

Maureen looked at her, feeling suddenly embarrassed.

"It's about . . ."

Seeing her red face, Sandra's wide mouth creased in a grin. "Not the birds and the bees at this late stage?"

"Don't be daft. It's just that . . ."

"Spit it out, for heaven's sake."

"You've got a mixed marriage, haven't you?"

"You know we have." Sandra waited patiently.

"Has it caused any problems?" Maureen felt awful asking her such a personal question, but Trevor's final words had left her in such turmoil, she didn't know what else to do.

But Sandra didn't seem to mind. "Oh, you mean the Church's teaching on birth control. No, kitten. We want lots of kids. Our problem is getting them, not stopping them." She looked curiously at her sister. "Why?"

Maureen told her what Trevor had said. "He means it too," she said miserably.

Sandra didn't say anything for a few moments. She was thinking how different John's reaction had been when she had wanted to get married in her church. "Isn't her wedding day supposed to be the happiest day of a girl's life?" he'd said. "You arrange whatever you like, love – I'll just fit in."

In truth, neither he nor his parents were members of any church, though his mother did sometimes go to the whist drives at the Catholic church hall. But then she also went to the anniversaries at the local Methodist church. "I like to see all the children dressed up in their new clothes," she'd say. "Any road, it all comes down to the same thing at the end of the day."

So Sandra had encountered no problems at all, which had been a tremendous relief for her religion meant a lot to her. A part of her could sympathise with Trevor, but she also understood the Church's attitude. After all, marriage was one of the sacraments, and if a couple wanted the blessing of the Church, then it was only fair to expect them to live their lives according to its teaching.

She looked at her sister, seeing with a pang the indecision and anxiety in her eyes. "Time to grow up I'm afraid, petal. You've got to decide which is the most important to you."

"You mean, it's definitely either one or the other?" Maureen whispered.

"Well, if you don't get married in a Catholic church, then you're more or less turning your back on your faith."

Maureen bit her lip in confusion. Perhaps if they'd become engaged for several months in the usual way, then these things would have been discussed. But nothing had happened in the way she'd expected. There had been no romantic proposal, no glamorous setting, soft music, red roses, her suitor down on one knee. Trevor had simply said one night as they walked home from the pictures, "I think we should get married before I go to do my National Service."

And when, after listening to his reasons, she'd agreed, he'd said that as time was so short, it wasn't worth them getting engaged. Maureen, who'd dreamed of a diamond solitaire ring, one she could flash around at work and show off to her friends, was bitterly disappointed. But Trevor had explained that they needed to save every penny for their deposit, although he had promised to buy her an expensive

68

ring once they were financially stable.

"It will be worth waiting," he said. "We'll be going to all sorts of functions later on. I intend to join the Round Table, for instance, and possibly join a golf club, so I'd rather you were wearing really good jewellery."

"Penny for them?" said Sandra.

"Sorry," Maureen said, then thought again about Sandra's statement. "You know my faith's never been as strong as yours," she confessed. "I only go to Mass these days to please Dad."

Sandra gave a wry smile. "I suspected as much."

"It means a lot to you, doesn't it? Being a Catholic, I mean."

"I can't imagine being anything else." She looked at Maureen's troubled face. "Have you tried praying about it?"

Maureen shook her head, then said with a note of desperation in her voice, "Don't you think Trevor's being unreasonable?"

"Not if he feels so strongly about it. Though you have a right to your opinion too, you know. But it does look as though one of you will have to compromise."

Maureen stared miserably at her, knowing her sister spoke the truth.

What could she do? If the alternative was to lose him, and sacrifice her dreams of their wedding, then being a Catholic in her opinion paled into insignificance. But with a sinking feeling in the pit of her stomach, she knew that her dad wouldn't see it that way at all.

CHAPTER SIX

Maureen's anxiety wasn't misplaced. Frank didn't shout and rave or even argue. But the shock, pain and bitter disappointment in his eyes was even harder to bear. She watched, frozen with apprehension as he sat quite still in his armchair, his empty pipe hanging loosely from his fingers. It seemed an eternity until he answered, then he said, very quietly, "You must do as you think best. But don't expect me to come to your wedding, because I won't."

His words resounded with finality. Stunned, Maureen looked desperately at Beryl, but she remained silent. Then, without another word, Frank got up, and taking his overcoat off its peg at the bottom of the stairs, walked through to the parlour and straight out of the front door.

Through a blur of misery, Maureen looked again at her mother – who still hadn't spoken.

"You did it," she whispered. "You compromised when you married Dad."

"Yes, I did," Beryl said, her face suddenly tired, "and it caused ructions. Your grandad nearly burst a blood vessel when I told him. He always was hot-tempered, which is probably what killed him in the end." She gave a wry smile. "I can hear him now, saying he didn't know whether I was married or living in sin, 'cos the service was gabbled in Latin, and it was that short! Because I was Protestant, we were in and out before you could blink."

"But you never converted," Maureen said. "Trevor seems to think the priest puts pressure on you."

"Oh, they made a few noises, but I wasn't having any," Beryl said. "Not that I've anything against them, mind. I agreed to have you and Sandra brought up Catholic, and I've never regretted it. I suppose I'm still a Baptist at heart, but as you know I don't think you need to go to church to lead a good life."

Maureen dabbed at her eyes, and looked down at the lace-edged hanky which had been a present from Aunt Vera. "You don't seem very surprised," she muttered. "About Trevor, I mean."

"I'm not, really." Despite the guilty reserve she still felt about her daughter's choice of husband, Beryl tried to be fair. "It's a big thing for some people, Maureen, getting married to a Catholic. There's a lot of ignorance and bigotry still around, you know. But it makes no difference to me where you get married, although I wouldn't be very happy if it was in a Register Office. That's asking for trouble, not taking your vows in church."

"What am I going to do?" Maureen looked at her in despair. "I can't get married without Dad." Her tears welled up again. "I've always imagined walking down the aisle on his arm, him giving me away."

Beryl could only stare helplessly at her. She had no consoling words, for if Frank remained adamant, there was nothing ahead but heartbreak for them all.

"I'll make a cup of tea," she said. Going into the scullery she lifted the kettle to check the weight of the water, and lit the gas. Folding her arms as she waited for it to boil, Beryl stared unseeing at the flaking distempered wall. Well, I can't say I'm surprised, she thought. I had a feeling nothing would be straightforward where Trevor's concerned.

For Maureen, the evening passed in a blur of misery. Unable to settle to anything, she was restless, her glance constantly darting to the clock on the mantelpiece.

Beryl retreated into her Fair-Isle knitting, furiously clicking the needles. "He'll be back, once the pub shuts," she said, but Maureen couldn't even manage a smile.

* * *

However, when Frank did return, all thoughts of trying to reason with him were forgotten. He came through the front door like a whirlwind, shouting, "You'd better get down to Elaine's, the pair of you! There's all hell let loose!"

Beryl and Maureen, who were just finishing their cocoa, grabbed their coats, and dashed out of the door after him. In alarm, her heart hammering, Maureen ran faster than her parents to find that several other neighbours were crowding on the pavement outside the small terraced house. From an uncurtained bedroom window, electric light blazed from a naked light bulb, and out in the street the noise of a fearful row could be heard. A woman shrieked, there came a crashing sound and loud thuds, and then there was a scream to chill the blood, a high-pitched scream of protest and pain, and at that Frank thrust his way to the front and hammered on the door.

"What's going on?" he yelled. "Open the bloody door, damn you!"

"I'll go to the phone-box and ring the police," someone said, and there were murmurs of agreement as, shocked and fearful, the small group of people waited to find out what had happened.

But Frank wasn't prepared to wait and he and another heavily built man, Len Hudson, put the full force of their shoulders to the door. With a loud splintering sound, the lock burst and they staggered into the parlour. "Come on!" shouted Frank, and ran through to the stairs door. He suddenly stopped as he saw the twisted body lying at the bottom, blocking his way. It was Elaine. Seven months pregnant, her swollen belly crushed awkwardly beneath her, she was unconscious, her lip bleeding and cut, a rapidly swelling bruise on her left temple.

"Holy Mother of God!" he muttered.

"Don't touch her," Len Hudson said, "I'll get an ambulance!"

Frank glanced upwards. This would be Bert's work! The street had been expecting trouble for years – the man was nothing but a drunken sot. But not this, not his own daughter! And pregnant, at that!

Another man rushed in to replace the one who

had left, and drew in a sharp breath as he saw Elaine's body.

"Bloody hell!"

"The only way to get over her is to bring that chair," Frank said and, dragging over an armchair, positioned it by the door.

One by one they stood on the arm and managed with difficulty to climb over Elaine's inert body. As they mounted the stairs, there was the sound of a scuffle in the front bedroom, followed by a woman's moan of pain.

Beryl and Maureen, held back with the other women from entering, were huddled together on the pavement.

"Where's your dad?" Beryl muttered. "What's he doing?"

"Mr Hudson said it was Elaine," Maureen whispered. "You don't think it's the baby come early, do you?"

"If it has, then from what we just heard it won't be nature's way!" Filled with apprehension and fear, Beryl shivered in the night air, then turned as she heard the distant sound of a police siren. A few moments later a police car swept round the corner and drew up beside them.

The crowd drew aside to let the uniformed officers

through, and Beryl breathed a little easier, feeling reassured now about her husband's safety.

Frank however, was far from safe. He and his companion were cornered in a bedroom, where Bert Jones was holding his wife before him, a broken beer bottle clutched in his hand, its jagged edge at her throat.

"Come one step nearer, and I'll mark her for life," he snarled, "and if not her, then I'll slash one of you interfering sods!"

Frank glanced quickly at his companion. He knew the man, had drunk pints with him, knew he'd seen active service in the last war. Dave Short had been in the Navy, had served on *HMS Cossack* during its heroic rescue of 300 British seamen from the German ship, *Altmark*. He was a good man to have with you in a crisis like this.

It was crucial that they didn't provoke the man before them. Inflamed by alcohol, his eyes were mad with both venom and cunning, yet they could have taken him on if it weren't for the ashen face of the woman held pinned against him. A stark red weal disfigured her swollen cheek, while her chin was bloodstained from an ugly cut on her mouth. Her eyes wild with terror, she mutely beseeched them to help her.

77

Frank had heard the sound of the police siren, but his brain, suddenly cold and reasoning, knew that if they burst into the room the shock might tip Bert over the edge. He made a slight movement of his hand, indicating to Dave to retreat, trusting him to play his part, as he tried to distract the swaying man before him.

"Come on, Bert," he pleaded, "what's all this about? Let Ida go, there's a good chap."

Bert's reaction was to tighten his grip on his wife's hair, jerking her head backwards. She winced with pain.

"The slut's got another man! That's what it's all about!"

Cruelly, he twisted her tear-stained face up to his, and from the corner of his eye, Frank saw Dave slip out quietly. Then Bert spat in his wife's face, before turning to Frank.

"I'm only doing what any man would do, teaching her a lesson!"

"And what about Elaine, what has she done?" Frank asked, struggling to keep his tone low and reasonable. He began to inch forward.

Bert stood, swinging his head from side to side, as he tried to focus his thoughts.

"Elaine . . . ?"

Suddenly his mesmerised wife found her courage and her voice.

"You knocked her down the stairs, you pig!" she screamed at him.

Frank seized his opportunity. "The ambulance will be here any minute! Come on, man, put that bottle down, you've done enough damage for one night!"

Bert was staring bulbous-eyed at him, and Frank met his gaze squarely, holding it, trying to transmit the force of his own reason into the other man's befuddled brain. With the obscene image of young Elaine in his mind, every instinct cried out to lunge, grab the brute, overpower him, but he knew such a move could be disastrous.

Then suddenly Bert's eyes flickered away from his to the two burly policemen who'd slipped in quietly to stand motionless just inside the door. Indecision and panic passed across his face, and for one moment he faltered, his hand, still clutching the broken bottle, wavering away from Ida. Swiftly, seizing their opportunity, the police made their move, and within seconds had him pinned against a wall and handcuffed.

"Well done, sir," one of them said, turning to Frank. "We could do with some like you in the Force." With Bert stumbling between them, they took him away.

As Frank leaned back against the wall, drained and shaken, Ida rushed from the room and down the stairs to her daughter and, amidst the sound of her sobs, he heard the ambulance men lifting Elaine on to a stretcher. He leaned against the wall for a moment, his legs strangely weak, then slowly he went down the steep stairs. He needed desperately to get out of the house, away from the place, out into the fresh air and some sort of normality. When he saw Beryl and Maureen waiting, their eyes filled with pride, it almost unmanned him and when Dave said in a gruff voice, "They should give you a medal, Frank," he could only shrug.

Beryl, seeing his drawn face, took his arm in hers, and with Maureen protectively on the other side, they pushed through the crowd and took him home.

"A drop of brandy, I think," said Beryl, pouring him a generous measure out of the half-bottle they kept for emergencies. "The police said they'll need a statement later, but they'll have to wait a bit."

Maureen was in shock, the horrifying sight of her friend being carried out on a stretcher still before her. Unconscious, her nose bloody and swollen, a grotesque lump on her forehead, Elaine had obviously not only had a violent fall, but had suffered a brutal assault.

Oh God, oh God, Maureen prayed silently, please let her be all right, please let her keep the baby!

And what about her dad? Suppose that maniac had tried to kill him, had succeeded? And only hours before she'd stuck her own knife into him. For that was how he must have felt. Guilt and remorse swept over her, and she said with despair, "Dad, I'm sorry, about the wedding and all that." She looked at him, her eyes brimming with tears.

Frank looked at her, at the lovely face which was his pride and joy, and muttered, "Don't worry, love. We'll try and sort something out." He stretched out an arm and, grateful for his words, Maureen moved into its circle, resting her cheek on his head.

For Frank now knew that some things were more important than defending a matter of principle. Against the enormity of the tragedy he'd just witnessed, his own desires and preferences seemed unimportant. Maureen's happiness must come first, for surely a child was one of God's greatest gifts. The vision of Elaine rose before him, and mentally he cursed the man who'd caused such havoc, that he might rot in Hell for what he'd done that night! Though if Elaine did not recover, then maybe he'd have his Hell on earth.

Elaine's husband, Brian, who was a shop-fitter, had been working away in Preston. Contacted by the police and rushed to the hospital, he arrived too late. The following day, in hushed tones, the shocking news spread throughout the neighbourhood. Elaine had died shortly after admission from a massive haemorrhage, and although doctors struggled to save her child, it was useless – the baby had died in the womb. It was a little girl.

White-faced, Carol came round to see Maureen, and the two girls wept together in the parlour, traumatised not only by the loss of their young friend, but also the brutal circumstances.

"I'd gone to do my cousin's hair for her engagement party," Carol said in a choked voice, "and stayed really late. I knew nothing about it until it was all over."

Beryl, devastated at the cruel waste of two young lives, dealt with the tragedy in practical terms. She organised a street collection for a wreath from the neighbours, although of course the funeral would have to wait until after the inquest. Everyone said it was the worst day in Oakvale's memory.

"He wants stringing up!" one old woman muttered.

"No, they won't hang him," Beryl said. "It was manslaughter. But they'll lock him away, that's for sure, and I hope they throw away the key."

"How's Ida?"

"No-one's seen her. She's gone to her sister's in Burslem."

"Aye, just as well."

No-one had seen Brian either. His father had fetched his belongings, and the street knew they might never see the popular youth again. He was going back to live with his parents, which they agreed was the only solution.

"Poor lad," Nellie said sadly. "No-one deserves what he's suffered."

Severely shaken, Maureen told Trevor, despite his protests, that she couldn't even think about their wedding until the funeral was over. There was time enough to plan their future. These few days she owed to Elaine.

CHAPTER SEVEN

The wedding took place on Boxing Day, a date chosen by Maureen because it was Frank and Beryl's own anniversary.

"It can become a family tradition," she said. "Besides, Trevor won't have any excuse to forget the date."

Appreciating the gesture, Frank had smiled. As he smiled throughout the service and throughout the reception. If his normal warmth and humour were missing, then only his immediate family were aware of it.

"The father seems all right," Henry commented.

"I'm not so sure about her, though." Norah indicated Vera – who, resplendent in a blue tailored costume with an imitation fox-fur around her shoulders, had already upset Trevor's cousin, an over-weight spotty youth.

She'd greeted him with the remark, "Well, you'd never think you were related to the bridegroom. Not much of a resemblance, is there?"

As her loud voice had boomed out, one or two people had turned, causing the unfortunate lad to redden with embarrassment, before muttering, "Obviously not."

Norah, overhearing the remark, had glared at Vera, who with one withering glance had made her feel even more aware that her sensible grey suit appeared dowdy compared with the smart clothes of the bride's relatives.

But Maureen was blissfully unaware of any under-currents as, hand in hand with her new husband, she drifted around the upstairs room at a local pub, her happiness apparent to all. Some of the older guests looked askance at the ballerina length of her white wedding dress. Her decision had dismayed Beryl too, but the bride-to-be was adamant. Trevor, she told her mother, considered the traditional long dress to be old-fashioned. And Beryl had to admit that the graceful style in Nottingham lace was perfect for Maureen's slender figure. In the flower-filled church, a painting of the young couple, Trevor fair and handsome, his bride dark and radiant, would have made an exquisite cameo. And as the winter sun poured through the stained-glass windows, there were several flutters of lace or embroidered handkerchiefs. If she hadn't been acutely conscious of Frank's disappointment, Beryl would have said that the whole day was perfect.

Both Frank and Maureen had been worried that their parish priest, on learning of the wedding plans, might, as Beryl warned, "give them a hard time," but before anyone outside the family had been told of the momentous decision, he was fortuitously transferred to another parish in the diocese.

"By the time this new priest gets himself organised, it'll all be over," Frank said, guilt warring with relief.

Vera, to everyone's surprise, had been compliant about the wedding ceremony.

"Makes no difference to me," she said. "One church is much like another. I don't hold with religion, it's caused too many wars."

As for Nellie, as long as Maureen didn't get married in a Register Office, she was happy.

Frank was an only child and, as his parents were dead and he had little contact with the rest of his family, the Matthews side hadn't caused any complications either.

Afterwards, he grudgingly admitted that the vicar had spoken well, and he'd been impressed with the lovely historic church. "Of course," he muttered, "if it hadn't been for Henry VIII, this would have been one of ours."

"Oh, give it a rest, Frank," Beryl said.

She was watching Sandra, initially a reluctant matron of honour, but the shantung silk dress in coffee and cream had been an inspired choice. Carol too, made a lovely bridesmaid. What a pity, Beryl thought, that her family were moving to Leicester where they had relatives. She'd always liked Carol. Maureen would miss her dreadfully, particularly now that poor Elaine . . . but Beryl firmly steered her mind away from thoughts of the tragedy. Such horror had no place at an occasion like this.

Glancing across the room she caught Norah looking at her and with an effort smiled, to receive only a slight nod in return. Beryl hadn't taken to either of the Mountfords, considering them stuck-up.

"I just hope they turn out to be good in-laws," she muttered to Frank.

Then, as Maureen caught her eye, she hurried across to go and help her change. In her going-away outfit of a blue fitted suit and white hat, she looked so grown up that Beryl had to turn away to hide her tears.

"He'd better be good to you, that's all," she said, as she removed a couple of stray hairs from her daughter's shoulders.

"Of course he will, Mum." Maureen looked at her in surprise, then held out her arms to hold her mother tight. "Thanks for everything," she said, and Beryl was about to speak when a sharp knock at the door caused them to move awkwardly apart, and she went to open it.

Trevor came in with impatience. "It's time we went – you've been ages."

"She looks lovely, though, doesn't she?" Beryl said.

He looked at Maureen, and said, "The word 'lovely' hardly does her justice." He smiled and said, "But I want to get there before it's dark, so . . ."

Hurriedly, Maureen picked up her handbag and followed him into the crowded room, to a chorus of approval.

"Ooh, you look lovely, doesn't she, our Vera?" Nellie, a little tipsy after two egg-flips, peered up at Maureen with misty eyes as she bent to kiss her goodbye.

"Aye, you'll do," Vera said. "Give my regards to the Great Orme. Eh, I had some happy times in Llandudno!"

Nellie raised her eyebrows to remind Maureen that the North Wales resort had been the one where Vera had met her soldier fiancé in 1916.

"I will," she promised, with a fleeting sadness for her spinster aunt. But it was only momentary, for soon everyone was showering them with confetti and, amidst laughter, they ran out to Henry's Morris Minor.

"Bring it back in one piece," he instructed.

"We will," Maureen said.

After pulling out the choke, Trevor eventually got the engine to start. Just a few seconds later, with Maureen waving furiously, they were gone.

"Well, that's that," Beryl said, suddenly feeling very flat, and Frank put his arm around her shoulders.

"They'll be back soon, and it's not as if anything's changed, not with them living with us."

Beryl looked at him and sighed.

"You're wrong," she said. "Things will never be quite the same, not now."

* * *

The decision about where to go for their three-day

honeymoon hadn't proved difficult. Maureen
wanted to go somewhere new. Trevor, who'd only
recently passed his driving test, hadn't wanted too
long a journey. So as they'd both already been to
Blackpool and Rhyl, Llandudno was the obvious
choice.

As the car sped away, Maureen said, "Everything
went really well, don't you think, and we were lucky
with the weather."

"Yes. But I need to concentrate now, Maureen, so
if you don't mind?"

Feeling snubbed, she turned her head away,
relieved when he stretched out his hand and
touched hers saying, "Sorry, sweetheart, but I daren't
let myself be distracted."

So, Maureen consoled herself for the rest of the
journey by reliving the whole day, right from the
time Beryl had brought her breakfast in bed. The
happiest day of my life, she thought with content.

The small inexpensive private hotel they'd
booked into was in one of the side streets leading up
to the promenade and as they drew up outside
Maureen could just glimpse the sea, grey and myste-
rious in the deepening gloom. Many of the windows
in the street were uncurtained, with their light
streaming out on to the pavement, and they could

hear strains of music as doors opened to let in guests.

"I keep forgetting it's Christmas," Maureen laughed.

Trevor hauled their suitcases out of the boot, before looking up critically at the outside of the hotel they'd chosen from the holiday guide.

"Could do with a lick of paint," he said.

"Oh, I'm sure it'll be nice inside. Have I got any confetti on me?"

"Not that I can see. How about me?"

Maureen brushed his shoulders. "You're fine."

To their relief, the interior of the hotel was warm and welcoming. Their bedroom could have been bigger, and the sea view they'd requested was only just discernible, but the room was clean and well-furnished, and when they drew the curtains and switched on the lamps, it looked inviting and cosy.

Maureen looked at the double bed, at the frilled eiderdown with its design of red roses, and tested it, bouncing on the sprung mattress.

"It's comfy," she said. "Try it."

"No, we need to get unpacked, the evening meal's at seven."

Obediently, she got up and went over to her case, while Trevor unlocked his own and began taking out his belongings.

91

"Hang your things in the right side of the wardrobe," he instructed. "You can use the top two drawers, and I'll use the bottom ones."

"Yes, sir!" Maureen saluted, but Trevor was preoccupied, already placing his clothes carefully on hangers, his socks and handkerchiefs neatly together, his underwear by their side.

Maureen sighed, and began to sort her own case out. She wished he'd lighten up a bit, but then decided she was being unfair. It had been a long day after all and he must be tired after the unaccustomed driving.

But the minute they went into the dining-room, she knew she should have changed. From the sidelong glances and half-hidden smiles, it was obvious that everyone knew they were a honeymoon couple.

"They've guessed!" she whispered to Trevor.

He looked around. "So what? It's not a crime, you know."

"Yes, but it makes me feel embarrassed. I mean, we'll have to face coming in tomorrow morning."

"You worry about some funny things," he said.

Maureen looked down at the festive menu. "What does Chicken Maryland mean?"

"Just chicken, only they serve it with a banana in batter."

It sounded a funny combination, but she wanted this night to be special and exciting, so she decided to be adventurous. "Okay, I'll have that, and just a fruit juice to start."

Trevor did the ordering, including a bottle of Blue Nun, and then, sitting back in his chair, examined the cutlery.

Maureen watched with amusement as he did what he always did: gave the perfectly clean utensils an extra polish with his napkin. But when he proceeded to turn over the side plates, she smiled. That, she could understand. "Where are they made?" she asked.

"Looks like Adderley."

"Our next-door neighbour works on their potbank – in the clay end."

"You know, people outside the Potteries wouldn't know what you meant by 'potbank'," Trevor said. "It's a local word – other people would say factory."

"I never knew that."

"There's a lot you don't know," he teased.

"Oh, and I suppose you're going to teach me."

"Who else?" Trevor said with a grin.

Later, they went for a short walk. It was cold and slightly damp, but they strolled hand in hand up to the promenade, walked a little way along and stood looking across the picturesque bay.

"It looks as though the sea could be rough tomorrow," Trevor said.

"Well, we won't mind – we'll be able to walk under the spray. I always loved doing that as a kid."

"Ah, but you're a married woman, now."

"I don't feel any different." Beginning to feel the chill, she turned up the collar on her coat and smiled up at him, her eyes full of meaning.

But Trevor didn't return her smile. Instead, he stared down at her for one long moment and then said quietly, "We can't have that, can we? Perhaps it's time we went back to the hotel."

CHAPTER EIGHT

An hour later, propped against the pillows in the unfamiliar double bed, Maureen waited in nervous yet pleasurable anticipation. As the minutes ticked by she began to feel uneasy and glanced at the alarm-clock. Trevor had been ages in the bathroom, which was inconveniently situated along the corridor and down a short flight of stairs. She whiled away the time by stroking the silky fabric of her cream, lace-trimmed nightdress. It had cost far more than anyone knew, but had been worth the expense, for it felt wonderful next to her skin. She looked around the cosy, inviting room, admiring her glamorous reflection in the triple mirror on the dressing-table. She was glad they had waited. It would make tonight so much more romantic.

But less than half an hour later, her dreams, her

hopes, lay in brutally shattered fragments. For there had been no love in what had just taken place. The harsh act that Trevor had performed was far removed from the passionate lovemaking of her dreams. In the darkened room there had been no soft words, no tenderness. Just a heavy silence as within seconds of returning, Trevor had switched off the lights, pulled her into a lying position and climbed roughly on top of her. Initially she was too shocked and confused to speak, but when she realised he was already fumbling inside his pyjama trousers and struggling with a packet of Durex, she protested, "What are you doing?" Her voice rose shrilly, "Trevor, wait!", but he ignored her, roughly pushing her legs apart. He entered her immediately, each thrust causing such pain that she thrashed her head from side to side, crying, "You're hurting me," pushing in vain at his chest – but he was already withdrawing, only to collapse weakly back on to the bed.

"Now you really are married!" he muttered, then turned abruptly on to his side away from her, and lay with hunched shoulders.

Maureen didn't speak, couldn't speak. She was too stunned at what had just taken place, and she lay frozen in silence until Trevor's deep, even breathing told her that at last he was asleep.

Then, her body and emotions battered and bruised, slowly the tears came, seeping beneath her eyelids, running hotly down her face, tears not only of bitter disappointment, but also of a burning anger. Uncaring, she ignored them, until they began to trickle down her neck and she wiped them away with the hem of the white cotton sheet. It shouldn't have happened like this, she wept in despair. She might not have any sexual experience, but even she had heard of foreplay. Eventually she pushed the folds of her nightdress between her sticky thighs, and realised she too had to get some sleep.

Retrieving the four hair-grips she'd hidden beneath her pillow, her throat swollen with tears, she wearily pinned up the side curls of her hair. A woman should keep some of her feminine mystery, that's what the magazines advised. But they don't tell us about sex, she thought with bitterness, nobody does. Oh, she knew what it was all about of course, and the subject was obliquely mentioned at times among her friends. But it was mainly sly comments such as "he can't keep his hands to himself", and the danger of "going all the way", in case you got pregnant, but no decent girl would go into personal details. Apart from sculpture, she'd never seen a man's naked body. And she still hadn't, she suddenly realised, for Trevor had kept himself covered during the whole degrading episode.

So much for admiring him for his restraint while we were courting, she thought bitterly. There was I thinking he loved and respected me. Well, he hasn't shown much of either on our wedding night.

The day had been long and tiring and finally she slept, only to wake with a heavy heart, feeling sore and uncomfortable. Stealthily removing the hair-grips, she fluffed out her hair and then flinched as Trevor, stirring, flung out an arm across her breasts.

Maureen stiffened with apprehension, terrified of a repeat performance, but he merely opened his eyes and smiled.

"Good morning, beautiful wife."

"Good morning." She could hear the chill in her voice, but Trevor just leaned over and kissed her, appearing not to notice her lack of response. "Come on, sleepyhead, I'm starving and they finish breakfast at nine o'clock."

He leaned over and picked up his dressing-gown from the floor, slipping it on before getting out of bed. "Shall I go to the bathroom first, or do you want to?"

Maureen hurriedly swung out her legs. "I'll go. I want a bath."

"Well, don't be too long, as I said –"

"You don't want to be late for breakfast, I know," she snapped, and trudged along the corridor, her shoulders tense with fury. How could anyone be so thick, so insensitive?

But as the day progressed, Trevor seemed oblivious to Maureen's resentment. He was attentive and tender, behaving just how she'd always imagined, and gradually she began to be won over by his charm, to soften towards him, to try to seek excuses for his behaviour. Although it had never occurred to her that a man could be nervous about such things, perhaps that was the reason. And he must have been tired too. He should have said, she thought, we could always have waited.

So, they spent the morning wrapped in warm scarves and gloves, walking along the wide promenade flanked by the Little Orme and the Great Orme, before going thankfully inside one of the few cafés open.

After ordering turkey rissoles, Maureen suggested, "We could walk and look at the West Shore, this afternoon."

"Oh?" Trevor said. "I rather thought we'd go back to the hotel."

With a lurch of her stomach, Maureen looked

down at the red-checked tablecloth, the colour rising in her cheeks. She was going to have to say something, if only because she was still sore – it even stung when she spent a penny.

"Trevor –" she began.

"Yes?" he said absently, examining the side plates.

"About last night . . ." she paused, waiting for him to react.

He did, looking up sharply. "What about it?"

Maureen floundered, trying to find the right words. "I'm not criticising, or anything –" she began.

"Then don't!"

"But –" she broke off as the waitress brought their food, and she subsided into resentful silence. Perhaps now wasn't the right time, but he was going to have to listen to her sooner or later – and he'd only got himself to blame, she railed inwardly. It was probably his guilty conscience that was making him so irritable.

Later, as they walked back to the hotel, she began to feel almost sick as anxiety gnawed at her stomach. But her worries proved unfounded, for when they went up to their bedroom, Trevor simply went over to his bedside table and took out his library book. "I thought we'd sit in the lounge and read – it's nice and warm down there."

She glanced at the title. It was George Orwell's *1984*.

"Is it good?" she asked.

"Brilliant, but you wouldn't like it."

"How do you know?"

Trevor looked at her and raised his eyebrows. "I only meant that you usually read romantic novels."

"Just because they're romantic, it doesn't mean they haven't any depth to them! Anyway, I didn't bring anything with me."

"There's a bookshelf, I noticed it last night."

And that's what they did, read. And when they were inside the hotel, day or night, that's all they did.

Outdoors they took the sea air, climbing the Great Orme to stand hand in hand looking out at the Lake District and the Isle of Man, walking past the outdoor theatre in Happy Valley, and exploring the town; but on their return, there was nothing. At least nothing, Maureen thought in confusion, to indicate they were on their honeymoon.

On the last night, they took a walk along the promenade, looking at the imposing hotels with their curtains undrawn, their golden light spilling out into the gloom. They paused outside one glittering façade.

"I'd love to be able to afford to stay there," Maureen said, looking at the chandeliers in a spacious dining-room overlooking the sea. She gazed at the women in their smart cocktail dresses, at their sparkling jewellery, at the formal waiters, and sighed with envy. Their own dining-room was in the basement, meanly lit, with cramped tables, and no-one really dressed up. Although it was called a private hotel, in reality it was only one step up from a boarding-house.

"Those places cost a fortune," Trevor said.

"Well, I can dream, can't I?"

"That's one thing you are good at."

Maureen glanced uneasily at him, wondering if he was being sarcastic, but he just smiled, put his arm around her waist and said, "Come on, let's go back. It's getting chilly."

* * *

And so they returned to Stoke-on-Trent, and to Maureen's home, where the parlour had been allocated for their exclusive use. Not that it was any great sacrifice, for it was only used at Christmas and on special occasions. The decision of where they should live had been one topic on which Maureen had been adamant.

"There's no point me moving into your parents'

house, not when you're likely to be away most of the time," she declared and, unable to argue with the logic of this, Trevor had reluctantly agreed.

"But I shall go over there for my baths," he said. "You can't expect me to rough it in your kitchen. And there's no sense in my moving in all my things until we buy our own house. I'll just bring a change of clothes and some books."

The pattern that had become established when they were in Llandudno continued over the next three weeks. Maureen's previous worries that she'd feel embarrassed and inhibited with her parents sleeping in the next room weren't put to the test, for the simple reason that Trevor never crossed the narrow divide between Sandra's old bed in which he was sleeping, and her own. Neither did he greet her suggestion that they should move them together with any enthusiasm.

"It's too small a room," he objected. "We wouldn't have space to move about."

In some puzzlement, and with the memory of their disastrous wedding night fading, Maureen waited in vain for Trevor to approach her again. Often, she would lie and watch him reading, thinking how handsome he was as the bedside lamp emphasised his profile. On a few occasions, she went over to

MARGARET KAINE

snuggle down beside him, her head resting on his chest. Usually she lay on top of the candlewick bedspread, but once or twice she slipped beneath the sheets, loving the feel of his warm body next to hers. But although Trevor put down his book to kiss and caress her, as soon as she tried to take things further, he distanced himself, saying, "We'd better get some sleep, I've got work tomorrow," or often just a dismissive, "Goodnight, Maureen".

Humiliated and embarrassed by the rejections, she stopped making the effort.

Frank and Beryl, too, were somewhat perplexed by their son-in-law. Oh, he was perfectly polite and well-mannered, but Beryl took exception to the way he always examined her cutlery, then polished it on a clean handkerchief.

"Does he think I'm not clean, or what?" she demanded.

"He does it everywhere," Maureen reassured her. "It's just one of his funny ways."

Another was his habit of removing himself from the family circle every evening to go and sit alone in the parlour reading. He wasn't interested in television, and when Maureen went into the warm kitchen to watch her favourite programmes such as *Take Your Pick*, or *Dixon of Dock Green*, he hardly seemed to notice her absence.

"He's not what you'd call sociable, is he?" Frank said one evening, after Trevor refused yet again to join him for a pint. He'd thought it would make a welcome change to have another man in the house.

"He's just quiet, that's all," Maureen said.

Beryl glanced at her, admiring her loyalty. She had her own worry. The young couple seemed happy enough, but hardly behaved like newly-weds. She remembered when they were first married Frank couldn't keep his hands off her, and many times she'd had to push him playfully away. But with Maureen and Trevor, nothing seemed to have changed. Their relationship was exactly as before; there was no sign of any increased intimacy between them. In the small, cramped house, not once did she see any meaningful glances, or come upon them "canoodling", as Frank called it. In fact, Maureen seemed to spend more time with them than with her new husband. They were all proud of Trevor of course, congratulating him on passing his final exams, but Beryl still couldn't warm to him.

"Is everything all right, love?" she said one night when she and Maureen were on their own.

"How do you mean?" Maureen was wary.

"With you and Trevor."

"Of course, why do you ask?" While part of her longed to confide in her mother, Maureen refused to believe that there was a problem. It's early days, she kept telling herself. I'm expecting too much, too soon. And how could she discuss such a private matter? Trevor would be livid, she knew he would.

"I just wondered." Beryl saw the defence in her daughter's eyes, and knew her intuition was correct. She sighed. The girl never changed – she'd always bottled up her problems. But whatever the trouble is, she thought bitterly, I'll bet it lies with him.

Then on Thursday morning, the long-expected brown envelope arrived. Trevor was called up, instructed to attend in two weeks at the Recruiting Office in Hanley, prior to reporting to RAF Cardington, in Bedfordshire.

CHAPTER NINE

The morning before her son-in-law was due to leave, Beryl had a word with Frank. "You're not out collecting tonight, are you?"

"No, why?"

"As it's his last night, I thought we'd give them the house to themselves."

Frank got out of bed and, stretching, went to the window and peered through the curtains. "Hell of a Jack Frost out there."

"It's Jack Frost in here. For heaven's sake, switch that electric fire on," Beryl said, shivering as she slipped her feet into warm sheepskin slippers. "How about going to the pictures, then to the pub afterwards?"

"But you hate the pub," Frank said.

"Where else can we go? It'll defeat the whole

object if we get back too early."

Beryl couldn't help feeling guilty that, since their wedding, the young couple had spent so little time on their own. But it had been such a bad month. First, Frank had gone down with flu on New Year's Day, then she'd caught it, with the result that even when they'd gone back to work, neither of them had felt up to a night out.

"So, that's decided, then?" Zipping up her flowered quilted housecoat, she turned to look questioningly at Frank.

"Whatever you say, my love."

* * *

Maureen waited until her parents had left for work, and then, putting Trevor's buttered toast in front of him, said, "We'll be on our own tonight. I thought I'd get a couple of steaks, and perhaps you could get a bottle of that wine we had in Llandudno."

"I suppose so," Trevor said.

"You don't sound very enthusiastic! You know you won't get leave until after your basic training."

"That's right, it'll be about six weeks."

"So," she said, taking off the cosy and pouring out his tea, "let's make our last night special."

Trevor looked up frowning, "I'd planned to go and see my parents, have a bath, pack up my things etc."

With an effort Maureen suppressed her irritation. "But I thought you told me you were finishing work early?"

"I am."

"So," she said, "you'll have plenty of time for both. But I want you here by a quarter past seven, mind."

"All right, Miss Bossyboots," he grinned.

"*Mrs* Bossyboots," she reminded him. "Right, I'm off to finish getting ready for work." Bending down she gave him a quick kiss. "See you later."

Maureen spent her lunch hour shopping in the market and, after buying mushrooms and tomatoes, hovered over a display of melons. The only time she'd tasted one was on their honeymoon.

"I want one I can use tonight," she confided to the stallholder, a thin, chirpy man whose beaky nose seemed to have a permanent dewdrop. "Sure sign you've never bought one afore, love," he chaffed. "If I kept 'em 'til they were ripe, I'd be running at a loss."

Embarrassed, she decided not to bother, and going to another stall bought a tempting-looking apple-pie and a tin of thick cream. Then spotting a bunch of early violets, she bought those too. And, buoyed up with plans for the evening, the afternoon passed quickly. Nothing could dampen her spirits, not even her growing resentment at the amount of extra work being piled on to her shoulders.

"They ought to make me manager – I do most of the work," she often grumbled at home. And Frank, who privately thought Maureen's boss was a lazy sod, agreed.

"Everyone knows you practically run the office," he said, "but you've got one thing against you."

"I know – no-one takes me seriously because I'm a girl. I tell you, Dad, I can run rings round anyone else there, but I get paid the least. It's not fair."

"Life isn't fair, love – I've told you that before."

Maureen glared at him. "You don't seem to care that I'm underpaid!"

Frank put his mug down, and looked at her reflectively, "You've got to remember that a man has a family to support. It's only right he should get paid more."

"I don't agree," she said stubbornly. "If a man and a woman are doing the same job, they should get the same wage."

"Absolutely," Beryl said. She glanced at Trevor, who for once was still sitting with them. "What do you think, Trevor?"

"I agree with Frank, and I also think most people

would resent working for a woman."

"Well, you won't convince me," Maureen retorted.

But today she balanced the books with a philosophical shrug. She had more important things to think about. She was convinced that it was the lack of privacy that was inhibiting Trevor. I mean, she reasoned, you can hear every sound through that bedroom wall. She knew just when Beryl switched the light off, and many a night Frank woke her with his smoker's cough.

That evening, it was almost seven before Frank and Beryl left the house. Running upstairs to the bedroom, Maureen put on both bars of the electric fire, drew the curtains and switched on the bedside lamps. Then, using a clean tablecloth, she reset the kitchen table, placing the violets in a pretty vase in the centre.

Trevor, as she expected, was punctual to the dot. "I don't know how you manage it," she said, bustling around the scullery. "Even relying on the buses, you're dead on time."

"I don't like sloppiness," he said. "Not in anything."

That was true, she mused as she heated the fat in the chip-pan. He was unbelievably tidy. Even his dirty washing, which he always insisted was loaded separately when she went to the launderette, was kept neatly in a small suitcase. "Did you bring the wine?"

"Of course. I'll put it outside the back door for a bit to chill."

She smiled at him as she turned the steaks. "Are you nervous, you know, about tomorrow?"

Trevor leaned against the doorframe watching her, as she dropped the chipped potatoes into the spluttering fat. "Thousands before me have survived, so it can't be that bad."

"I can't wait to see you in your uniform," she said. "I bet you'll look like one of the stars in *Reach for The Sky*, or *The Dambusters*."

"You've watched too many war films," he grinned.

"Mum thinks I've watched too many films, full stop!"

"She might have a point."

"What do you mean?"

"You're such a romantic. Real life isn't like that."

I found that out on our wedding night, she thought, but resolutely pushed the memory away. "Yes, well, in this real life, it's time you opened that bottle," she replied.

Later, both mellowed by the food and wine, they

curled up on the sofa in the parlour.

"Don't you want to watch TV?" Trevor asked eventually, and Maureen saw his eyes stray to his library book.

"Not tonight," she said. "I'll have plenty of time for that when you've gone. I'll put some music on, though."

She chose a Frank Sinatra LP and, with the crooner's seductive tones filling the small room, leaned over the back of the sofa and wound her arms around her husband's neck. "Will you miss me?" she murmured, her face against his.

"Of course I will!" Trevor caught her hand and kissed the inside of her palm.

She leaned closer, her breasts pressing against his head. "It's lovely to have the house to ourselves," she whispered. "They won't be back for ages, and it's nice and warm upstairs."

Trevor remained silent for so long she thought he wasn't going to answer her. Then at last he said, "All right. You go on up."

With exhilaration, Maureen went quickly up the steep stairs and turned down the bedclothes. Excited and nervous, she wasn't sure whether she should get undressed or not. Then she decided to strip down to her bra and pants, sprayed herself with perfume, and got into the chilly single bed, cursing that she'd forgotten to put in a hot-water bottle. Well, they'd just have to cuddle up to get warm, for this time she was determined that things would be different. But she lay shivering and alone for what seemed like ages, and a glance at the alarm-clock told her she'd been waiting nearly fifteen minutes. What on earth could Trevor be doing? Her excited anticipation beginning to turn to anger, she was about to fling back the bedclothes and go and find out, when she heard his tread on the stairs.

"At last! I wondered where you'd got to."

"I had the last glass of wine," he muttered.

Confused, Maureen stared at him. She could have sworn they'd finished the bottle. But not wanting to spoil the mood, she teased, "Just waiting for me to get the bed warm, you mean."

Trevor turned his back and began to undress. Taking off his jacket, shirt and tie, he put on his dressing-gown before taking off his trousers, and then keeping it on, climbed in beside her. "It's freezing!"

Maureen wound her arms around him and snuggled close. "You're lucky," she smiled. "You've got your own personal bed-warmer."

And so at last they made love. And it *was*

114

different, well slightly anyway. For this time, to Maureen's relief, Trevor began by kissing and caressing her. She responded eagerly, but to her dismay almost immediately he was climbing on top of her, and the final act was over even more quickly than before. But at least they'd 'done it', she consoled herself, and although she'd been dreading the searing pain she'd felt before, all she experienced this time was a certain amount of discomfort.

Yet later, as she lay with her head on Trevor's shoulder, Maureen's feelings were not of happiness, but bitter disappointment. Is that it? she thought. Is that what all the fuss is about? Feeling an urgent need to touch him, to have some sort of skin contact, she nestled closer and began to gently stroke his bare chest.

"I'm glad you haven't got a lot of hairs," she said. "I don't like hairy men."

"I didn't know you'd seen many," Trevor said, but his tone wasn't easy and relaxed like her own. It was stiff, and she looked at him in surprise.

"I do go to the open-air pool at Trentham, you know."

"Oh, I see what you mean."

"You're a funny one, Trevor Mountford. You soon get jealous."

"I certainly do." He moved away from her and sat up in the bed, wincing as the hard wooden head-board cut into his back. "So you'd better remember that while I'm away."

"Same goes for you," she retorted promptly. "None of these WAAFs, mind."

"You don't need to worry about me."

Maureen smiled up at him and kissed the top of his arm. "Come back down and cuddle."

But he was already getting out of bed and, still wearing his dressing-gown, reaching for his trousers. She watched him get dressed and then with a sigh got up and, fetching a clean pair of pants, put her own clothes on. Once downstairs, while Trevor returned to his reading, Maureen cleared the table and began to wash the dishes. From the boudoir to the kitchen-sink, she thought with a wry smile. I wonder how many women have said that in the past!

But she felt unsettled and vaguely irritable, and halfway through paused in resentment. Hey, some-thing was wrong here. Even her dad used to wipe up sometimes.

"Trevor!" she called.

There was no answer, so wiping her hands on the tea towel, she marched through to the parlour. "How about giving me a hand?"

He looked up with a puzzled expression. She dangled the tea towel in front of him. "I'll wash, you dry."

"But ..."

"But what?"

"Surely that's women's work. I mean I'm just in the middle of this chapter."

She looked down at his book. It was *The Devil Rides Out*, by Dennis Wheatley. "Isn't that about witchcraft?"

"More the supernatural really."

"Well," she said tartly, "we live in the natural world, and I'd like you to dry up for me. Didn't you ever dry the dishes at home?"

"No, never."

She kissed the top of his head. "But you will for me, won't you?"

With an exasperated sigh and obvious reluctance he followed her into the scullery.

One up to you, Maureen, she thought, although Trevor's tightened expression told her that he regarded the menial task as totally beneath him.

CHAPTER TEN

After a few days at Cardington, Trevor was posted to RAF Bridgnorth to do his "square bashing", and apart from their letters, Maureen sometimes felt she'd dreamed all that had happened over the past few weeks. There was only her gold band and the presents to remind her of her married state.

"We'll store them for you," Henry had offered, immediately after the wedding, and Beryl had agreed they should.

"There's no room here, love," she said, "and you don't want anything to get broken. Let the Mountfords keep them until you have your own place."

And so Maureen relaxed back into her previous role, no longer having to iron Trevor's shirts or press his trousers, her evenings spent reading, chatting or watching TV. Occasionally, remembering the parlour was still designated as "hers and Trevor's room," she would go in to listen to her transistor radio, or put a record on the Dansette record player, but each time she switched on the bars of the fire, she felt guilty. It seemed selfish to burn up electricity just for one person, and it took so long to heat the room up. It was much cosier in the kitchen. As for going out, now she was married it was unthinkable that she should go dancing, so that just left the cinema.

"What are you girls going to see tonight?" Beryl asked one foggy evening.

"*The Big Country.* Jean Simmons is in it," Maureen said, winding a red scarf around her neck.

"That should be good. When is it Carol moves away?"

"Next Tuesday."

"You'll miss her," Beryl said.

"That's stating the obvious," Maureen muttered.

"Sharpness is for knives, young lady."

"Sorry, but of course I'll miss her. With Elaine gone . . ." She bit her lip. It gave her the shudders every time she passed the bleak and empty house. As everyone said, the landlords would be lucky to find anyone who wanted to live there, after what had happened.

Beryl frowned. The problem was worrying her too. For it wasn't as if Maureen had friends at work. Oh, there were agents and clients coming in and out, but there were no other girls in the office to gossip with. She knew, from her own experience at the clothing factory, how much she depended on the company of other women. The humour and gossip made her days bearable, together with programmes like *Music While You Work*, and *Workers' Playtime*, broadcast over the Tannoy system.

"Don't forget to put your scarf over your mouth," she called.

"I will." Maureen closed the door behind her and pulling up the collar of her Harris tweed coat, hurried down the dark street.

Frank looked up from the *Radio Times*. Beryl didn't think he'd been listening. The terrible news that the plane carrying Manchester United, indisputably Britain's best club side, had crashed on take-off at Munich Airport, had affected him deeply. "All those young lives," he kept saying. "All that talent. It's a huge loss for football, not only in this country, but everywhere."

"At least they weren't all killed," she tried to console him.

"That's not much consolation to the families of

120

those who were."

So now Beryl was surprised when he said, "Are you thinking the same as me?"

"About Maureen being lonely?"

"Aye. It's strange how things change. I mean, who'd have thought this time last year, these three girls would be split up like this."

He sank into a reverie for a few moments, remembering with sadness the pleasant little girl he'd watched growing up. Elaine had been in and out of their house most days, and he knew the memory of her brutal death and the horror of that night would haunt him the rest of his life. And Carol had often come round, asking Maureen for help with her homework.

Maureen's only other outing was to go once a fortnight to have Sunday tea with her in-laws. She dreaded it. The first time had been the worst. For one thing she'd been fifteen minutes later than the appointed time, arranged by a series of three-way letters.

"*Mum says to come at four o'clock,*" Trevor had written. Although he now had a car, Frank had a heavy cold, so Maureen set out in what she thought was plenty of time. But she could have walked while she was waiting for a bus to arrive. In fact, if it had been the summer she might have done so, as it would only have taken about forty-five minutes. But it was cold, with a piercing north-westerly wind, and so she stood shivering at the bus stop, wishing she was at home, listening to Gran and Auntie Vera's sparring.

"Was the bus late?" Norah greeted her with a frown, as she opened the front door. "Oh well, you're here now. How are you, Maureen?"

"Fine, thanks, and you?" Maureen followed her into the lounge, where a tea trolley set with sandwiches and a Victoria sponge was waiting.

"Henry's not been well this past couple of days, coming down with the 'flu, I think."

Great, Maureen thought, a dose of the 'flu is all I need.

That was the easy bit. Henry, after getting up to greet her, was in a morose mood, and Norah subdued and polite. Maureen watched as her mother-in-law's pale hands hovered over the teacups, thinking yet again how colourless she was. With her face devoid of make-up and wearing a plain grey skirt and cardigan, she was the most self-effacing person she'd ever met. The most interesting thing in the afternoon was to see that the sandwiches had their crusts cut off.

"A wicked waste of good bread," Nellie would

122

have said, but Maureen had to admit they were much daintier to eat.

The second visit was marginally more relaxed, but an atmosphere of duty being done hung in the room like a shroud. At times, the only sound to break the frequent silences was the chiming of the Westminster clock on the mantelpiece.

But gradually the weeks passed, until to her relief it was time for Trevor's first leave. *"I'll be issued with a rail warrant,"* he wrote. *"Otherwise I'd have hitch-hiked. Apparently, most people will pick up a National Serviceman. I'll come after the passing-out parade so can't tell you exactly what time I'll arrive. By then, I should know where I'm posted."*

So, just after six on Friday night, they heard a sharp rap on the front door, followed by the sound of his key in the lock.

Maureen jumped up from the kitchen table and rushed into the parlour, only to halt in admiration. Trevor seemed to fill the tiny room, as he stood there in his "best blues", still wearing his peaked hat, and with a large kitbag by his side.

"Gosh, you look gorgeous," she said.

"Hardly the right term for a member of HM forces," he teased, removing his hat and smiling at her.

123

She went to him, her arms outstretched.

"I've missed you," she whispered.

"I should hope so," he said, kissing her. "I've missed you, too."

"Come on, I'll get you some tea," and he followed her into the kitchen, where Frank stood up to greet him.

"Well, Trevor, don't you look every inch an airman!"

"I should do, after the last six weeks," he said.

"Tough, eh?"

"You could say that. Why it has to be so, well, almost brutal, I don't know." There was resentment and bitterness in his tone, and Beryl, who was busy setting another place at the table, looked up sharply.

"Ah, they have their reasons," Frank said. "It's the discipline, you see. It teaches you to obey orders without question, to be part of a team. Could save not only your own life but your fellow airmen's too in a war."

"Do they still insist on all that bull?" Beryl said. "I remember Frank complaining about that."

"Oh, I don't mind that," Trevor said. "Or the insistence on keeping the billet immaculate. It's some of these Warrant Officers, they think they're gods."

Frank broke into a guffaw. "Equivalent to our Sergeant Majors, eh? I could tell you a thing or two. There was this bloke . . ."

Maureen, who was in the scullery grilling some sausages, listened with pleasure to the two men talking. Perhaps now they'd find some common ground. In fact she was hoping that being in the RAF, spending so much time with other young men, would make her husband lighten up a bit.

"Where've you been posted?" she asked, as she put his meal in front of him.

"Cosford, just outside Wolverhampton. Pay Accounts," he said.

"That's ideal," Frank said. "You'll be able to get home easily from there. How long have you got?"

"A 72-hour pass," he said, polishing his cutlery on a clean handkerchief. Beryl glared at him and went into the scullery to make a fresh pot of tea. What is it with you, she scolded herself? He's only been in the house a few minutes, and already you're bridling.

Maureen was overjoyed to have Trevor home.

But when they eventually went upstairs, he just yawned, "Thank God for a quiet bed. You've no idea what it's like sleeping in a hut amidst twenty other men."

He was obviously too tired even to read, and

within minutes was asleep.

On Saturday he said he was going over to see his parents, and hastily she suggested he went alone.

"I was only there last week," she said. "In any case, it's you they'll want to see, not me."

Instead she took his washing to the launderette, ironed his shirts, and then prepared to go dancing at Trentham in the evening. She'd wanted to show off Trevor in his uniform, but he'd flatly refused.

"No," he'd said. "I don't mind wearing it today when I see Mum and Dad, but once they've seen me, that's it."

Frank was on Trevor's side.

"He's worn nothing else for six weeks, love. You can't blame him."

But in Beryl's eyes, it was another black mark.

"I still think he should have given in to her," she grumbled after the young couple had left. "It's not much she asks of him."

"You worry too much," was Frank's only reply. He was sitting at the kitchen table, trying to balance his takings. Saturday was a busy day for him, the best day for catching people in and collecting their premiums.

"It's no use," he said in exasperation. "I'm thirty bob out somewhere."

"Oh, leave it," Beryl said comfortably. "Ask Maureen to sort it out later. Anyway, we've got an accountant in the family now." But she only meant it as a joke. Frank would never ask for Trevor's help.

The following day proved to be a momentous one for the Matthews family. Sandra and John had been invited for Sunday dinner, and the moment she saw her elder daughter, Beryl guessed.

Maureen, who was peeling potatoes at the kitchen sink, heard the squeals and laughter and came out, wiping her hands on a tea towel.

"What's going on?"

Sandra beamed at her, while John stood, embarrassed by all the attention.

"You're not …?"

Sandra laughed. "Yes, I am. It's early days, but I don't think there's much doubt."

"Oh, Sandra!" Maureen flung her arms around her sister. "I can't believe it. When?"

"Well, the doctor will have to confirm it, but I reckon late November," she said proudly.

The three women went into the kitchen, full of excitement, while John remained in the parlour.

"Congratulations," Trevor said, looking up from the Sunday papers.

"Thanks. Where's Frank?"

"He went to the eleven o'clock Mass, then said he'd call and have a pint."

"Oh, do you fancy going down? We could wet the baby's head, so to speak."

Trevor hesitated, then said, "Oh, I see what you mean. Yes, all right then."

John went through to the kitchen. "Okay if we have a pint with Frank and tell him the good news?"

"Don't be any later than two o'clock though, I'm doing Yorkshires," Beryl said.

"We'll be lucky if we get any dinner at all, the amount of chat there'll be going on," John grinned.

"Only one pint, mind," Sandra said. "Remember you've got responsibilities now."

John looked at his wife, her face alight with happiness, and kissed her on the cheek.

"I took on one big responsibility the day I married you."

"Oh, go on."

Maureen watched them, envying the ease of their banter. No-one could be in the same room with Sandra and John without being aware of their love for each other. Did she and Trevor seem like that, she wondered? But if she was honest, it was doubtful. Trevor was so serious for one thing. Although he might tease her in private, it was rare that he joked in public. Look at today, for instance. Gran and Auntie Vera would be coming round at teatime, but while the rest of them would see the funny side of Vera's outrageous remarks, she knew Trevor would be stiff and disapproving. "I just wish he'd relax, be more sociable," she thought wistfully, but any niggling criticisms disappeared when he came into the kitchen. She still only had to look at him to melt inside.

Trevor said, "I thought we were . . ."

"Don't fret, I'm coming."

The two young men left, and Maureen went back to finish peeling the vegetables, while Beryl began to question Sandra.

"How are you? Any morning sickness?"

Maureen smiled, knowing her mum's knitting-needles would be clicking away over the next few months. I'll get some patterns when Trevor's gone back, she planned, have a go at a matinée jacket myself.

Then, to her consternation, later that afternoon just after Sandra and John left, she felt a familiar ache in the pit of her stomach. Oh no, it can't be, she thought, not now! But half an hour later, on going out to the lavatory in the backyard, she discovered that yes – her period had started. What

129

brilliant timing, she thought, miserably, and went into the parlour to tell Trevor.

"I'm sorry," she said. "I'm not really due until Tuesday."

"Don't worry about it, it's fine," he said, hardly looking up from his reading.

Feeling perplexed, and with menstrual cramps already beginning, she went to fill a hot-water bottle. His leave's only short – he could at least have sounded disappointed, she thought. But then she was beginning to realise that she could never anticipate Trevor's reaction to anything. Complicated, that's what he is, she determined as she went upstairs to lie down. Not that she'd change him of course, but she was beginning to wonder whether she'd ever understand him.

CHAPTER ELEVEN

During the next three months, Trevor came home whenever he could get leave, but with only a 48-hour pass, his visits seemed fleeting and, to Maureen, something of a disappointment. Although they often went out on Saturday night, usually dancing or the cinema, any time they spent at home he sought the solitude he obviously missed so much in his crowded billet. Then there were his Sunday visits to his parents, but now, realising it was one way to spend more time with her husband, Maureen went with him. Another advantage was that then she could miss one of her fortnightly visits, for as she said brightly, "I don't want to wear my welcome out."

Norah had just smiled, the tight little smile that Maureen hated. She could never work out just what was going on in her mother-in-law's head. She would sit and watch the interplay between parents and son, wondering at the cold detachment of it all. It had mystified her when they were courting, and she'd put it down to her own unfamiliar presence. But over the past few months, she'd begun to realise that this was the inhibiting atmosphere in which Trevor had grown up. It was no wonder he was so reserved, she told herself, preferring books to people, and her heart filled with pity as she thought of how lonely he must have been, growing up in this repressive house.

But, along with the pity, was a growing bewilderment. For although weeks would pass between leaves, it was a rare occasion when they made love. And always, Maureen had to make the first move.

"Mum and Dad are going out tonight," she'd say, looking at him suggestively. And always she had to wait for an answer. Never did Trevor show any enthusiasm, often making the excuse that he was tired. When it happened, nothing changed. Although she kept trying to infuse some warmth and passion into their lovemaking, a couple of kisses, a token caress and seconds later the whole thing was over. Her bewilderment was turning to embarrassment and resentment. After all, what had marriage brought her? She didn't mind too much not having her own home to furnish and care for, she'd expected that. Nor did she ever complain about their separation. But she had hoped, even expected, that their relationship would become closer, more intimate – that they'd have fun together as a couple. Yet the only change in her life seemed to be that she had lost her freedom. Going dancing without Trevor wasn't an option and even the cinema wasn't so much fun on her own. The loss of her friends, Carol and Elaine, had left a huge gap, and she missed them both dreadfully. There were no girls at work to gossip with, as the only other female employee was a middle-aged typist, and although Maureen got on well with her, it wasn't the same as being with someone her own age.

Then, after he'd been at Cosford for three months, Trevor was posted overseas to RAF Gütersloh. He came home, and told them the moment he arrived.

"Germany! But that means I'll never see you!" Maureen stared at him, her eyes wide with shock.

"You can count on that," Frank said drily. "Not until he's demobbed, anyway."

"But that'll be another eighteen months!" Maureen turned away, her eyes misting over, as she struggled to come to terms with the news. How could she face eighteen months without seeing him? It was bad enough now. After all, what else did she have to look forward to?

"So this is your last time?" she whispered.

"I'm afraid so," Trevor said. "Don't look so upset, you must have known it was a possibility."

"Yes, but you said you hadn't requested an overseas posting!"

"I didn't. Don't ask me how their minds work."

"There's nothing anyone can do about it, lass," Frank said. "Just be thankful we're at peace, at least he'll be safe."

"I know, it's just . . ."

"Can you come and give me a hand, love," Beryl called from the scullery.

"Did you hear that?" Maureen hissed, as she helped to strain the vegetables.

"I did." Beryl saw the distress in her eyes. "The time will soon pass," she consoled, "and you'll have buying your own home to look forward to when he gets back."

"I know," Maureen said. Standing at the sink, she stared through the lace curtain at the brick wall which divided their backyard from the one next door. Well, she was determined they'd make this leave one to remember, for they'd almost be strangers by the time they saw each other again.

This time, Trevor's leave was longer. As usual, Sunday was sacrosanct for the visit to his parents, but on Monday they went to Blackpool for the day. Maureen had to take a day off work, but she didn't care. They could manage without her for once and she felt no compunction about ringing in sick. They had their lunch at Woolworth's café, and after an afternoon's dancing with Reginald Dixon playing the organ in the Tower Ballroom, made their way to the noisy and crowded Pleasure Beach. Although Trevor refused at first, he relented and took her on the Big Dipper. Gripping the rail until her knuckles were white, Maureen screamed with fearful exhilaration as they hurtled down the steep slopes and even Trevor was laughing. Then he took the wheel as they squashed into a car and swerved around bumping and chasing on the dodgems. Hand in hand they wandered around, rolling pennies on to a chequered board, where Maureen proudly won ninepence.

"Look, there's the Ghost Train," she pulled him towards the entrance.

"You don't want to go on that thing, surely?"

"Yes, I do."

He looked down at her, his expression indulgent.

"Go on, then."

The weather was smiling on them, and for the first time since their wedding Maureen felt truly happy, as later they strolled along the wide, busy promenade. Despite Trevor's protests that it was a childish habit, she bought a pink candy floss and grinned up at him, aware that her mouth was smeared with the spun sugar.

"How about a kiss?" she teased, delighting in his look of mock horror. But he drew the line at buying her a Kiss Me Quick hat. "Have you no dignity at all?" he complained.

"Oh, don't be so stuffy," she said, but didn't push the issue. She was too happy that he was in such an open, friendly mood, to risk spoiling it. Although they were both exhausted when they got home, they agreed it had been a wonderful day.

However, Maureen's happiness didn't last. At least, it wasn't that she became unhappy – just confused. Trevor might be affectionate with her during the days but, as so often happened, once they went upstairs to bed, he showed more interest in continuing to read his current book, than in her. Desperately, she tried to rationalise the situation. It was because they didn't have a double bed. Then there was the inhibiting proximity of her parents in the next bedroom, with only the thin wall between them. Perhaps he was afraid she'd get pregnant, for no contraception was a hundred per cent safe. Reasons and excuses whirled inside her head, yet she couldn't bring herself to share her worries with Trevor. It would sound as if she was asking for sex, a shameful thought, or even worse, being critical of him. It wasn't even that she enjoyed it when it happened, but she had a desperate need to know that her husband found her desirable. And she longed for the warmth and closeness of lying in the same bed. If only they had their own home, she railed inwardly, none of these problems would have arisen.

On Trevor's last night Beryl and Frank, trying to be diplomatic, went out.

There was nothing they fancied on at the cinema, so Beryl said, "Oh, come on, I'll just have to sit and watch you play darts for a few hours."

"The self-sacrificing mother," Frank grinned.

"Well, it's no thrill, I can tell you." An evening sitting in a pub's crowded, smoky atmosphere, sipping a sweet sherry, wasn't Beryl's idea of entertainment.

"We don't have to go to my local. We could have a run out to a country pub if you like."

Beryl brightened. "That would be nice. Why not take Gran and Auntie Vera? It would give them a treat."

"If that's what you want," Frank shrugged, not exactly keen on spending an evening listening to what he called women's chit-chat. However, he knew how close Beryl was to her mother and aunt and, as he had no close relatives of his own, Nellie and Vera had in a way taken their place. And she was right, he thought guiltily, it would be a treat for them. He ought to do it more often. Perhaps this summer he'd make more of an effort.

Maureen watched the car pull away from the kerb and turned round to Trevor.

"So," she said brightly, "we've got the house to ourselves."

"Yes." Trevor smiled at her, and she waited.

She didn't know quite what she was waiting for, but it was suddenly crucial that he should do something, say something, anything to change the ambience of that ordinary day. Would he hold out his hand, pull her on to his knee, tease her, look at her with warmth, or even desire?

"How about a cup of tea?" he said, his gaze falling to the page he was reading.

Suddenly the bubble of resentment and bewilderment, that had simmered inside her for months, burst.

All her reservations and reasoned caution were forgotten as unable to control her rage she shouted,

"Is that all you can suggest? A cup of tea! What's the matter with you, Trevor? Or have you gone off me now we're married! Because if you have, I wish you'd tell me why! You're leaving tomorrow for months on end, in case you've forgotten! What's the point of Mum and Dad going out so we can have some privacy, if we don't take advantage of it?"

The bitter words poured out of her and, as Trevor stared at her in shock, she realised that this was the first time she'd ever attacked him. They'd never even had a row and perhaps that had been the trouble, she thought grimly. She'd been too wary of upsetting him, had been treading on eggshells for too long.

But Trevor was looking at her with distaste.

"I didn't know I'd married a fishwife," he snapped.

"A fishwife – me? And what do you think you are? You're a cold fish, that's what you are, Trevor Mountford! I sometimes wonder why you wanted to get married in the first place." She held up her hand. "No, don't remind me, it was so that we could get the Marriage Allowance."

"That's a dreadful thing to say."

"Well, that's what it looks like from where I'm standing."

"And this outburst is just because I wanted a cup of tea? Is your monthly due or something? You know how ratty you get."

"No, it bloody well isn't," she blazed. "Don't you go putting this on me! I think I've a right to expect a romantic evening with my new husband before he clears off for the next eighteen months!"

"We went to Blackpool yesterday!"

"Yes, and it was lovely. But that's not the point, Trevor. You just can't see it, can you? A girl needs to know she's attractive, you know, physically, and," she began to stumble now, "you don't seem inter-ested, that's all," she ended flatly. There, she'd said it, after all these months of bottling it up, and her temper began to subside, leaving behind a sick pounding in her throat as she stared in misery at the white-faced man before her.

"You obviously think the best way of spending our last evening together is to have a row, is that it?"

"No," she said. "I never intended to, it's just that . . ."

"You felt like giving me a tongue-lashing."

"No. It's not like that," she protested.

"Well, it's hardly going to put me in the mood for 'romance' as you call it," he said coldly.

"Does anything?" she said bitterly.

He stared at her for a moment, and his gaze dropped before hers. For several minutes there was a heavy silence, and then, gazing down at the floor, he said with a note of desperation in his voice, "These things need to happen spontaneously, Maureen. Not to order just because your parents have gone out."

"But –"

"Let me finish. You're not a man, so you wouldn't understand. It will probably be different when we've got our own home."

His explanation floundered her. So, she was right – he did feel inhibited because of the lack of privacy. She could only say lamely, "Would you like that cup of tea?"

"Yes, please."

Feeling somewhat defeated, Maureen went into the scullery and filled the kettle. But then as she lit the gas she told herself it was a good thing that she'd brought the problem out into the open. For although Trevor's words "to order", had been hurtful, at least she now had a reason. I've got a lot to learn about men, she thought with a sigh, as she put some custard creams on to a plate. So in the end, they spent their last evening listening to records, and when he left the next day, she returned his parting kiss with warmth and affection.

"Write often," he muttered.

"I will," she promised, and stood on the platform waving as his train drew away from Stoke station, watching until it disappeared from sight.

CHAPTER TWELVE

It took just one month after Trevor left for Maureen to realise that she had to take drastic action about her way of life. One month of living like a middle-aged woman at the age of nineteen was enough for anyone. All she did was go to work, come home and eat her dinner, help Beryl to wash up, and then watch television. If she went to see a film, it was usually with her parents. And so, she made her decision.

"I'm going to look for another job," she announced one weekend.

Frank and Beryl looked up from their newspapers and stared at her.

"What's brought this on?" Beryl said.

"I've thought about it before. I'll never make any

progress in that office, Dad knows that. But most of all I need some company of my own age – I'll go mad otherwise."

Beryl nodded, she could understand that.

"Have you mentioned this to Trevor?" Frank said.

Maureen bit her lip. She'd brought up the subject once, before Trevor went away and remembered how she'd been taken aback by her young husband's reaction.

"You've already got a secure job," he'd said.

"That doesn't mean I won't find another, one where I can make new friends."

"I'd rather you stayed where you are, working with people I can trust."

At first she was unsure what he meant, but then said, "Are you talking about men?"

"Naturally."

Maureen stared at him in disbelief.

"You really do suffer from the green-eyed monster, don't you?"

Trevor's expression had hardened. "Well, if you can't differentiate between jealousy and genuine concern for your welfare, that's your problem, not mine."

So now, in reply to her dad's question, Maureen admitted, "Yes, I did once."

144

"And?"

"He thought I should stay where I was," she said in a flat voice.

Yes, he would, Beryl thought. He knows she's safe there, no temptations or anything. He wants her closeted at home, never mind her young life going by.

"Well, I can see your point," she said. "There's no harm in having a look round, anyway. What do you say, Frank?"

He grinned. "I'm just thinking of the chaos in the office if our Maureen goes. No, I'm all for it. You never know, love, you might get a job which pays a bit more."

"I certainly hope so." Maureen's two years in the insurance office had revealed a talent for organisation, and she was confident she could handle more responsibility. Besides, she thought, if I earn more money towards the house deposit, Trevor can't possibly object. So she decided not to say anything in her letters, not until it was a fait accompli. I don't see why I should have to do everything he says, she determined, just because I'm married to him. Heavens, this is the 1950's, not the Victorian age!

And so Maureen began to wait eagerly for the *Evening Sentinel* to arrive, when she would scour the

Situations Vacant page. But job-hunting wasn't as easy as she'd imagined. The public bodies, such as the City Council, or the Health Authority, required certain qualifications, even stating that accepted levels of achievement would place an applicant higher up the salary scale. And there was no doubt that the salaries were good, much better than the one she was getting at the moment. With reluctance, she turned to the private firms, but they were mainly insurance companies or solicitors. The pay in the offices of solicitors was notoriously low, and she was unlikely to find what she was looking for in yet another small insurance firm. No, she wanted something different, something – she thought for a moment and then came up with the word she was searching for – something livelier, that was it.

"What's wrong with an office on a potbank?" Vera barked, the following Sunday, when as always family affairs were aired.

"Absolutely nothing," Maureen said, "except that there haven't been any jobs advertised."

"There's always been a member of our family working on a potbank," Nellie grumbled. "It doesn't seem right, somehow, not to have anybody there. Thirty years I worked on one, and our Vera did."

"Yes," Beryl said, "most people round here work

on the pots. But I always liked sewing, and our Sandra was the same, unlike someone else I know."

"All right, all right," Maureen laughed. "Mind you, I'm not doing too badly with those bootees."

"Is there nothing at the Michelin?" Vera said. "After all, they are one of the largest employers round here."

Maureen shook her head. "No, nothing. Still," she said airily, "at least I've had one decision made for me!"

"What's that, love?" asked Nellie.

"Whether to be a debutante or not. I see they're stopping it this year."

"Oh, what a shame," Nellie said dreamily. "I used to like to see pictures of all those lovely frocks."

"Where's your socialist principles?" Vera said sharply. "Look at our Maureen here, as lovely a girl as you're likely to meet. Does she get a chance to be introduced to the Queen? No, and we all know why," she sniffed. "Not top drawer, that's why not. It's time all that nonsense was done away with. We're all equal in the sight of the Lord."

Maureen laughed, but although she enjoyed being with her family, she couldn't help feeling stifled as she sat with the three older women. I'm only just nineteen, she thought, there'll be plenty of time when I'm old and past it for gossiping over the teacups. Restless, she got up. "I'm going for a walk, get some fresh air."

In the warm sunshine, Maureen walked slowly down the street. One or two children were playing hopscotch on the pavement, but otherwise everywhere was deserted. Sunday afternoon, she thought, it's always the same – there's never anything to do. She averted her eyes as she passed Elaine's forlornly empty house. Bert's trial, referred from the Magistrates Court to Sessions, was due to be held in the middle of August. Frank had been called as a witness and he was dreading it. The knowledge that his evidence would help convict a neighbour of manslaughter lay heavily on his shoulders. I don't care what they do to him, Maureen thought bitterly, I hope they put the monster away for life.

Carol had written that she was working in a fashionable hair salon and had quickly made new friends in Leicester. I'll go over and visit her soon, Maureen determined, although she'd promised Trevor not to spend any of her salary on what he called non-essentials. Well, keeping my sanity is essential, she decided, and I've got to have something to write to him about.

Then the following week a large firm who made

electrical insulators advertised for a sales ledger clerk. Experience essential, the advertisement said. There was no mention of the dreaded word qualifications. So Maureen drafted a letter of application, copied it out in neat handwriting on blue unlined Basildon Bond paper and, to her delight, within a few days, she was invited to attend for an interview.

"You'll need to wear a suit," pronounced Vera. "I've read about these things, and a hat."

"A hat?" Beryl protested. "Oh, I don't think so, Vera."

"I had a lovely hat once," Nellie reminisced. "Maroon velour it was, with a long, curling feather."

"I don't mean that sort of hat," Vera snapped. "One of those smart little straw ones."

Maureen grinned to herself. She'd already decided to wear her blue going-away suit, but as for a hat – well, that was going a bit too far.

"Hold yourself up straight, and look them in the eye," advised Vera. "Shows strength of character, does that."

"And smile," Nellie said. "You've got a lovely smile."

So, armed with their advice, Maureen presented herself at the entrance to the large factory. With more confidence than she felt, she showed her letter to the lodgeman, then made her way through a side door, up some stairs and so to a corridor lined with offices. There was a small window set in a wall to her left, with the word *Reception* on the glass, and she tentatively pressed the bell at the side. When the glass slid back, a girl of her own age, with long brown hair looked up at her.

"I've come about the interview. My name's Maureen Mountford."

"Oh yes. I'll ring through. I won't keep you a moment."

Maureen waited, the knots in her stomach tightening with apprehension. She'd never been interviewed before, not properly, and there were bound to be other applicants.

Almost immediately a middle-aged woman came to meet her. "If you could just come this way," she said. "Mr Sims will be interviewing you. He's our Financial Director." She ushered Maureen into a large oak-panelled office. Facing her, seated behind a mahogany desk, was a balding silver-haired man, whose podgy pink and white features made her think irreverently of Santa Claus. He only needs the whiskers, she thought, hoping his personality would be as genial. It wasn't, but neither was it unduly harsh.

"I'm a strict employer, Mrs Mountford, but a fair one," were his opening words, and although at first she felt nervous, when he went on to question her about her work in the insurance office she was on safe ground. Accounts held no fears, and when he detailed the job description, she knew she was more than capable of it.

"Is there anything you'd like to ask me?" he said.

She wanted to ask how much the salary was, but instead, instructed by Frank, she said, "I wondered whether the job carried any prospects."

"I like my staff to be ambitious," he said, "and I can only say that, if possible, I always promote internally." After detailing holiday entitlement and hours of work, he paused, adding, "I have one other, more personal question."

Maureen waited.

"I see that you've recently got married. May I ask whether you're intending to start a family in the near future? Only I wouldn't like to take you on, to have you leave in a few months' time. I mean, you are very young, so naturally I did wonder . . ."

Maureen went hot, not only with embarrassment but with anger. What was he implying? With a struggle, she managed to keep her expression blank but there was an edge to her voice as she said, "We

151

got married before my husband went to do his National Service. I'm not pregnant now, and he'll be serving in Germany for the next sixteen months."

"Fine," he rubbed his hands together, and then said, "Thank you for coming – you'll hear from us within seven days."

He stood up and held out his hand. Maureen shook it awkwardly, and then waited as he pressed a button on his intercom. "Please show Mrs Mountford the Accounts Department on her way out, Miss Walker."

"How did you get on?" his secretary asked. "He's not such a bad old stick, can be a bit tricky if you don't do your job properly, but otherwise he's a right softie at heart."

"I don't know," Maureen confessed. "Have you had many applicants?"

"Six, and he's interviewing three."

They were walking along a corridor lined with offices, and as the walls were only half partitioned, their occupants and desks were on view through the upper glass sections. Not much chance of slacking here, thought Maureen, so at least it meant everyone would have to pull their weight. She was fed up of doing other people's work.

"That's the typing pool," Miss Walker said, indicating an office containing four desks, where the sound of pounding typewriters and the ping of carriages returning could be heard even through the closed doors. As they passed, all four heads turned in their direction, looking with blatant curiosity at Maureen, and she smiled, before being ushered into the next office. It was a large room, with six desks in two lines of three, one larger one facing them. Seated at this was a thin man of about forty. He had an anxious but kindly face, and smiled a welcome. Maureen stood in the doorway and glanced quickly around, noticing that there were two girls of her own age, and two others in their late twenties. One male clerk was about forty, and another looked near retirement age. It was a vast improvement on her present working conditions. And then there were the typists next door, several of whom were of a similar age to herself. This will do me very nicely, she decided.

She was introduced to the Chief Clerk, Colin Campbell, and said, "It all looks very efficient. I'd love to work here – everyone seems so friendly."

He beamed at her. "Yes, we like to think of ourselves as a happy ship." He held out his hand, and Maureen shook it, smiling. She sensed, rather than saw, Miss Walker's nod of approval, but when she was leaving noticed with a pang of anxiety an older applicant than herself, severely dressed in black, with her hair skewered into a bun, being given directions at the lodge. "Oh, well," she thought. "I did my best – now it's in the lap of the gods."

But the gods were smiling on her, for exactly four days later the letter arrived offering her the position. With a wage of two pounds a week more than her present one, Maureen was highly delighted and wrote back immediately accepting.

"Trevor can't have any objections," she said gleefully, telling Beryl the good news. "Just think how much more money I'll be able to save."

"When do you start?"

"After I've given my week's notice."

"Clever girl, I'm proud of you." Beryl gave her a hug, not only for her achievement, but because she had, in a small way, asserted her independence. Times are changing, she thought, and I for one am glad for both my daughters' sakes. Not that she herself had experienced much domination from Frank, but the tales she heard at work were a real eye-opener. There was one woman, a thin tireless worker, who not only had to account to her husband for every penny she spent, but defer to him about every trivial decision. Having seen her two timid daughters, Beryl could well imagine how his tyranny had broken their spirit at an early age.

Frank too, approved, particularly when Maureen told him what Mr Sims had said about on promotion.

By the time she received Trevor's reply to her news, Maureen had finished working her notice at the insurance office. Tearing open the thin blue airmail letter, she read it in disbelief.

"I'm really surprised at you," Trevor complained. *"I thought we'd discussed this before I went away. Oh, I know you'll be earning more money, but I'm sure if you'd threatened to leave the insurance office, they would have offered you a rise. You obviously didn't think of me, Maureen, stuck over here. Now, in addition to everything else, I've got to worry about you, in a different environment, coming into contact with all sorts of undesirable influences."*

Maureen flung it on to the bed. God, anyone would think he was her father! Not that her dad would be so pompous she thought, her temper flaring. For heaven's sake, how old was Trevor? Ninety?

Beryl took one look at her stony expression as she came downstairs, and said, "He wasn't too pleased about it, then?"

"No!"

"Don't you worry, love," Beryl advised. "You did the right thing. He'll come round to it."

"I just don't understand his reaction," Maureen confessed.

"I think he's just being a bit possessive. Perhaps he's afraid you'll meet somebody else while he's away."

Maureen stared at her in horror. "I'd never do that. I'm married!"

Beryl frowned. Her younger daughter was still hopelessly naïve. Perhaps moving to a more worldly environment would encourage her to take a more realistic view of life. But she didn't say any of this, merely replied, "I know that, Maureen, and I'm sure he does too. In any case, I might be wrong, it's only my opinion."

CHAPTER THIRTEEN

Within a couple of weeks of starting her new job, Maureen couldn't imagine being employed anywhere else. Working with figures came easily to her, and she sailed through the days, stress-free and enjoying the easy companionship of her colleagues. She became especially friendly with Barbara, a bubbly frizzy-haired redhead, who worked on the switchboard. Like herself, Barbara loved anything to do with Hollywood and film stars, and the two girls often went to the pictures together, although Barbara complained that Maureen cramped her style.

"I mean," she grumbled, "look at those two lads last week in the row behind. They obviously fancied us, but of course with that gold band on your finger you're enough to put anyone off!"

"You get plenty of chances when you go dancing," Maureen retorted. "Anyway, they were hideous."

"Oh, you did notice then. I thought you were above those things!"

"Just because I'm not buying, it doesn't mean I can't look in the shop window," Maureen laughed. And she laughed a lot these days. A fact that did not go unnoticed at home, particularly by her gran and Auntie Vera.

"She seems a different lass," Vera pronounced one Sunday.

"Yes, I think it's the new job. She's got more company there," Beryl said. Her own opinion she kept private. But she soon realised that she wasn't the only one who thought Trevor had shortcomings.

"Aye," Vera said. "Well, I'm beginning to wonder about that husband of hers. I didn't like to say anything Beryl, but we've had our doubts, haven't we, Nellie?"

Nellie, her kindly face troubled, looked across at her daughter.

"It's only since the wedding," she explained. "She's seemed a bit too quiet for my liking. I mean, our Maureen's always had a bit of spirit, liked a bit of

158

fun, but she's been so serious, too much so for a young girl."

Beryl hesitated, diplomacy warring with a desire to unburden herself. But what could she say? It was only her own intuition that something was wrong with the young couple's relationship. Also, she was well aware that words uttered could never be withdrawn, and caution made her keep her true feelings about Trevor firmly under wraps. "I think it's just that she missed her friends. After all, those three girls went everywhere together."

The women sat in silence for a moment, each of them calling to mind the street's worst ever tragedy. Also imminent was Bert's trial.

"How's Frank feeling?" Nellie said.

"Worried sick. He's never been inside a court before, never mind as a witness in a murder trial."

"I suppose they'll call Ida?" Vera commented.

"I thought a wife couldn't give evidence against her husband," Nellie said with a frown.

"I don't think she can be forced to," Beryl explained, "but from what I gather, Ida didn't need any persuading."

"They ought to stand him in the middle of the street, and let us women get hold of him," asserted Nellie. "When I think of that little innocent babe –"

"Oh yes," interrupted Vera. "I can just see you laying into him. I mean, you've always been known for your violent nature, haven't you?"

Beryl had to smile at an image of her mild-mannered elderly mother setting about the burly Bert.

"You can scoff," Nellie retorted, "but I might surprise you."

"Aye, and pigs might fly," Vera muttered. "Right, it's time we were off." She stood up and put on her coat, taking a pleated plastic rainhood out of her pocket to protect her perm against the grey drizzle. "Talk about summer," she grumbled. "We ought to have been born with webbed feet."

"Just a minute," Beryl said. She went into the kitchen and brought in a couple of bottles of milk stout. "Enjoy these while you watch the telly."

"Thanks, love," Nellie kissed her cheek. "You're a good lass."

"Careful how you go, now." Beryl watched them make their way along the wet, narrow pavement, arms linked and walking slowly, then turned to go and wash up the tea things. Frank was still in bed, getting over a summer cold, while Maureen had gone to visit those snooty in-laws of hers.

Beryl was looking forward to an hour or so of

peace and quiet. She could get on with her baby-knitting, and listen to the wireless without interruption, even indulging in a few chocolate caramels. There was something about being cosy in your own home, listening to the rain beating on the window panes, that brought peace to the spirit. But her respite didn't last long, for soon Frank thumped on the bedroom floor, a sure indication that he wanted yet another of his endless cups of tea.

* * *

Due to a cold, it was the first time Maureen had been to visit Trevor's parents since she gave in her notice at the insurance office, and Henry opened the door to greet her with the comment, "I hear you've been a bit impulsive, Maureen."

"Oh, why's that then?" she said coolly.

"Deciding to change your job. Trevor tells us he advised you against it, but . . ."

With a sigh of exasperation she followed him into the airless, tidy lounge, where Norah waited, hands primly folded on her lap. The tea trolley, laden with the usual cucumber sandwiches and Victoria sponge cake, stood in readiness. Maureen sometimes fanta-sised that she'd arrive to the huge excitement of cream as well as jam in the sponge, or perhaps even a chocolate or fruit cake. Would there be ham sandwiches, or beef from the Sunday joint? But no, every visit it was the same, and she wondered how anyone's life could be so ordered, so unimaginative. She didn't even like cucumber sandwiches for heaven's sake, but it had never occurred to Norah to ask her.

"Cheap entertaining, that's what it is," was Beryl's opinion. "I mean, how much is half a cucumber? A nice bit of boiled ham, or ham off the bone like your dad likes, now you have to get your purse out for that!"

Maureen's hackles were already up at the realisation that Trevor had written to his parents complaining about her. It's none of their business, she thought angrily. I'm certainly not answerable to them.

But she merely said, "Well, he wasn't here to discuss it with, so I had to make my own decision."

Henry glanced sharply at her, but Norah just gave a little sniff – she was too busy looking askance at the Maureen's clothes.

"Obviously new," she said to Henry later. "And did you see the length of the split in that pencil skirt? Not to mention those fancy heels on her stockings. A bit tarty, I thought. We're going to have to keep an eye on that girl, Henry, you mark my words."

But Maureen forgot about them between her fort-nightly visits, and her life settled into an enjoyable if predictable routine. With Trevor's Marriage Allowance being paid regularly into the Trustees Savings Bank, and the amount she managed to save from her own salary, the balance crept satisfactorily upwards. The account was in their joint names, although of course it needed both signatures before any money could be taken out. Trevor had been most insistent about that. It did mean that she had to budget carefully, for once her money was paid in, she couldn't touch it until he was demobbed.

Bert's trial, now over, gradually receded to the back of their minds, although in Frank's case, the image of the wretched accused man being led away to serve his sentence of nine years would always remain with him. Bert's face had been pale and drawn, his eyes shadowed with grief, remorse and guilt. Frank knew he'd never find peace again, not in this world, but he couldn't feel any sympathy for the man, not with a young lass and an unborn baby being his victims.

* * *

And so the summer passed. There was no holiday that year for any of them. Beryl preferred to spend the money on a fitted carpet and new curtains for front and back, while Frank was quite content with a couple of day trips out. Once they went to Rudyard Lake, taking a picnic, Nellie in the front, and Beryl, Vera and Maureen squashed together on the back seat. Another time, they went on a PMT bus trip to Rhyl. Nellie and Vera hitched up their skirts and paddled in the sea, laughing like children as the waves swept up their calves. Maureen, wearing a turquoise swimsuit lay stretched out on a beach towel by the side of Frank and Beryl's deckchairs. "You won't get a tan in one day," Beryl told her.

But Maureen didn't care. "The way this summer's going, we may never get any more sun," was her philosophy, so she was making the most of it. Wistful, she watched the young couples, and wished Trevor was with her. They exchanged letters every week, although at times she struggled to find something to write about. It wasn't as though he was interested in office gossip, although she always told him if she'd been to the cinema. Films were always a safe subject. And then she could tell him she'd seen his parents. Henry and Norah had gone away for their annual fortnight in Scarborough. They'd been going to the same guesthouse for the last twenty years, and as Norah said, "The air is very bracing, and suits us, so we don't see any reason for a change."

At first Maureen looked forward to receiving her husband's letters in their blue airmail envelopes. Religiously, one would slip through the letterbox every week, and eagerly Maureen would scan their contents. *Dear Maureen*, he would begin. Never *Darling Maureen*, or *Hello, sweetheart*, she'd given up hoping for that. Then he would tell her what the weather was like, or complain about the food, or how one of the Warrant Officers was always trying to undermine him. He would ask for the current balance in their savings account, tell her if he'd been off the station, and finish, *I hope you're keeping well, all my love, Trevor*. She'd hoped for love letters to keep and adorn with pink ribbon, but after he didn't respond when she wrote back in a more romantic manner, there seemed no point. Eventually, her own letters followed the same pattern, and the postman's visit became just routine.

When winter came, all talk in the tea-break was of the forthcoming Christmas Party at the end of November.

"We hold it here," Barbara said, "in the canteen. You wouldn't recognise it when it's all decorated up. You'll be coming, won't you?"

Maureen wasn't sure at first. However, encouragement came from an unexpected quarter.

"Of course you must go! You work there, don't you?" Beryl said. "It's a totally different thing than going dancing at Trentham or the Crystal."

As December approached, so did the date of the firm's auditors' annual visit. There were three of them, two solemn men of middle age, and a tall young man in his early twenties. Dark, with laughing brown eyes, he had the office girls in a tizzy within hours. Every time he walked along the corridor, he would glance over the partitions, to find several pairs of bright eyes hoping to meet his gaze. He smiled at them all – a warm, teasing smile – making each girl feel that she was the special one, the one he really fancied. Maureen tried hard, she really did, not to join in the fun, but there was something so irresistible about it all, so diverting in the day's normal routine, she found herself laughing with the rest of them. And was it her imagination, or did his gaze really rest on her for a moment longer? And why was it always her desk that he looked at first?

"His name's Stuart Copestake, and he's coming to the party," came the whisper, and Barbara began to take bets on who would be the lucky one.

"I've seen the way he looks at you, Maureen!" she teased.

"He won't be interested in me, I'm married," she pointed out. "Anyway, how do you know he won't bring someone?"

" 'Cos I've asked him!" Barbara tossed her head, and gave a wicked grin. "Well, if he gets past my cleavage, he'll be hard to please. I've bought a new dress and you should see it." She sketched with her hands the plunging neckline.

"Go on," scoffed one of the typists, a buxom blonde girl of about seventeen. "He's the type who'll go for experience. I mean Maureen knows what it's all about, hey Maureen?"

"Not that she ever tells us," Barbara complained.

"And I won't either," Maureen retorted. "Such things aren't for young maiden ladies."

"Hark at her, maiden ladies indeed! What century were you born in?" Barbara grinned. "Why don't you say the word 'virgin', or don't you think we've got any?"

She nudged the girl next to her who said, "You speak for yourself, you fast cat!"

"Well, I'll put my money on you, Barbara," Maureen said. "Here's half a crown."

"Last of the big spenders, eh?"

"You know I'm on a tight budget." Sometimes Maureen hated the fact that she couldn't go out and spend her wages like the other girls. They were always showing off new clothes, experimenting with make-up and buying records. She made sure she looked reasonably smart for work, but apart from that, spent very little. Even the planned visit to see Carol in Leicester hadn't materialised, her conscience overruling her previous decision. She had no excuse to buy a new outfit for the party either, for she had clothes in her wardrobe no-one at her new firm had ever seen.

So one cold Friday night, Frank drove Maureen to the factory and dropped her off at the lodge. Watching her walk towards the entrance, her slim legs elegant in their stiletto heels, he felt a qualm of uneasiness. She was a looker, no mistake, and in that flimsy green dress she'd draw admirers like a magnet. Not for the first time did he wonder whether his girl had tied herself down too early in life. But it had been what she wanted and, as his old mum used to say, you made your bed and you lay on it.

Maureen however, was oblivious to her father's anxiety. Excited at the thought of an evening of music and dancing, the adrenalin was running high as she left her coat in one of the offices, and went to join the others. Her friends looked up and waved, and she began to weave her way across the room.

But she made slow progress, as colleagues stopped her to introduce their husbands, or boyfriends. It was fascinating to see how they differed from the mental picture she'd formed of them. The small band, seated on a raised dais at the end of the room, was playing a lively quickstep and already her feet were itching to get on to the dance floor.

"He's here!" Barbara hissed, but Maureen was staring in alarm at her friend's low-cut black dress, which was even more daring than she'd described.

"Aren't you scared you'll pop out of there?"

Barbara grinned. "Nope. It's the force of gravity, it keeps them down – that's the advantage of being well-endowed."

Maureen laughed. That was one of the things that attracted her to Barbara – her wit and humour. Earthy at times maybe, but she was very genuine and the most good-natured girl she knew – after Sandra of course.

And almost as though Barbara had sensed her thoughts, she said, "Any news on that baby yet?"

"No. It was a false alarm, but it's due any day now."

"Rather her than me," Barbara shuddered. "The very thought of giving birth scares me to death."

Maureen thought of her elder sister, and of her

joyous anticipation of holding her first baby in her arms. She'd asked Sandra if she was worried about going into labour, but she just shrugged and said, "Naturally, I'm a bit nervous, but if millions of other women can do it, I can."

But then Barbara was nudging her as the handsome young auditor made his way over to them. "Evening, girls."

"Evening, Stuart." Barbara looked archly up at him.

"And who's this?" he said, his gaze sweeping over Maureen.

"Maureen. And don't say you haven't noticed her, 'cos I know different."

"I've noticed all of you."

"Yeah, you're a right Lothario!"

"I just like to share myself around," he grinned. "I don't like anyone to feel left out," but as he spoke his eyes were on Maureen's and she felt the heat rise in her cheeks. Embarrassed, she brought up her left hand with its gold wedding ring to flick back her hair, but he just smiled and said, "May I have the pleasure?" and, taking her hand, led her on to the dance floor. He was an accomplished dancer, and for the first few minutes Maureen gave herself up to the pleasure of a slow, dreamy waltz as the band played

Connie Francis' hit, 'Carolina Moon'. There was also the unfamiliar sensation of being held in arms other than Trevor's and, to her discomfort, she was beginning to realise just how much she was enjoying it. I'm only dancing, she consoled herself, and anyway he knows I'm married.

"Where have you been all my life?" he murmured, as holding her ever closer, he rested his cheek against her hair.

"Nowhere particular," she said, suddenly feeling somewhat unsure how to react to his flirting. She was out of practice, that was the trouble. Relax, she told herself, he's only having a bit of fun. And Stuart was fun, and she found herself laughing at his light banter as they swirled around the floor. The next number was 'Jailhouse Rock', and they went immediately into a rock and roll routine as though they'd been partners for years. Exhilarated by the beat of the music and the breathless dancing, Maureen hadn't enjoyed herself so much for years. I really haven't, she suddenly realised with dismay. How long is it since I've felt like this?

Stuart didn't seem interested in dancing with anyone else and with reluctance, after half an hour, Maureen pulled away from him. "I think I'll sit the next one out," she said, feeling awkward, aware that by dancing so long with him she was attracting attention. Besides she wasn't happy about the way his hands were caressing rather than holding her.

"Right, what would you like to drink?" he said.

She said quickly, "Oh, I'm all right. You go and dance with one of the others."

"But I don't want to. Now, what do you want to drink?"

"I'll have a lemon and lime, please."

"Come on, it's nearly Christmas! How about a gin and orange?"

She pulled a face. "No, but all right, I'll have a snowball."

"That's my girl!"

Feeling uneasy, Maureen watched him go over to the bar. She was definitely attracted to him, a feeling that filled her with both fascination and guilt. She'd never looked at anyone else, not since she'd met Trevor, had never thought she'd even want to.

Barbara sidled up to her. "Looks like you've made a conquest."

"Don't be daft!"

"You'd better watch yourself," Barbara warned. "He's a born ladies' man, that one."

"Stay with me," Maureen urged. "Perhaps he'll ask you to dance."

"No thanks, I take nobody's cast-offs. Besides, I've got my eye on that new bloke in the labs." She drifted off, a cloud of perfume wafting behind her.

"How much of that stuff has she got on?" Stuart complained, returning with their drinks.

"Her father won it in a raffle," Maureen said. "It's Chanel No.5."

"I suppose you know," he said with a grin, "that Marilyn Monroe is supposed to wear nothing but that in bed?" He looked around making sure they couldn't be overheard. "I'll have to buy you some," he whispered.

"You can't do that!" She smiled, feeling sure he was joking.

"Why not?"

"You know why, I'm married. What would my husband think?"

He slipped his arm around her waist, and leaning closer, murmured, "Who cares? You told me he's out of the country. And don't tell me you're not missing the sex, a gorgeous girl like you!" His hand moved against her waist, caressing her skin through the silky fabric, and Maureen tried to pull away. But he held her tight, and bending, whispered in her ear, "How about my getting you another snowball, and then we could sneak away to one of the offices. No-

173

one would know."

Shocked, Maureen looked up and realised to her horror that he actually thought she was going to agree. She was so angry that her hand shook, almost spilling her drink. Hot with mortification, she wrenched herself away. "Get lost, Stuart!"

He took a gulp of his beer. "Come off it, Maureen, don't play hard to get with me. You're begging for it, any man can tell that!"

Before she could stop herself, Maureen flung the contents of her glass in his face. As he staggered backwards, frantically trying to mop up the spillage, people nearby turned at the commotion, the men nudging each other and grinning. With her cheeks flaming, Maureen marched to the safety of the other end of the canteen, where some middle-aged couples were sitting at tables.

"Mind if I join you?" she asked Colin Campbell, who introduced her to his wife, Janet.

"Make a pass, did he?" Janet said. "Just ignore him, love!"

Deciding to stay where she was for a while, Maureen tried to simmer down while Colin went to fetch her a cold drink and Janet chatted to her about their family. Eventually, the couple went on to the dance floor, leaving her alone at the table, and soon

Barbara came over. "What's been going on?" she hissed. "I've just heard you threw your drink over Stuart?"

"He deserved it."

"Why?"

"He propositioned me," Maureen said shortly.

"What? I wish someone would me. That bloke from the lab was a right wimp." She looked suspiciously at Maureen. "Don't tell me that's why you did it?"

"Of course it was," Maureen flared. "I'm married, for heaven's sake! And even if I weren't, I wouldn't want anyone thinking I was a slut!"

"You really don't live in this world, do you?" Barbara said. "Surely you know most blokes will try it on if they can. In their twisted little minds they think they're paying you a compliment."

"Within a few hours of meeting you?" Maureen snapped.

"Yeah, well, that is a bit much, I have to admit. But that's what men are like, Maureen. They've got sex on their minds twenty-four hours a day."

Not the one I'm married to, Maureen thought grimly. She looked at Barbara and said, "Well, I don't think all men are like that. There must be some decent ones around."

"When you find one, pass him over to me," Barbara grinned. "Anyway, come over and join the rest of us. As for Stuart, apparently he's left."

The rest of the evening passed uneventfully and, once home and in bed, Maureen tried to sort out her jumbled thoughts and emotions. Her big mistake, she realised, was to assume that her wedding ring would act as a sort of armour, that her marital status would be a barrier, a protection. Now she could understand why convention frowned on a married woman going out dancing or socialising without her husband. It was stupid to lay oneself open to temptation, and that was the most shocking thing to Maureen. She *had* been tempted. Oh, not to be unfaithful – she'd never be able to live with the guilt, but she couldn't deny that she'd enjoyed the physical contact of dancing in Stuart's arms, and basking in his admiration. She tossed and turned on her narrow bed, staring blankly into the darkness. I just don't understand, she muttered to herself. I love Trevor, for heaven's sake. How could I even look at anyone else, let alone a snake like that?

By the time she drifted off to sleep in the early hours of the morning, Maureen had come to a decision. It wouldn't happen again, because she refused to get into that sort of situation again. On the

evening of the next annual Works' party, she
planned to have the flu.

CHAPTER FOURTEEN

Maureen's niece was two days old before she saw her. Sandra and John, paranoid about anyone passing on germs to their precious newborn baby, had requested no visitors for forty-eight hours.

From the first time she saw the tiny crumpled face, Maureen was overwhelmed.

"Just look at her fingernails, Sandra – they're like little pink shells!"

"Isn't she beautiful?"

"She's wonderful!"

"Do you want to hold her?"

"Can I? I'll be really careful."

Sandra held out her precious bundle, and gingerly Maureen cuddled the baby in her arms. "She looks like you."

"Hope not," Sandra said with a grimace. She

looked tired and pale, her hair greasy and lank, but there was no mistaking the look of happiness in her eyes.

"What was it like?"

"Bloody awful!" Sandra said. "I suppose I shouldn't tell you that, but I believe in being honest. I can't stand these women who have babies just like shelling peas. It makes the rest of us feel like wimps. But don't you worry about it, pet, every pain was worth it." She looked at Maureen, thinking what a lovely picture she made. "It suits you," she said.

Maureen smiled. "Oh, I think I'll have to wait a few more years before it's my turn. I hear you got your own way about the name."

Sandra laughed. John, an avid fan of Buddy Holly, had been pressurising her to call the baby Peggy Sue. "Peggy, I drew the line at. But we've compromised and she's going to be Susan."

"He'll only shorten it to Sue!"

"I don't mind that. In fact, I think it suits her." She looked up at Maureen. "How are things with you?"

"Fine." She'd decided not to say anything to her family about the Christmas party. She'd only get an earful about how important it was not to give the wrong impression!

Carefully passing the tiny baby back to Sandra, Maureen opened her handbag and put an envelope on the bedside table. "I bought her a couple of these new Premium Bonds," she said. "I thought she's bound to have rattles, and you and mum have done enough knitting for quads!"

Sandra beamed. "Oh, thanks, pet. Hey, wouldn't it be great if she won a prize!"

Later, as Maureen made her way home, she thought about the empty months stretching ahead, and wondered how on earth she could fill them. It was going to seem so strange without Trevor. However, she was determined not to fritter away the time. Once Trevor was demobbed and she had her own home to run, plus a full-time job, then life would be too busy to allow much time for her own interests.

But now . . . I could have a project, she decided. Improve myself. Since she'd met Trevor, Maureen had often felt inadequate, aware that she was woefully ignorant in many ways. Lack of a decent education – that was the problem, she reasoned. She had to think about the future, for when Trevor returned after serving abroad, he was bound to have changed. Travel was supposed to broaden people's outlook. What was it her gran always said? They went into the Forces as boys, and came out men? Well, she wanted to show him that she too had matured.

"Go to night school," was Frank's advice.

At the word "school", Maureen blanched. "I'm not taking any exams," she protested.

"They can't force you to now," he said mildly. "You're an adult, attending a class on a voluntary basis."

She looked at him with suspicion. "You mean I can learn things, then just not sit the exam at the end?"

"I don't see why not."

Frank didn't say any more, just lit his pipe and retreated behind his newspaper. 'Softly, softly, catchee monkey,' he thought. Studying in an undemanding adult environment, Maureen might at last find her courage.

So then it was a decision of what to study. What she was striving for was to be a more interesting companion, a suitable partner for Trevor when in the future they attended social functions. Above all, she didn't want to let him down. And that included the way she spoke.

"What's wrong with the way you talk?" Beryl said indignantly at the very mention of the subject. "You don't speak 'pottery'. Neither you nor Sandra."

"That's because you and Dad don't, not really. Even Gran and Auntie Vera aren't what you'd call 'broad'," Maureen said. "But I have got a Stoke accent, you can't deny that."

"I think the true Potteries dialect is dying out," Frank commented. "I notice it all the time on my rounds. I think it's a great shame." He looked at Beryl and grinned. "I remember your dad, the first time I went to your house. He greeted me with, "Ast thee gorrany fags on yer, lad?"

Beryl laughed. "I know. Funny my mum never picked it up."

"That's probably because she was born in the country, out at Tittensor. The same goes for your Vera."

"How about you, Dad?"

"Most of mine seemed to disappear when I spent all those years in the Army," he said, putting the newspaper down. "The way you speak has a lot to do with whoever you mix with." Holding his pipe in his hand, he pointed the stem at her. "So, if you want to develop a BBC accent, Maureen, the best thing is to make friends with people who talk like that." Then he added, "Personally, I can't see there's anything wrong with having a regional accent – it adds colour to our language – but if you feel self-conscious about it . . ."

Beryl looked up from her knitting, where she'd been concentrating on a lacy pattern. "Just don't start talking with a plum in your mouth," she said, and Maureen laughed.

"Not much chance of that!"

Later, she began to wonder who she could ask for advice. Henry would have been the logical answer, at least as far as night classes were concerned. After all, he was involved in education. But he was the last person she wanted to consult. If she did succeed in improving herself, then she wanted to surprise Trevor, for him to become gradually impressed with his wife. A wife he would be proud to take anywhere. Cultured, that's what I want to be, she determined.

So, she asked Bernard Clewlow. A short, serious, bespectacled man of early middle age, he was a bachelor who lived alone, content with only a cat for company. His desk was situated on Maureen's right, and his dry wit contributed much to the friendly working atmosphere in the office. A fount of irrelevant information, his opinion was widely sought on a variety of subjects and would always be given after quiet deliberation.

Maureen had noticed that he often took his mid-morning break later than the others, and so on the next occasion she remained behind too, pretending to be immersed in a work problem. When he eventually left, she followed him down to the canteen.

"Mind if I join you?" she said, taking her coffee over to his table.

Bernard looked up from his book. "No, of course not."

She sipped the hot coffee as he carried on reading. He was always reading; even in his lunch-hour he ate his sandwiches poring over some tome or other.

"Bernard . . ." she began.

"Yes, Maureen," he said absently.

"Can I ask your advice?"

"Certainly, although Colin is really the one to ask."

"Oh, not about work," she said quickly. "It's more of a personal matter."

Now he really did pay attention, looking slightly alarmed as he replied, "Don't you think one of the girls . . ."

"No," she smiled. "Not that sort of personal."

"Thank God for that!"

She laughed. "It's just that . . ." Put into words she thought it might sound daft, but ploughed ahead. "I want to improve myself. You know, increase my general knowledge, make up for not having been to a grammar school."

"I wondered about that," he said. "You're an intelligent girl, Maureen, streets ahead of some of the others, although you mustn't repeat that. Wouldn't your parents let you go?"

She shook her head. "No, they were very keen. It was my own fault." She told him about the scholarship, how she'd been so nervous she'd vomited all over the test paper, how ever since she'd had a phobia about taking exams. "It's silly, I know," she said lamely, "but I just can't help it."

"The mind's a strange thing," Bernard said. "You mustn't blame yourself too much. Anyway, tell me how I can help."

Maureen hesitated for a moment, then seeing the friendly concern in his eyes, told him. She explained about Trevor being a chartered accountant, how she felt ignorant about so many things, and how she wanted to acquire what she could only describe as "polish".

Bernard leaned back in his chair, glanced at his watch to ensure they still had time left from their break, and gazed at her. "You say your father suggested going to night school. In view of what you've just told me, how do you feel about that?"

"Sick at the thought," she confessed.

"And you wouldn't sit an examination, not even to gain a qualification?"

"Definitely not." Her voice was emphatic, and Bernard frowned.

"Then I don't think that's the answer. Besides, you'd be studying a single subject, whereas you need a broader outline."

"Do you have any suggestions?" she said hopefully.

He ran his finger inside his shirt collar to loosen it, and sat for a moment in thought. "Leave it with me, Maureen, I'll come back to you."

And he did, the following day. When the others left for their break, he glanced across and caught her eye.

"Are you coming, Maureen?" one of the girls called.

"I'll take mine later, I want to finish this," she said.

When Bernard left, Maureen waited a few moments and then followed. She'd already decided to keep her plans to herself, for she could just imagine the ribbing she'd receive. In any case, she didn't want people thinking she had ideas above her station, as Auntie Vera would call it. She'd ask her

186

mum and dad to keep it to themselves, too. She didn't want to change drastically anyway; just a subtle sophistication, that was what she was aiming for. Pleased with her choice of phrase, she repeated it to Bernard when she joined him.

His face creased in a smile, rather an attractive one she noticed suddenly, and wondered why he'd never married. Not that one could ask him, of course. "Right," he said. "First question. Do you read?"

"Yes," she said. "I go to the library every week."

"Good. What are you reading at the moment?"

Maureen frantically tried to remember the title of the book. She didn't look for any particular author, merely picking out a book with an attractive cover which looked as though it would be romantic. "I can't remember," she confessed.

"Well, who's your favourite author?"

She shook her head. "I haven't really got one. I just go to the shelf where it says romances."

"Ah." He smiled gently at her. "Nothing wrong with that, Maureen – we all need escapism in our lives. But you see, you can self-educate yourself by reading the right sort of books, but you have to choose carefully. Have you ever read Shakespeare, for instance?"

She pulled a face, remembering the English lessons at school, where the teacher had sat at the front droning on. Talk about boring!

"Well, perhaps not Shakespeare then. But the classics, that's what you need. Or perhaps we'll build up to them. I'll give you a list of authors, ones whose writing will extend your vocabulary, give you a wider glimpse of life. Words and stories to fire your imagination."

Inspired by his enthusiasm, Maureen said, "Thank you, Bernard, that would be great." Then she asked, "What about improving the way I talk?"

"Amateur dramatics," he said promptly.

"Oh, I couldn't go on the stage!" She was horrified. She'd forget all the words, she knew she would.

"You don't need to. A lot of effort goes into putting on a play or a show, much of it backstage. You could be a prompter, for instance. That would be ideal, for then you'd be forced to listen to other people reading, a good way of hearing how words should be pronounced."

She looked at him in admiration. "Gosh, you are clever, Bernard! That's a wonderful idea."

He looked embarrassed, but she could see he was pleased. "You're young," he said suddenly. "Don't make the same mistake as me, get stuck in a rut."

Maureen looked at him, then said tentatively, "You know, some of us have wondered why you stay here. I mean, you could do so much better, Bernard."

He shrugged. "Like you, I have no qualifications. In my case, it was money, or rather the lack of it. I was down the pit at fourteen. At least I got out of that – this job's utter luxury in comparison. I've no family to support, enough for my needs, and not being overburdened with responsibility it leaves my mind free. Mental freedom and the time to think, Maureen, are worth more than any fancy title."

"He makes a lot of sense, that man," Frank said, when she repeated the conversation. "You could learn a lot from him."

Beryl was silent for a few minutes and then asked, "What's he like, this bloke?"

"What, Bernard?" Maureen said. "Oh, he's quite old, in his forties I should think, looks a bit like Dad." She glanced at her mother, and exploded into laughter. "You weren't thinking . . . oh, I don't believe it!"

"She's just being protective, love," Frank said.

"Well, there's no need, not in this case. I mean, he's a really nice person, but as for anything else, never in this world. Anyway, I think he sees himself as a born bachelor."

Frank grinned, "There's many a married man thinks the same, only too late."

"Oh, yes. Does the cap fit, then?" Beryl bantered.

"I'm keeping quiet," he laughed, but his eyes were soft as he watched his wife struggling with the pram-suit for her new granddaughter. He'd struck gold when he'd married Beryl, and had never for one minute regretted it.

"I've thought of something else," Maureen said. "Do you remember Trevor taking me to a concert at the Victoria Hall once? I'd like to go again, only I haven't anyone to go with. I don't think any of the girls at work would be interested."

"I'll come with you," Beryl offered. "In fact, I'd like to. I went to see the D'Oyly Carte Opera Company once at the Theatre Royal, in Hanley. It was Gilbert & Sullivan – *The Mikado*, but I've never been since. You weren't keen, were you, Frank?"

He shook his head.

"We could go there as well," Maureen said, growing excited. "I'll find out what's on."

Now, with her head buzzing with plans, the months ahead didn't seem so much like an arid desert stretching before her. With her organisational skills coming to the fore, within two weeks she'd applied to join a local dramatic society, booked tickets at the Theatre Royal, and had a programme of concerts to consult Bernard about.

"Not that one, nor that," he advised. "Chamber music isn't to everyone's taste. Now this one would appeal, I think. When you go, note which ones you particularly like, and when you go to the library, read up about the composers."

"You should have been a teacher," she told him.

"Maybe," he smiled. "Perhaps in the next life."

She looked at him, frowning.

"Reincarnation," he said. "Look it up."

And gradually over the next twelve months, Maureen slowly and surely grew in confidence. Not only that, but she felt invigorated. She loved the time she spent rehearsing with the dramatic society, where, just as Bernard had suggested, she acted as prompter. It was not a popular job, requiring intense concentration, so her offer had been accepted with alacrity. Although, with her vivid colouring and slender figure, she attracted many admiring glances, Maureen had learned her lesson. "Friendly but distant" was her motto when dealing with any male under forty. If there were times when her heart beat faster – particularly in the case of one young actor who resembled Gregory Peck – then she kept it firmly under control. But she listened. Listened to the differing way that actors read the words on the sheet before her, noting the inflexion of their voice, the rounding of their vowels. And her own speaking voice slowly became more distinct, her pronunciation no longer lazy, her opinions more articulate. The latter was due to following Bernard's advice to watch the news, keep abreast of current affairs, and follow political debates broadcast on television.

"Observe how people communicate," he advised, and Maureen could sense his approval when she joined in discussions in the office, confidently expressing her opinion.

Frank didn't make any comments, but he watched his younger daughter's progress with keen interest, and not a little pride. "I always knew she had it in her," he said to Beryl. "She could have gone to university, that girl."

"Well, it's too late now," she said. "Anyway, you need exams for that."

"It's a weakness in her character, you know, Beryl. She should have put that behind her long ago. I still feel a bit disappointed she decided not to go to night school."

But Beryl's thoughts were of the future. A future

which was quickly approaching, for in two weeks Trevor would have finished his National Service. Well, he would find his young wife changed, for Maureen had developed a mind of her own, and, Beryl thought smugly, not before time. I mean, she thought grimly, how many newly married men would have chosen not to come home on leave? There was our Maureen, pining to see him, and what did he do? Spend his time off traipsing around Germany – travelling, he called it. Selfish, was her word for it!

With a self-satisfied smile Beryl, filled three hot-water bottles. The next few months promised to be very interesting, very interesting indeed.

CHAPTER FIFTEEN

Maureen wasn't sure exactly when Trevor would arrive and, restless and impatient, she drove Beryl mad as she paced up and down. "I wish we had a telephone," she grumbled. "It would save all this uncertainty."

"Oh yes," Beryl said, "and who'd pay the bills? Anyway, what's the point? We don't know anyone with a telephone."

"I suppose you're right. But Bernard says most people will have one within the next ten years."

"That's it, then. If Bernard says it, it must be right." But there was no rancour in Beryl's voice. She'd come to have a lot of respect for this man who acted as mentor to her daughter. She'd suggested inviting him for tea, but Maureen hadn't been keen.

"I think it would embarrass him," she'd evaded. But that hadn't been the truth. For some reason she couldn't explain, even to herself, the platonic friendship she shared with Bernard was a separate entity from her everyday life. To Maureen it was something private, and at work, they were always very careful to be unobtrusive with their special relationship.

But now, her thoughts were all of Trevor. She'd spent ages getting ready, shampooing her hair and varnishing her nails. She held them out admiringly, deciding she liked the deep crimson. She'd never bothered much with her nails before Trevor went away, but she had watched the actresses at the dramatic society, noticing how gracefully they used their hands. And always those elegant hands were tipped with polish. So now, a weekly manicure had become part of her routine. What to wear for their reunion had caused her much deep thought. Lately, she'd taken to wearing more positive colours: emerald green, deep blues and reds which contrasted so well with her dark hair. Encouraged by her friends at the society, Maureen had learned how to make the best of her natural good looks and as Vera and Nellie told Beryl, she'd blossomed.

"He'll have a shock when he gets home," Vera had pronounced, settling her spare frame on the hard chair she favoured. "She's grown up a lot, that girl."

"He's probably changed too," Nellie said. "They'll be all right, just you wait and see."

"Well, I hope so."

Beryl had remained silent.

Now, she looked at Maureen and scolded, "For heaven's sake, come and sit down. You'll be worn out by the time he gets here."

"I know." Maureen sat in the chair nearest the parlour window, so she could see the moment Trevor's shadow passed.

"You decided against the red one then?" Beryl said, nodding at the pale camel sweater Maureen was wearing.

"Yes. He always liked me in this colour. It's probably how he remembers me. Why, do you think I should get changed?"

There was anxiety in her voice, and Beryl stifled a smile. "Good heavens no, you look fine. Stop worrying! He'll be so pleased to see you, you could be wearing a sack for all he'll care. And do stop fidgeting! What exactly did he say in his letter?"

"That it would be either Friday or Saturday, and he didn't arrive yesterday, so it's got to be today."

"I remember when your dad came home after the

war," Beryl reminisced. "Do you know, I felt quite nervous about it." Her lips curved in a smile as she remembered the passion of their reunion. Then she nodded at the electric fire, switched on since early morning in anticipation of Trevor's arrival. "At least it's nice and warm in here – you'd have caught pneumonia the amount of time you've spent at that window."

"What about his dinner?"

"I've put the plate on top of a saucepan of hot water, it'll keep. For a while, anyway." Beryl had made them all a steak and kidney pie.

"Proper English home cooking, that's what he'll want," Frank had declared.

But the day wore on, the meal dried up and Maureen still waited, disconsolate and frustrated, unable to settle to anything except to wait at the window. And then, just before seven o'clock, the longed-for shadow passed the window and with a surge of joy she flew to greet him, her face wreathed in smiles.

"You look surprised," Trevor said. "Weren't you expecting me?"

Maureen laughed. "Expecting you? I've been waiting all day." She hesitated for a moment, feeling suddenly shy, and then held out her arms, and they kissed, her mouth warm and eager, his lips cold from the east wind outside. "I expected to see you in your uniform."

"Oh, that," Trevor said, coming into the room and putting down a small suitcase. "I went home first and got changed."

Maureen drew away and stared at him. "You went home? Before coming here? Why, what time did your train get in?"

"About eleven o'clock," he said easily. "I thought I'd go and see my parents first, and have a bath."

Stunned, Maureen could only think that he must have passed the end of their street, either in a taxi or on the bus! She should have been the one to see him first, not his parents! He'd been sitting in that stultifying room chatting, having a bath, no doubt eating a meal, while all the time she'd been waiting, counting every minute.

"Mum made you a steak and kidney pie," she muttered, "but it's spoilt now."

Trevor didn't answer, just sat on the sofa and held out his arms, pulling her on to his knee. Maureen couldn't stop looking at him. She'd forgotten how different he looked with a short haircut, almost like a stranger, and she longed for him to grow it, remembering how she used to love the way it flopped on to his forehead.

"You look well," he said.

Self-consciously, she patted her own hair. "I'm wearing my hair differently. Do you like it?"

"It looks fine." But Trevor wasn't looking at her hair, he was staring at her hands, taking one of them in his own, examining her nails. "You never used to wear this stuff."

"What, nail varnish?"

They turned as the front door opened letting in a cold blast of air, and Frank came in from the away match at Derby. "Trevor! Welcome back, lad!" He shook his son-in-law's hand. "Did you have a good journey?"

"Fine, thanks."

"He's only just arrived, Dad," Maureen pointed out, wanting Trevor to herself.

But Frank didn't take the hint – he was too busy unwinding his red and white scarf. "You'll be wanting a cup of tea then. Come through, the football results are coming on – Stoke lost by the way, but I don't know how Port Vale got on."

Maureen got up and Trevor followed him into the kitchen. Reluctantly, she trailed behind.

Dutifully, Beryl went to kiss his cheek "How are you, Trevor? You're looking very fit."

"Of course he is, woman. He's in the Forces," Frank growled.

"I can see Stoke lost," Beryl said tartly. "Sit yourself down, Trevor, I'll put the kettle on. Your dinner's dried up, I'm afraid."

"It doesn't matter, Mum," Maureen said quickly. "Trevor went to see his parents first – he's already eaten."

Beryl glanced at her daughter, and then swiftly away again. With set shoulders she went into the scullery and, striking a match, lit the gas under the ready-filled kettle. Her girl had been waiting for hours! As if he couldn't have called in on the way and taken her with him!

Later that evening, she vented her feelings to Frank. "I just can't get over it," she declared. "If that doesn't take the biscuit for insensitive behaviour, I don't know what does!"

"Don't keep going on about it, Beryl. Happen he just wanted a bath, like Maureen says."

"Our house should have been his first port of call and you know it, Frank Matthews."

Frank got up to get her another drink. They were in his local, trying to give the young couple some time on their own. So, they sat in the bar lounge, although he could hear the familiar noise and bustle coming from the saloon, and couldn't help missing the friendly atmosphere in there, where men would be playing darts, or table-skittles or maybe dominoes. That was what a real pub was all about in Frank's opinion, none of this genteel sitting at little tables making a couple of drinks last all night. But as he waited to be served, Beryl's words lingered. Perhaps, he thought, trying to be charitable, the lad had wanted to spruce himself up a bit before seeing Maureen. And Frank knew only too well how it felt to be away from your wife for months on end. Mixing solely with men all the time it was easy to forget that women often put a different interpretation on your actions. For instance, it was obvious that Beryl had taken umbrage at Trevor's late arrival, and he had himself seen the hurt in Maureen's eyes. Yet to him it was no big deal. Or was it? Uncomfortably, he cast his mind back and remembered how when at last he'd been demobbed, his one burning desire had been to see Beryl, to hold her, to know she was still there for him. Everything else had paled into insignificance. He sighed as the barmaid gave him his change, and she said, "Come on, Frank, it can't be all that bad."

"Just life, Betty, just life."

* * *

Maureen and Trevor were curled up on the sofa, enjoying the warmth of the front room and listening to Glenn Miller. She turned to look up at him. He looked older, and she wondered what sort of experiences he'd had over in Germany, and whether they would have changed him. "I have missed you," she murmured. "It's so good to have you back."

"It's good to be back."

"Go on, then, tell me all about it."

His face closed. "There's nothing to tell, really. I sent you postcards of where I'd been. Life in the Forces is pretty much the same anywhere. You did like your present?"

She looked down admiring the silver bracelet on her wrist, and smiled happily. "Yes, it's lovely."

"A lovely present for a lovely girl," he said, and she kissed him, a long lingering kiss.

"Oh," she said again, "it is good to have you home!"

Trevor ran his finger over the bracelet, tracing the pattern. "I bought my mother one as well, they were such a bargain."

Maureen froze. "You mean," she said slowly, "that your mum has a bracelet exactly like mine, the same design?"

"Yes. They're nice, aren't they?"

She nodded, unable to speak for disappointment. She looked down at the bracelet again. It was lovely, and she'd been so thrilled when he gave it to her. But now, instead of seeing it as a romantic and loving gesture, her mind conjured up an image of Trevor trailing around trying to find bargain souvenirs. Why didn't he go the whole hog, she thought, and buy Mum, Vera and Gran one as well?

In frustration, she glanced up at him in annoyance, but his expression was relaxed and he was obviously completely unaware of the effect of his words. Maureen almost ground her teeth in exasperation. Well, what did she expect? That he'd have had a complete change of personality over there? Trevor had always been the same, incapable of sensing any change in her mood. But then, it was well known that men weren't as sensitive as women. She couldn't help wondering whether everyone had these mixed-up feelings when they loved someone. I mean, she thought, he always did make me feel as though I was on a seesaw, up in the air one minute, and crashing to the ground the next. But then, as Trevor drew her closer and she nestled into his arms, Maureen lifted her lips to his and tried to banish her feelings of resentment. She'd waited so long, why spoil her delight in his homecoming.

There were more important things than bracelets, after all.

CHAPTER SIXTEEN

As Trevor was taking a week off before returning to work, Maureen had arranged to take a week of her holiday entitlement at the same time.

On the first morning, as soon as Frank and Beryl left for work, she prepared a tray, and took it upstairs. "Wake up, sleepy head," she teased. "I bet you didn't get waited on in the RAF."

Trevor raised a tousled head from the pillow. "No, you had to be an officer for that!"

"Well, I think you deserve a bit of pampering," she said.

"Of course I do, I need waiting on hand and foot, woman! How about a kiss, as well?"

Willingly Maureen complied, kissing him on the lips as she lowered the tray on to his lap. Not only did she consider he deserved a bit of pampering but, by sitting on the side of his bed as he ate, she could prolong their intimacy. He always looked so boyishly handsome in his blue pyjamas. But although so far he'd hugged and kissed her, there had been no hint of anything further. Maureen, remembering Trevor's outburst on the night before he left for Germany, was determined to wait for him to make the first move. She'd obviously approached the issue in the wrong way before. In any case, unexpectedly, she was feeling a little shy and constrained. Eighteen months was a long time, and she'd become used to her privacy, her own space. Now, Trevor's male presence in their small bedroom seemed intrusive, disruptive. She'd even woken several times in the night, disturbed by the sound of his steady and sometimes noisy breathing. And it must be the same for him, she thought, getting used to being with me again. Resolutely, she managed to banish her lingering resentment about the previous day, and smiled brightly at him. "What's the plan, then?"

Trevor, finishing his bacon and eggs, yawned. "I haven't a clue. What's the weather like?"

"Raining."

He sipped his tea and grimaced. "It's gone cold."

"Oh, sorry. I'll fetch you another."

"Bring the paper up with you!" he called after her.

When she handed him the paper, Trevor opened it, and without a word settled back against the pillows. Maureen hovered uncertainly for a few minutes, longing to go over to him, to curl up beside him on the bed, then with a sigh went downstairs to wash up. There was still the clutter of the usual hectic breakfast rush to clear up, but when she'd finished that she sat on one of the kitchen chairs, feeling unexpectedly flat. Then she gave herself a mental shake. "It's just the anticlimax," she scolded herself. "All that waiting for the day to come. And there's bound to be a period of readjustment. You expect too much, that's all." Exactly what she did expect, she wasn't sure. After all, experience had shown her that Trevor wasn't the fun-loving romantic type. He was unlikely to immediately "pounce" on her, as the girls at work called it. But for Maureen, the old attraction was still there – it had flared up the moment she'd seen him. Still, she consoled herself, we have a perfect opportunity this week. With Mum and Dad out at work, we'll have the house to ourselves.

Eventually, Trevor got up, and wasted no time in wanting to talk of their future. It was obvious what was foremost in his mind. "We need to get a foot on the first rung of the housing-ladder," he insisted, leaning against the wall in the kitchen, as Maureen made coffee. "Buy our own home, as soon as possible."

Maureen wasn't sure she liked his reference to the housing-ladder. It had a sort of temporary ring to it, while she was longing to create a proper home, one in which she could feel really settled. "What do you mean? Are you saying you're only looking for a stopgap?"

"Not exactly. But I shall be looking to trade up eventually." Seeing the expression on her face, he said, "Don't look so surprised. You expect me to make progress in my job, don't you? Perhaps even work for myself eventually?"

"Yes, of course."

"So," Trevor said, "hopefully, by that time we'll be able to afford a bigger and better house. Have you got the Trustee's passbook?"

"Of course. Here, you take these in, I'll bring the biscuit tin, and then I'll get it."

Maureen also provided a pad and pencil, and watched as Trevor began to work out a budget.

She waited for him to pass the figures to her and when he didn't, said, "Let's have a look then."

"No need," he said, snapping the pad shut. "It's all organised."

"Surely I can see?" she insisted.

He hesitated, then passed the pad over.

Maureen ran her eyes down the calculations. It was simply a projection of monthly commitments, rates, heating and lighting, insurance, household expenses, etc. At the side was the current balance in their savings account. There was no mention of income. As Trevor had never divulged his salary, she had no idea just how high a mortgage repayment they could afford. Maureen sometimes wondered why she didn't ask him straight out. She often heard the girls at work complaining about the same thing, with dark mutterings of, "I'm sure he earns more than he tells me," and "He can always find the money for his beer and fags, even when things get tight". She wondered whether her dad was in the minority. For as long as she could remember, at the end of every week, Frank had handed his unopened wage packet to Beryl, seeming content just to receive his 'pocket money'.

Now, glancing at her husband's closed expression, Maureen realised that the omission was deliberate. He didn't want her to know how much he earned, even though they were discussing their finances. Perhaps it was one of these "male ego" things she read so much about. Anyway, she thought, I'm blowed if I'm going to lower myself and ask!

"Have you been keeping an eye on the housing market?" he said.

"Yes, but I didn't know which price range to look in, what our ceiling was." She glanced at him, hoping for illumination.

"It all depends," he said.

Feeling annoyed that he couldn't give her a straightforward answer, Maureen got up. "Right, let's go around a few estate agents while we've got the time."

Later, after Maureen had cooked them egg and chips, they caught a bus up to Hanley and, thankful that it had stopped raining, wandered around, gazing in the windows of estate agents, and browsing around the displays. At first Maureen studied the prices of terrace houses, then noticing that Trevor was looking at properties in a higher price bracket, said, "We don't want to burden ourselves with too high a debt. In any case, your salary's the only one they'll take into account for a mortgage."

"Of course," he said. "A woman can leave her job for lots of reasons, having a family for instance."

"That sounds nice." She tucked her arm into his and smiled up at him. "How big a family shall we plan for?"

Expectantly she waited for his answer, but Trevor didn't reply. He was staring at a notice on the wall, and said, "What about a brand new house? Look, they're building out at Trentham!"

Maureen was drawn like a magnet to the plans and drawings displayed at the back of the office. "They've got several different designs," she said with excitement, "and there's a show house."

Trevor stood thoughtfully in front of the stand. "You know, we might be able to afford one of the semis, and a new house would be a better investment. Mind you, it would be pushing it a bit."

Maureen was already fired with enthusiasm. Just think, she thought, everything would be new, no moving in after other people, having to put up with their tatty carpets. I could choose the colour scheme for the whole house. Adrenalin coursed through her veins, as she gazed avidly at the architect's drawings.

"It's a good area," Trevor said, "so they should increase their value."

Maureen turned to him in eagerness. "Shall we go and look at the show house? It's open on Sunday afternoon."

"Why not?"

All that evening, Maureen poured over the plans and brochure, discussing with Beryl the merits of different designs. Trevor, however, only gave them a cursory glance. "I'll form an opinion when I see them," was all he'd say, and reverted to his previous habit of going to read in the parlour.

Frank, tiring of all the house-buying chat in the kitchen, wandered in. "Fancy a pint?" he said.

Trevor looked up. "I won't if you don't mind."

Frank shrugged. "Please yourself." He went to fetch his coat and hat. So what, he thought, there's plenty of company down the pub. Still, after eighteen months he did feel his son-in-law could have made an effort, if only to be sociable. Neither did he seem to want to talk about his service overseas. Frank had been looking forward to exchanging reminiscences and jokes about the Forces, but when he'd broached the subject, Trevor said, "That part of my life's over now, I'd rather put it behind me if you don't mind." At first, Frank had felt rebuffed, thinking that Trevor just couldn't be bothered to make the effort, but when questioned, Maureen said, "It's the same with me, Dad. He doesn't seem to want to talk about it."

But Trevor wasn't left in peace for long. Maureen, on a high, was restless and excited, wanting to talk about the new estate, whether they would like to be in a cul-de-sac, which design of house he preferred.

"Mum says –" she began.

"Oh, for heaven's sake come here!" He pulled her down on to his knees. "Calm down a bit, we might not even like the development."

"Maybe," she said contentedly, "but it's still exciting." She rested her head against his chest. She loved it on the rare occasions when he was spontaneously affectionate. "How about going over to see Sandra tomorrow? I'm dying for you to see little Sue."

"I think we should carry on house-hunting. Okay, one of these new houses might be perfect, but we need a yardstick to measure them by."

"You're right, of course," she admitted. But she was determined that some time during the week they would visit her sister. Sandra had at last been allocated a council house, and had moved in only the week before. Maureen was dying to see it. In any case, she hadn't seen little Sue for nearly two weeks. She adored her niece, whose winsome ways enchanted everyone.

But somehow, they never did go to visit. Each day appointments were made to view properties, and time had to be made to visit Trevor's parents. However, Maureen insisted on dragging her newly returned husband round to see Gran and Auntie

Vera. "They'll be really hurt if we don't go," she
pointed out.

Nellie and Vera lived in the rented house in
which they were born. When Nellie married shortly
after the deaths of her parents from influenza, she
was the sitting tenant, and it seemed only practical
for her husband to move in too. Beryl, her only
child, always said that she grew up with two
mothers, one soft as butter, and the other with a
tongue on her like a rasp.

Maureen always found the house claustrophobic,
cluttered as it was with old-fashioned heavy furniture and thick dust-collecting curtains. But the one
feature which always repulsed her was the sticky fly-
paper that the two women insisted on hanging from
the mottled glass-bowl light-shade suspended on a
chain from the centre of the ceiling. When the light
was switched on, the bulb inside illuminated the
many bloated, gruesome outlines of dead bluebottles
and flies which adorned the hanging strip.

Maureen noticed Trevor's glance of repugnance
and said, indicating the offending article, "Why do
you keep that disgusting thing, Gran? Nobody has
them these days."

Vera answered for her sister. "Aye, well if they
don't mind the little buggers leaving their filth over

214

their food, then more fool them."

"I'd have changed it for a new one if I'd known you were coming," Nellie apologised. "You always were a fussy young madam!" But she was smiling, her eyes gentle as they rested on her granddaughter – her family meant everything to Nellie.

Vera went and busied herself making the tea, then brought the tray through including a plate of home-made shortbread.

"I bet you couldn't get this in Germany, Trevor. I hear the Jerries eat nothing but sausages."

They were sitting in the kitchen, Nellie and Maureen on two wooden-armed easy chairs adorned with antimacassars, while Vera and Trevor sat side by side on two dining-chairs.

Trevor took a biscuit with a smile. "Well, it's true, sausages are very popular. But remember we had a NAAFI canteen on the station so we weren't exactly deprived."

"Well, I must say you look well on it."

There was a short silence, then Maureen told them about the show house.

Nellie frowned. "You want to be careful. I hear all these new houses are built with breeze-blocks. Now the older houses are solid built, they've stood the test of time."

"We've been looking at some, Gran," Maureen explained. "Anyway, we're only going to look at the show house."

"Trentham, eh," Vera said. "You'd be living among the toffs there, you know. Have to watch your ps and qs!"

Maureen laughed. "Oh, I don't know, I think they'd be lucky to have us."

"Of course they would," Nellie said indignantly. "You're as good as the next, and a lot better than some. Just you remember that."

"I will, Gran."

They finished their tea and, sensing Trevor's impatience, Maureen said, "We'd better be off, we've got loads to do."

"Gosh, they're like a pair of dinosaurs," Trevor complained, as they walked back down the hill. It was a clear day, the first they'd had for a week, and Maureen who'd felt her spirits lift at the glimpse of blue sky turned on him. "What do you mean?"

"Wearing those flowered crossover pinafores, and talking of living among the toffs! As if anyone thinks like that any more."

"Oh, for heaven's sake Trevor, they're old ladies, and it was only a comment," she said crossly.

He looked down at her, then said with a smile,

"Okay, you're right. So, when's our next appointment?"

"Half past six. It's a 1930's semi in Trent Vale. Why?"

"I was just thinking that gives us the afternoon free."

"Yes." Maureen held her breath, and waited. Did he mean . . .

"Good. I thought I'd nip along to the library."

And that was how the week passed, filling in time between appointments to view. But although Maureen mentally shortlisted a couple of properties, the new show house was never far from her mind.

* * *

On Sunday afternoon, after the long-awaited visit, the young couple burst into the kitchen.

"Six weeks?" Beryl stared at them in amazement. "And you've made your decision, just like that?"

Trevor frowned at her. "There's no question that it will be a good investment."

"Yes, but . . ." Beryl turned to Frank for support.

He drew on his pipe and paused a moment before saying, "I think what your mum means is, do you think you're being a bit impulsive? I mean, wouldn't it be wise to take a few days to think about it?"

Maureen shook her head. "We can't afford to

hang about. The house is gorgeous, you'll love it, I know you will."

"How come you can have one so soon?" asked Frank. "I thought it usually took months."

"Someone's dropped out," Trevor said. "We were just there at the right time. It's a good plot too, at the end of a cul-de-sac."

"That's why we had to make a snap decision," Maureen said. "We've put down a deposit, and now everything will depend on whether we can get a mortgage."

But with Trevor's previous record of employment, and his future prospects with the same company, this didn't prove to be a problem.

"Just think," he said, picking up Maureen and twirling her around. "In another five weeks, we'll have our own home."

"I can't wait," she laughed, and then, looking down into his blue eyes, her heart lifted with the thought – perhaps then our married life will really begin.

CHAPTER SEVENTEEN

Maureen laughed as little Sue stamped her feet on the stairs. "It makes a nice noise, doesn't it?" she said, holding her hand securely. "A stair carpet will have to wait," she said over her shoulder to Sandra.

"You could have my old thing if it would fit. Then perhaps John would agree to replace it." Sandra picked up the toddler to carry her in safety along the landing and into the bedrooms. "Oh, this is nice, pet. What a lovely view!"

"Yes." Maureen smiled at her in delight, enjoying showing her new home to her sister. They'd been in the house a month now, and already the lounge was looking less bare. Not that she hadn't had to do battle with Trevor over buying things on hire purchase but, as she pointed out, they had to have a bed and something to sit on at least. Beryl had run them up some bedroom curtains from remnants off the market, although Trevor had insisted on lined curtains for the front of the house.

"Typical," Beryl had sniffed. "Just to impress the neighbours. I like to see a nice bit of colour from outside, myself."

But Maureen wasn't complaining. She was in love for the second time in her life. She still couldn't help touching the walls and the paintwork, hardly able to believe that this pristine new house was actually hers. Her head was full of colour schemes, visions of how her home would eventually look, plans to invite her friends to tea. She'd have to be patient, of course, but she didn't mind that. And the kitchen! She loved the cleanliness of it all, the simple lines, the modern fitments. Everything would be perfect, if only there wasn't that one cloud . . .

She glanced uncertainly at Sandra.

"What's up? Sue, don't pull on the curtains, there's a good girl!"

Maureen shook her head. No, she couldn't. It would be a betrayal, and a humiliating one at that. It was her problem, or rather theirs. Not something to be discussed with anyone, even her sister.

"Nothing," she said. "Come on, I'll show you the garden, although we haven't had time to do anything with it yet. Here, I'll take Sue."

Sandra followed her thoughtfully down the stairs. It wasn't the first time she'd seen that shadow in her younger sister's eyes. Her eyes narrowed, recalling the first time Maureen had brought Trevor to visit them in their new council house. Remembered the look of disdain on his face as he'd sat on a sagging chair watching Sue drag a truck of bricks across the cracked lino. Okay, the wallpaper with its pattern of green ivy and pale green paint wasn't what she'd have chosen, but as the house had only recently been decorated, it had seemed silly to waste their meagre savings on changing it. But what had really disconcerted her was the scant attention he'd paid Sue. She could have sworn no-one could resist that impish smile, but Trevor had seemed to regard her as a noisy nuisance, rather than an entertaining child. Sandra sighed. She hoped Maureen was happy, that he treated her well, because after all, as her gran often said, "You never know what goes on behind lace curtains." She thought of her John's open, kindly face, knowing that her husband might not have matinee-idol looks, but she wouldn't swop him for Trevor, not for a thousand pounds.

"What about the Dramatic Society?" she asked. "Are you going to join again?"

Maureen shook her head. "No, it's too time-consuming. You have to be able to give up at least a couple of evenings a week, particularly when a production is coming up. And then there's the buses – they're not so frequent from here. Anyway, it wouldn't be fair on Trevor."

Later, she watched her sister put Sue in her pushchair and walk down the cul-de-sac before turning left to make her way to the bus stop.

Maureen turned away from the wrought-iron gates, and went back into the house. The hall had black and white gleaming Marley tiles, the choice of the original buyers, and Maureen noticed that the pushchair had made scuff-marks. Hurrying to the kitchen, she restored the floor to its original splendour, and then wandered with pleasure into the large through-lounge. It was so spacious - much better than the traditional two small rooms with a dividing wall. Most of the the new houses were now being designed in this way. She loved the light, airy feel of the house, and tried to console herself that once they were really settled in, then the 'bedroom thing,' would sort itself out. She'd been bitterly disappointed when nothing had changed as soon as they were in their own home, but she tried to reason that it had been a very busy time, and most nights they were tired after a day at work and a bus journey home. Only now did she appreciate all that Beryl had done over the years, working full-time, and bringing up two children as well. Of course as they grew older, she and Sandra had been given their chores, but most of the domestic responsibilities fell on Beryl's shoulders. Frank would light the fire, clean shoes, offer to peel vegetables and occasionally wield a tea towel. He was also quite at home with wallpaper and a paintbrush but, like many men of his generation, he thought the regular and monotonous cooking, shopping, dusting, cleaning and laundry came under the category of "women's work".

She went up to the back bedroom to tackle the ironing and, gazing through the window at the small, as yet unturfed back garden, she wondered whether to suggest they opened the bottle of wine someone had given them as a housewarming present. Perhaps she should immerse it in cold water in the sink in the bathroom, and try to pick the right moment. Surely wine would relax them both and perhaps . . .

She had just finished ironing Trevor's shirts when she heard the front door open. He always went to the public library in Stoke on Saturday afternoons.

"Where's my tea, woman?" he called.

She smiled and went down into the hall to kiss him.

"I thought we'd have sausage and mash."

"Great! How about a cup of tea?"

Maureen filled the kettle and, waiting for it to boil, took some potatoes from the vegetable rack and began to peel them. Saturday night – it still felt strange not to be able to watch *Dixon of Dock Green*, although Frank was looking out for a second-hand television set for them. She paused, peeler in hand, her mind, as always, swinging back to *their problem*. She was becoming increasingly aware that she'd made a serious mistake in agreeing to have twin beds. But at the time, in all the chaos of moving in, she'd allowed herself to be persuaded by Trevor that double beds were old-fashioned.

"It's a modern house," he pointed out. "Twin beds will look better."

"They're not very romantic," she muttered.

"Of course they are. Just look at all the films – you'd never see Rock Hudson and Doris Day in a double bed together, now would you?"

That was true, although when Maureen mentioned it to Barbara at work, she'd hooted with laughter.

"You are a twerp! That's because of censorship. It

wouldn't do to show a couple in a double bed – twin beds are the only way they can get away with a bedroom scene."

Frank had been scandalised. "Twin beds! Recipe for disaster, if you ask me. What's up with them?"

"Some people say they're more hygienic," Beryl pointed out, who secretly rather liked the idea of not lying next to Frank with his everlasting twitching legs.

"Rubbish! Either you're married or you're not. And that means sleeping in the same bed as far as I'm concerned!"

Another reason Maureen had given in was because she was getting her own way on everything else. Apart from insisting on quiet colours, Trevor had let her have a free hand, and it was only now that she wondered whether he'd had a hidden agenda.

Once the meal was organised, she went into the lounge. Trevor was reading the paper, but she gently removed it and curled up on his knee

"Hey, I was reading that!"

"Well, I needed a cuddle," she said, smiling up at him.

He looked down at her, and with relief she saw his eyes soften.

"You're looking very lovely, Mrs Mountford."

"You're looking very handsome, Mr Mountford."

He kissed the top of her head, and stroked her hand, holding it up to inspect her nails.

"Ah, no varnish, I see."

"Well, I know you don't like it. Mind you, that doesn't mean I'll stop wearing it completely," she warned.

"If you must. But keep it quiet and restrained. I don't want you looking as though you've dipped your fingertips in blood!"

She hesitated, then nestling closer, said softly, "How about we open that bottle of Mateus. We could have a glass with our meal, and then finish it off later."

"Sausage and mash and wine? I hardly think they go."

"Does it matter?" Looking down at him, she saw unease in his face.

Then he said, "I suppose not. But it needs to be chilled."

"That's where you're wrong. It's already organised," she proclaimed in triumph, and thought: right, that's the first hurdle over.

Getting up to put the sausages under the grill, she called over her shoulder, "Did you bring my book?"

226

Trevor followed her into the kitchen. "Yes, although I think you'll find Jane Austen a bit heavy going."

Maureen smiled to herself. She'd done little reading since Trevor had returned; all her spare time had been spent poring over colour charts, swatches of material, and catalogues of household goods. Now, she was looking forward to getting back into 'her books', as Beryl called it.

"I didn't find *Pride and Prejudice* heavy going," she smiled. "I thought Elizabeth Bennett made an excellent heroine." She glanced questioningly at him, "Have you read many of Jane Austen's books?"

He looked discomforted, "No, actually I haven't. I always think of her as more of a women's author."

"You don't know what you're missing," she said lightly. "You should try one some time."

He stared at her. "You know, you're different."

"In what way?" She busied herself setting the small formica kitchen table. "More confident, somehow. I can't put my finger on it exactly."

Maureen leaned up and kissed him on the cheek. "Perhaps I've just grown up." With a secret smile of pleasure, she returned to the cooker and tested the potatoes with a fork.

"It'll be about ten minutes. Why don't you fetch

the wine down? It's in the sink in the bathroom."

"Quite a little schemer, aren't you?"

As he went out of the kitchen, Maureen stared after him. Was he being sarcastic?

But Trevor seemed in a good mood as they ate their meal at the small kitchen table, raising his glass and toasting their new home.

"It'll be nice when we've got a proper dining-table," Maureen said wistfully. She held her glass out for a refill and, smiling, tried to introduce a lighter topic of conversation. "I'm looking forward to going to your annual dinner-dance next week."

"It'll just be full of boring chartered accountants," he smiled.

"Are you sure my dress is all right?" It was her first long evening dress, and Trevor had insisted on going with her to choose it.

Maureen had fallen in love with a glamorous dress in shimmering emerald green, but he'd shaken his head and said, "Why not try this one on?"

Maureen had looked dubiously at the insipid shade of blue. "It's a bit boring."

"Good taste, Maureen, that's what it is." Trevor frowned. "I don't know why you've suddenly started wearing these loud colours. Probably the influence of that dramatic society you used to go to."

"The colours aren't loud, they're bright," she retorted. "And if I can't wear them while I'm young, when can I? Anyway, everyone else thinks they suit me."

"Well, remember at this dance, you're going as my wife. Something quiet and unobtrusive is called for."

And so, they'd bought the blue dress. It had a high neckline and lace-trimmed long sleeves, fitted her slim figure perfectly and the full skirt swished satisfactorily when she walked. But it wouldn't have been her own choice.

"You look lovely in it," he said now.

Maureen's eyes held his. "We could always take the rest of the bottle upstairs, and really celebrate moving in," she said softly.

As Trevor's eyes slid away from hers Maureen felt her stomach lurch – he wasn't going to agree, she knew it. What was wrong with him? Or, perhaps she thought miserably, there's something wrong with me.

But Trevor didn't turn her down. After a few seconds he said, "I suppose we could."

Maureen stood up and picked up the two wine-glasses, leaving Trevor to bring the wine. She went unsteadily up the stairs. Now that at last the time had arrived, she suddenly felt unaccountably nervous. It's only natural, she tried to reassure herself

– after all, it's been nearly two years. But it wasn't just nerves; her anticipation was running high. While Trevor was away, her reading had brought her an increased awareness of the passion and joy two lovers could share, and Maureen longed for this experience. Surely this time, their lovemaking would be spontaneous, full of desire and loving. I want it to be, I need it to be, she thought fiercely.

Yet once again half-heartedly, almost with reluctance, Trevor performed what he obviously thought was his duty. At least that was how it seemed to Maureen. When at first she'd lain by his side and tried to draw the sheet away, wanting to touch him, to arouse him, he'd taken her wrist and moved her hand firmly away. Oh, he kissed her, even briefly caressed her breasts, but then as before it was all over within seconds. Maureen lay afterwards awash with disappointment and bewilderment. Trevor didn't give himself to her at all, not even allowing her a glimpse of his nakedness. And as far as her own body was concerned, he knew it no more intimately than before they were married, for 'everything', such as it was, took place under the covers.

Eventually, as Trevor didn't speak and she felt too vulnerable to trust her own voice, Maureen got up. Trevor was lying with his eyes closed, and gathering up her clothes she went along to the bathroom. It was all wrong, even she knew that. Now, they should have been lying in each other's arms, sated – that was the word used in literature – sated with love, not feeling as she did, cold and demeaned in some way. She leaned her head against the cool, distempered bathroom wall, and felt full of despair. She'd seen the sly, secretive glances of girls at work when the subject of sex was mentioned. Heard the teasing and ribbing. Never anything dirty of course, they were a decent bunch of girls, but enough was said to make her realise that it should be a pleasurable experience. Perhaps it's me, she thought miserably, perhaps he just doesn't fancy me. Then why had he married her? It's his parents' fault, she decided miserably, for bringing him up in that stifling atmosphere. She couldn't imagine them ever being young and full of fun. The problem was, she didn't know what to do about it.

CHAPTER EIGHTEEN

The Institute of Chartered Accountants held their annual dinner-dance at the imposing North Stafford Hotel in Stoke. Although she'd often seen it, Maureen had never been inside and was full of anticipation as they got out of the taxi and Trevor escorted her through the double doors and into the foyer. She was looking forward to dancing too, for they hadn't been since Trevor's return. She hadn't gone to her own firm's Christmas party. She'd felt guilty at lying, but it hadn't been difficult to invent a sore throat then confess to flu symptoms during the day. Not that she'd have been in any danger, for to the female staff's disappointment the auditors that year had been silent and morose. As Barbara acidly observed, "Dry as dust, all three of them".

Once she'd left her coat in the cloakroom, and

checked her make-up and hair, she rejoined Trevor. "Do I look all right?" She glanced up at him anxiously.

"You look fabulous," he assured her, as they walked through a long corridor and into a small already crowded bar. Maureen looked around – the scene wasn't anything like the dances she used to go to at Trentham ballroom. Everyone was in evening dress for one thing, the women with hair stiffly lacquered, their ears and necks glittering with jewellery. She glanced at the hands of a woman sitting at a nearby table, noticing how her pudgy fingers displayed massive diamond and ruby rings. She glanced down at her own left hand with its simple gold band. Still, she thought, at least I've got my silver bracelet. Maureen followed Trevor who looked impossibly handsome in his dinner jacket as he led the way to a small table in the corner.

"What would you like to drink? Don't forget you'll be having wine with the meal," he cautioned.

"I'll have an orange juice, then." Maureen watched him go to the bar. Cary Grant, she decided. That was who he reminded her of, dressed like that. A suave and sophisticated hero, exactly as portrayed on the silver screen. *But certainly not the great lover!* The criticism flashed through her mind, and she felt instantly ashamed. You should count your blessings, she told herself, I bet most of the women here are jealous. And it was true; already Trevor was attracting admiring glances.

He returned with their drinks, and they watched other guests arrive, Maureen studying their clothes and hairstyles, Trevor filling her in on anyone he recognised.

"I don't suppose we'll be on one of the main tables," he said, "only these occasions are very useful for making contacts. I want to get on, Maureen, and it's who you know, not what you know, that matters."

"But it must count that you're qualified."

He frowned. "Naturally. Otherwise we wouldn't even be here. Oh, there's Alan!" Trevor put up a hand to attract attention, and Maureen saw a slightly balding man in his late thirties. The woman with him was wearing what looked to Maureen like an imitation funeral shroud! In a dull grey lace, her skirt hanging limply, she looked almost lifeless, and with an inward giggle Maureen could imagine it being the sort of dress that Norah would choose.

"Trevor!" With a surprisingly booming voice for a small man, he held out his hand. "How are you?"

"Fine, Alan. Can I introduce my wife, Maureen."

"And this is my better half – Mary."

The two women smiled at each other.

"Alan used to be with us, but he left for greener pastures," Trevor explained. "How's it going?"

"Marvellously," Alan said promptly. "More responsibility, of course, but the salary reflects that. Have you looked at the table plan yet?"

"No," Trevor admitted.

"Come on, let's go and see if we're sitting with the high and mighty." The two men left and Maureen turned to Mary with an awkward smile, "It's my first time – you know, to one of these functions."

"Oh," Mary said, "they're quite pleasant usually. I just hope they haven't got smoked salmon as a starter. I can't stand it, can you?"

Maureen didn't like to admit she'd never even heard of it, let alone tasted it, so she said, "Not particularly."

Mary's small brown eyes swept Maureen's hair, face and figure. "Have you and Trevor been married long?"

"Since before he went to do his National Service – nearly two and a half years." There was a short silence, then Maureen asked, "Do you and Alan have a family?"

Mary's face closed. "No."

Maureen reddened, hoping she hadn't touched on a sensitive subject, and was relieved to see Trevor returning. "Alan's just been waylaid," he explained to Mary, and without a backward glance she went to search for him.

Trevor sat down with a self-satisfied expression. "We've got John Hawthorne on our table."

"Who's he?"

"Only head of the biggest accounting firm in Staffordshire. As I told you, Maureen, this is what these occasions are all about. Now we must be sure to make a good impression. There are only limited prospects where I am. You heard Alan, and I'm a damn sight better accountant than he is."

Maureen stared at him in surprise, seeing the steely glint in his eyes, his whole body tense with suppressed energy. This was a side of Trevor she'd never seen before, full of adrenalin and enthusiasm. Pity he couldn't feel the same about making love to me, she thought, and then, startled that her resentment should surface yet again, pushed the thought away. "I asked Mary if she had a family, but I've got a feeling I said the wrong thing."

"Not really," Trevor said. "They made a decision not to have any. I just think they get fed up with people asking."

"I can't understand people not wanting children."

"Oh, I don't know," he said. "It has its advantages."

As people began to drift towards the ballroom, they followed and at the entrance, Maureen caught her breath. Towering vases of flowers stood on either side of the stage, and the tables – so many of them – were resplendent with pretty floral arrangements and pink linen napkins folded into fans on the immaculate white tablecloths. With the settings of silver and sparkling glasses, it was to Maureen the most sophisticated scene she'd ever been part of.

"We're on table seven," Trevor said, and with excited anticipation she followed him to a large round table on one side of the room. They circled, looking for their place-names, and then stood behind their chairs, waiting for the other diners to join them.

John Hawthorne, a middle-aged man with a pronounced paunch and a short, goatee beard, was the first to take up his place opposite. His wife, in a black evening dress which displayed far too much of her ageing upper arms, and wrinkled cleavage, beamed at them.

"Nice to see we're sitting with some bright young people," she said and Maureen smiled back.

"We're young, I'm not so sure about the bright bit," she joked, and felt Trevor stiffen. Oh, Lord, she thought, I've said the wrong thing already!

The rest of the table filled up. They were mostly older people, with the wives mainly wearing black, or what Maureen thought were drab colours, with the exception of one woman in her early thirties. Seated next to John Hawthorne, she was wearing a white, halter-neck dress, with a plunging neckline which left little to the imagination. Blonde and curvaceous, she seemed totally unsuited to her pale, bookish-looking husband, and immediately turned her back on him to smile bewitchingly up at John.

As they took their seats, Maureen looked in alarm at the array of cutlery before her, and glanced in panic at Trevor. "Just work from the outside," he whispered. "Watch the others."

But no sooner had she settled than the toast-master announced, "Would you all please rise for Grace," and there was a scraping of chairs while 150 people stood up. Once seated again, she read the menu, and couldn't help smiling as she saw the first course was, indeed, smoked salmon. Well, at least she'd find out whether she liked it or not. The main course was crown of lamb. She'd seen a picture of that in a cookery book: it was all bones with miniature chef's hats on.

Trevor was busy consulting with the rest of the table about wine. "A claret, I think," John suggested.

Claret? Maureen thought only the Victorians drank claret – it was often mentioned in Dickens, for instance. At least she'd never seen any in their local off-licence. Although she had to admit they didn't stock much wine; it was mainly sherry, port, and spirits. You could buy egg-flip, or advocaat, and Tia Maria or Drambuie, but the wines were limited to one or two bottles of Mateus or Blue Nun. But then, in a working-class area, people were hardly going to be able to afford claret.

And so the meal passed pleasurably, Maureen really enjoying herself. If she found it noticeable that Trevor ingratiated himself at every opportunity with John, she soon forgot in watching with fascination the way the 'woman in white' outrageously flirted with him. So, that's what furthering your husband's career entails, she thought, secretly amused, although John's wife wasn't, judging by the irritation in her glances. But when her gaze met Maureen's, there was in them a mischievous glint, and once she raised her eyebrows in mock exasperation. I bet he gets this all the time, Maureen thought, and looking across at the influential accountant realised that although he might enjoy the flattery, he knew exactly what was going on.

Then, during the interminable speeches, she saw him. It was only a glimpse at first, and then he turned his head and she was sure. It was Stuart Copestake, that lousy, insulting moron – he was one person she'd hoped never to see again! She supposed it was only to be expected that he'd attend an event like this, as an auditor.

Once the tables were cleared, a band appeared on the small dais, and Maureen was delighted to recognise a familiar crooner at the microphone. He was a regular singer at Trentham Ballroom and she remembered how Elaine used to fancy him – but her mind shied away from the memory.

"Try and remember the good times," Beryl kept telling her. "Think of her smiling and happy," and Maureen did try, but found she could cope better by keeping that particular door in her mind firmly closed.

The music chosen to begin with was sedate, and at first only a few couples braved the dance-floor in a slow foxtrot. Maureen and Trevor remained at the table watching, but then slowly people began to get up and when the band played a lively quickstep, the floor was soon crowded.

"Shall we?" Trevor said and, nodding, Maureen took his hand.

"They're playing one of our favourites," she whispered, as the familiar strains of 'When the Saints Come Marching In', began. "Are you enjoying it?"

"Very much, are you?"

"Oh, yes," she said dreamily. She felt as though she was in a film, surrounded as she was by the men in their dinner jackets and the women swirling by in evening-gowns. She looked up at Trevor – he was the handsomest man in the room, although she had to admit that most of them looked distinguished. What was it Auntie Vera always said – "Fine feathers make fine birds"? Well, now she knew what she meant.

Later, they wandered out into the bar where it was cooler, and while Trevor ordered the drinks, Maureen went to the ladies' cloakroom. There was a queue for the toilets, and it was nearly fifteen minutes before she was able to rejoin him, only to recoil as she saw his furious expression.

"Get your coat!" He spat the words at her.

"But . . ." Bewildered, she stared at him, seeing their drinks still on the bar counter, untouched. "It's only eleven o'clock, the taxi's not due until one!"

"Just do as I say!" he shouted.

Trembling in shock at the cold implacable anger on his face, she backed away before hurrying to the cloakroom and, her eyes stinging with tears of humiliation, handed in her ticket.

Minutes later, she stood in the foyer, huddled into her coat and clutching the white, tinsel-fringed stole she'd borrowed from Barbara, waiting while Trevor went to phone the taxi firm. He didn't speak as he returned to her side, and such was the aura of fury emanating from him that she didn't speak either. She remained in rigid silence, not daring to ask what was wrong. All she wanted to do was to get out of hotel, away from curious eyes, and back to the refuge of home. The icy silence continued throughout the journey, her enjoyment of the evening shattered, her confidence in tatters. What had she done? In misery, she sat staring out of the window, every nerve aware of the stiff figure of her husband beside her.

Once inside the house, Trevor had hardly closed the door before he turned on her.

"Well," he said, and his tone was vicious, "that was an education!" Taking off his coat, he flung it over the balustrade in a heap and stalked off into the lounge. Shaking, Maureen stared at the coat. Never, in all the time she'd known him, had she seen her husband treat his clothes like that. She took off her own coat and put it on top, an action which normally would have brought about a reprimand, but she was past caring. She was frightened, afraid of the violence she could sense in him, and with some trepidation she followed him.

"Whatever's the matter?"

"Matter?" he shouted. "Matter? You have the gall to stand there and ask me what the matter is?"

In a choked voice, she said, "Trevor, I haven't the faintest idea what you're talking about?"

"Stuart, that's what I'm talking about. Stuart! You didn't know I knew him, did you? Do you know what he said to me? Do you?" He thrust his face threateningly against hers, and Maureen blanched, tears springing to her eyes.

"No, I don't."

"Then I'll tell you! 'See that girl in blue,' he said, 'the one over there? She's a right little raver. I met her at a firm's dance where I was auditing. Gagging for it she was. Play your cards right, and you'd be in there like a shot!' And I had to stand there, knowing he was talking about *my wife*!"

Flabbergasted, Maureen stared at him. "And you believed him?"

"Well?" he shot at her. "Are you denying you know him?"

243

"No, I'm not – "

"I thought so!"

"You don't think anything, Trevor Mountford," Maureen flashed, her temper rising now that she understood the situation. "If you'd thought even for one minute you'd have asked *me* what happened. As you say, I *am* your wife!"

"Go on then, I'm waiting," he said, but his expression was hard, his eyes cold.

"He asked me to dance," she tried to explain. "At the firm's Christmas party."

"And?"

"He made a filthy suggestion, saying that as my husband was away in the Forces, I must be missing it – 'gagging for it' just like he told you. So in front of everyone, I threw my drink over him." She looked at him, her face flushed with anger. "He was just getting his own back tonight, trying to cause trouble between us."

For a moment there was silence, then Trevor said, "Are you telling me the truth?"

"Have you ever known me to lie?" she challenged, her tone now as hard and cold as his. She was fuming, livid that he could ask her such a question, that he'd put her through such an unnecessary ordeal. Feeling she couldn't bear to stay in the same room with him for another moment, she snapped, "I'm going to make some tea," and marched off to the kitchen. Furiously, she filled the kettle and switched it on, clattering the cups into their saucers, and slamming the cupboard door as she took out the sugar. Stuart! What a vindictive . . . she searched her mind for a suitable swear word . . . vindictive sod! The sheer malice and nastiness of his action appalled her. And to think that for a fleeting few moments she'd been attracted to him! And as for Trevor – well, it just showed how much trust he had in her. She'd certainly seen another side of him tonight! Hot tears began to well in her eyes, and going back into the hall she began to search for her hanky which was in her evening bag. The shiny silver bag she'd been so proud of, and now look how the evening had ended. She'd been so happy . . .

Trevor stood in the doorway of the lounge.

"Maureen . . ." he began.

"Don't you 'Maureen' me," she snapped, and headed back to the kitchen.

He followed her. "What was I to think?" he said. "How would you have felt if the position had been reversed?"

"I wouldn't have made the scene you did. Have you any idea what you put me through? We live in a country where you're innocent until proved guilty, or doesn't that rule apply in this house?"

He didn't answer, and in silence Maureen made the tea and then, taking a biscuit from the tin, took a bite and began to chew it furiously, trying to ease the sick feeling in her stomach. Seething, she picked up her cup and stormed upstairs. But even as she went she realised she had no alternative but to sleep in the same room. The other bedrooms were still bare, and as yet they didn't possess a sofa. Just let him try to touch me, she railed, and then collapsed on the bed in despair. She was kidding herself – there wasn't the remotest chance.

CHAPTER NINETEEN

Maureen pretended to be asleep when Trevor came up to bed, not trusting herself to even speak to him. The following morning, she got up early and before he was awake, she had already burned off some, if not all, of her anger in a frenzy of cleaning.

He was late coming down, and by then Maureen had pulled the twin-tub washing machine in front of the sink, and was busy sorting their laundry into piles on the floor.

"Don't forget that I like my shirts and underwear to go in first," Trevor reminded her as he came into the kitchen.

Glaring at him, she retorted, "I don't know what you think you'll catch – you were just the same at Mum and Dad's, insisting your washing was done separately."

"Just put it down to one of my funny little ways,"

he said, and sat at the kitchen table to wait for his breakfast.

You've certainly got enough of those, she thought and snapped, "What do you want? Cornflakes?"

"Fine."

Huh, he hasn't the nerve to ask for a cooked breakfast, she thought with satisfaction. As she put the dish in front of him, Maureen began to wonder whether he was going to refer to the previous night's row at all. Eventually, she could stand it no longer.

"And how are you this morning?" she said icily.

"Okay," he said. "How are you?"

"I'm how you'd expect!"

He turned to face her. "Look, Maureen, I thought we'd sorted all this out last night."

Sorted it, she thought. Sorted it? When he hadn't even apologised! Stiffly, she removed his empty dish, and filled the kettle ready to make his coffee. "I think you owe me an apology."

"All right, I apologise. Now can we forget it?"

Maureen turned off the hot tap and removed the rubber hose. As she bent down to pick up an armful of Trevor's shirts, she could only think, you might be able to – I'm not going to find it so easy.

Her instinct was correct, for over the next few weeks she was dismayed to find that, in a subtle way, her feelings towards Trevor had changed. His willingness to believe the worst of her had shaken her confidence in their relationship, and the violence of his reaction, his threatening attitude, had made her wary. But their lives fell into a pattern, as they settled down in their brand new house, and eventually Trevor began to work on the garden, clearing away the builder's debris, and preparing the ground for a lawn. "I think I'll buy turf," he said, one Saturday morning, "rather than seed it."

"Whatever you say." Maureen was standing at the window, arranging flowers in a vase. She peered out. "It looks as though someone's moving in next door."

He got up and joined her. "You're right."

"They're a young couple, like us."

"I hope they haven't got any children."

She stared at him. "Why ever not?"

"Well, they're noisy, aren't they? Always knocking a ball into your garden, that sort of thing."

"You won't say that when we've got some of our own," Maureen said, and then bit her lip.

There had been no sex at all since that first time soon after they'd moved in. Lovemaking never seemed to occur to Trevor, and fed up with his lukewarm reaction to her own advances, she'd stopped making any effort. And strangely, Trevor seemed more relaxed and affectionate as a result.

"I think I'll come with you when you go to the library," she said. "Drop in and see Mum and Dad."

"Do you need your book changing?"

"No, thanks, I haven't finished it."

Maureen always looked forward to an afternoon at home. And that was still how she thought of the small terraced house in Oakvale. As the football season was over, Frank was there, and it felt like old times as they settled down with tea and biscuits for a cosy chat. At least Maureen and Beryl did; Frank retreated behind his newspaper. They talked about little Sue and her latest antics, and their concern that Sandra, now pregnant with her second child, was suffering so badly from morning sickness. Then there was Beryl's latest catalogue to look through and discuss in endless detail, all of which Frank put up with in silence. When he heard the sharp knock on the front door, he went to open it with profound relief.

"Thank goodness you've come!" He grinned. "Any more of this female gossip and I'll go spare."

Trevor smiled. "I know what you mean."

"Do you fancy a cuppa in here?" Frank said. He never gave up hope that he and this distant son-in-law of his could find some common ground.

"Why not?" Trevor put down his books and sat on one of the armchairs, stretching out his legs.

"Right, I'll switch the fire on. It's as cold as February out there. It's Trevor," he announced, going back into the kitchen. "How about some tea and biscuits in the parlour – there's too much chat in here."

"Oh, all right," Beryl said, getting up, although when he'd gone she muttered to Maureen, "You'd think men weren't given arms and legs like the rest of us!"

Maureen laughed. "I know what you mean."

"You're finding out, are you?"

"I certainly am."

In fact Maureen was finding out a lot more. As the months passed, the extent of Trevor's fastidious habits was becoming increasingly apparent. It wasn't that she minded his excessive neatness, because at least that meant she didn't have to tidy up after him, but when he tried to inflict it on *her* domain, that rankled.

"Why are all these tins put in higgledy-piggledy," he'd complain, opening the kitchen cupboard and taking them out to re-arrange according to size. Then he'd 'tut' if he came in and found the tea towel not hung up neatly on its hook, or the jar of

251

coffee left out on the work surface. "A tidy house – a tidy mind," he'd say, and Maureen would put her tongue out at his back as he left. Once, she'd even caught him running his finger along the top of a doorframe for dust, and at that she'd exploded.

"I'm not a maid you employ, you know, Trevor. I do go out to work!"

He'd had the grace to look discomforted, but she'd have been more impressed if he'd offered to pick up a duster. As it was, he did little to help in the house. But when she complained about this at work, it simply unleashed a barrage of similar complaints.

Joan, one of the typists, had them in stitches. "The first time I asked my husband to wipe the dishes," she said, "he drew the curtains so the neighbours couldn't see him. Honestly, I'm not kidding!" But there were others who admitted that their husbands did help a bit with the housework. Few did any cooking, yet as Maureen pointed out most famous chefs were men. But it was reassuring to find that her husband wasn't any different from many of his contemporaries.

"I think we've been downtrodden for too long," she declared. "All through history women have been taken advantage of. Call us the weaker sex? Not in my book."

"You'll never change things," Barbara said airily. The group of women were in the staff canteen having their coffee break. Demolishing the last mouthful of chocolate éclair, she licked the stickiness from her thumb, before adding, "It's a man's world, always has been, always will be."

Maureen was finding it more and more difficult to accept this. She found herself observing social conditions in the area, comparing them to articles she read portraying a movement towards more freedom for women, more choice in their lives. Not that she had any ambitions to be a career woman – she'd always known what she wanted: her own home and children. Well, she had her own home, and hopefully, once they were 'on their feet' financially, then babies would follow. For surely then, Trevor would make more of an effort to be a proper husband – or rather an 'improper one', she thought with a wry smile.

Yet again she wondered just how much his home environment had contributed to what she saw as his lack of passion. Even now, when Norah and Henry came to tea, Maureen would watch the interaction between the Mountford family with incredulity. Trevor's parents would behave as though they were in the home of a complete stranger, rather than that of their only son, while their conversation consisted of polite small talk. Any attempt by Maureen to lighten the proceedings always met with coolness, and eventually she gave up. She took care to prepare a dainty tea, following Norah's preferences, and saw their visits as a depressing but necessary duty. Where, she thought, was the affection in this family? Certainly none was shown either in their greeting or their farewell. It was no wonder that Trevor, growing up in such a sterile existence, was so inhibited.

"Penny for them," Beryl said, looking up from her knitting. Sue and her expected new grandchild kept her fingers busy clicking away, and it was her favourite relaxation to knit while listening to the wireless – particularly The Home Service. "Give me a good play I can listen to, any day," she'd say. "I can't do with the box being everlastingly on."

"Oh, nothing," Maureen said, "I was just thinking."

Beryl looked up at her, her eyes shrewd. "Not getting broody, are you? I've seen you looking at the baby patterns."

Maureen flushed. "Well, sometimes, but I'd like to get the house how we want it first."

"That's only sensible and you've plenty of time. In any case you need a couple of years on your own," Beryl said. "Unless any come along by accident," she added hastily.

Maureen kept her thoughts to herself.

In the parlour, the two men had finished their tea, and while Trevor looked at the flyleaf of his new library book Frank tried to think of a topic of conversation. He never had this trouble with John, but then Sandra's husband was easy-going and sociable, whereas he always felt awkward with Trevor.

"You must be proud of the way our Maureen's come on," he said at last.

Trevor frowned. "Sorry?"

"Maureen. You must have noticed a difference in her since you've come back."

"She does seem a lot more confident – she's lost some of her Stoke accent too."

"I think you can thank the Dramatic Society for that. She did a lot of reading while you were away as well."

"Yes, I'm pleased to see she's reading the classics now."

"That's because of Bernard. He's been a tower of strength if you ask me," Frank said. "I wanted her to go to night school, but to be honest I think he's done far more for her."

"I'm not sure I know what you're talking about, Frank."

Frank stared at him. "Hasn't she told you about Bernard? Now that's just like Maureen – deep as they come, always has been."

Trevor put down his book, and said slowly, "Told me what?"

By his tone, Frank suddenly became aware that this wasn't turning into a casual chat at all. He looked at the younger man, taken aback by the coldness in his son-in-law's eyes. "Just," he said uncomfortably, "that Bernard, someone she works with, has been giving her advice."

"I see." Trevor's lips tightened, and Frank wished he'd kept his mouth shut.

"Why all the secrecy about Bernard?" he said to Beryl as later in bed they huddled together trying to get warm.

"What do you mean?"

"I mentioned something to Trevor, and he about froze the pants off me."

"Oh, for God's sake, Frank, what did you have to do that for? You know what a funny devil he is. And keep your cold feet to yourself!"

"Can't think what all the mystery's about," he grumbled, turning over.

* * *

Maureen, always acutely attuned to Trevor's mood,

had known immediately she went into the parlour that something was wrong. Uneasily, she kept glancing at his closed-in face. With anxiety gnawing at her stomach, she forced herself to wait until they got home. "What's the matter?" she demanded, the moment they got in.

"Nothing."

"You can't fool me. Have I done something to upset you?"

"You tell me."

Maureen stared at him. "What do you mean?"

Trevor looked at her, his lips drawn into a thin line.

"Who's Bernard?"

Taken by surprise, she stammered, "He's a bloke at work."

"I see. And why have you never mentioned him?"

"I didn't have any reason to."

"So you don't think it's important that your husband should know another man's been your 'Svengali'. I had to wait to hear it from your father!"

Maureen groaned inwardly, but couldn't blame her dad. She was the one who was so secretive about the friendship.

"He's a very well-educated and intelligent man," she explained. "And he's been kind enough to take an interest in me, you know – my education, that sort of thing."

"As long as that's all he's taken an interest in!" Trevor looked at her with suspicion. "I don't remember meeting him."

"Oh, he doesn't like parties, he never goes."

"And how old is he, this paragon of learning?"

"I don't know, middle-aged I suppose – and you needn't look at me like that, you haven't got competition. He's not interested in women, not so far as I know, anyway."

"You mean he's . . ." Not even saying the word, Trevor's tone was one of outrage.

"No, of course not," she snapped. "Why do you jump to that conclusion? He just likes living on his own, with his books and cat. I don't know why you're getting jealous – it's possible for a man and woman to have a platonic friendship, you know."

"Who said I was jealous?"

"Oh, pull the other one, Trevor. I know you! I just wanted to improve myself, that's all."

"That's very commendable, Maureen," Trevor said stiffly, "but I still don't understand why you never mentioned him."

"As I said, there was no reason to." She held his gaze steadily, and his eyes searched hers for a minute.

Then, to her relief, he said, "All right, if you say so. But I wish you wouldn't be so secretive."

"And I wish you wouldn't be so jealous and possessive!"

"I'm not," he protested, and then pulled her close. "You're just so beautiful," he said, his face muffled in her hair. "You can't blame me for wanting you all to myself."

Maureen raised her head and, as his lips met hers, she kissed him with tenderness, trying to convey her longing, hope leaping within her that the charged emotion between them would lead at last to further intimacy.

"You've *got* me all to yourself," she murmured, kissing him again with increasing warmth. She pressed even closer, her hands caressing the back of his neck.

But Trevor didn't respond. Instead he drew away, gave her a quick kiss on the cheek and then going over to the television switched it on. Maureen stared at him in bewilderment and disappointment.

"Trevor …" she said hesitantly,

"Mmn?" He was only half-listening, and when he didn't turn to look at her, Maureen realised the moment had passed.

"Nothing, it doesn't matter."

Going into the kitchen she dispiritedly began to prepare their tea. Well, what did you expect, she told herself. You should be used to it by now.

CHAPTER TWENTY

And so life went on. During the following year, Maureen continued with her job, and did most of the housework, keeping the modern semi 'like a palace', as Beryl once remarked. Trevor mowed the small lawn in their back garden, planted a narrow border around and kept it neat and free of weeds. He'd taken out a loan to buy a second-hand Mini, and gradually, staying within their budget, and using hire-purchase carefully, they furnished the house. It meant rarely spending any money on entertainment, and going dancing or even to the pictures became a thing of the past. Sometimes Maureen would look at her fitted carpets, teak dining-table and chairs, modern check three-piece suite, and refrigerator, and wonder whether they were worth all the sacrifice.

MARGARET KAINE

Not that she didn't love her home – she did, but part of her yearned for bright lights, music and the heady atmosphere of a ballroom. She missed seeing the latest films too, but with reluctance had accepted that their self-denial was necessary, at least for now. Instead, she consoled herself with romantic novels, interspersed between the classics. She discovered historical fiction, reading Baroness Orczy's *The Scarlet Pimpernel* and Norah Lofts' *The Town House*, while Bernard recommended *Jane Eyre*, and *The Mill on the Floss*. Their love of books was one thing that she and Trevor really did share, and many evenings were spent in companionable silence. At least most of the time it was companionable, but sometimes Maureen would sit and gaze at her handsome husband totally absorbed in his library book, and wonder if this was all there was going to be to their lives. To live in the same house, eat the same food, and share a bedroom just to sleep. It will be different when children come along, she kept telling herself, and she told herself so more and more often as one year led into another. Maureen wanted to have her babies – and she planned to have at least two – while she was young. Of course, she said nothing of this to Trevor. Not yet, but she knew the crucial moment couldn't be delayed for much longer.

262

Then one Monday, when she went into work, Bernard wasn't there. And neither did he come in the next day. This was unusual in itself, for he was rarely ill, but more so was the fact that there hadn't been a phone call.

"His next-door neighbour rang last time he was off work," Colin said. "It's a bit odd, because you know what Bernard's like for following the rules."

"Perhaps he'll be back tomorrow," Maureen suggested.

But when there was no sign of him the following day, she became concerned. No-one, as far as she could find out, had ever been to Bernard's home and she knew he guarded his privacy fiercely, but that afternoon she went to Colin.

"Is it okay if I leave early, and go to see if Bernard's all right?"

Colin looked at her. "It's fine with me, Maureen. And perhaps you're the best one to go, seeing as you're such good friends."

The office had long accepted that she and the quiet bespectacled man were 'bookish', and her initial fears about ribbing or sly remarks had proved unfounded. It was probably because once they'd met Trevor, the girls couldn't imagine her ever being interested in anyone else.

"When you've finished with him, you can pass him over to me," Barbara had quipped, and many flirtatious glances were aimed in her husband's direction when he came with her to the Christmas parties. Each year, Maureen held her breath as the time for the annual audit arrived, but so far, to her relief, there had been no sign of Stuart. Neither, for some reason, had he attended The Institute of Chartered Accountants' dinner-dance again.

Now, she had to find out exactly where Bernard lived. She knew it was local, so hopefully it wouldn't be too far to walk. Issued with his address by the Wages Office, Maureen left at four o'clock, and began to walk through the narrow streets. It was a hot July day, and she was glad to be out in the fresh air. Lately there had been a restlessness within her, a chafing at being confined, her freedom restricted. She thought of Sandra, picturing her sister sitting out in the garden, relaxing and enjoying her two children. Maureen was well aware that with babies came hard work, but at least, she thought, you were in control of your own life, not a 'wage slave'. But it wasn't just that – increasingly lately she'd found herself envying Sandra and her simple, homely lifestyle. She may not have a smart new house, Maureen thought, but how can you compare such things with Sue's happy face, and little Stevie's affectionate hugs. Her heart softening at the thought of being able to cuddle her own tiny baby, Maureen made her decision. Tonight she would talk to Trevor about starting a family! And perhaps, she thought wistfully, things will be different this time. For although she'd eventually accepted the limitations of their relationship, Maureen was acutely aware of a need within her for . . . she searched for the word and came up with . . . fulfilment. That was it, there was a space within her, a sort of loneliness, a need to give – to . . . oh, I don't know, she thought miserably, but surely there must be more to love than this.

She turned into the street where Bernard lived, looking around her curiously. She always found it fascinating seeing where other people made their homes. Financial necessity of course limited their choice. But even then just by looking at the outside of a house, how the windows were curtained, the colour chosen for the front door, the condition of the woodwork, whether the step was clean – all could give an indication of the personality of the occupants.

Bernard's house was in a 'dead end', a cul-de-sac of Victorian terraced villas facing each other, their small square bay windows glinting in the afternoon sunlight. Number twenty was at the far end, and she walked slowly along, mentally picturing Bernard's life in this quiet backwater. In the distance a bottle-kiln overshadowed the horizon, its blackened brick a permanent testament to the industrial nature of the area. Apart from a mongrel relieving itself against a lamppost, there was no-one about, and Maureen pushed open the single wrought-iron gate at the front of Bernard's house, lifted the small black knocker above the letter-box and tapped on the door. She looked around at the tiny garden with its neatly trimmed privet hedge and single bush of pink tea roses. Bernard's door, she noticed was freshly painted black and free of dust, unlike the one in the adjoining house where the paint was peeling, and the knocker rusty. So much, she thought, for the common perception that men living alone are scruffy. After waiting for a few moments without a reply, Maureen retraced her steps until she found an entry between the houses, and walking through turned left to Bernard's back gate. Fortunately, it wasn't locked and going through she found herself in a small, but painstakingly kept garden. Sticks of sweet peas, rows of lettuces, cabbages and carrots were wilting badly, and she frowned. Bernard must really be feeling ill to neglect his beloved vegetables.

A tabby cat was prowling around and Maureen bent to stroke it briefly before knocking on the back door. There was no answer. She knocked again while the cat fussed around her ankles, mewling piteously, and Maureen stood back feeling disconcerted. Should she try the door? Did she have the right to intrude in such a way? Then, the niggling worry about Bernard's welfare overcame her doubts and she tried the doorknob. It moved easily and as she tentatively opened the door, the cat leapt in, brushing against her legs.

Following, she stepped inside and called, "Bernard? It's Maureen!"

But there was only silence. The back door had opened directly into the kitchen, and she went through and opened the door to a small living-room. She never got further than the doorway.

Bernard was sitting in an armchair facing her, his hands hanging stiffly over the wooden arms, his spectacles askew. The right side of his face was twisted into a grotesque leer, his sightless open eyes staring at her, while in the silence bluebottles buzzed obscenely around his body. The stench emanating from the decaying corpse in the stifling, foetid room was overpowering, and bile gushed into her mouth, to splutter into her covering hand as she fled, just managing to reach the back door, before vomiting until her throat was raw.

Shuddering in horror at what she'd just seen, Maureen wiped her sticky hand on some grass, and then dried it and her mouth with a handkerchief. Stunned, she leaned for support against the wall that divided the two small gardens. He was dead! Bernard, her friend – only now did she realise just how fond she'd been of him, how close they'd become – was dead! She couldn't believe he'd died alone like that, with not a soul aware of it. It was terrible! And he must have been dead for days! On trembling legs, Maureen made her way out of the garden and back along the entry, fumbling at the gate to the neighbouring house and hammering angrily at the front door. Were they blind? Hadn't they noticed that something was wrong?

A voice called, "All right, hold your horses, I'm coming!" The door swung open, and a 'bottle-blonde' of indeterminate age stood before her. "Yes?" she snapped.

Now that the time came for her to speak, Maureen found her voice was shaking.

"It's Bernard," she managed. "Mr Clewlow, next door . . ."

"Well, what about him?"

"I've . . . just found him . . . round the back . . ."
Maureen was choking on the words, as a sob caught
in her throat, and unable to control her tears they
ran unheeded down her cheeks.

The woman's attitude changed. Brusquely, she
brushed past Maureen and began to run to the entry.
Maureen followed and the two women went through
the gate to Bernard's house, the neighbour's face
flushed and anxious, Maureen hanging back, not
only unable to face the horrific scene again, but
feeling that she owed it to Bernard not to 'gawp' at
him in death. He'd been such a private man, so
fastidious about his appearance, and his home
portrayed that. He'd have hated this, she thought,
would have loathed being a public spectacle.

The neighbour, who later told Maureen her name
was Evelyn, came out, her face pale with shock.

"The last time I saw him was at the weekend," she
said in distress. "I don't understand it – I mean,
where's his milk?"

"That's what I wondered," Maureen said. "Do you
think we'd better call the police?"

Evelyn nodded. "Mrs Waters over the road's got a
phone. I'd better feed his cat as well."

Within minutes the call was made, and then as
one neighbour after another heard the news, a small

group of women gathered on the pavement, arms folded over flowered pinafores, shocked that one of their kind could die without anyone noticing. Maureen stood by awkwardly, shaken and stunned. It was the first time she'd ever seen anyone dead, and nausea rose again in her throat at the memory of the pungent and sickly smell which had emanated from the body. And all the while, her mind struggled to come to terms with the fact that Bernard had gone, that she'd never see him, talk to him again. Her friend, her true friend, in an unusual relationship the like of which she might never again experience. And he died alone, she thought with bitterness, but then on its heels came another thought – perhaps he would have chosen to die alone, in privacy as he had lived.

Soon, the police arrived, and once she'd agreed to make a statement later, Maureen left. She felt no inclination to remain among the groups of neighbours, talking in hushed tones. She wanted to have some time to herself, to try to come to terms with what had happened. When she arrived home, pale and tearful, Trevor looked up from the evening paper.

"You're late . . . what's the matter?"

"It's Bernard," she said in a tight voice. "I went

round to his house and found him dead in an armchair. It looked as if he'd had a stroke."

Trevor stared at her, but instead of getting up to comfort her, as she needed, he said, "What were you doing at his house?"

His tone was sharp and accusing and, taken aback, Maureen stammered, "I'd gone round to see if he was all right. We hadn't heard anything from him."

"Have you been before?"

"No, of course not!" This time her voice rose in anger. "What are you suggesting?"

"I'm not suggesting anything – I was just asking, that's all."

Stunned, Maureen stared at him in bewilderment. Not a word of sympathy had he expressed, not even to say he was sorry Bernard had died. Feeling suddenly dizzy, she put out a hand to steady herself on the doorframe, and then went slowly into the kitchen to get a glass of water. All thoughts of having a discussion with Trevor were postponed. She was too upset even to think of it, not only by Bernard's untimely death, but also by what she saw as Trevor's callous and insensitive reaction. He hadn't even offered to make her a cup of tea.

But Trevor must have realised that his questioning had hurt her, because he followed her into the kitchen, and at last took her in his arms and held her close. "It must have been an awful shock," he said. "Look, you go and sit down, I'll make you a hot drink."

* * *

It was a bright but windy day when Bernard was buried, the only sound the rustling of the leaves of the old oak-trees in the small churchyard. There were scarcely any relatives to mourn, just a couple of cousins, and feeling somewhat self-conscious, Maureen threw a single pink rose down on to the coffin before, with eyes blurred by tears, she turned away to join the others from the office. Evelyn was there, and drew her to one side.

"The milk," she said. "Do you remember, we wondered about the milk?"

"Yes, I remember."

"Been on my conscience, it has, him being in there dead and nobody noticing. We like to keep an eye out for each other in our street." There was an angry glint in Evelyn's eyes as she muttered, "Well, I found out what happened – that new family who've moved in opposite, they were only pinching it, weren't they? I caught one of 'em, a lad about ten, taking a bottle off my step the other morning."

Maureen saw the genuine distress in her eyes, and

said reassuringly, "You're not to blame yourself, you probably couldn't have done anything anyway."

"That's not the point. It's no way to go, is that. Still, that little toe-rag won't do it again, not after I put the fear of God into him."

So that solved that mystery, Maureen thought as she travelled home from work on the bus later that night. And now, she needed to look to her own future. She would talk to Trevor about starting a family, but not yet – she'd give herself time to get over this trauma before she embarked on another.

CHAPTER TWENTY-ONE

It was over a month before Maureen could nerve herself to broach the subject. Not just because she was still upset over Bernard's death, but every time she thought about Trevor's possible reaction, she had a sick feeling in the pit of her stomach. She was well aware of her husband's coldness towards little Sue. He'd never once picked the child up, or suggested taking her a present. Whenever they visited Sandra and John – which wasn't as often as Maureen would have liked – he took no interest in the child's play and chatter, he merely sat in an armchair and unsociably read a newspaper. No matter how she tried to persuade herself that he would feel differently about his own children, as the time approached her anxiety increased. And conversely, so did her longing for a baby and her conviction that now was the right time for them to start a family.

She waited until after Sunday lunch, when Trevor was normally in a good mood. After washing and wiping the dishes, she checked that the cooker was gleaming and the work surfaces spick and span – he was very particular about that – before hanging the dishcloth over the taps to dry. Going upstairs to their bedroom, Maureen sat before the kidney-shaped dressing-table, brushed her hair and freshened her make-up in an effort to to give herself more courage. Then she gazed at her reflection for a moment, squared her shoulders and went downstairs, where Trevor was reading the Sunday papers in the lounge.

She sat in the armchair opposite.

"Trevor . . . ?"

"Mmn . . ."

Maureen waited until eventually he looked up. "Can we talk? Really talk, I mean."

With a frown, he put down the paper. "Of course. Is it about this Cuba crisis? Don't worry, Maureen, I don't think Khrushchev is stupid enough to risk a nuclear war."

Maureen shook her head.

"No, it's not that. I wanted to ask you . . ." she drew a deep breath, and the words came out in a rush, "how you felt about starting a family?"

Trevor stared at her for a moment, then his eyes narrowed. "What's brought this on?"

"Nothing's 'brought it on'. I just think it's time, that's all."

"And have you done your sums?" he asked, raising an eyebrow.

She was prepared for this. "Yes, I have. We could manage on your salary now most of the house is furnished. And we always intended to have children, didn't we?"

Trevor gazed steadily down at the carpet, while Maureen waited.

The silence lengthened, until unable to bear it any longer, she said, "What do you think?"

He said, still not meeting her eyes. "You've rather sprung this on me. I'll need to consider it."

But this wasn't enough for Maureen; now that she'd plucked up the courage, she wasn't prepared to be fobbed off.

"You need to think about whether it's the right time?" she probed. "Or . . ." and here her nerve almost failed her, "whether you want children at all?"

Hardly able to believe that she'd actually put into words her fearful suspicion, she waited tensely for her husband to speak. For what on earth would she do – could she do – if Trevor said he didn't want a baby? But Maureen pushed this thought from her mind, as she had so many times before – it was too terrible even to think about. Instead, she just waited . . . and waited as the seconds slowly ticked by.

She watched his face, saw the tension in his jaw, saw a hint of glistening sweat on his upper lip as he struggled with his answer.

An answer which didn't come, and when at last he met her eyes, Maureen forced herself to say, "That's it, isn't it? You don't want children at all."

"As you hadn't mentioned it for ages, I thought you felt the same," was his muttered excuse.

"That's not true," she defended. "I've often referred to it. And," she pointed out, her voice rising in hysteria, "we talked about children before we got married. If you remember, you made quite an issue of the birth-control thing."

"Maybe, but time and experience change things." His tone was heavy and, bewildered, Maureen stared at him. Time and experience changed what? Surely you either saw your future life holding children or you didn't? Was it something deeper than that? All this time she'd reluctantly accepted their platonic relationship, reasoning that perhaps they both merely had low sex drives. Certainly, her own desire to try and repeat the lacklustre performance had slowly waned. For a few moments she sat in silence, as with desperation she tried to understand what he meant, then with a sudden flash of insight – she knew.

"You don't like it, do you? Sex – or marital relations, or whatever you want to call it?"

Startled, he looked up at her, and fiercely Maureen held his gaze, searching, probing his face until she saw the truth in his eyes. She turned her head away, her face crimsoning with embarrassment and shame. The memory of how in the past it had been she who'd set the scene, coaxed him, blatantly offered herself.

"Tell me, Trevor," she said quietly, "for God's sake, talk to me!"

With a trembling hand, he lit a cigarette and took a couple of ragged puffs, then stubbed it out in the ashtray by his side.

"I didn't know," he said in a tight voice. "Before we were married, that is. It's just that when it came to it I found the whole act, what was expected of me . . . well, distasteful, degrading even. I mean, it's so undignified, like animals."

Maureen could only stare at him in utter

incredulity. "But it's supposed to be a wonderful thing, a way of two people expressing their love for each other." Now her voice was no longer under control, as her mind struggled to take in the monstrous concept of what this might mean to their lives.

He looked at her, and there was a hardness in his eyes, a cold determination and she felt a sudden stab of fear.

"That may be how you see it," he said. "I just know I have no intention of ever repeating the experience, *ever* . . . do you hear me? And you've accepted our life without it, I know you have. Sex is only a very minor part of marriage – it's really about working together, supporting each other. You know I love you, and you love me – you do, don't you?"

"You know I do," Maureen said with bewilderment. "But . . ."

"Tell me honestly, Maureen. Did you enjoy it . . . what we did?"

She could only stare mutely at him, misery in her eyes, and he said, "There you are then, so what's the point?"

"But what about children? Are you asking me to go through life without having any? I want a baby, Trevor!" There was agony within her, as she began to realise that this miracle might never be hers, that she was destined to be – what did they call it? – barren, for the rest of her life. How could he possibly expect her to agree to such a sacrifice?

"I'm not so hardhearted that I'd deny you that," he said. "For your sake, I'd be quite willing to adopt a child. But it would have to be an older one, not a baby, they make too much mess."

Maureen was stunned – no baby of her own? No baby even to adopt? What sort of man had she married, for heaven's sake?

"Suppose," she said slowly, "I say that I can't accept that. I want my own child, Trevor – I want to hold my own baby in my arms."

"Then it won't be mine."

The cruel finality of the words was like a knife-wound to her, and she turned her face away struggling to control blinding tears. For even if his answer had been different, how could she ever consider conceiving a child with someone who found the very act degrading? 'Like animals' he'd called it, and she recoiled at the coarseness of the term. How could any woman live with that? Suddenly, Maureen knew that she would never be able to bear Trevor to touch her again.

She stood up, and in a voice thick with emotion

and anger, snapped, "I'm going for a walk!"

Desperate to get away from him, once outside the house, she kept her head bent to hide her distress as she hurried along the quiet roads and out of the estate. Desperately she looked around for some sort of refuge, a place of privacy. I am like an animal, she thought bitterly, looking for somewhere to hide while I lick my wounds. And still walking at a fast pace, she turned into a tree-lined road. Trentham Park, that was where she would go; unlike the Gardens with its many attractions, it would be quieter, free of crowds. It was a lovely early autumn afternoon and Maureen looked up at the clear blue sky, glad of the soothing touch of a gentle breeze on her hot face, and found a secluded spot beneath a large tree. Curled up on the grass, she rested her tense spine against the solid strength of the ancient oak and thought. Thought of all the devastating words that had been said, thought of her future, thought of her past. She stared down the years yet to come, years without physical affection, years without love. For Trevor had killed the love she had for him that afternoon as surely as if he had taken an axe to it. If he'd shown any sign of distress, guilt, or shame at his predicament, had admitted even that the problem was his, she would have rallied to his side, suggested he seek help, offered to go with him, would have supported him. It was the sheer selfishness of his stance that devastated her. That he could make a clinical statement which affected her so profoundly without apology, without showing any concern for *her* feelings, *her* needs.

Maureen was unaware of time passing as she sat and relived over and over again the recent scene. Just a freshly decorated room, proudly displaying its modern furniture, in an ordinary semi on a new housing estate, yet what heartbreak had been played out within its thin walls. My whole life, she thought bitterly, summed up in a few sentences. And then there was the shameful rejection. Maureen looked down at her body, and knew she was desirable. Why, she couldn't even walk along the main road without some bloke whistling at her. Yet her own husband was refusing to sleep with her *ever again*.

She buried her head in her hands, trying to remember whether there had been any clue in Trevor's behaviour during their courting days, any hint that he had this . . . she searched for the word . . . peculiarity, for that was what it was. It wasn't normal to feel as he did – he was sick, he had to be. But she knew her husband well enough to know that he'd never admit it. No, she thought with bitterness, he'd rather parcel up the problem into a neat package and leave it to me to carry the burden. Maureen didn't cry easily, but now, as the hot tears rained down her face, she reached for a hanky, only to realise that in her rush to leave the house, she didn't have one with her – she hadn't even brought her handbag. She pulled at the cuff on her sleeve, stretching it and tried to wipe away the tears. The wool was Aran and rough on her skin, but she didn't care, she felt as though she would never care about anything ever again.

CHAPTER TWENTY-TWO

Beryl waited until after Christmas and New Year before she admitted to Frank that she was worried about their younger daughter. Frank, who'd spent much of the morning trying to thaw out the outside toilet, was immersed in *The Sunday People*, reading how the freezing winter was heading to be the worst since 1947. With a resigned sigh he put his paper down.

"How do you mean, 'worried'?"

Beryl waited for a moment, then said quietly, "I don't think she's happy."

Frank stared at her. "Has she said anything?"

Beryl shook her head. "Very little. But she isn't, Frank, I can see it in her eyes."

He drew his brows together in a frown. "Have you mentioned this to Sandra?"

"I sounded her out the other day, but she doesn't see that much of Maureen these days. She blames it on Trevor, says he thinks he's too superior to go visiting a council house. She thinks I could be right, though."

Frank smoked his pipe, deep in thought. He'd noticed himself that the girl had been a bit quiet lately. But then he didn't always listen as she and Beryl gossiped over the teacups. Over the years, living with three females, he'd perfected the art of closing his ears to their chatter.

"I have noticed one thing," he said slowly. "Not just recently either. But do you remember how when Trevor was away in Germany, our Maureen used to dress in bright colours? They suited her, too!"

"Exactly," Beryl seized on his words. "Now all I ever see her in is dull colours. Sometimes with a pastel top, yes, but it's as though the life has gone out of her. I mentioned it once, and do you know what she said?"

"What?"

"That Trevor didn't like her in loud colours, he thought they were common." She glared at him in anger, almost breaking her rule of not criticising her son-in-law. That was dangerous ground, almost as dangerous as interfering between husband and wife.

But if I find out he's making my lass unhappy, she resolved, I'll not hold my tongue then!

Frank sat brooding for a few minutes, then said, "I don't think there's much we can do, love, not unless she confides in us. You could try and draw her out, I suppose."

"Easier said than done," Beryl replied, getting up to clear the table. "You know what she's like for bottling things up."

Frank watched his wife take the dishes into the scullery. He'd never actually said as much to Beryl, but right from the start he'd never been that keen on Trevor. Later, after Trevor returned from Germany, his uneasiness had increased. He remembered how after his first rebuttal, he tried once again to talk to him about the time he'd spent over there.

"I expect," he'd said conversationally, "you miss the RAF, you know – being with the other men."

"Not really," Trevor replied, and there was a bitterness in his tone. "I'm not keen on all this men together stuff."

Seeing the hard expression in his eyes, Frank hadn't pursued the matter. But he'd thought about it, wondering if there was a reason why Trevor didn't seem to have made any particular mates in the RAF. He'd never mentioned any airman by name either to him, or apparently to Maureen.

But now Frank wondered whether, when marriage had first been broached, he'd done the right thing in keeping his misgivings to himself. But Maureen had been starry-eyed about the chap, and he'd convinced himself that her happiness was paramount. Afterwards, he'd held back because he didn't hold with talking about members of the family behind their backs, and also because as far as Beryl was concerned he'd sensed that it would be tantamount to holding a match to a tinder-box. He valued harmony in his home; he'd had no desire to create an atmosphere where Trevor's shortcomings were continually aired. But now, as he sat looking in vain for comfort in the glowing imitation coals in their new electric fire, Frank thought uneasily that he should have been stronger, taken the long-term view. For if Beryl said their younger daughter was unhappy, and she was usually right about such things, then he was only too conscious that he must shoulder his share of the blame.

* * *

Although she sensed that Beryl was worried, any attempt to invite confidences Maureen brushed aside, for how could she tell anyone the true cause of her unhappiness? For better for worse, in sickness

and in health, were the vows she'd taken, and if
Trevor was sick and as she saw it an emotional
cripple, that was their tragedy, theirs alone. She
might not love him any more, but she owed him
that loyalty, if nothing else.

And as one month dragged into another, Maureen
tried to continue her life as before. Well, almost as
before, because now when her husband went to kiss
her goodnight, she just offered him her cheek. Gone
was any spontaneity in their life together, any
laughter, any fun. She felt as though she was living a
lie. Oh, she went to work, sat quietly among the
banter of the other girls, cleaned her house, did her
domestic chores. But there was no joy in her life, no
happiness. It amazed her how easy it was to hide her
true feelings, to portray an image of a normal young
married woman leading an ordinary life, like thousands of others. And Trevor had no inkling of how
she really felt, she was sure of that. Maybe he was
aware that she wasn't as affectionate as before, that
she didn't seek his company, often busying herself in
the kitchen or elsewhere in the house, but he didn't
say anything. In fact he said very little, and certainly
the emotive subject of children was never raised
again. In any case, feeling the way she did, there was
no question of adopting a child. What sort of home

could she offer it? A child needed love and security, warmth and affection. And so do I, she thought miserably, so do I.

And as slowly, so slowly, the weeks passed, Maureen began to sink into depression. In the evenings, she would sit before the television screen, but her mind was oblivious to the programme showing, as she stared blankly ahead. She was even finding it difficult to concentrate enough to read. She went through the motions of living, at times sleeping so deeply it was like being sucked into a dark womb, yet at others she would wake in the early hours to lie sleepless for the rest of the night, tears trickling down her face.

At the office, which at one time would have proved a distraction, Bernard's absence was not her only loss. Barbara had left to join her sister in the accounts department at the local council offices, and her replacement was a girl Maureen didn't much care for. Fortunately, the work she was doing had become simply repetitive and she managed to cope despite her lack of mental energy.

Vera, whose sharp eyes missed nothing was, as usual, vociferous with her opinion.

"There's something wrong with that girl, Beryl," she boomed. "Is she keeping her bowels open?"

Nellie snorted. "Don't be daft, our Vera, young girls don't have that sort of trouble."

"You may scoff," Vera said. "The girl looks tired to death and she's sluggish. You tell me if they aren't symptoms of constipation!"

Beryl remained silent. She hated hearing Maureen talked about like this.

"Is everything all right, Beryl?" Nellie asked. "Between her and Trevor, I mean."

"So far as I know – she doesn't say much."

"Well, I've been wondering myself," Nellie said. "I don't suppose you could ask her – straight out, like?"

"I did once," Beryl admitted. "I said that she seemed a bit down, was anything wrong, but she said no, everything was fine." But Beryl wasn't convinced. Maureen had serious problems; it didn't take a genius to work that one out.

* * *

One evening a few months later, Maureen walked wearily through the estate after a day at work. She didn't know how she'd got through it, didn't know how she would get through the rest of her life. Constantly exhausted, her mind struggled against a blanket of darkness, and all she wanted was to get home, have a meal and go to sleep.

Trevor was there before her, reading the *Evening*

Sentinel. He looked up as she came in through the front door, calling into the hall, "Had a good day?"

"Fine, thanks. And you?"

"Not so bad. What are we having for dinner? I'm starving."

Maureen looked at him. He must have been home for at least half an hour, yet it never seemed to occur to him to make her a cup of tea after her long bus journey. But she couldn't be bothered to make an issue of it, and just said, "I'm tired. How about fetching in fish and chips?"

"Must we? I don't really fancy them tonight."

Maureen sighed. She didn't care what she ate, just as long as it didn't take any effort. "I suppose I could do bacon and eggs, that's easy enough."

"Fine. Although we mustn't make a habit of it," he said, following her into the kitchen. "Good health springs from well-balanced meals, you know."

Maureen hadn't even the energy to feel irritated, and quietly she put on her apron and switched on the grill. "Will you set the table for me?" Although she was vaguely aware that Trevor did the task with ill grace, it didn't bother her. Tonight, she couldn't be bothered with anything.

The following morning the alarm's shrill bell failed to wake her, and when Trevor shook her

MARGARET KAINE

shoulder she had to struggle to surface from a death-
like sleep. When eventually she managed to drag
herself out of bed it was to experience a strange
heaviness in her limbs, a cold detachment in her
mind. Her brain seemed slow, but she managed to
get ready for work. While Trevor, who never spoke
first thing in the morning, was doing his exercises,
she went down to carry out her normal routine. Half
an hour later, she glanced at the clock. *In the silent
kitchen, Maureen lifted out an egg from the frying-pan
and placed it carefully on top of a triangle of fried bread.
Already on the warm plate were two rashers of smoked
bacon, and two links of pork sausage. Her husband was
very fussy about his cooked breakfast. It had to be
precisely the same every morning, and she knew that in
five minutes he would come downstairs expectantly,
wearing the suit she had pressed, the shirt she had ironed.*

"*I'll say one thing for her,*" she'd once heard her
mother-in-law say. "*She turns him out well.*"

*And Maureen did. Just as her own appearance was
always neat. Not flamboyant mind, he wouldn't have
liked that, any more than he liked her to wear nail
varnish. In the two years since he'd returned from doing
his National Service in Germany, Maureen had discovered that her husband didn't like a lot of things.*

She peered through the net curtain. It was raining; not

292

a heavy downpour, but the sort of misty dampness which clung to your hair and clothes.

For one long moment, she remained motionless, then putting on her coat she picked up her handbag, unlocked the back door and stepping out closed it quietly behind her. On tiptoe, she crept down the side of the house and turned into the narrow road. With the sound of her high heels tapping on the pavement, she saw no-one, not even when she turned the corner.

Inside, the table was set in readiness, the brown teapot was snug under its knitted cosy. The note, already beginning to curl over at the top, was propped against a bottle of HP sauce. Just an ordinary piece of lined paper torn out of an old exercise book, it held one line:

Gone for a walk, M

CHAPTER TWENTY-THREE

Maureen's pace was steady as she walked through the streets of the modern housing estate and out on to the main road. The tree-lined pavement at the side of the A50 was damp with dew, and as yet traffic was light. If she saw anyone at all, they were just a blur to her, and when after passing through Hanford she reached Oakvale her step never faltered as, in the fine rain, she walked blindly past the street where her parents lived. Maureen felt as though her body was imprisoned in a vice as her mind focused on one objective, one overwhelming desire. She needed to – *had to* – get as far away as she could – away from Trevor, and from her travesty of a marriage. She walked on and on, oblivious to the distance, until, as she waited at a kerb to cross a side road she realised she was within yards of the city's main railway station. A train! That was her solution. With a train journey she could go miles away; surely then she'd be able to think clearly, surely then at last she would be free of this dreadful lethargy and greyness in her mind.

Turning right, with the same steady pace, Maureen passed before the unseeing gaze of the statue of Josiah Wedgwood which faced the station, and without pausing went through the entrance. In the distance she could see a train standing at the nearest platform and, going straight to the booking office, she said, "A ticket for the next train, please – the one on the platform."

"The London train?"

She nodded. She didn't care where it was going.

The clerk, a small man wearing rimless spectacles, peered through the glass at her. "Single or return?"

She floundered. "Single."

"One pound, ten and sixpence." He pushed the ticket towards her as she began to fumble in her handbag for the money. Her movements were slow and clumsy and he glanced at the clock. "Come on, love, it's due out!"

With an effort, she managed to pass over the right money and clutching the ticket in her hand went to the barrier. The collector took it from her, clipped it, and urgently indicated the waiting train. As a guard walked along slamming doors, Maureen hurried across the platform to grab the door-handle of the first carriage she saw. She stumbled in and even as she closed the door, the guard blew his whistle and the train began to move. Steadying herself, she looked around – the carriage was empty. She sank into a seat by the window and soon, overcome by drowsiness, fell asleep.

It was the noise and draught of the door opening which awakened her and a silver-haired woman, struggling with a large suitcase, stubbed her toes. "I'm so sorry!" she said.

Maureen drew her legs in, murmuring automatically, "That's all right," and once more drifted off into sleep. It was only when she felt her shoulder shaken that she stirred.

The same woman was looking down at her with concern. "We've arrived at Euston. Are you all right? You're looking very pale."

"Yes, fine, thank you." Maureen managed a slight smile and, satisfied, the woman pulled down the window, reached outside and opened the door. She left it open, and gradually Maureen pulled herself together enough to follow. As she stepped down on to the platform, her mind could only seize on one word. Euston! Numbly, she remembered the clerk saying the train was going to London. London! Maureen had never been to the capital – when her school had visited the Festival of Britain, she'd been ill with tonsillitis. She'd been one of the last passengers to alight from the train, so the platform was fairly empty as she walked slowly along. Totally unprepared for the mass of people waiting beyond the barrier, Maureen, in her weakened state, found it exhausting to push her way through and when she saw the sign of a station café she headed straight for it.

Her mouth felt dry with a metallic taste, and suddenly conscious that she'd eaten nothing since the night before, she went up to the counter and stood looking at the sandwiches. Most, despite the glass cover, were already curling at the edges, but the only other choice was a slab of dry-looking fruitcake. She asked for a cup of tea and a ham sandwich, paid for them and turned to find a seat. The room wasn't particularly crowded, and she tucked herself away at a table in the far corner. The ham in the sandwich was thin and tasteless, but she ate hungrily and then put two spoons of sugar in the strong tea and began to sip it. Meanwhile, she opened her bag, took out her purse and with a slightly trembling hand checked its contents, relieved to see she still had that week's housekeeping intact. Her head ached and when, rubbing her eyes with weariness, she looked up it was to see a small boy staring at her with curiosity, only to be reprimanded by his mother.

With a sudden urgent need, she hurriedly finished her tea and left the café to find the station toilets. When eventually she went to wash her hands, she looked at her reflection in the mirror. Horrified, she saw that not only had her mascara run – giving her blackened panda eyes – but her hair, uncombed since early that morning when she'd walked so far in the rain, was hanging in what Beryl always called 'rats tails'! Ten minutes later, feeling a bit better now she'd freshened herself up, Maureen went uncertainly to the station exit.

The noise of the dense traffic seemed deafening, and she took a step backward, looking right and left at the impressive architecture of the capital. The buildings seemed so tall, intimidating even, and she hesitated, wondering which way to turn. By now, her feet were beginning to hurt in their tight-fitting court shoes and she loitered, trying to think, to work out a strategy. It's no use just wandering around wearing yourself out, she told herself. You need more time – to sit quietly, to think things through. She turned to go back into Euston and then, noticing all the names of the cities along the railway line displayed on the brickwork, her gaze travelled up until she saw the name of her home town. It was the first listed and she remembered Frank's football joke that 'the only time you'd see Stoke at the top of the league was outside Euston Station!' In a small way, the memory warmed her and she walked with a slightly lighter step back to the café and ordered another cup of tea, together with a bar of Cadbury's milk chocolate. She'd read somewhere that chocolate was very sustaining, and she knew she couldn't afford to spend money in expensive restaurants. It was said that you had to take out a mortgage to buy a decent meal in London!

This time the corner table was taken, and so she sat at a one adjacent to the wall. And sat, and sat – just staring blankly into space, her shoulders hunched inside her beige mac. What was she doing here? Why had she come? But she knew that she'd had no control over what had happened that morning; it was as though a force greater than herself had propelled her out of the house, and away from her husband. Husband . . . what sort of husband would deprive his wife of children, of love, of everything that marriage stood for? Her loyalty had been misplaced – Maureen could at last now see that. I don't owe him anything, she thought, and bitterness filled her throat. Not a single thing.

I'm not going back! The decision flooded into her heart, her mind, her very being. *I am never going back to him!* And as though her body responded to her vow, her shoulders straightened, she lifted her head and for the first time looked around the room. Her gaze caught that of a middle-aged woman who smiled, a comfortable and motherly sort of smile, and got up from her own table and brought her cup and saucer over, saying, "Mind if I join you, dear? I could do with a bit of company."

Startled, Maureen muttered, "No, of course not."

"Can I get you another one? Yours must be cold by now."

Maureen looked down, realised she hadn't touched it, and felt the thick earthenware cup. "Oh, so it is. No, it doesn't matter, honestly."

"If you say so." The woman sipped her tea slowly. She had a sort of currant-pudding face, Maureen thought, with small brown eyes. But she was friendly enough, unlike what she'd heard about Londoners. The problem was, she didn't really feel like chatting, exchanging small talk. She had to decide what she was going to do! There was no question of her catching a train back to the Potteries. She couldn't bear the thought of all the questions, the discussions, the endless traumas that her decision to leave Trevor would cause. And she'd have to face *him* – there would be arguments, persuasion, shame heaped upon her. No, this was a crisis in her life she had to deal with alone. She had to stiffen her resolve, regain her energy and strength.

Maureen could see now that it had been the strain of living a lie, of trying to hide her unhappiness at being married to someone she no longer loved, or, now she admitted the truth, even liked any more, that had caused her depression. What she needed was somewhere to hide away from all that was familiar in her life – for a time, at least.

"Are you just up for the day?" The woman, who had been sitting quietly, put down her cup and dabbed at her mouth with a paper serviette.

"No . . . at least . . ."

"Thinking of staying on a few days? London's a fascinating city."

"Possibly," Maureen admitted.

The woman held out her hand, "My name's Mary, Mary Fellows."

Maureen took her hand and gave it a quick shake.

"I'm Maureen . . ." she glanced down at her wedding ring, hesitated, then added, "Maureen Matthews." She felt she couldn't bear the thought of even carrying Trevor's name and, hiding her hands in her lap, removed the slim gold band and slipped it into her handbag.

Mary leaned back in her chair, and began to tell Maureen about the business she'd recently started. "Just a modest little guest house, you understand, but I offer people clean rooms and a decent breakfast. Reasonable rates too. I'm doing quite well. Some places in London – well, you'd never believe what they charge. Immoral, I call it. Of course, you probably already have somewhere in mind . . ."

There was a sudden movement as a man who had been sitting with his back to them at another table got up, pushing his chair roughly back. The chair-legs scraped on the floor and, startled, Maureen turned round. He was about thirty, wearing a belted raincoat, his features unremarkable except for piercing grey eyes, which were staring at Mary with an unnerving intensity. Maureen glanced at her, surprised to see alarm and unmistakable fear in her eyes. The man came and stood at the side of their table, but now his intense gaze was on Maureen's upturned face. She stared back at him, puzzled and a little apprehensive, until he looked away, back at her companion.

"Well, Mary, up to your old tricks, I see!" His deep voice was curt, harsh even, and Maureen looked from one to the other in bewilderment.

"Just having a nice, cosy chat," Mary muttered, and stood up, averting her face as she picked up her belongings. "I was just leaving."

He stood impassively until the door to the café closed behind her, while Maureen sat in stunned silence, wondering what on earth was going on.

"I don't understand . . ."

"You've had a lucky escape," he said. "It was just fortunate that I was here, waiting for a train." Even as he spoke there came an announcement over the tannoy. He leaned forward to emphasise his next words, "Don't ever accept hospitality offered to you by a stranger, particularly on a railway station!"

His eyes bored into hers and, startled, Maureen stammered, "No, of course not."

"Right. Enjoy your stay." Then, he was gone.

Shaken, Maureen sat for several minutes longer, remembering something she'd read once in an article, about how seemingly ordinary, kindly women preyed upon young girls arriving in the capital. How once under their control, they were eventually led

303

into prostitution. She spent a few moments trying to recall where she'd read the article, and suddenly Elaine came into her mind. That was it, they'd read it together in a women's magazine in carefree, innocent days which now seemed so long ago. She shuddered at the thought that perhaps, just perhaps, in her mentally weakened state, she might have been taken in. It was true what people said – London was a dangerous place.

She eventually got up and, going out into the station again, noticed for the first time the signs to the Underground. She'd read about the system in various novels and it had sounded exhilarating, glamorous even, to hurtle around the capital underneath the traffic. But now she halted, undecided. If she did go down the steps, where was she aiming for? She didn't know anyone in London, in fact she didn't know anything about it! As people began to push past her, she moved aside in confusion, then suddenly heard a familiar word.

"Leicester?" A porter stood in front of a young woman not much older than herself. "You need St Pancras. Turn left outside the station and it's about ten minutes' walk."

Leicester! That was where Carol lived! Maureen found herself moving as though in a dream towards the exit, following the girl. Leicester – that was the answer, her solution! She could go and stay with Carol – for surely her childhood friend would give her sanctuary.

CHAPTER TWENTY-FOUR

Maureen climbed the steps leading up from the platform and made her way out of the redbrick building that fronted Leicester Railway Station. Emerging from its impressive portals she stood in confusion on the pavement outside. Although she'd dozed on the train, the sensation of fatigue and heaviness, the inability to think clearly, which had been so much a part of her life in recent weeks, was returning. She tried to concentrate, force herself to think, to remember. Exactly *where* did Carol live? But she didn't have the address with her, and no matter how she tried, her brain was too foggy even to recall the district. Undecided which way to turn she looked in both directions, and then began to head for what seemed to be the main road into the centre. With her court shoes now pinching, she walked slowly and painfully, eventually pausing outside a café. She glanced up at its decorative tiled frontage, wondering whether she should get a cup of tea and something to eat. Then as she reached out to open the door, suddenly one word came into her mind. 'Dolores'. That was it! The name of the town-centre hairdressing salon where Carol worked! She could go there! Almost dizzy with relief, all thoughts of the café were forgotten. She started to walk again, but a few seconds later came to a halt, looking around her in bewilderment, feeling overwhelmed by the strangeness of her surroundings. An elderly woman passed her, hesitated and then coming back, said, "Are yer lost, me duck?"

"I'm looking for 'Dolores'. It's a hair salon."

"Oh, it's not far, it's just off the Town Hall square. See the Midland Bank on the corner over there?"

Maureen nodded.

"Right, walk up by that. You'll see the square and the fountain, and 'Dolores' is opposite." With a cheery smile, she hurried on her way.

Maureen made her way as directed and was soon crossing a square, with an imposing Town Hall facing a circular treed area where pigeons hovered and pecked at the ground. Even though the weather was chilly and damp, there were one or two people sitting on the benches facing the fountain which was fronted by majestic statues of lions. Maureen limped across, feeling more weary with every painful step and then at last she saw the sign. 'Dolores'. The salon looked exclusive, but she was beyond being intimidated. There was only one thought, one desperate aim in her mind – she had to find Carol, *she had to*, and almost in tears, she pushed open the door.

A tinkling bell sounded, causing a tall, slender receptionist to look up from a desk just inside. Her black hair sharply cut in a straight bob, she raised her finely plucked eyebrows, one glance sweeping disparagingly over Maureen's dishevelled figure.

"Can I help you?" Her tone was cool.

"Could I see Carol, please?"

The receptionist looked down at her appointment book.

"She's fully booked I'm afraid until the twenty-seventh. She could fit you in then, at nine-thirty."

"No," Maureen tried to explain, "I don't want a hair appointment – I'd just like to see her – I'm an old friend of hers."

"Oh, I see. Well, I'm sorry, she's with a client at the moment."

Maureen glanced around. There were three gilt and red velvet chairs, none of which was occupied. "I'd like to wait, if that's possible."

"Certainly. But she could be another half hour."

"That's all right." Thankfully, Maureen lowered herself into one of the chairs. Her feet were now hurting so much that as soon as the receptionist was looking the other way she eased them slightly out of her shoes. It wasn't enough – she didn't dare to be too obvious – but it helped. The minutes slowly ticked by, and clients emerged to pay their bills, escorted by their pink-uniformed stylists, while one or two other expensively dressed women arrived for appointments. Oblivious to the curious glances, Maureen fought a battle to stay awake and then when an elderly woman, her sparse hair fluffed into a silvery-blue-rinsed bouffant, came through, Maureen heard at last Carol's distinctive husky voice. "Just brush it through, Mrs Martin, and use a tiny amount of Vitapointe. I'm sure you'll find it easy to manage." She emerged and, taking a fur coat from a cupboard, she helped the woman on with it and then with a smile took the proffered tip.

Maureen waited, staring at the transformation in her childhood friend. Gone was the curvy young girl she remembered – in her place was a slim, confident young woman, manicured and made-up to perfection.

Maureen suddenly felt grubby and unkempt, and nervously pushed back her hair as the receptionist leaned forward and, nodding in Maureen's direction, whispered to Carol.

Carol turned round and looked into the corner where Maureen was sitting. For a split second she stared, and then exclaimed in astonishment, "Maureen! What on earth are you doing here?"

Maureen began to stand up, but her legs wouldn't obey her, and she had to grasp at the arm of the chair for support. "I . . ." Suddenly, to her horror, her eyes filled with tears, and Carol hurried to her in concern.

"Are you all right? Fiona," she said over her shoulder, "can you get her a glass of water? Here," she took Maureen's arm, "take your time, just sit quietly a minute."

Maureen dabbed at her eyes with her hanky, and gratefully took the glass of water. "Sorry."

"Don't worry!" Carol looked at her closely, seeing the pallor in her cheeks, the dark circles under her eyes. She was dishevelled too, which was unlike the Maureen she remembered.

"I'll take her home, Fiona. Marcia can do Miss Prendergast."

"But you know she always asks for you!"

"Tell her I've had to look after a friend who's been taken ill. It's the truth, after all, and I think her need comes before someone's weekly shampoo and set!" She took Maureen's limp hand and held it for a moment. "Just stay here while I get my things."

Within a few minutes, Carol was ushering Maureen out of the salon and across the road towards a taxi rank. "I know we were brought up to think taxis were a luxury to be used only in emergencies," she said, "but from the look of you, this is one!" She opened the door of the first cab and they both clambered in and sat on the spacious back seat, while Carol gave the address.

Maureen sat clutching her handbag. Any lingering energy she possessed had drained away as if, now she had achieved her objective, her body had given up the fight. By the side of her silent friend, she gazed passively out of the window, seeing nothing, feeling nothing.

Carol sensed that this wasn't the time for questions, each anxious darting glance at her friend's strained face giving her more and more cause for alarm. Then she saw Maureen's left hand with its bare third finger. Her wedding ring! Where was her wedding ring? What on earth had happened to bring

Maureen here? And in this state? As the taxi drew to a halt, she rummaged in her bag for money and house keys, paid the driver, and helped Maureen carefully out of the cab. The other girl was now so pale that Carol was becoming alarmed.

"Hang on," she said, "Mum should be in – she'll soon get you a cup of tea." Swiftly, Carol inserted her key and opened the door. Taking Maureen's arm she propelled her into the hall. "Mum!" she called urgently. "Look who's here!"

Freda Farmer came forward from the kitchen, and stared in surprise.

"Well, I never – Maureen! But what on earth . . ?"

Carol put her finger to her lips. "I think she could do with a cup of tea, Mum."

Freda looked more closely at Maureen's pallor. "Right, love. Take her in and get her comfortable by the fire. I'll put the kettle on."

Carol helped Maureen to take her coat off and then led her into a cosy sitting-room. The gas fire was on, the red curtains already drawn against the grey sky with its April showers. Maureen sank thankfully into the downy cushioned seat of an armchair, saying, "Do you mind if I take my shoes off?"

"'Course not. Here, give them to me and put your

feet up." Carol dragged a leather pouffe in front of the chair. "Now, just rest for a minute, you look all in."

With a backward glance at the wan-looking girl, Carol took the shoes with her into the kitchen, putting them by the back door.

Freda was spooning tea into a teapot. She glanced at her daughter with a frown. "What's going on?"

Carol held up her hands. "Don't ask me! She just turned up at the salon looking like death. She's hardly said a word. Perhaps after a hot drink and something to eat . . ."

Freda nodded. "I'm making a cottage pie for dinner, it'll stretch to three. In the meantime, give her a slice of this." She opened a cake tin and cut a slice of home-made cake, then went to a cupboard. "Here," she passed a quarter bottle of brandy to Carol. "Open that, and I'll put a drop in her tea."

But when they went back into the sitting-room it was to find Maureen slumped in the chair and fast asleep.

"Shall I wake her?" Carol suggested, holding the tray.

Freda shook her head. "No, leave her be. Sleep will do her more good at the moment."

As she helped her mother to set the table in the

small square kitchen, Carol said, "Did you notice?"

"Notice what?"

"She hasn't got her wedding ring on."

"No! You don't mean she's taken it off!"

Carol shrugged. "Unless she's lost it."

"You don't lose wedding rings," Freda said sharply. "Once they're on, they're on for good."

"Obviously not in Maureen's case," Carol pointed out. She sat and fiddled with the cruet. "Do you think we should do anything?"

"How do you mean?"

"Well, let someone know where she is."

"What makes you think they don't?"

"I don't know," Carol said slowly. "It's just a feeling I've got. I mean, it's so odd for her just to turn up like that, without letting me know, and in such a state."

"Let's see how she is when she wakes up. I mean, we don't want to go interfering unnecessarily."

"Perhaps you're right. I'll just pop upstairs and get out of this uniform."

Freda watched her go and smiled to herself. It had done Carol the world of good moving to Leicester. Not that there was anything wrong with the Potteries, she thought hastily, not wanting to be disloyal, but living in a more cosmopolitan city had

314

opened up opportunities to both of them. Carol had been taken on at 'Dolores', where the salary she earned was far higher than anything she'd achieved before. And she herself had trained as a silver-service waitress at the Grand Hotel. It was a job she enjoyed, and she loved working in such elegant surroundings. For so many years in the struggle to raise their only child after her husband was killed at Dunkirk, she'd had to take cleaning jobs, where the hours fitted in with Carol's needs. In her present job she could not only earn good tips which helped to pay their bills, but also meet other people. It was only lately that she had become aware of how lacking in friendship and good times her previous life was. There had never been the money or the time to seek entertainment, yet now, with Carol for company at home, and a little bit extra each week for 'spends', she was happier than she'd been for years.

Maureen slept for two hours and when she awoke it was to look around her at first with dull incomprehension, and then gradually alarm. The square room, warm with the heat from the gas fire, was unfamiliar as was the red moquette three-piece suite, the matching curtains, the black half-moon rug before the tiled hearth. For a moment she closed her eyes again, and taking a deep breath tried to collect her thoughts. She'd walked out, that was it, this morning. Caught a train to London and then . . . Carol! She'd come to find Carol in Leicester! This must be where she lived. Struggling to her feet, Maureen went to the door and opened it, peering into the narrow hall. A door was ajar at the end, and she could hear a radio playing. Tentatively, she went into the kitchen and Carol came forward immediately.

"Maureen!" She put her arms around her friend and drew her into a hug. "How are you feeling now? You've certainly had a good sleep."

"I'm okay, thanks, Carol." She turned to Freda. "Hello, Mrs Farmer. It's nice to see you again."

"And you, Maureen." Freda kissed her cheek. "You've just timed it right, I'm about to dish up. Cottage pie okay?"

"It smells lovely." Feeling her legs begin to tremble, Maureen pulled out a chair from beneath the table and sat down. Freda darted a sharp glance at her, and hurried up with serving the meal.

Freda watched Maureen pick at her food, eating slowly, and waited patiently long after she and her daughter had finished their meal before she removed Maureen's plate. Seeing that Maureen was sitting motionless, her face closed and without expression, she put out a hand and touched her shoulder.

"Why don't you go into the other room, while we see to the dishes?"

Slowly, without looking at either of them, Maureen left the kitchen. Carol followed her into the sitting-room and switched on the television. "I won't be long," she said. "I'll just wipe up for Mum before she goes to work. She's working as a waitress, now – she likes it better than cleaning for a living."

But Maureen didn't answer.

Lost in a world of her own, thought Carol, and hurried back to the kitchen. "She looks awful – just sits staring into space."

Freda was running the hot-water tap, and squirting a minute amount of washing-up liquid over the dirty plates. At first she didn't say anything, just carried on putting in the cutlery to soak, then she turned round, leaning back on the sink with folded arms.

"I've seen that look before," she said slowly. "Do you remember me talking about our Muriel? That cousin of mine who emigrated to Australia?"

Carol nodded. "The one who married the widower with two children?"

"Yes, that's the one. She got engaged in 1939 – in

317

the August it was, just before Hitler invaded Poland. Of course he went, like everyone else, and was reported missing in 1942. He ended up in a prisoner-of-war camp, died of pneumonia. She took it very hard, did Muriel. She was just like Maureen. Sat there in the same room, but wasn't with you, if you know what I mean." She turned and began to wash up, putting the dishes to drain so that Carol could wipe them.

For a few moments they worked together, then Carol said, "How long was she like that?"

"Oh, she came out of it eventually. The doctors called it depression, but in my opinion she was suffering from a broken heart."

"Do you think that's what's wrong with Maureen?"

"Who's to say, but I wouldn't be surprised."

Freda emptied the bowl of soapy water into the sink, and dried her hands.

"I don't know what to do, Carol," she said, anxiety creasing her forehead.

"I mean, why has she come *here*? If she's in trouble, I'd have thought she'd go to Beryl, or to their Sandra?"

"Do you think I should ask her, straight out, you know – what the matter is?"

Freda shook her head. "No, I don't think you

should probe. Let her come to it in her own time."
She glanced at her watch. "I'll just go and get
changed, and then I'd better be off. Will you make
up that other bed in your room?"

"Yes, of course. I'll just see if she's all right first."
Carol quietly opened the door to the sitting-room.
Maureen was still sitting in the same position on the
sofa, facing the television set. But her eyes weren't
on the flickering screen; she was gazing downwards
at the mottled cream tiled fireplace, her expression
abstracted, her fingers plucking at her skirt. She
didn't turn or even notice her friend in the doorway
and, taking care not to disturb her, Carol closed the
door and followed her mother up the steep, thinly
carpeted stairs.

Fifteen minutes later, mother and daughter stood
in the hall conferring.

"What do you think?" Freda said. "You know —
about whether she told anyone she was coming?"

Carol shrugged. "I haven't a clue. She looked so
exhausted when I first saw her, I didn't ask any questions. But the state she's in, I doubt it."

Freda thought for a moment. "I'm going to have
to ask her, otherwise she could be reported missing
or something. Frank and Beryl wouldn't want the
police involved."

"What do you think *I* should do?" Carol asked, frowning.

"Nothing." Freda said briskly. "Obviously Maureen trusts you, otherwise she wouldn't be here. If she wants to tell us, she will. If not, then it's none of our business. The best thing we can do for that girl is to give her refuge until she comes out of it. She needs a breathing space, away from pressure. It's my guess that's why she's ended up here and not with her own family."

Carol stared at her mother. "You know, Mum, you never cease to amaze me. You should have been a psychiatrist."

"Ah, well, you need an education for that and there was no chance in our house. I was out at work at fourteen, and had to turn up all my wages, as well. Not like you, miss, with money to spend on make-up and nail varnish." But she was smiling as she added the last words, and impulsively Carol leaned forward and gave her a hug.

"I'm very lucky," she said. "I know that."

Freda smiled with pleasure but, as so often happened lately, there was a slight chill around her heart. Whatever would she do when Carol eventually got married and left home? Her life had for so long been built around her only child, who had repaid her care with a bond so close that it almost hurt. But the time had to come, because she wouldn't wish Carol to go through life without a partner, as she'd had to.

Wearing her coat and gloves, with Carol close behind, she opened the sitting-room door. "Maureen?" There was no response. Freda raised her voice, "Maureen?"

Vaguely, Maureen heard her name called and, rousing herself from her reverie, turned round. She blinked, then seeing that Freda was ready to go out, began to stir.

"No, don't get up," Freda said. "I'm just off to work. Did Carol tell you that I'm working as a waitress, now?"

Maureen struggled to think. Had she? The words did sound familiar. "Yes, I think she did."

"Maureen . . ."

"Yes, Mrs Farmer?"

"Does anyone know you're here?"

Maureen didn't know what was happening to her; it seemed as though she drifted in and out of reality. At first she couldn't remember, then she slowly shook her head.

"Don't worry, that's fine," Freda said. "You'll feel better after an early night – I'm sure Carol will make you both some cocoa."

"Of course I will," said Carol.

"You're both very kind," Maureen muttered. "I'm sorry to be such a nuisance."

"Nonsense, that's what friends are for, and I know Carol's missed you a lot since we moved. Anyway, I'll have to go, see you in the morning." Indicating with her eyes that Carol should follow, Freda went into the hall and opened the front door.

"I'll try and get in touch with Beryl," she whispered. "Better her than Trevor in view of the wedding-ring thing. But don't say anything to her."

"I won't." Carol closed the door behind her mother, and leaned back against it. She hated seeing Maureen in this state, remembering when she'd last seen her, dark hair blowing in the wind, her face alight with enthusiasm. They'd been to the pictures on Carol's sole visit back to the Potteries. Maureen had been laughing and joking about the film they'd just seen, *Some Like it Hot*. It was hilarious, and both girls had been doubled up in the cinema. Now, thinking of the silent girl in the other room, Carol could hardly believe she was the same person.

CHAPTER TWENTY-FIVE

Frank and Beryl were immersed in *No Hiding Place*, when the clap of the doorknocker caused them both to look round in annoyance.

"Who can that be?" Frank grumbled. "Tell me what happens!" Going through the parlour, he opened the front door only to stare in surprise at a small red-haired boy. "Grandma says can Mrs Matthews come to the phone?" he panted, breathless from running up the hill.

Startled, Frank said quickly, "Yes, lad, she'll be right there!" He closed the door, shouting, "Beryl!"

Annoyed, Beryl got up as Frank came back. "Who is it?" she hissed. "Not Mrs Waters on the cadge?"

"No, it was Rita's grandson. You're wanted on the phone!"

Beryl stared at him in amazement. Wanted on the

323

phone? The only people she knew on the phone were Trevor's parents and they certainly wouldn't know Rita's number. Or would they? Could Maureen have given it to them for an emergency? Grabbing a coat, she was out of the house in seconds and, hurrying down, she tapped on the partly open front door. Rita was notoriously house-proud; Beryl hesitated and then went in, careful not to tread on the red Cardinal-polished step.

The phone stood proudly on the sideboard in the parlour and without a word Rita laid the receiver on the polished surface and left the room.

Nervously, Beryl picked it up.

"Hello . . ."

"Hello, Beryl?" a woman's voice came out of the other end. Fumbling, Beryl turned the receiver round. "Hello, yes?"

"Beryl, it's Freda, Freda Farmer. I'm ringing from Leicester."

"Freda! What's wrong? It's not Carol, is it?"

"No, love, Carol's fine. Beryl – is anyone listening?"

Lowering her voice, Beryl said, "No, no-one."

"Only the thing is – I've got your Maureen here."

"What! You mean in Leicester?"

"She just turned up at Carol's work. Look, Beryl, I

324

don't know what's going on – she's never said a word. But I didn't want people thinking she was missing and getting the police involved."

Beryl was struggling to take in what Freda was saying. Maureen had gone to Leicester? Without telling anyone? Why? "You mean even Trevor doesn't know she's there?"

"Apparently not, and it's my guess she won't want him to know."

Confused, Beryl said, "You mean they've had a row or something?"

"I think it's a bit more than that." There was a silence, then Freda added, "She isn't wearing her wedding ring, which might go some way to explaining the state she's in."

"What sort of state?" Beryl's voice sharpened.

"I'm no expert, but I'm sorry, Beryl, I think she's either had or having some sort of breakdown."

"Breakdown?" Bewildered, Beryl seized on the word. "How do you mean, breakdown?"

"It's the way she is, the way she looks. Just stares into space, doesn't say anything."

"I'd better come!"

There was a pause, and then Freda said, "Beryl, I'd leave it a few days. I get the feeling she needs time, you know . . . not to have to answer questions, that

325

sort of thing."

Bristling at being told to stay away from her own daughter, Beryl said firmly, "But if she's ill . . ."

"We'll look after her, I promise. Look, Beryl, this is very awkward for me. I've no idea why she came here, and not to you," Freda tried to explain. "I can only think she had this sudden urge to get away, put some distance between herself and . . . whatever the problem is. Damn, there's the pips and I haven't any more change. I'll write to you tomorrow," she gabbled, "Don't worry and . . ." The rest of the sentence disappeared as the line went dead.

Stunned, Beryl replaced the receiver. Her palm was damp with nervous perspiration, and she wiped it down her coat, before tapping on the middle door which was opened so quickly she suspected Rita had been trying to listen.

"Everything all right?"

"Yes, fine," Beryl was trying to stay calm. "Thank you, Rita, sorry to disturb you."

"Oh, that's all right, Beryl. Nice to see you anyway – it's been a while."

"I know," Beryl said, beginning to edge with impatience towards the front door, "but you know what it's like when you're working, you never seem to have the time."

"Frank all right?" Rita crossed her arms over her ample breasts and was obviously in the mood to chat. She was inordinately proud of being the first person in the street to have a telephone installed, and had sent little cards to everyone she knew to announce their number.

"Fine, and Bert?"

"His chest's playing up a bit, but apart from that he's all right. It wasn't bad news, I hope?"

"How do you mean?"

"The message for your Maureen from Carol?"

"No, not at all!" Then aware that Rita was waiting to be enlightened, Beryl added, "She just wanted to know if Joe Loss was on at Trentham Ballroom next week."

"Oh." Obviously disappointed, Rita opened the door.

"Thanks again," Beryl said and, conscious of Rita on the doorstep, forced herself to walk home at a normal pace. Whatever had happened? Stricken that her daughter hadn't turned to her, or even to their Sandra, she burst into the kitchen.

"Who was it?" Frank looked round from the television.

Beryl didn't answer, just went to the set and switched it off.

327

"Hey, I was watching that!"

"We've got more important things to think about," she said tersely. "That was Freda Farmer, ringing from Leicester."

"Something wrong with Carol?"

"No. It's our Maureen! She's turned up there – in Leicester, Frank, in a right state according to Freda." Beryl's voice began to tremble, and she realised she needed to sit down.

Frank was staring at her with incredulity. "How do you mean? And what on earth is she doing in Leicester of all places?"

Haltingly, Beryl told him what Freda had said. "I don't understand it," she went on. "Frank, if she was in trouble, why didn't she come to us?"

"I don't know, Beryl," he said heavily. "I'm more worried about what's got her in such a state."

"You don't think she really is having a break-down?" Beryl looked at him with fear in her eyes.

"Freda was always a sensible woman," he said, his brow furrowing with worry. "I think we can take it she's not making it up."

"But why? What's been going on?" Agitated, Beryl got up and began pacing the kitchen. "And as for saying I shouldn't go – well, I resent that, I can tell you! Can you understand it?" Beryl demanded.

There was a short silence, then Frank said slowly, "Yes, I think I can. Perhaps she couldn't face us, Beryl. I'm damn worried, I don't mind telling you. There's something seriously amiss . . ."

They both turned at the sound of a loud and imperative knock on the front door.

"It'll be Trevor!" Beryl hissed in panic. "What are we going to say? Don't you think he's got a right to know?"

But Frank was already on his feet, his mind grappling with the problem.

"Freda said she doesn't want him to! I'll deal with it – just pick your knitting up as though nothing's wrong. Remember – leave the talking to me!"

Beryl sat tensely on the edge of her chair, straining her ears to hear what was going on in the other room. She heard Frank say, "Trevor! Come in, we've been expecting you."

"You have?"

"Come on through where it's warm."

Beryl looked up and managed a smile of welcome.

Trevor looked pale and distraught, but Beryl tightened her lips. He'd get no sympathy from her, driving her daughter away like that. For it stood to reason she wouldn't have gone if she'd been happy!

"Why were you expecting me?" he demanded. "Is Maureen here?"

"No, she isn't." Frank crossed over to where his pipe-rack was at the side of his armchair and taking one out sat down and began to fill it. "But she's sent a message. I was going to come up, but the car wouldn't start. It's those damn spark-plugs again, I'll have to get them seen to."

Beryl darted a glance first at Trevor, and then at Frank, marvelling at his composure.

"I must admit," Frank said, sucking on the stem until the tobacco in the bowl smouldered, "I wondered what was going on. When did she go?"

"Go?" Trevor repeated. "Go where? All I know is she left a note first thing saying she was going for a walk!" He sat on one of the dining-chairs, his normal self-possession deserting him, as he looked at them both with bewilderment. "I know she didn't go into work, because I phoned. I thought it was a bit odd, you know, going off like that before we'd even had breakfast. She still hasn't turned up, so I thought she might be here."

"We've never seen hide nor hair of her, have we, Beryl?"

Beryl shook her head and, hoping to prevent Trevor asking her any awkward questions, began to count the stitches on her needle.

"You said you had a message?"

"Yes. I didn't speak to her meself," Frank tried to keep his voice casual. "I was out collecting, but one of the clerks took the call. She said to tell me not to worry, she's gone away for a few days' break, and would I pass the message on."

Trevor stared at him. "Gone away for a few days' break?" he repeated. "On her own, without a word? What on earth is she thinking of? And I'm sorry, Frank, but I'd have thought she'd have rung me, not you!"

Frank didn't reply immediately, he spoke instead to Beryl. "How about a pot of tea, love. I'm sure you could do with a cup, eh, Trevor?"

He nodded and, getting up, Beryl went into the scullery, taking care to leave the door open so that she didn't miss anything.

"I've told you all I know, lad," Frank said, "and don't ask me how women's minds work! I've been married nearly thirty years and I'm still no wiser." He glanced at the young man sitting stony-faced a few feet away from him, and said, "Had you had a row or summat?"

Trevor's expression tautened. "No, we hadn't had a row! As far as I know everything was normal."

"Only," Frank said, drawing deeply on his pipe, "I've noticed she's been a bit quiet like, lately."

Trevor looked away from his father-in-law's gaze, and muttered, "Can't say I'd noticed anything."

"Aye," Frank said, keeping his tone comfortable. "Happen it'll be something or nothing. She was always deep, was our Maureen. Anything worrying her, she'd never bring it out into the open."

"And I suppose I'm just to wait, am I? Until she feels like coming back?" Trevor snapped.

"From where I'm sitting, you've not got much choice. Ah, here's the tea, and how about a biscuit, love?"

Beryl went back to fetch the tin, and then occupied herself with the ritual of pouring the tea. Trevor, stiff and tense, moodily took two teaspoons of sugar.

"I still don't understand why she didn't ring *me*," he said, stubbornly refusing to drop the subject.

Beryl intervened. "Perhaps she thought you might be busy with a client. She'd be trying not to embarrass you, Trevor – a message like that might have caused gossip."

"You know, you could be right," he said, obviously slightly relieved. "It's just a pity our phone at home isn't installed yet, but the GPO said it would be another three weeks. Mind you, it still doesn't explain what's going on!"

"I suppose we'll just have to be patient," Frank said, "and give her time." He paused, then shot the question, "She's not pregnant, is she?"

Trevor's face suffused with colour. "No, she's not!"

"Only," Frank continued, ignoring his son-in-law's answer, "women can go a bit funny, you know, in the early stages. Might explain a lot."

"Well, I can assure you, it's definitely not that!"

Watching him Beryl thought, no, but Frank hit the spot there all right. So, that's what all this is about, not being able to conceive. Her heart filled with compassion for her daughter. It was a terrible thing to be denied motherhood. But why hadn't Maureen confided in her? After all there was a lot that could be done these days to help childless couples. Not for the first time did Beryl wish her daughter would share her problems; it wasn't healthy bottling them up the way she did.

Frank exchanged glances with her. "Nothing more we can do, Trevor," he said. "Just wait until she gets in touch, or comes back. At least we know she's all right."

"If you say so," Trevor said, his tone stiff with anger, "but I can't say I take your philosophical attitude. She's no right to go gallivanting off like that!"

Beryl, resentful of his criticism, and finding the situation increasingly stressful, became desperate for Trevor to leave. "Shall we just wait until we hear the whole story?" she said.

They sat in silence for a bit and then, standing up, Trevor said with a shrug, "I suppose I'd better get off."

Frank went to see him out. "Try not to worry, I'm sure it'll come right in the end." He knew it was essential to mollify Trevor, to keep his anger curbed, if only to give Maureen time. Frank had no idea what had been taking place in that house at Trentham, but, until he knew the full story, his loyalty lay firmly with his daughter.

CHAPTER TWENTY-SIX

Maureen slept for twenty-four hours. Freda regularly tiptoed up the stairs to softly open the door and peer into the bedroom. Reassured by the sleeping form's even breathing, she left a glass of water by the side of the bed, and in her usual practical manner got on with her day. The morning was spent doing housework, although she didn't vacuum because of the noise.

Carol told curious colleagues at work that Maureen had recently been ill and had found the journey exhausting.

"If she's come to stay, she didn't have any luggage with her!" Fiona always had her nose into everyone's business.

"She'd already been to the house and left it there," Carol lied.

"What was wrong with her?" the other girl persisted.

Carol thought quickly. "Appendicitis."

Fiona promptly lost interest.

Carol, however, couldn't dismiss the subject so lightly, and often during the busy day, as she expertly styled and set hair, she thought about Maureen, and of course, Trevor.

Carol had always fancied him, not that she'd ever breathed a word to anyone. The tall young man's film star looks had attracted her the moment she saw him, but Trevor had never had eyes for anyone but Maureen. Now, if his relationship with Maureen failed, then who knew what could happen? But as swiftly as the disloyal thought surfaced, she squashed it. Her duty to her friend was to help her, not take advantage of her problems! You can be a selfish bitch at times, Carol Farmer, she told herself, trying not to wrinkle her nose at the pungent smell of perm solution. She expertly wound the last strand of her client's hair around a small blue roller and, once she was under the dryer, retreated to the tiny staffroom for a break and lit a cigarette. What she needed was to find a man of her own, not try to pinch someone else's.

* * *

It was seven o'clock that evening before Maureen stirred. She lay awake for a while in the darkened room, trying in bewilderment to remember the confused events of the previous day, and then noticing the glass of water drank it gratefully. Her mouth felt parched, but her head was clearer than it had been for a long time. The door was slightly open and she could hear sounds of movement downstairs, so eventually she got up and gave a wan smile as she looked down at the pink baby-doll pyjamas she was wearing. They were *so* Carol, and with a pang of nostalgia she remembered how they used to trail around the shops together on Saturdays, looking for the latest fashions. All that filled their heads in those days was clothes, make-up and records. We didn't realise how lucky we were, she thought wistfully, the three of us, for as always Elaine's memory was inextricably entwined with those carefree years.

Feeling crumpled and grubby, Maureen looked for her handbag and finding it by the side of the bed combed her hair and ran her tongue over her coated teeth. I need a bath, she thought, and taking down a threadbare candlewick dressing-gown hanging on the back of the door, she stepped into it, zipped it up to her neck and barefoot went downstairs.

Carol heard her coming, and came out of the kitchen.

"Well," she smiled, "Sleeping Beauty awakes at last!"

"I didn't see the handsome prince!"

"I always thought you'd married him!" The riposte came out impulsively, and she could have bitten her tongue, as she saw a shutter come down on Maureen's face. Her mum had told her to be careful what she said. "Keep the conversation light," Freda had advised. "Away from Stoke and her life there. Give her time to come out of it." Cursing her stupidity, Carol said lamely, "You've timed it quite well, your dinner won't be too dried up."

As Maureen sat at the kitchen table, Carol placed a plate before her, and then carried on with the washing-up. "Mum's gone to work. She told me to let you sleep." Maureen looked down at the lamb chops, mashed potatoes and cabbage, and picked up her knife and fork. "I can't believe I slept so long," she confessed. "I suppose I must have needed it."

"Here's the mint sauce," Carol said. "Eat it all up now, it's the real thing – there's none of that Smash in this house!" She watched Maureen begin to eat, noticing she had more of an appetite than the night before. "How do you feel?" she said after a while,

338

hanging up the tea towel to dry on the handle of the oven door.

Maureen finished off the last of her meal. "Much better. I could do with a bath though, and you wouldn't have a spare toothbrush, would you?"

"I've got one in my toilet bag," Carol said promptly. "I only bought it last week, ready for my holiday."

"Where are you going?"

"Get a load of this!" Carol reached for a brochure stuffed behind some cookery books on a shelf and handed it to her. "Page nine," she said with pride.

Maureen turned the pages, and then looked up at her friend, "Spain! Carol Farmer, you're never going abroad!"

"Yes, I am. Benidorm it's called. I'm going with a couple of girls from the salon on one of these package holidays."

Maureen was reading the description of the resort, and the self-catering apartment the girls were going to share. "I'm jealous to death," she confessed. "It looks fantastic."

"And fantastic is the word for the tan I'll have when I come back," Carol laughed. "Just three weeks to go, and then it's sun, sand, and maybe even romance." She looked at Maureen. "It's nice to see you smiling again," she said gently.

Maureen looked down. "I must have looked a right mess when I got here. I can't remember much about it after I left London."

"London!" Carol stared at her. "What on earth were you doing in London?"

Maureen shrugged. "Nothing, I just got on the first train I saw."

Carol gazed at her in puzzled and curious silence, and then asked, "Do you want to talk about it?" She held her breath, hoping she wasn't probing too soon.

Maureen shook her head. "I won't if you don't mind." She looked away in distress. She knew she owed both Carol and her mother an explanation, but as yet her emotions were too raw, too confused.

Carol just said, "No problem. Right, you go and have your bath – I'll make you a cup of tea to take up with you." Once the kettle was filled and switched on, she lit a cigarette and offered the pack to Maureen. "Have you started yet?"

Maureen smiled, "No, I leave all the vices to you."

Carol grinned, it was an old joke between them. "You never know, you might find it helps."

"I could do with something," Maureen admitted, "but I don't think smoking's the answer."

Carol turned to make the tea. "Still taking sugar?"

"One please." Maureen got up and waited to take her cup. "I'll go up then and make myself decent." She hesitated, "You haven't got any clean knickers I could borrow, have you?"

"Of course I have. And I'll sort out a pair of nylons as well."

"Thanks. You're a good friend, Carol."

"We go back a long time. I've missed you, Maureen. Oh, I've made new friends, but there's no-one quite like the one you grew up with, is there?"

Maureen realised that the pretty blond girl's front of sophistication was a veneer – her childhood companion hadn't really changed. She smiled with shaky relief. "I feel the same."

Carol gazed at her thoughtfully. Despite her long sleep, Maureen was still very pale, with dark shadows under her eyes. Had Trevor been unfaithful? It wouldn't surprise her – a man with his looks was bound to attract other women. Had Maureen just found out and was suffering from shock? Or was it something darker? There was a woman at the salon whose husband beat her. Not that Joan came in covered with bruises, he was too devious for that. But they could tell. Often wincing as she lifted her arms or bent down, she always made the excuse that she'd knocked herself, was naturally clumsy. The owner of the salon said Joan was too ashamed to admit it, women often were. But they all knew the truth. Surely Trevor hadn't hit Maureen? Carol shuddered at the ugly image. Yet violence had always been one of the main reasons why women left their husbands. *Had* she left Trevor? It certainly looked like it.

After her bath, Maureen came downstairs with her hair hanging in damp tendrils. "Can I borrow your hairdryer?"

"Sure," Carol followed her up the stairs, and watched her friend dry her hair. "You're lucky, you know," she said, "having dark hair like that. You should see how much women spend on having theirs coloured."

Maureen glanced at her. "Have you had yours lightened?"

"Just a bit," Carol confessed. "Goes with the working image."

"How about the personal image?" Maureen twisted round to face her. "For instance, how's your love life?"

Carol laughed. "Oh, I've had my moments, but nothing really serious. Except once." She hesitated then added, "I only found out he was married, didn't I!"

"Carol!" Maureen was shocked. "You mean he

never told you?"

"Nope! We went out for six months, he came here, met Mum and everything. Then one Saturday afternoon, I nipped out from the salon to change something in Marks, and there he was. Him, his wife, and a baby in a pushchair." Carol's eyes darkened with pain at the memory, and Maureen's heart went out to her.

"Oh, Carol, I'm so sorry. That must have been awful."

"It was," Carol said bitterly. "Do you know, I felt quite dirty afterwards."

"It wasn't your fault."

"No, but it left a nasty taste in my mouth. He'd even talked of getting engaged!"

"The scumbag!"

"Yeah. But you'd never have thought it – talk about charming! Mind you, he didn't fool Mum, people rarely do. But I wouldn't listen, would I? Perhaps we have to learn the hard way!"

"I think we do." There was a flat tone to Maureen's voice, followed by a short silence.

Then Carol said, "Do you want to go out or anything, or stay in and watch telly for a bit?"

"I'd rather stay in and watch telly, if that's all right with you."

And that's what they did. Or rather, Carol did, for whenever she glanced at Maureen, it was to see her staring blindly at the hearth, deep in thought, oblivious to the action taking place on the screen.

Maureen was struggling to recall the events of the previous day, to mentally trace each step she had taken. She could remember standing in the kitchen – and she had written a note! Yes, that was it – to say she was going for a walk! And, unbelievably it seemed now, for the first time the full implications of her actions struck her. That was yesterday morning! Trevor must be worried sick! Not that she cared, she thought with bitterness. But so would Frank and Beryl, because their house would be the first place he'd go to look for her!

In panic she said, "Carol! I didn't let anyone know I was here!"

"That's all right. Mum rang Rita up the street. Your parents know."

"Thank goodness for that!" Maureen sank back into her reverie, then as she looked down her face paled. She wasn't wearing her wedding ring! "My ring," she said frantically. "I haven't got it on!"

"You weren't wearing it when you got here!" Carol looked at her with concern. Maureen might be better than yesterday, but she was far from her usual self. "Have a look in your handbag," she suggested. "No, you sit there – I'll fetch it."

The ring was found. Noticing that she didn't put it on, Carol remained silent, and returned to watching *The Avengers*.

Maureen lay back in her armchair, her eyes closed. The café on Euston Station – *that* was when she'd taken off her wedding ring! She looked down at it lying in the palm of her hand, and felt a wave of unspeakable sadness. The gold band had been a symbol of all she wanted in life, a promise of love and happiness, a glowing future. Now, all it meant to her was repression, both of her sexuality and her maternal longings. For although she'd had her doubts, Maureen didn't really think she was a cold person. For surely if that was the case, she wouldn't have been so physically attracted to Trevor in the first place. Tears came to her eyes as she remembered how she'd felt about him when they were courting, how she'd often wished he wouldn't be so self-controlled. A control she'd mistakenly thought was due to respect for her. Well, now she knew better, and a deep sigh of despair escaped her, causing Carol to glance at her sharply.

"You okay?"

"Yes, fine, just thinking." Maureen managed a smile.

Carol returned to her programme, and Maureen got to her feet. "Shall I make us a cup of tea?"

"Shall I do it?"

"No, you'll miss the plot. I'm not an invalid, you know."

In the kitchen, Maureen found the things she needed, and waited for the kettle to boil. Then a sudden thought struck her, and she hurried back into the sitting-room. Why hadn't she thought of that before?

She burst in. "Carol, if your mum rang and told Rita, I suppose that means Trevor will know where I am!"

Carol shook her head. "Mum doesn't read Sexton Blake for nothing – you were a bit of a mystery when you turned up out of the blue. As you weren't wearing your wedding ring, she thought you wouldn't want him to know. Don't worry, your mum won't have told him. But at least he'll know you're all right, so he won't be reporting you missing or anything."

"Thanks," Maureen turned her head away, embarrassed by her weak tears of relief. "I can't thank you both enough. Mum and Dad must be so worried. I'd better write to them first thing in the morning."

And the following morning, firmly pushing all

thoughts of Trevor out of her mind, Maureen did just that.

Dear Mum and Dad – she frowned at her shaky handwriting, and made an effort to write firmly. *I hope you haven't been too worried about me. I'm going to stay with Carol for a few days until I sort myself out. For the time being, I'd rather Trevor didn't know that I'm in Leicester. I'll write to him shortly, I promise. Hope this doesn't make things too difficult for you. I'll be in touch soon, Love, Maureen.*

Ps. Please could you ring work and tell them I've got flu or something?

She looked at it doubtfully. It seemed very short, but there wasn't much else she could say, not yet. She needed more time to think; hopefully soon she'd begin to feel better, more in control. She was aware that she wasn't well; even now her mind kept clouding over. To her surprise, despite sleeping most of the day, she'd slept deeply the previous night, yet she still felt tired. Fresh air, that's what I need, she decided, and licking the flap of the envelope went into the kitchen.

"Have you got a stamp, Mrs Farmer? I'll pay you back later."

"Nonsense. Yes, I have got one somewhere." Freda rummaged in a drawer. "There you are."

"Thanks. I thought I'd go out, get a breath of fresh air," Maureen said.

Freda beamed. "Good idea. A walk would do you good." She paused, "In fact, the ideal thing would be to stroll down New Walk. It's lovely and peaceful."

"Is it far? Only my feet are a bit sore and blistered from the other day, and I've only got those court shoes."

"What size are you?"

"Five and a half or six."

"Hang on." Freda went upstairs and returned with a pair of brown suede calf-length bootees. "Now, I know that normally you wouldn't be seen dead in these, but no-one knows you round here, and it's still cold enough."

Maureen looked at them doubtfully.

"Try them on," Freda urged.

Maureen pulled them on, zipped up the sides and stood up. A look of delight crossed her face, as her tender feet sank into the fleecy lining. "They're so comfortable!"

"That's why we oldies wear them. We've got a bit of sense at our age!" Freda began to write on the back of an old envelope. "Follow these directions, it's quite straightforward. If you feel strong enough to walk all the way down, you'll come to the shops, so get yourself a bowl of soup or something. You need to build your strength up. This is the bus you'll need to catch back. Have you got any money?"

Maureen nodded, and then impulsively hugged her. "You've been so kind, Mrs Farmer, I'll never forget it."

"Oh, go on with you," Freda said, embarrassed, and then watched from the front door as Maureen began to make her way along the street.

* * *

The day was chilly but fine, and the air felt clean and invigorating as Maureen walked along the unfamiliar streets, then turning right on to the main road she crossed over to the pavement at the side of a large open space of grassland. Victoria Park it was called, according to the note Freda had written. Maureen, used to the formal Victorian parks at home with their bowling greens and laid-out flower gardens, thought it was unlike any she'd seen before. There were a few people exercising their dogs, others were simply walking along the paths enjoying the crisp air.

She found University Road without difficulty, and saw the ornate black and gold posts Freda had mentioned, signalling the beginning of New Walk. The long tree-lined thoroughfare with its ornate iron lamp-standards was almost deserted as she walked along, and she looked around curiously, seeing a terrace of Regency houses with pretty balconies, and then buildings of differing, but distinctive architecture. Eventually she passed a museum with a large classical portico, and then hesitated when a few minutes later she saw a church on the right-hand side. On the board outside was the name: Holy Cross Priory. Maureen began to walk on, and then gradually her steps became slower. Should she? It had been a long time since she'd been inside a Catholic church, or indeed any church – not since her wedding. But now, she felt a sudden need for the familiar peace and tranquillity and, pushing open the studded oak door, she went inside. Immediately the faint scent of incense brought back her formative years, yet she'd never been inside a church as large as this one. Austere, its atmosphere of coolness and calm in the middle of the busy city was like an oasis. Slowly and quietly, she made her way to a side altar dedicated to Our Lady, and knelt just inside one of the pews. She buried her face in her hands and prayed. Prayed desperately for help, prayed for grace to guide her. All her life she'd been brought up to believe in the Sacrament of Marriage, and the enormity of what she was proposing to do was a

heavy burden. *I tried so hard, I really did.* With the
heartfelt plea, her eyes filled with tears, and she
remained on her knees, repeating the prayers she'd
learned in her childhood. *Hail Mary, full of grace.*
The familiar words brought their own comfort, and
it was some time before she sat back on the bench.
Just sat and gazed at the flower-bedecked altar, at the
blue and gold statue of Our Lady, with the rows of
flickering candles before it. Although there were
faint sounds of movement behind her, as the door
occasionally opened and closed, the overall silence
surrounded her like a cocoon, and slowly the feeling
of desolation which had been her constant
companion during the past months began to lift.
She'd made her decision, and it was the right one.
Maureen had no reservations, no doubts. She recognised now what her body had been telling her. The
life she was living with Trevor, the future she had
with him, was empty and barren. Theirs wasn't a
marriage, not in any sense of the word, and now
what she had to do was to be practical, to look
forward. The fatigue and depression would pass; they
had simply been a reaction to the strain she was
suffering in her marriage. Now, that was over, and
although there would be huge difficulties ahead,
Maureen was prepared to face them. *I only have one*

life, she thought with determination, and Trevor isn't worth wasting it for.

She began to rise, intending to light a candle before she left, but sank back as a tall young man passed her and stood inserting his money in the slot. Remaining in the pew, Maureen watched as he knelt for a few moments on the padded kneeler. She lowered her eyes as he got up and returned down the aisle, failing to see his sharp and curious glance as he passed where she was sitting. Nor was she aware that he turned and looked back before opening the heavy door and quietly leaving.

CHAPTER TWENTY-SEVEN

Greg Barlow walked down Wellington Street to where he'd parked his car, and drove through the busy traffic to the Leicester Royal Infirmary. Ten minutes later, he began to make his way along the long polished corridors, his thoughts returning yet again to the girl in Holy Cross. He knew her, had met her, he was certain of it. The fact that he couldn't remember where he'd seen her before was annoying him, for Greg prided himself on his retentive memory. It was an essential part of his job.

Once at the correct ward, he waited with the other visitors until the main doors were opened. The Sister was obviously a stickler for routine, and he glanced impatiently at his watch. One minute to go! Almost to the second, the visitors were allowed to file in.

Sarah Barlow looked up with relief and pleasure as the impressive figure of her son entered the ward and walked past the long central table with its vases of flowers, to where her bed was in the far corner. At least he was impressive to her, for Greg wasn't handsome in the conventional way. Rugged, that's how she fondly thought of him, a man with a bit of strength in his face. She'd never liked what she thought of as 'pretty boys'. It took a woman of perception, she thought with pride, to appreciate men like mine.

"I was just thinking," she greeted him, "how like your dad you get."

Greg smiled as he kissed her cheek. "I take that as a compliment." He hesitated before saying quietly, "I still miss him. There's not a day goes by that he doesn't come into my mind."

"And mine, lad."

"How are you?" He looked searchingly at her. "I must say you look better than you did last night."

"I am. The doctor says I might be able to go home in a few days."

Greg frowned. "So soon?"

"It was only a mild heart attack, you know. There was no need for you to come rushing down from London."

"There was every need." When the hospital had rung to say his mother had been admitted, he'd felt his world threaten to crash about him. With the shocking scenes he encountered in his job, Greg knew how blessed he'd been to have such a happy childhood and supportive parents. Now, with this alarm about his mother's health, he was only too conscious that, as an only child, the sole responsibility for her welfare was his.

He gazed at her intently. Sixty years of age, Sarah Barlow had only recently retired from working as a hospital orderly. His father had never earned an enormous wage as caretaker at the local grammar school. But he'd loved his job, and the pupils came to have enormous respect for the quiet man who was always ready to help with a problem, his courteous manner and sound advice having guided many a young mind.

"It's odd," he used to say, "how they'll come and ask me instead of a teacher. Not that I can always answer, mind, but I do my best."

And his best would be just that, Greg recalled. Born too soon and with the wrong background to have received much of an education, nevertheless Arthur Barlow had been an avid reader, and his fund of knowledge had never ceased to amaze his university-educated son. Sarah had soon recognised the intelligence of the young man who was at that time working as a hospital porter. It was always a joke between them as to who pursued the other but, so far as Greg knew, neither had ever regretted it.

Now he frowned as he looked down at the thin hand lying on the grey regulation blanket. She'd always been wiry, his mum, full of energy and drive. Work was second nature to her, she used to say, yet even he could recognise the signs of fatigue in her eyes.

"I won't be a moment," he said, and walked back down the ward. Tapping on the door of the door marked *Sister*, he went in. "Excuse me, Sister, I'm Greg Barlow, my mother is Sarah Barlow. I wondered if you could tell me exactly how serious her condition is."

Sister Forbes stared up at him, her eyes keen behind her rimless spectacles.

"She's due to go home soon."

"Yes, but that's the problem," he told her. "She lives alone, and I work away, in London."

"Oh, I see." She bent down, her stiffly starched apron crackling as she retrieved a file from a drawer in her desk. She read it for a few moments and then said, "Perhaps you'd better have a word with the doctor. You're lucky, he's coming in specially to see a patient." She glanced at her watch. "He should be here just after visiting time."

"I'll wait, if that's all right."

"Of course."

The regulation hour allowed for visitors – it was only half an hour during the week – soon passed and when the bell went, Greg bent and kissed his mother goodbye.

"I'll be here tomorrow," he smiled. "Behave yourself, now."

"I'd like the chance to do anything else!" Sarah's eyes were soft as she watched her son leave, but as the doors closed behind him her smile faded, and with a sigh she turned her head away.

Half an hour later, Greg drove back to the neat semi-detached house where he'd been born. He let himself into the familiar small hall, redolent of the smell of lavender furniture polish, and after making a cup of tea, slumped into the chintz armchair and gazed despondently out at the garden. The garden his father had loved, had planted diligently so that the view through the French windows would be pleasing to the eye. The garden his mother now struggled to keep tidy.

The doctor had said that this heart attack had

been a warning, and far more serious than Sarah had led him to believe.

"She needs to take life easy, Mr Barlow," he'd stressed. "Slow down, not do too much."

"Try telling *her* that," Greg had said.

Now, he sat deep in thought. He had a problem, there was no getting away from it. He knew his mother. Used to a busy life, she'd always found it difficult to relax; he couldn't ever remember her sitting without her hands busy. Either knitting or sewing, even when she watched television. She baked her own cakes and pastry, grew all her own vegetables, and cleaned and polished with a strict routine. Even as a child he'd had to leave his shoes inside the door when he came in. But that had been her way, and he and his dad had exchanged indulgent glances, suppressing – at least in Greg's case – their own untidy inclinations. Slow down? Impossible, at least without someone to insist. And that person had to be himself. There were kind neighbours certainly, but Sarah wasn't on such friendly terms with them that she'd welcome what she would see as interference in her life. His father's relatives were scattered throughout the country, and Sarah didn't have any brothers or sisters. For a long time Greg remained seated, staring into the embers of the open fire Sarah insisted on keeping. He had a mental vision of her carrying in coal from the outside bunker, and emptying the ashes. Even if he could persuade her to have a gas or electric fire installed, there would still be shopping to fetch and carry. The cleaning he could pay someone else to do, although his mother wouldn't like it. But that still meant she'd be living on her own, having to cope with any emergencies that arose. He was also uncomfortably aware of Sarah's loneliness since his father died, and not for the first time Greg wished he hadn't been an only child.

He sat for a long time in the gloom, neglecting to switch on the lamps and draw the curtains, and then got up, squared his shoulders and went into the kitchen to forage for something to eat. The decision had been a hard one, in many ways unwelcome. But convinced that he had no choice, Greg determined that as soon as he returned to London, he would apply for a transfer.

CHAPTER TWENTY-EIGHT

Sunday was usually Carol's one opportunity to spend some time alone. It was a busy day at the hotel for Freda, so Carol would have a lie-in, a leisurely bath, do her ironing and generally lounge around the house. And when she told this to Maureen, the plan was met with an appreciative smile. And Maureen *was* smiling more, at least sometimes. At others, she still seemed withdrawn, but as Freda said when she came home, "She's coming out of it, Carol, whatever it was."

* * *

Beryl's nerves were, as she said to Frank late on Sunday night, 'run ragged'. Over the weekend, she'd had to put on a front, pretending nothing was wrong not only with Sandra and John, who'd brought the children round on Saturday afternoon, but also with

Vera and Nellie when they came for tea on Sunday.

"You're not to say a word," Frank had instructed. "This might all blow over, and the last thing Maureen and Trevor will want is for everyone to know their business."

But it was hard, for Sandra was disappointed that Maureen hadn't come along to join them, and Vera and Nellie always asked after her welfare. Beryl hated lying, she wasn't any good at it, and Vera's sharp eyes soon noticed something was amiss.

"You're not yourself, our Beryl," she barked. "Something bothering you?"

"No, not at all, Vera," Beryl said, reddening. "Just a bit of headache."

Fortunately, all the talk was of the new National Health hearing-aid that Nellie had been issued with. "Eeh, it's marvellous," she enthused, showing it off. "None of that crackling, and the reception's wonderful."

"Reception! It isn't a television aerial, you know."

"It's my aerial, our Vera."

"At least you'll be able to hear the numbers when he calls them!" Vera and Nellie had started to go to bingo, and Vera never missed an opportunity to remind Nellie that she'd once missed a full house.

"Oh, don't rub it in," Nellie snapped.

Beryl let their bickering pass over her head; she was just hoping and praying that Trevor wouldn't turn up. He didn't, not until after they'd gone, and Beryl realised she should have known he'd deliberately try to avoid them. He usually did.

His first words when she let him in were, "Any news?"

Beryl shook her head, not trusting herself to speak.

Stony-faced, Trevor strode into the kitchen. "Four days," he said, "Do you realise she's been gone four days! What the hell's she playing at?"

"I don't know, Trevor. Frank's gone down to the pub – just the outdoor – so he won't be long. Would you like a cup of tea?"

"Thanks." He frowned. "She must be somewhere we know! I thought she might have gone to Llandudno – you know, that hotel where we stayed. But she's not there. I've been thinking, what about that friend of hers, Carol?"

Beryl felt herself freeze in panic. "I don't think they're in touch," she evaded. "She moved away when her mother did."

"Exactly. I've been going through Maureen's address book. You know – that big one she had for Christmas."

"Yes, off Nellie and Vera," Beryl said, cursing the size of it. If they'd bought a small handbag-sized one, Maureen would probably have had it with her.

"Carol's address is in there. Leicester, that's where she lives. I've been wondering if that's where she's gone. In fact, the more I think about it the more likely it seems." He drummed his fingers impatiently on the table, and in the silence Beryl escaped to the scullery and began to fill the kettle. Now what could she do? Nellie's favourite saying of 'least said, soonest mended' came into her mind, and in this case it was sound advice. "Would you like a piece of my fruitcake," she called, hoping to change the subject.

"Yes, please."

She cut a slice and took it in.

"I could have starved to death for all Maureen cares," Trevor said bitterly.

Beryl refrained from pointing out that he had two hands like everyone else. Instead she went back into the scullery, praying Frank would soon get back, and at that moment she heard his key in the lock. Right, she decided, I'll let Frank handle this.

"Hello, Trevor," Frank said. "Any news?"

"Not a dickey-bird. I was just saying to Beryl that I reckon she's gone to visit that Carol, the one who was bridesmaid."

Beryl stood at the door to the scullery, her eyes frantically signalling to Frank.

"I suppose it's possible," he said, giving Beryl even more cause for panic. "Leicester, wasn't it, where she moved to?"

Beryl brought in the tea tray. "Yes, that's right."

"Difficult for her to get to, I would have thought," Frank said. "I don't think there's a direct train or anything."

"Even so, have you got a better idea?" Trevor took another bite of cake, his eyes fixed on Frank's.

"There's Llandudno," Frank said after a pause.

"I've tried there."

"What about work?" Frank said. "Have they any idea?"

Trevor looked sharply at him. "I haven't told them anything. I just rang and said she had the flu. After all, she won't want to lose her job."

You don't want to lose her salary, you mean, Beryl thought uncharitably.

"Aye," Frank said. "It's best to keep these things to yourself."

"I trust you haven't been spreading it about?"

"We've told no-one. It's your business, Trevor, yours and Maureen's. What about your parents, have you told them?"

Trevor shook his head. "I've said nothing."

Frank was trying to make a decision. He deplored parents who interfered in their children's marriages, but his girl had been driven away by something. And unless he was very much mistaken, sitting before him was the man responsible. Steady, he told himself, don't make matters worse, but in the end he had to ask the question.

"Have you got any idea at all," he said slowly, "what's made our Maureen go off like that? I know you said you hadn't had a row, but have things been all right between you two?"

Beryl held her breath, watching the expression on Trevor's face change.

"I don't know why," he said through thin lips, "you assume that *I'm* to blame in some way for your daughter behaving like this. How do you know it isn't something else? She could be running away from something she's done, or maybe," he paused, and stunned they both waited until he added, his lips twisting in distaste, "*to* someone."

"What are you implying?" Frank's voice was deceptively calm.

"I'm not implying anything. But Maureen does have a life outside our house. I don't know everything she gets up to."

Horrified, Beryl could only stare at him. "I hope you're not suggesting she's gone off with another man?" Her voice was shrill with indignation. Trevor shrugged. "How would I know? She's a very attractive girl, and I do know that when I was away in Germany . . ."

He didn't finish the sentence, and Frank leaned forward, his hands gripping his knees.

"What?"

"Well, there was an incident at the firm's Christmas party. Nothing came of it, or so she says. But according to him . . ."

"Are you calling our Maureen a liar?" Frank's tone was harsh, loud.

"No, of course not. It's just that when this happened, well," Trevor spread his hands helplessly, "it does make you wonder."

Beryl, frightened of Frank's reaction if Trevor said anything else, tried to diffuse the situation.

"Look," she pointed out, "all this is pure guesswork. Maureen said she'd be in touch, and it's Monday tomorrow, so why don't we wait and see." But she couldn't help adding tartly, "And I'd thank you, Trevor, to have more faith in your wife!"

Anyone else, she thought, would have had the

grace to look discomforted, but not him! Oh no, Trevor just gave that shrug which always irritated her, and then stood up.

"Right, I'd better go."

As neither moved to see him to the door, he said, "I'll see myself out," then turning as he left the kitchen he added, "I'm going to take the day off tomorrow and drive over to Leicester! At least I can find out whether she's there."

He didn't wait for an answer, and a few seconds later they heard the front door close.

Beryl opened her mouth to speak, but Frank put his finger to his lips, and then getting up went to check that Trevor had indeed gone.

"I wouldn't put it past him to have tried to pull the wool over our eyes," he said. "You know, drop his bombshell and then listen to see if it had any effect."

"You think he suspects we know something?"

"I don't know, I just wasn't taking any chances."

"What are we going to do?" she whispered.

"There's nothing more we can do, Beryl," Frank's voice was heavy with defeat. "There's no way we can warn her in time. We haven't even got the address – and you say Freda's not on the phone?"

"No, she rang from a call-box."

Frank sighed. "In any case, it's up to them to sort

it out. Perhaps it's all for the best, she's got to see him sooner or later."

* * *

On Monday morning, Maureen lay in the narrow bed listening to the footsteps on the landing and stairs, staying out of the way while Carol got ready for work. Once again she'd slept deeply throughout the night, and felt hugely relieved that the disturbed sleep pattern which had so depleted her energies seemed to be over. She turned over, trying to think, to plan. She couldn't keep on borrowing Carol's underwear and clothes, but what was the alternative? Go into Leicester and buy new ones? But that would mean dipping into the housekeeping money which was all she possessed. Although Maureen knew that she could draw cash out of their joint account at the Midland Bank, she didn't know whether the location of the withdrawal would show up on the bank statement, and she didn't want to face Trevor until she was ready – stronger, more sure of her plans. Then – what plans, she thought miserably, you haven't got any! There was a limit to how long she could impose on Carol and her mum; she certainly couldn't expect them to house and feed her much longer.

Eventually Maureen got up, dressed and went

downstairs. After getting herself a bowl of corn-flakes, she said, "Is there anything I can do to help, Mrs Farmer?"

Freda looked up from sorting out piles of washing on the floor. "No, you're all right, love, you have a rest."

Maureen watched for a moment as Freda pulled out the twin-tub washing-machine from underneath the work-surface and pushed it before the sink. She was a woman of medium build, neither slim nor fat, but she had good posture and somehow on Freda Farmer, clothes always looked 'just right'. With her fashionably cut light-brown hair, she was an attractive woman, and Maureen wondered why she'd never married again. Suddenly, before she could stop them, the words were out of her mouth: "Did you never think of getting married again, Mrs Farmer?"

Freda looked at her in surprise and then seeing that Maureen genuinely wanted to know, said, "I've thought about it, love, but just never met the right man. After being so happy with Don, I don't want to accept second best. Mind you," she gave a conspiratorial grin, "I've had my chances, just don't tell our Carol."

Maureen laughed. "I won't. Perhaps you'll meet

someone at the hotel."

"Maybe." Freda turned away, not wanting Maureen to see the heightened colour in her cheeks, as she thought of the new chef who had just been appointed. Not that she had any hopes. In her experience, men like that were usually married.

"I've got to be off at eleven," she said. "Will you be all right?"

"I'm fine, Mrs Farmer," Maureen said. "I've got a couple of letters to write and, well, some thinking to do."

Freda shot her a sharp glance. "Don't forget we're both here if you want to talk."

"I know, thank you. And do leave me a few jobs – I'll go spare with nothing to do, I'm not used to it."

Freda pursed her lips. She could understand that.

"Okay, but only if you feel like it. The downstairs windows need cleaning inside, that would be a great help."

And so, it was about half an hour after Freda had gone, that Maureen, busy with a chamois leather, saw to her horror the familiar red Mini cruise up the street. She drew back quickly, but it was too late! Framed as she was in the front window, Trevor had already seen her. She stepped back in panic, almost stumbling against the back of an armchair, and rushed into the kitchen, throwing the chamois into the sink, and pushing back her hair with a suddenly shaky hand. Frantically, she looked at the back door, but realised it was futile. What would be the use? He knew she was here – if he didn't speak to her now, he would only wait and she'd have to come back sometime. Even though she expected it, the loud rap of the knocker caused her heart to hammer against her ribs and she didn't answer at first. Then when the knock, even more insistent, came again, she forced herself to open the front door.

Trevor stared at her, his face like granite. "Remember me?"

Maureen drew aside and he stepped inside the hall. Playing for time, she slowly closed the door and in silence led the way into the sitting-room.

"How did you know where I was?"

"Powers of deduction and your address book."

"Oh." She couldn't think of anything to add, except, "Would you like a cup of tea?"

"Thanks. It's been a long drive."

Maureen went into the kitchen, and Trevor followed her. She kept her back to him as she filled the kettle, the cups rattling as she placed them on the saucers, and forced herself to take deep breaths.

"I think you owe me an explanation." Trevor's voice was cold, controlled, to Maureen more menacing than if he'd ranted and raved.

Not answering, she opened the back door to fetch a new bottle of milk. Automatically, she poured some into a jug, put some biscuits on a plate, and made the tea. The familiar ritual helped to calm her, and she was able to say, "Perhaps you'd bring the tray in," before going back into the sitting-room.

Trevor sat on the sofa, and Maureen in an armchair on his left. It began to rain, the noise it made pattering on to the windows sounding unnaturally loud in the silent room. Maureen poured out the tea, and watched as Trevor ate a couple of biscuits and sipped at his drink. Her own she left on the tray, untouched.

"So," Trevor repeated after a couple of minutes. "I'm waiting?" He glanced up sharply, his eyes hard as flint, challenging hers.

To her dismay, Maureen felt her own prick with tears. It was one thing to lie in bed, certain of the rightness of her actions, but to actually face her husband, look at the so-familiar handsome face, feel the force of his strong personality – she was too vulnerable yet, it was too soon!

In the end, she said, "I just had to get away."

"Away? Away from what?"

Miserably, she said, "From you, from our marriage."

There was an ominous silence.

"And who did you have to get away to?"

Maureen was shocked. It had never occurred to her Trevor would think she'd gone off with another man. Then anger set in. "That's just typical of you!" she flared. "You always were jealous and possessive."

Trevor ignored her outburst. "You still haven't answered my question."

"I shouldn't need to. I haven't had to get away to anyone."

"Then what suddenly made you go off like that?"

Maureen tried to explain. "I didn't plan it, Trevor. It just came over me that morning, a sort of compulsion." She paused. "To be honest, I think I was ill."

"Ill? How do you mean, ill?"

But Maureen noticed his tone wasn't one of concern; it was still cutting, harsh.

"I don't think you've even noticed," she said, fighting treacherous tears, "but I've been very depressed, very unhappy, for quite a long time. On Thursday, I think something just snapped. According to Carol, I was in quite a state when I got here. I didn't even know where she lived. I ended up going to the hair salon."

"If you were feeling like this, why didn't you tell me?"

She looked at him. "You're not the easiest person to talk to, Trevor, not about emotional things."

He suddenly stood up and began to pace about the small room. "I'm not sure what you're getting at," he said.

"We've got problems," she said desperately, "serious problems. Surely you can see that."

He turned to face her. "Not as far as I'm concerned, we haven't."

"That's just it," she said bitterly. "If you're not affected, then the problem doesn't exist. Are you ever aware of anyone else's feelings beside your own? Did you even know that I've been going through hell these past months?"

"You're being hysterical," he said. "Is it that time of the month, or what?"

Her patience snapped. "Don't you dare throw that at me," she was shouting now, "You, you patronising –"

"Oh, calm down," he said icily.

"I'll calm down as you call it, when you agree to listen to me!"

He sat again on the sofa and spread his hands. "Okay, I'm listening."

Maureen tried to breathe more calmly. She mustn't let him get under her skin, she must be rational, that was the only way she'd get him to understand.

"Can you honestly sit there," she said, "and tell me that we've got a happy marriage?"

"I thought so –"

Maureen interrupted him. "Don't!" she said through clenched teeth. "Don't you dare to answer me by saying that *you're* happy. For once in your life, why don't you ask me if *I'm* happy?"

He just looked at her and then said in a flat tone, "I take it you're not then, which is why you decided to traipse across half the country."

Maureen looked at him in despair. "Can you blame me, Trevor? Can you honestly blame me? And don't pretend you don't know what I'm talking about!"

His face reddened. "I thought we'd sorted that out," he muttered.

"Sorted what out? Come on, Trevor, what did *we* sort out? *You* told *me*, that you weren't prepared to ever make love again, not even so that we could have a child. What sort of marriage is that?"

375

"There's more to a relationship than sex!"

"Agreed. But what about caring, what about consideration for each other's needs?" Maureen looked at him and said sadly, "Do you know what hurt the most? That it never occurred to you how your decision made me feel. You just seemed to think that you could proclaim and I would follow. Well, I tried, but just became more and more depressed until I nearly had a breakdown. And you never even noticed."

For a moment there was silence as Trevor sat with his head lowered, staring at the floor, then Maureen added, "If only you'd admitted that you had a problem and sought help, we might have overcome it together, but I knew there was no use suggesting it. I know you too well."

At that he raised his head and stared at her in anger. "Then you were right!" He almost spat out the words. "Don't you *ever* think that's an option!"

Maureen, now feeling emotionally exhausted, could only look away, her eyes filling with weak tears. It was hopeless.

"There's no alternative, then, is there?" she said, her voice breaking on the words. "I'm not prepared to go through life on your terms, so," she looked despairingly at him, "I'm not coming back, Trevor.

In fact, I think it would be better if we got a divorce."

There, she'd said it, actually said the words, and Maureen felt as though a heavy block of concrete had been lifted from her heart. Relief flooded through her, and that together with the emotion of the moment caused her tears to flow so profusely that she had to rush from the room. Upstairs she went into the small spare room to rummage in her bag for her crumpled and slightly grubby hanky, angrily drying her tears. She didn't want Trevor seeing her weakness, only her strength, because she knew she was going to need it.

Her intuition was proved correct as soon as she returned to the sitting-room, to find Trevor standing before the window. His back was to her, but the tension and anger in his posture, in the set of his shoulders was palpable.

Maureen sat in the armchair and waited.

Trevor turned. His face was pale, taut, his pale blue eyes hard like pebbles. "I can't force you to come back, but as for a divorce – you can forget it!"

CHAPTER TWENTY-NINE

After Trevor had left, Maureen felt exhausted, emotionally drained. She opened a can of tomato soup, heated it, and sat forlornly at the kitchen table. What was she going to do if Trevor refused to divorce her? Surely by leaving him she'd given him grounds: desertion it was called. Not that she knew anything about divorce proceedings. But one thing Maureen did know was that she wasn't prepared to go through life with an anchor weighing her down. And that was what it would be, a lifelong handicap called 'separation'. No, she wanted a divorce. Inside her was a hard fist of resolve that she would settle for nothing else.

She couldn't even bear to think of her family's reaction. Both Frank and Beryl believed firmly that marriage meant what it said, 'till death do us part'.

As for Sandra, her devout Catholic faith would never accept that Maureen was doing the right thing. Separation, she could hear them saying, maybe, but divorce? Never! But separation was not an option, as far as she was concerned. Neither single nor married, what future would that hold for her?

"Can you tell me you don't love me any more?" Trevor had flung at her.

She'd turned away, too upset to answer, silently closing the front door behind him, but now she thought of his parting words. *Did* she still love him? Maureen only knew that over the past months, whatever love she'd had for Trevor had been superseded by another emotion. Anger. Anger at what she saw as his cruel selfishness. She resented bitterly that he expected her to live a half-life, deprived of intimacy, deprived of ever having a child. Also, she realised that with that anger had come a loss of respect. She'd always looked up to Trevor, almost in awe at times of his better education, his profession, his confident manner. Now, she could see him for what he really was – an emotional cripple.

With a sigh, Maureen got up. It was no use sitting and brooding. She'd finish cleaning the windows and then, despite the weather, go for a walk. Perhaps the fresh air would help to clear her mind. But she'd no sooner finished her task than a horrifying thought struck her. Suppose Trevor went to see her parents when he got back? What if he told them what had happened, that she'd asked for a divorce? They'd never forgive her if they heard it from him first. In panic, she rushed upstairs and grabbed her coat and handbag, blessing the fact that as Frank and Beryl were both at work, he wouldn't be able to see them until the evening. Hurriedly, she scribbled a couple of lines for Freda and Carol, and within fifteen minutes was walking in lightly falling rain down London Road to the railway station.

* * *

Travelling to Stoke-on-Trent from Leicester wasn't as easy as she'd imagined. There was no through train, which meant she would have to change at Derby. She booked her ticket and went down to the cold and draughty platform, thankful there was a waiting-room where she could wait until her train was due. Three hours later, she was walking back along the route she'd taken only five days ago. It was still raining, the air damp and misty. Just like before. And she realised suddenly she would never again be able to walk with soft rain on her face, without it being a sad reminder of these two traumatic journeys. And this one *was* traumatic for the simple reason that Maureen knew she was going to bring disappointment and shame to her family. People in the Matthews' social circle didn't get divorced; in fact Maureen didn't think she'd ever met anyone who was. She'd heard of people of course, usually discussed in lowered, shocked tones, inferring that the person concerned was of questionable character. According to the newspapers, times were changing, but that didn't mean a thing as far as the parochial working-class morality of the Potteries was concerned.

Maureen glanced at her watch as she walked past the black and gold iron gates of the Spode China factory. It was nearly five o'clock, just before her parents would be coming home from work. Not that it mattered that the house would be empty as she had a front-door key in her purse.

And so it was that when Frank let himself in, he could hear movement in the scullery and the sound of the kettle boiling.

"You're home early, Beryl?" he called as he came through.

"Hello, Dad." Maureen stood in the doorway, smiling uncertainly, and Frank came forward and enveloped her in a bear hug.

381

"Oh, lass, it's good to see you! We've been that worried!"

Tears sprang to Maureen's eyes, and she brushed them away. She'd been more tearful during these past few days than she'd been in her entire life.

"I'm sorry, Dad."

"That's all right, love. Here, let's have a look at you." She was pale, yes, and there were purple shadows beneath her eyes, but she held his gaze steadily, and although he could see anxiety there, she was in control. With a sigh of relief, it was only then that he realised just how frightened he'd been. On the verge of a breakdown, that was what Freda had implied. And his imagination had worked overtime, envisaging his lovely, spirited daughter incarcerated in St Edward's Mental Hospital out at Cheddleton.

With a nod of approval, he said, "Right, you can keep explanations until your mum gets here. Let's have a cup of tea."

"I'm dying for one," Maureen said. "I walked from the station. I've only just got here."

"Change at Derby, did you?"

"That's right."

"Freda and Carol all right?"

"Fine. They've been real friends."

"Well, you can't have too many of those."

They both drank their tea in silence, and then turned as one when they heard Beryl come in. She stopped in surprise as she entered the sitting-room, her face lighting up.

"Maureen!"

Maureen got up and went to kiss her.

"I'm that pleased to see you!" Beryl exclaimed, and drew back, looking at her keenly. "Are you all right?"

"I'm okay," Maureen turned away, her eyes pricking with tears. Why was it that kind words provoked such an emotional reaction? Irritated, she brushed the tears away, and went to pour her mother's tea.

Beryl glanced questioningly at Frank, but he shook his head.

"I'm doing lobby for tea, so there should be plenty for all of us," Beryl said as Maureen handed a cup and saucer to her. "That's if you're staying for a meal, of course. Or are you going . . ." she almost said 'home', but substituted the words, "to Trentham?"

"No, I'm staying."

Maureen's tone was short, and Beryl glanced sharply at her. "Right, as soon as I've drunk this, I'll get started. It won't take long."

"No, Mum, wait a bit." Maureen gathered up her courage. "There's something I want to tell you, and if I wait until later, we might be interrupted."

Frank, as was his habit in times of stress, reached for his pipe. "By that, I suppose you mean by Trevor?"

She nodded. "Yes, that's why I suddenly decided to come back this afternoon. He came to see me this morning."

"He said he was going to," Beryl told her, "but there was no way we could let you know – we hadn't even got Freda's address."

Maureen frowned. "But I wrote to you, I posted it on Saturday."

"Ah, well, Saturday's post is never very reliable. It'll probably come in the morning." They both looked expectantly at her. Frank kept his expression non-committal as he carried on with the ritual of lighting his pipe. But every sinew was tense. Beryl sat with her hands folded on her lap, trying not to betray her anxiety. She knew from her daughter's expression, her tensions, that whatever Maureen was going to say, it was serious, very serious.

"I've asked Trevor for a divorce."

The bald words hung in the air, and for one long minute neither Frank nor Beryl spoke.

Then Frank said quietly, "Do you mind telling us why?"

Maureen swallowed. This was going to be hard, so hard she didn't know how to begin. In the end, she just said, "I can't."

Beryl, still reeling from the shock of her daughter's statement, said sharply, "Can't or won't?"

Maureen looked at her in despair. "I can't."

Frank, whose hands had stilled, sat with his unlit pipe in his hand, and stared at his daughter. "You'll have to do better than that, Maureen."

The note of authority in his voice, so well remembered from childhood, almost defeated her resolve, but stubbornly she said, "It's no use asking me, Dad. I can't, it's as simple as that!" Maureen knew that at all costs the real reason her marriage had broken down mustn't be revealed. Her knowledge, and her capacity to keep it a secret, were the only weapons she had.

Frank felt a slowly rising anger. "Simple! There's nothing simple about your daughter telling you she's seeking a divorce!"

"I'm sorry, Dad, I know how disappointed you must be in me. But if you knew the reason . . ." her eyes filled yet again with tears. It wasn't *her fault*, she thought childishly, none of it was!

But Frank's anger was now running high. "For once in your life, Maureen, will you unload your problems! You never change, do you? Haven't you learned yet that bottling things up never solves anything?"

Beryl, whose emotions were in complete turmoil, was still trying to grasp the implications of her daughter's dramatic announcement. She glanced from her husband to her daughter, seeing the frustration in one face and the distress in another.

"Maureen," she coaxed, "listen to us, love. Perhaps if you share what's troubling you, we can help. Don't you think it's a bit drastic, going for a divorce just like that? Every couple has their ups and downs, you know."

Maureen shook her head. "It's not like that. This isn't because we've been rowing, or not getting on, and it isn't something sudden. And before you ask, there's no-one else involved on either side." She looked pleadingly at their concerned and bewildered faces. "Can't you just trust me? I wouldn't contemplate such a terrible thing if I had any choice."

Beryl's control crumpled as she saw the anguish in her daughter's eyes, heard it in her voice. "Oh, love," she said, "I'm so sorry. A lot must have gone on for it to come to this."

Maureen couldn't reply; once again her emotions were out of control. She fished for a hanky, and dabbed at her eyes. "I seem to have become a crybaby all of a sudden," she said, with a weak smile.

"It's the stress," Beryl told her. She got up. "Well, I don't know about you two, but I'm starving. I'll go and peel the veg." She looked at Maureen. "Give me a hand?"

"Of course," Maureen stood up and followed her into the scullery.

But if Beryl had thought that her daughter might confide in her, she was mistaken. Maureen remained silent as she cut the remainder of the weekend's joint of beef into small cubes. Beryl chopped onions, carrots, parsnips and celery, and tossed them into a saucepan. While her mother crumbled an Oxo cube and prepared the stock, Maureen peeled two large potatoes, cut them into small squares and placed them in water to be added later.

"There," Beryl said, washing her hands and drying them. "That didn't take long. It's surprising what another pair of hands will do. I wonder how many other people in Stoke on-Trent are having lobby tonight, just like us? Old traditions die hard around here. Monday was always wash-day, and people had to do it the hard way. You'll remember yourself when

I had to heat the copper, and use a mangle. So they'd get the lobby ready first thing, and then switch it on just before lunch-time. It didn't need any attention, you see, and they were ready for a hot dinner by the time they'd done a family wash." Beryl kept talking, keeping a watchful eye on her daughter, relieved to see the set of her shoulders begin to relax.

"You were dreading telling us, weren't you?" she said softly.

Maureen nodded. Beryl busied herself in tidying up around the sink. She didn't know how she felt about it all. Shocked yes, and appalled that such a thing as divorce should happen in her family, but beneath it all she was ashamed to feel a slight sense of which she could only describe as relief. She'd never liked Trevor, she could admit that to herself now. Her girl deserved better and with grim satisfaction she hung up the tea towel. She didn't know what this 'reason' was that Maureen couldn't tell them about, but whatever the cause, Beryl was firmly on her daughter's side.

She turned and, holding out her arms, drew Maureen close to her. "You can count on my support, love, but it will be a rough road, you know."

"I know, Mum." Maureen went back into the

kitchen and taking a blue check cloth out of a drawer in the sideboard began to set the table.

Frank watched her with a heavy heart. Who would have thought it? Maureen, his lovely little girl – getting divorced! Frank wasn't bothered what other people would think. His daughter's happiness was the important thing. As for this 'reason', he didn't dare to open his mind as to what that might be, but if Trevor Mountford had harmed Maureen in any way – and Frank had heard of women being ashamed to confess to violence in their marriage – then he'd have him to answer to. His eyes suddenly narrowed. There was one question they'd forgotten to ask.

"I take it Trevor's agreed to this divorce, then?"

Maureen turned and faced him. "Not yet, but I think he will."

"You're sure of that?"

"I'm not sure of anything, Dad," Maureen said wearily. It had been a long day, and the journey had tired her more than she'd realised. "I'll have to take legal advice of course, but I think he can divorce me on grounds of desertion."

Beryl came in, having heard the conversation. "You're definitely not going back, then?"

Maureen shook her head. She couldn't take the

risk of slipping into that awful depressive state again.

Frank hesitated. "You are sure about this, Maureen? I mean, have you thought it through. You are a Catholic, after all, and you know the Church's views on divorce."

"I'm a lapsed Catholic, Dad," Maureen said, choosing to forget those moments in Holy Cross.

It was just after they'd finished eating the lobby, which Beryl served in earthenware basins, that they heard the sharp knock on the front door.

Maureen blanched and, seeing the sudden pallor in her face, Frank said grimly, "Leave this to me."

With squared shoulders as if for battle, he opened the door. Trevor moved to step inside, but Frank barred the way.

"She's here, Trevor," he said. "And at the moment, I don't think Maureen wants to see you."

"Here!" Trevor's expression was incredulous. "How did she get here?"

"By train."

"By train," Trevor repeated. "When I could have brought her in the car. That just shows, Frank, what a state she's in. She's just not thinking clearly. Personally, I think she should see a doctor."

"To be honest, I think she decided to come after you'd left," Frank told him. "But I'd be grateful if you could leave it for now, Trevor. Another time, perhaps."

Trevor stared at him in amazement, then his jaw clenched and he put his foot on the step. Frank began to close the door, unwilling to actually shut it in his son-in-law's face, and for a few seconds the two men's eyes locked in a battle of wills. Suddenly, to Frank's relief, Trevor turned on his heel and, his shoulders stiff with anger, went back to his car.

Maureen, who'd been listening behind the middle door, said, "Thanks, Dad."

"What are you going to do about your things, love?" Beryl said.

"I'll have to do something, I've only got the clothes I'm wearing." Maureen turned to her father. "Would you have time tomorrow to run me to the house?"

He nodded. "I'll make time."

Maureen looked at them both. She might strive to improve herself, to seek knowledge and broaden her horizons, but she knew how lucky she was. Her roots would always be here, with her family.

CHAPTER THIRTY

"Auntie Maureen!" The childish treble echoed through the house, as Maureen, after knocking lightly on the back door of Sandra's house, went into the kitchen. Sue scrambled down from where she was crayoning at the table and Maureen swept her up, giving her a hug and a kiss. "Hello, scrumptious, what are you doing?"

"Drawing." Proudly Sue fetched her piece of paper.

"That's lovely, you're a clever girl. Where's Mummy?"

"She's changing Stevie's nappy." Sue pinched her nose with her fingers. "Pooh!"

Maureen did the same, pulling a face, which made the little girl squeal with laughter.

"What's all this noise?" Sandra exclaimed, coming

in, her toddler in her arms. She came over to her sister, and Maureen kissed them both.

"Hello, sweetie," she touched little Stevie's cheek, and he beamed. "Another tooth, I see."

"Yes, he drove us mad with it!" Sandra put her son in his playpen and gave him some toys to play with. "What brings you here? Aren't you at work today?"

"No." Maureen said. That was one problem she was going to have to deal with and soon. Apparently, Trevor had told the office she had flu, but she was only allowed seven days off without a medical certificate.

Sandra raised her eyebrows. There was something about the tone of Maureen's answer which rang alarm bells. "Something wrong?"

Maureen nodded, and Sandra said briskly, "Right, I'll put the kettle on, you get the choccy biscuits."

Maureen couldn't help but smile. That was Sandra's remedy for everything, food. And it showed. She was always grumbling about her weight, constantly going on a diet, but although she would try for a few days, she always gave up in the end. Maureen looked at her sister's ample figure, as she busied herself with the teacups, at her two happy and contented children, at her shabby but comfortable home, and said, "Don't ever change, Sandra.

You're the happiest person I know."

She turned round in surprise. "Why, thanks! I wouldn't mind a figure like yours, though!"

"You don't need one," Maureen said. "Your beauty is all on the inside. And on the outside, of course," she added hastily. And it was true, for although Sandra was plain, her good humour and generosity shone through.

"Oh, I accepted years ago that I'd never be an Ava Gardner," Sandra brought the tea and biscuits over to the table. "Now then, you tell your big sister all about it."

And so, as Sandra began to nibble a chocolate digestive, Maureen told her how unhappy and depressed she'd been over the past few months, and saw her sister's eyes widen when she revealed that she'd been staying with Carol in Leicester. But the one thing she didn't tell her was the shameful reason for her misery.

Sandra, who'd put down her biscuit in dismay, opened her mouth to speak, but before she could, Sue clamoured for attention. "Not now, sweetheart! Look, it's time for Andy Pandy!" She took the little girl into the small sitting-room and settled her before the television, then went back into the large dining-kitchen.

Maureen looked directly at her. "I've left him, Sandra. I've told Trevor I want a divorce."

Sandra caught her breath. Her eyes wide and incredulous, she said sharply, "You've done what?"

"Told him I want a divorce. And I do, Sandra. No matter what you say, I won't change my mind." Maureen felt her voice rising, already defensive.

Sandra bit back her words of censure, studying her sister's face, seeing the strain in her eyes, which were full of misery. It's not going to help if I add to it, she thought, profoundly shocked by Maureen's announcement. "I won't try to make you change your mind, pet," she said. "You're big enough now to make your own decisions."

At her gentle tone, Maureen's eyes pricked with tears. "I suppose *you* think I'll go to Hell."

It was a half-hearted joke, but Sandra answered her seriously. "Just because my faith is so strong, it doesn't mean I expect everyone else to live by it." She got up and cleared the used crockery from the table. Keeping her back to her sister, she asked, "Has he got another woman?"

"No, it's nothing like that," Maureen said. "And before you ask, I haven't been playing away either."

"He hasn't been beating you up?" Sandra turned and her expression hardened. She wouldn't put anything past him! If there was ever a bloke who proved the truth of the old saying, 'never judge a book by its cover', it was Trevor Mountford. John couldn't stand him either. If that arrogant louse had laid a finger on her younger sister she'd . . .

But Maureen was shaking her head.

"Then what's the problem?" Sandra looked closely at her. "Is just that you've been rowing? Everyone does that, Maureen, it's part of marriage."

"No, Sandra. I know everyone has their ups and downs, it's . . ."

Maureen swallowed hard. They'd always been so close, she and Sandra. It seemed almost traitorous not to confide in her. But she couldn't take the risk. Secrecy was her only weapon.

"I'm sorry, Sandra," she said in despair, "I can't tell you why I want a divorce, I just can't."

There was a short silence, then Sandra, recognising from experience the finality in her sister's voice, the mutinous look in her eyes, sighed in resignation. "It's no use my asking then?"

Maureen gazed into Sandra's concerned brown eyes. "No," she said quietly. "I'm afraid not."

Later, after Maureen had left, Sandra rinsed the cups and saucers, and began to prepare the children's lunch. She felt terribly upset by Maureen's news, and hated to think of the little sister she'd always protected and loved being made so unhappy. Of course she should never have married him. No-one in the family had ever admitted it – that wasn't their way – but Sandra knew neither of her parents had taken to him. She sighed. Maureen had been too young, her head full of Hollywood glamour. How could she fail but be flattered when a young man as handsome as Trevor courted her? But a divorce! She still couldn't take it in! It was a cause for shame and scandal within any family, let alone a Catholic one, but not even to know why defied belief. It was just typical of our Maureen, she thought. Deep as they come, always was.

* * *

In the afternoon, Frank drove Maureen to the small semi-detached house on the new estate at Trentham, and promised to pick her up in a couple of hours. She carried upstairs the suitcases she'd brought, and dumped them on one of the neatly-made twin beds. For a few moments she slumped on the yellow quilted bedspread, feeling utterly defeated. She'd put such love and care into this, her first home, their first home, and now she could hardly believe she was planning to leave it. For Maureen knew that once she walked out of that door with her belongings, she would never set foot inside the house again. Suddenly she couldn't face the thought of packing her things, and wandered around the house, touching the teak dining-suite, the natural stone fireplace with its Westmoreland slate hearth, stroking the green geometric-patterned curtains she'd taken so much care in choosing. It was such an irrevocable step she was taking, giving up her home, the life she had built. In panic she wondered whether she was doing the right thing, and sat for a while on the sofa, her head cradled in her arms. Here, in the home she and Trevor had furnished together, the enormity of her decision to divorce him and its consequences seemed frightening. Maureen felt sick with doubts, as she wandered over to the French windows to look out over the garden. Although Trevor had planted a hedge, it was only partly grown yet, and she could see her next-door neighbour taking in her washing. She was a pleasant girl, and Maureen had hoped they'd become friends. But Trevor had objected.

"It doesn't do to become too friendly with neighbours," he'd insisted. "The next thing you know, they'll be knocking on the door, being nosy – we'll never have any privacy."

The memory profoundly disturbed her. Maureen

wandered into the kitchen and switched on the kettle to make herself a coffee. If she did stay with Trevor, assuming of course that he'd have her back, then that was what her life would be like. Full of repression. He wants to mould me into his mother, she thought, and remembering Norah's colourless personality, she was suddenly filled with horror. What was she doing? Allowing a few material possessions to influence her? How could she even think of changing her mind? You're mad, she told herself. Stupid! Where's your guts, for heaven's sake? So you've got to say good-bye to your house? So what, it's only bricks and mortar! Maureen sat at the blue formica kitchen table and sipped the hot, sweet coffee. She remembered Bernard once saying, "If your life doesn't fit, then it's up to you to change it." Suddenly, the doubts which had flooded her drained away. She'd made her decision, she knew it was the right one. Taking the rest of her coffee upstairs, she began to pack her belongings.

* * *

It was not until later that evening when Maureen, having unpacked a few of her clothes and left the rest in suitcases, fished inside her handbag to retrieve a couple of letters which Trevor had left on the hall table.

One envelope contained a get-well card from one of the girls at the office, causing her a pang of conscience, and she turned the other over, trying to guess its contents. It was a local postmark, type-written, and the fact that the envelope was such good quality intrigued her. It seemed a pity to rip it open so she went downstairs and took a knife out of the sideboard drawer. Frank and Beryl were immersed in *Take Your Pick*, and Maureen slipped into the scullery to open it in private.

When she saw the embossed heading, her heart skipped a beat. She stared at the words – *Cartlidge & Leadbetter, Solicitors*. But, she thought wildly, Trevor had said he wouldn't agree to a divorce! But then as she began to read, her eyes widened in astonishment.

Dear Mrs Mountford,

<u>*Bernard Clewlow, deceased.*</u>

I would be most grateful if you could telephone this office to arrange a mutually convenient appointment, when you may learn something to your advantage.

Yours faithfully,

Henry Cartlidge.

Maureen read the letter again to be sure she wasn't mistaken, then leaned against the draining-board, the sheet of paper held limply in her hand.

Bernard must have left her something in his will, perhaps a couple of his favourite books or something. How typical that was of his kind nature, his thoughtfulness. Sadness swept over her, at the memory of their unique friendship. She'd so valued his gentle guidance, his belief in her potential. Poor Bernard, to die alone, to remain undiscovered for several days. He'd been worth far more than that. Maureen knew she owed the solitary man a huge debt of gratitude. Do people come into your life by pure chance, or is it something deeper, she wondered. It was inevitable that whoever you met influenced your life in some way, but was it pre-ordained?

Her musing was interrupted as Beryl called, "Maureen? Make a cup of tea, there's a dear."

"Okay." She turned the cold-water tap on, and with the kettle held beneath it, made a decision. Tomorrow, she'd go into work. Not that she'd say anything about what had really been happening in her life; she'd just have to pretend to have recovered from flu. Feeling as wretched as she did, it wouldn't be difficult to convince them. And while she was there, she'd ring the solicitor and fix up an appointment.

CHAPTER THIRTY-ONE

As with the night before, the following evening they all waited with increasing tension for Trevor to come back. But there was no knock at the front door and eventually, when the clock struck ten, Maureen in particular breathed a sigh of relief.

"Trevor won't come now," she said. "I'll make us all some cocoa." She'd shown her parents the letter from the solicitors and hated to think what Trevor's reaction would have been. He was so jealous, he'd have put the worst possible interpretation on it, probably accusing her of having had an affair with Bernard. I'm well out of it, she told herself for the umpteenth time, but that didn't take away the feeling of failure.

When she took in the cocoa, Beryl looked at her with concern. "Maureen, love," she began, "I've been thinking. Do you think it would be a good idea to go and see the doctor – you know, after the way you've been feeling, the depression and so on." She frowned, her face showing her worry. "I mean, it's not normal, what happened, is it?"

Maureen looked at them both. "If you mean the state I was in when I travelled to Leicester, then no, I agree. But I went up to the library in Hanley yesterday in my lunch-hour and did some reading. Apparently there's something called reactive depression and I think that's what I had. Now the cause is removed, I'm sure I'll be okay. I'm still a bit shaky at times, but I'm feeling more like my old self every day."

Beryl looked at her doubtfully. "If you're sure . . ."

"Look, if it comes back, I promise you I'll go. How's that!"

Beryl nodded, satisfied.

Frank blew his nose. His throat was a bit sore, and he was trying to ward off a cold. "You'll have to see Trevor soon, you know. There's things to sort out."

Maureen nodded. "I know. I'm just giving myself a breathing space. I'll ring him at work in a couple of days."

And she did, suggesting they meet for a drink at a quiet pub they sometimes visited in Stone, a pretty market town a few miles away. Neutral ground, she decided, and a public place. Then there would be no chance of a shouting match. She dressed carefully, deliberately choosing a beige sweater and camel and beige check skirt. She looked in the mirror – sedate, that's how she looked, and that was how Trevor liked her. She didn't want him to be irritated in any way; she needed him to be in a receptive mood, because she knew that this meeting was going to need all her powers of manipulation. When, at eight o'clock to the second, the red Mini drew up outside the house, she thought Trevor's face could have been carved out of granite, it was so cold and set. She slid into the passenger seat. Without a word, he did a three-point turn, and then drove back down the street. Within minutes they were on the main road which would lead them directly into Stone. Trevor was wearing a black polo neck and trousers, clothes she had chosen for him, ones he knew she liked. Was that a good sign? Did it mean he was prepared to listen to her, to be reasonable?

After a couple of miles, Maureen broke the silence. "Are you okay?"

"Fat lot you care," he muttered.

"Don't be like that, Trevor, of course I care! Just because –"

"Just because you've left me, you mean?" There was a hard edge to his voice and, clenching the wheel in fury, he put his foot down on the accelerator. As the car sped along, Maureen darted an anxious glance at the speedometer, wishing she'd never spoken. The rest of the short journey was taken in silence and, as Trevor's driving became more and more erratic, it was with relief that Maureen saw the carpark of the pub looming ahead. Swerving into it, Trevor slammed on the brakes. Silently, Maureen got out and waited while he locked the door, then began to walk towards the entrance. Trevor followed and her nerves, still not completely stable after all that had happened, caused her stomach to churn as she entered the pub and headed for a table in the far corner. There were few other couples in the lounge as yet, and she chose to sit with her back to the room. Trevor was more likely to control any outburst if other people could see him. She turned, but without the courtesy of asking her what she wanted, he had gone to the bar to order their drinks. Maureen sat down and, in an agony of apprehension, tried to control her breathing. After a few minutes, Trevor brought the glasses over, and sat opposite.

They both sipped their drinks in silence, Trevor

not even looking at her as he pretended to take an interest in the room, his gaze wandering over the display of copper ornaments and brass horseshoes over the bar. But she knew he was just marking time, waiting for her to begin. A tense silence built up between them until Maureen broke it.

"We need to talk, Trevor!" The words came out sharply, and his eyes met hers at last, the expression in them cold and challenging.

"That's an understatement!"

"I meant what I said, you know. I want a divorce."

"And I meant what I said when I told you to forget it!"

Maureen took another sip of her drink. "I don't think you're in any position to refuse."

His eyes narrowed. "How do you mean?"

Maureen felt the heat rise in her cheeks. She hated the stance she was taking, but what alternative did she have? "What I mean, Trevor, is that I've given you grounds for divorce . . ."

He cut her short. "Ah, you admit it at last! And there I was, thinking you Catholics were above such things! It just shows how wrong you can be. Come on then – who is he?" Trevor spat the words at her, his eyes blazing not only with anger but with triumph.

Maureen stared at him in disgust. He'd always been willing to think the worst of her. "You're on the wrong track," she snapped. "There isn't anyone! I meant I'd given you grounds by walking out. You can divorce me for desertion."

"You know that, do you? You've taken advice?"

His tone was sarcastic and, stung, Maureen snapped. "No, but I have made an appointment with a solicitor!" It was none of his business that it was to do with Bernard.

"A solicitor? Well, don't think you can use my money to pay him!"

Maureen struggled to remain calm. "Trevor, I want a divorce! So far," she gazed intently at him, " I haven't told a living soul the reason – you know what I'm talking about." Her eyes held his, and his lips tightened. She forced herself to speak slowly, emphasising every word. "You don't seem to realise just how serious I am. If you refuse to divorce me, then that loyalty will be cancelled out. Do you understand what I'm saying?"

Trevor's face was ashen. "You wouldn't do that, Maureen."

"Try me," she said, deliberately hardening her expression. "Of course, when I see the solicitor, I could ask him whether our *peculiar situation* constituted grounds for divorce. In that case, *I* could divorce *you*." She took another sip of her sweet Martini and finding her hand was trembling carefully put down the glass. Then she fabricated, "It would probably be in the papers. The *News of the World* would just love to pick up a story like that."

Trevor's hand jerked, almost knocking over his glass, and he picked it up, drained the rest of its contents, and without a word went over to the bar. Maureen, whose insides felt like jelly, was fighting to control her nerves. Only she knew how many hours she'd spent in the middle of the night, lying awake in the dark, agonising over what she should say.

Trevor returned, not with another half-pint of beer, but with a large brandy. He looked at her and, seeing the misery in his face, Maureen's heart filled treacherously with compassion. Although she didn't love him any more, she hated the thought of hurting him like this. To her distress, she saw tears in his eyes. Seeing a man cry was a shocking thing to Maureen. In her world, men didn't show emotion – tenderness maybe, and certainly anger, but everyone knew that men didn't cry – even little boys were discouraged from doing so. Were they tears of self-pity? Or perhaps he did love her – inasmuch as he was capable of loving anyone. But it's no use, she thought wearily, I've just got to get out of this sham of a marriage. She opened her handbag and pretended to rummage through it, wanting to give Trevor time to get his feelings under control.

Eventually she looked up to see him swallow the rest of his brandy.

His pale blue eyes were full of defeat. "You win," he said in a flat tone. "I'll do whatever is necessary."

Maureen reached out and touched his hand for what might be the last time. "I'm sorry," she said. "I wish things had turned out differently," but he turned away.

Later that evening, instead of feeling, as she'd anticipated, full of relief, Maureen felt an overwhelming sense of sadness. She lay in the bed which had been hers since childhood, and glanced across to where Trevor had once slept, remembering her confusion and uncertainty in those early days. She'd never imagined that she'd become divorced. In common with most of her friends, she'd grown up dreaming of Mr Right and living happily ever after. Why did it have to be different for me, she thought in despair. It was a long time before she was finally able to sleep.

CHAPTER THIRTY-TWO

It was decided that Frank and Beryl would tell Nellie and Vera about the impending divorce. Maureen couldn't face it. Not that she lacked the courage, but she knew that Vera would interrogate her about the reason. So, on the evening her parents departed to convey the dramatic and upsetting news, Maureen took advantage of the quiet household to think about her future. Her return to the office had only intensified her restlessness – it was time to move on, she knew that. Bored with the work, she was chafing to take on more responsibility, more challenge. She also desperately needed a distraction to help her to recover from the depression and emotional turmoil of the past few months.

Aware that there was an ideal solution, thoughtfully she fetched a writing-pad from the sideboard drawer, and began to write.

* * *

In the Farmer household the post didn't arrive until mid-morning, so it was after she got in from work, and while Freda was cooking their tea, that Carol read Maureen's letter.

"One egg or two?" Freda was making a mixed grill, and the bacon, sausages, small pieces of steak and tomatoes, were sizzling gently under the grill.

"One," Carol said absently. She looked up. "They're getting divorced."

"You're joking!" Freda was profoundly shocked. She would never have imagined that young Maureen Matthews would end up divorced. She'd always been such a nice girl! But then, she thought, it's getting more common than it used to be. One of the chambermaids at the hotel had just got divorced. Mind you, she thought darkly, from what I've heard, I'd have divorced him myself. "On what grounds?

"Trevor's divorcing her for desertion," Carol said. "I wonder what happened to make her leave? She was always crazy about him, right from the start."

"Handsome is as handsome does," Freda said, tartly. "You never know anyone until you live with

411

them, I've always said it." She spooned the fat over the eggs and slid them on to warm plates, adding the rest of the food. "What else does she say?"

"How grateful she is for all we did for her." Carol pushed the letter aside as Freda brought over her plate. "She also says she needs a complete break." She looked across at her mother uncertainly. "She's asked me if I think it would be easy for her to get a job over here, in Leicester."

Freda paused with the saltcellar halfway in mid-air. "You mean leave Stoke?"

Carol nodded. "I think it's my fault in a way. I told her how much higher the wages are here."

Freda didn't reply for a few moments, as she began to eat her meal, then paused and exclaimed, "You can say that again! Do you know an overlocker in a hosiery factory can earn as much as twenty-five pounds a week?" At Carol's gasp of incredulity, Freda explained, "I know, because one of the waiters is gutted that his daughter who's barely twenty is earning more than he is. As he says, it doesn't do much for a man's ego."

"But how on earth do they earn that much?" It was inconceivable to Carol that a woman could earn such a high wage.

"Piecework!" Freda said shortly. "When I think of

how much the skilled paintresses and pottery-workers earn, I could spit. Talk about justice – it doesn't exist, at least that's been my experience!"

"But Maureen's not an overlocker!" Carol grinned, "She's not likely to make one either, not from what I can remember about her sewing!"

"But seriously, she probably would get more money working in an office in Leicester than she would in the Potteries."

"I know, but I've never understood why."

"Because Leicester is currently one of the richest cities in Europe," Freda said promptly. The new chef, Vincent, was not only good-looking, but well-informed, and in Freda he found a rapt audience. Freda picked up the teapot and began to pour. "You know, it might be a good thing for Maureen. Can you imagine what it would be like, once it got out about the divorce? People looking sideways, and knowing they were talking about you?"

"But renting somewhere to live would eat away at the extra money she earned," Carol pointed out.

Freda glanced at her. "That's true. Unless . . ."

Carol stared at her. "You mean . . . here?"

"Why not?" Freda said briskly. "Of course that spare room's a bit poky, but you two girls could redecorate. And the extra cash would come in handy. It'd be far cheaper for her than living anywhere else!"

"Yes, but . . ." Carol looked at her mum doubtfully. "Wouldn't you find it too much – two of us in the house?"

Freda shook her head. "Not really. I've always liked Maureen, and you get on well." She paused, "Or are you saying you're not sure it's a good idea?"

"No, not at all, I'd love it," Carol said with alacrity.

Freda turned away with a secret smile. It was early days yet where Vincent was concerned; after all it was only two years since his wife had died. But if her intuition was right, and there was a mutual attraction there, then Maureen's presence would help to deflect any resentment Carol might feel. Freda treasured the close bond between herself and her daughter, but knew that the time was fast approaching when they both needed to make separate lives for themselves. And now, she thought as she cleared the table, I think at last I may have a second chance.

* * *

When it was time to see the solicitor, Maureen had to ask at the office for time off, and gave the excuse that she had a dental appointment.

"Have you got your appointment card?" Colin Campbell asked. "Sorry to ask, but you know the rules. It's not that we don't trust people, but you're supposed to provide proof that the appointment's genuine."

But Maureen was prepared. "Sorry, Colin. Mum made the appointment, and she can't find it."

He sighed, then warned, "Just this once, mind, seeing as it's you."

So now, Maureen walked through the centre of Hanley, past C & A's, across the Market Square, threading her way through the shopping crowds until she turned into a quiet side road. Apart from an elderly man walking a Staffordshire bull terrier, the area was deserted, and halfway along she saw the shiny brass plate, *Cartlidge & Leadbetter, Solicitors*. The offices were in a converted Victorian villa. Maureen walked through the open gate and, feeling slightly nervous, rang the bell. Within seconds the door opened.

"Mrs Mountford," she announced. "I've an appointment to see Mr Cartlidge."

A grey-haired woman, with spectacles dangling on a chain across her ample breasts, stepped aside for her to enter. Maureen looked around curiously. The hall was long and narrow, with a red and black diamond-patterned tiled floor, and a plain red carpet running along the centre. The secretary asked her to wait in a small ante-room, but within minutes Maureen was ushered into a large, square office, where a tall, thin man, of pale complexion and thinning hair, rose from behind an imposing but file-littered mahogany desk, and came round to greet her.

"Mrs Mountford," he shook her hand. "Thank you for coming."

Maureen smiled, feeling a little awkward, and took the chair he indicated. He retreated behind his desk, and opened a file.

"Ah, yes, Bernard Clewlow." He leaned back in his chair and put the tips of his fingers together, making an arch. "You know, this has restored my faith in human nature." He smiled at her. "But of course, you have no idea what I'm talking about."

Maureen shook her head and smiled. "No, I'm afraid not."

"You were a good friend of Mr Clewlow, I take it?"

"Yes. We worked together."

"Mmn. Well, Mr Clewlow left all his estate to his two cousins. There was no mention in his will of any other bequests, which is why you didn't hear from us sooner." He looked at her and smiled, and unable to think of anything to say, Maureen smiled back and feeling slightly puzzled, waited.

"However," Henry Cartlidge continued, "one of his cousins, David Weston, recently found Mr Clewlow's diary. It was in a small drawer in his bureau among some other papers. And in it, he'd expressed an intention to make a bequest to you. The majority of people would have ignored such a discovery, but David Weston is a religious man, and so is Mr Clewlow's other cousin," here the solicitor referred to the file, "John Asprey. After due consultation, they have decided to honour Mr Clewlow's wishes." He looked keenly at her. "I think you can consider yourself fortunate: it's a rare thing when money is concerned to find such principles."

Maureen felt bewildered. Money? Bernard had left her money? But why would he do that? His own salary hadn't been much more than her own.

Henry Cartlidge was watching her and explained, "Mr Clewlow had made some very wise invest-ments." He took out a sheet of paper from the file. "I wouldn't describe the bequest as substantial, not by any means, but he thought you might find it useful."

Maureen waited yet again, her mind whirling with

excitement. If ever there had been a time she needed extra money it was now.

"There is, however, a condition to the bequest," the solicitor continued. "Mr Clewlow left you the sum of five hundred pounds, and his exact words were," he read from the sheet of paper, *"That she should use the money in any way she deemed necessary, to further her education and achieve her potential."*

Maureen's eyes suddenly stung with tears. The sentiment brought back the memory of Bernard's kindly and intelligent face so vividly, it was almost as though he was with them in the room. Five hundred pounds! It was a fortune!

"I don't know what to say," she managed eventually. "I never expected anything like this. When your letter came, I thought Bernard might have left me a few books." She looked at the solicitor. "We shared a love of reading, you see. He became a sort of mentor for me, a teacher, almost."

Henry Cartlidge nodded. "Yes, I can imagine that. I had a lot of respect for Mr Clewlow."

"What about the two cousins – should I write and thank them?"

He shook his head. "No, they're both very private people. I will furnish them with the details of today's meeting, and express your appreciation. I can only repeat that you are very lucky indeed. I have a cheque here for you, and I'm sure you will honour Mr Clewlow's wishes in the way you use it."

"Of course, " Maureen assured him. "I'll put it in a high-interest savings account until the right time."

With a nod of approval, the solicitor got up and coming round the desk, handed her an envelope. Maureen held out her hand, and he shook it warmly. "Thank you," she said. "Thank you so much."

Almost in a daze, she retraced her steps and began the long walk back to work. Five hundred pounds! What faith Bernard had in her abilities. She mustn't let him down, she must try and continue to improve herself. How and when, she had no idea, but if such a miracle as this could happen, then Maureen felt confident that some time in the future an opportunity would present itself. It was a pity in a way that she couldn't use the money for other things, but that would betray Bernard's trust. With her spirits higher than they had been for some time, she eventually turned in the firm's gateway. Waving at Sid, the lodgeman, she made her way back to the Accounts Department, wondering how on earth she was going to be able to concentrate on the mundane figures in a sales ledger.

* * *

Maureen's health gradually improved, although she still couldn't dismiss an underlying sadness at the way her life had turned out. The neighbours had obviously noticed that she was again living at home, and Beryl had borne the brunt of their curiosity.

"Just tell them the truth," Maureen had told her. "That I've left my husband. And if they pursue it, say we're separated. They'll find out soon enough about the divorce when they read it in the *Sentinel*."

"That will take years," Frank said. "Three isn't it, before you can sue for desertion?"

"I think so," Maureen shrugged. "It's up to Trevor to consult a solicitor. I don't see why I should have the expense."

Frank frowned. "I don't agree, Maureen. I think it would be worth the money to find out the facts. You need to know where you stand, what's involved."

"Your dad's right," Beryl said, coming in from the scullery. "I'm going upstairs to change before Mum and Vera get here. Will you wipe up for me, love?" The last remark was directed at Maureen who, although she got up willingly, knew that if she hadn't been there Beryl would have asked Frank who was sitting reading the paper wearing a smug expression.

Why washing dishes and housework was regarded

as 'women's work', she'd never understood, for after all didn't men eat off plates, use lavatories, drop cigarette or pipe ash on the carpet? Why should they always expect someone else to clean up after them? It made sense if their wives didn't work, but in common with most of the women in the area, Beryl managed to combine a job in a factory with running a home. Oh, her dad would help if her mother asked, but even then his attitude would be that he was doing a job for *her*, not simply because it needed doing.

When Nellie and Vera arrived, Frank made his escape upstairs, and Maureen went back into the scullery to make a pot of tea. She took her time, knowing that when she went into the parlour it would be to see Nellie's concerned expression, and feel Vera's gimlet eyes boring into her.

She didn't know how Frank had achieved it, but apart from a muttered, "I'm sorry, lass," not a question had Vera fired at her, while Nellie had simply hugged her tight and shed a few tears. However, it was all there in the atmosphere, and she could almost hear the invisible words. *Why did she leave him? It must be something terrible for her to want a divorce!*

What Trevor had told his parents, she had no

idea. She didn't care if she never saw Henry and Norah again. She'd never liked them, and had always felt that they didn't approve of her, didn't think she was good enough for their precious son.

As the weeks passed, her restlessness increased, and at last she told Frank and Beryl of her plans, hoping desperately they would understand her reasons for moving away.

* * *

And so, at the end of June, Frank drove Maureen and her luggage to the small terraced villa where Freda and Carol awaited her. Beryl sat in the front passenger seat, somewhat excited at the prospect of travelling to somewhere other than Blackpool, or North Wales. Immediately they approached Leicester on the main A50 and she saw the wide tree-lined roads, she decided she liked it. She was sad, of course, that her daughter was going to live so far away, but was sensible enough to recognise that this was what Maureen wanted, and perhaps needed. Maureen, sitting in the back, was glad that the journey was quiet. She was fighting her own fears, fear that she might be homesick, anxiety about getting another job. But underneath it all, there was a keen anticipation within her, a determination that she was going to make a new future for herself, one that wasn't dependent on another person's whims and moods. I won't have to answer to anyone, she thought, and it was a heady and welcome sensation.

CHAPTER THIRTY-THREE

The February sky, which had looked so promising earlier, was threatening rain as Greg Barlow entered the side door of Holy Cross. He was late, the eleven o'clock Mass had already started, but it couldn't be helped. His job with its uncertain hours made it difficult for him to keep to a regular routine. He slipped into a seat at the end of a pew and automatically murmured the responses as the priest intoned the *Kyrie*. Although it wasn't his parish church, he sometimes found the Dominican priory more convenient to use, particularly when he was working. There was an added incentive too. Was she here? Discreetly he turned his head, his eyes searching the congregation – and then he saw her. Head bowed, her black lace mantilla framing her profile, she was heartbreakingly lovely. He could remember the first time he'd seen her at this church. It had been here, by Our Lady's altar, on the day he'd come up from London to visit his mother in hospital. He'd spotted her again about six months ago, shortly after his transfer had come through and he'd moved back to Leicester. Listening to the sermon, his attention had wandered for a moment and he'd suddenly noticed her, sitting in a pew on his right. He now looked for her whenever he came, and felt a sharp stab of disappointment if she wasn't there. Greg admitted to himself that he found her fascinating. But he *had* seen her somewhere before, he was sure of it, and he found it frustrating that he couldn't remember.

When it was time to leave, he hung back as he always did, hoping she would look his way. Sometimes she did and would catch his eye. Then he would give a half smile, which she would return, causing his heart to miss a beat. But today, she didn't see him, and he was close behind her as members of the congregation queued to get out. It had started to rain, and people were pausing in the doorway to put up umbrellas. Greg saw the girl turn up the collar of her coat and lower her head to dash through the rain, which suddenly became a downpour. Still sheltering in the porch, Greg saw her stop, obviously wondering whether to run back, and as she looked over her shoulder, *he knew!* Her face, pale in the eerie light of the threatening storm, her normally bouffant hair now damp and hanging limply, brought a vivid scene to his mind. *Euston! The station café.* That was it! That was where he'd seen her before.

It was a triumphant feeling to have solved the mystery at last and Greg, suddenly making a decision, ran to where she stood. "I'll give you a lift," he called, and fumbled with the ignition key in the lock of his car, parked nearby. He saw the indecision on her face, and added, "I'm very respectable, quite holy really, after Mass," and she laughed.

Realising her hesitation was causing them both to get drenched, Maureen hurried to the passenger door and got in. She brushed her damp hair away from her forehead, and looked at her companion. She'd noticed him in church a few times, a pleasant enough looking bloke, tall with a somewhat craggy face.

"Thanks," she said, "but what if I live miles away?"

"Then I shall honour my promise," he smiled. "But as you were obviously on foot and there are few buses on Sundays, I'm not too worried."

"I could have come by train," she teased, surprised

at how comfortable she felt with him.

"Then I'd simply drop you off at the station!" Greg started the engine, and looked at her. "So, where do I head for?"

"I live just off the Evington Road," she told him, and he nodded.

"No problem. I'm Greg Barlow, by the way."

"Maureen," she said. "Maureen Matthews." She tended to use what she thought of as her 'real' name, whenever she could.

"I've noticed you in church before," he said.

"Yes, I know."

Greg frantically tried to think of something intelligent to say. He'd like to ask her out, but it seemed a bit bad form in the circumstances. He didn't want her to think that his offer of a lift had a hidden agenda.

"You're not from Leicester, are you?"

Maureen looked at him and grinned. "You guessed! No, I come from the Potteries."

"Ah! Good old Stoke. Hey – Matthews? You're not related to . . ."

"Stanley?" Maureen laughed. "If only! Gosh, there'd be no living with my dad, if we were."

"It's a pity Stoke City ever let him go!" Greg glanced at her. "Sorry, I'm a bit of a football fan."

"I've grown up with one," she smiled. "I suppose you support Leicester."

"I most certainly do."

The distance was short and all too soon in Greg's opinion he was drawing up outside the Farmer's house. Maureen hesitated, wondering whether she ought to ask him in for tea or coffee, but a vision of Carol's horror at being caught in her dressing-gown, devoid of make-up, and painting her toe-nails, made her realise it was impossible.

"Thanks a lot," she said, as she opened the door. "You'll get your reward in Heaven."

He smiled and raised a hand in farewell, before drawing away. Oh no, he thought, I intend to get my reward far sooner than that. The next time I see you at Mass, Maureen Matthews, I'm going to ask you out.

* * *

There was a hint of spring in the air, as Maureen walked briskly across Victoria Park the following Sunday afternoon. During the past few months, she had made a habit of spending time here, grateful for the fresh air of the green expanse, enjoying the relaxed atmosphere, watching with amusement the dog-owners vainly trying to recall their pets. She liked to watch the children too, and the university students walking along, heads bent in thought, or alternatively laughing and joking with their friends. It was hard to imagine that during the Second World War, in 1944, the American 82nd Airborne Division had been stationed there. But now it was a lovely day, and somehow the coming of the new season felt significant, as though it signalled a new beginning, a fresh start. I know what it is, she thought in surprise – I feel confident, happy. Could it be that at last she'd let go the unhappiness and frustration of her marriage, the guilt that had plagued her ever since she'd asked Trevor for a divorce? Suddenly, Maureen realised how little her husband had been in her thoughts lately, how free she felt, how full of optimism.

Of course, she mused as she watched the antics of a puppy, it could be as a result of all the candles I've lit. The return to her faith had happened gradually, born out of the feeling of homesickness and loneliness that she'd felt shortly after her move to Leicester. Remembering the comfort she'd experienced in the tranquillity of Holy Cross, and needing some form of structure to her weekend, Maureen had tentatively begun going to Mass. At first, it had been purely for selfish reasons, wanting to give herself and Carol some space, and going to church had been a convenient way to do that. But slowly, she became conscious that the hour she spent each Sunday morning, the quiet time sharing familiar rituals and prayers, gave her solace and spiritual refreshment.

Something of the change in her must have shown, for when she went back to the small terraced house, Carol looked up from her magazine with raised eyebrows. "What's up with you? You look all excited!"

"I feel it." Maureen plopped down on an armchair. "You see before you a newly-born friend, ready to face the future – ready, in fact, for anything."

Carol's face lit up. "Well, hoo-bloody-ray, it's about time!"

"Have I been a pain?" Maureen looked at her ruefully.

"Nope. But we never expected it to go on for so long. Not that you've been a misery or anything, but at our age, there should be more to life than work and sleep." She glanced at her friend. "I thought you looked a bit more perky last week, after that bloke brought you home from church. Wouldn't have anything to do with that, would it?"

"No, of course not. I kept telling you just to give me time!"

"I know – but it's been months!"

"I needed it, Carol," Maureen said stubbornly. "I just wanted time to switch off." What she didn't say was that it had taken far longer than she'd expected to recover from her depression. It was insidious; she'd find it beginning to creep back and had been tempted at times to go and see her doctor, perhaps take some of the Valium she kept reading about. But she had argued with herself that she was luckier than most – she'd been able to eliminate the reason for her depression. She felt desperately sorry for anyone trapped in a similar predicament. I'd rather have a physical illness, Maureen thought, than a mental one. And according to statistics she'd read, the problem was far more widespread than most people realised.

"Penny for them?" Carol was looking at her quizzically, and Maureen laughed.

"Oh, they're not worth that much!"

"Does that mean you'll come to the Palais this week?" Carol waited, watching her friend with keen anticipation, and her face lit up as Maureen nodded. It would be just like the old days, the two of them going dancing together. Perhaps it would bring her luck, as apart from a couple of disastrous dates, Carol's love life was non-existent.

"You're too fussy," Freda had scolded. "I'm sure

lots of young men ask you out."

"Yeah," Carol had answered. "Morons, most of them. Anyway, you can talk, it took you over twenty years to find someone."

Freda turned away, pleased that Carol had accepted Vincent so well. When he'd first asked her out, she'd been hesitant and wary at the prospect of telling her daughter, but Carol, once she'd met him, had been all for it.

"Time you had a bit of romance in your life," she had said, grinning. "If you'd left it much longer, you'd be past it."

"Cheeky madam!"

"He seems very quiet. I thought chefs were supposed to be temperamental – you know, throwing tantrums and things."

"Not Vincent," Freda said proudly. And it was true, although he could be a bit of martinet during working hours, he rarely lost his temper. He's just the sort of man I always hoped to meet, she thought with satisfaction, and so far she had seen nothing to change her mind.

Now, Maureen, pleased to see Carol's delighted reaction when she agreed to go to the Palais, went into the kitchen to make some coffee. And, she decided, thinking affectionately of Sandra, we'll have chocolate biscuits as well – I feel like celebrating.

CHAPTER THIRTY-FOUR

The following Saturday, Maureen sat in her tiny bedroom, peering into the small double-sided magnifying mirror which, propped on the battered chest of drawers, transformed it into a dressing-table. The light was poor for applying make-up, but she applied her Max Factor foundation with a practised hand, blended rouge subtly into her cheeks, and dithered over whether to apply blue or green eyeshadow. Then as a finishing touch, she back-combed her hair into a fashionable bouffant style. It was so long since she'd been dancing that her stomach was fluttering with nervous anticipation. She'd spent her lunch-hours searching Lewis's, the large department store where she worked as a cashier in the Accounts Department, for the right dress to wear. Her staff discount meant that she could have a wider choice, and eventually she'd chosen a cocktail dress in a vivid emerald green. I can wear whatever I like now, she decided, loving its tiny straps, fitted waist and slightly flared skirt, which worn with a pair of silver high-heeled strapped sandals, showed off her long slim legs to perfection. Maureen loved the wide variety of shops in Leicester, and although she couldn't afford their prices, often wandered around Marshall & Snelgrove, the opulence of the expensive shop wrapping itself around her like a warm cocoon. Then there was Joseph Johnson, and Morgan Squires, all catering not only for the city but for the county as well. One could buy smart clothes for 'town', and, 'Lovely for a weekend in the country' an assistant would purr, as Maureen browsed. Chance would be a fine thing, she'd grin to herself and move on. But it was a game she loved to play, pretending she could afford all these luxurious things.

"Have you finished tarting yourself up, yet?" Carol appeared in the doorway, wearing black, her blonde hair in its crisp bob giving an impression of ultra-sophistication.

"How do I look?" Maureen twisted to face her.

Carol considered. "Stunning. Come on, I've a feeling it's my lucky night!" She went down the

stairs humming. She hadn't been dancing for weeks
– her friend from the salon had found herself a
boyfriend, while Fiona, the receptionist, had moved
to Skegness, where her parents had bought a seaside
hotel.

Freda had already left for work, so the two girls
checked the house was locked, and set off to walk to
the bus stop. The night air was chilly and they both
wore their winter coats and shoes, carrying their
strappy sandals in small carrier bags. When the bus
arrived, the conductor greeted them with a cheerful
grin. "Good hunting," he chaffed, and there were a
couple of wolf whistles as they made their way down
the narrow aisle. Maureen glanced at Carol and
their eyes met in merriment. It wasn't necessary to
say, 'Just like old times'. Maureen was tempted to
murmur, 'If only Elaine could have been here', but
decided against it, pushing away the unhappy
memory of her untimely death. "I shall miss the
conductors," she said instead, "when they bring in
these one-man buses."

"My Uncle Sam's a bus driver," Carol said. "He's
in the Transport & General Workers' Union –
they've been fighting it, so he said in his last letter,
but I think it's a losing battle."

The Palais Ballroom was in Humberstone Gate,

only seconds away from where the bus dropped them off, and a doorman, dressed in a black jacket and dicky bow, gave them an appraising glance as they entered. After paying, Maureen followed Carol upstairs to the ladies' cloakroom, where they checked in their belongings. Minutes later, they were downstairs, searching to find an empty table. Spotting one, Carol said, "Do you want a drink?"

"Why not? I'll have a Babycham for a change." Maureen put her sequinned evening bag on the table and sat down, looking around her. With the glittering silver ball rotating on the ceiling, and the generally festive atmosphere, she was already enjoying herself and wondered why she'd held out so long before coming. She'd gone with Carol regularly to the cinema, and they'd queued unsuccessfully for tickets to see the Beatles on tour at the De Montfort Hall, but she'd been hesitant about dancing. Perhaps, she reasoned, it had to be the right time. And it was, for she felt gloriously alive again, at last accepting that she was no longer married, but free to make a new future for herself. The divorce would take time and she itched to have it finalised, but she was determined not to live in a sort of limbo – my Catholicism coming to the fore, she thought ruefully – any longer. Feeling relaxed and happy, she watched the couples on the dance floor circling to the catchy rhythm of the new Bachelors' hit, 'Diane', until Carol returned with their drinks. "What do you think? The dance-floor's sprung, you know."

"I like it," Maureen said promptly. "Mind you –"

"I know, it's not as big as Trentham!"

"Who was it who said 'comparisons are odious'?" Maureen frowned, trying to remember.

"Don't ask me," Carol laughed. "You're the one who's always got her head in a book."

"Oscar Wilde," Maureen said triumphantly. "That's who it was."

"Whatever you say." Carol's eyes were scanning the room. "Can't see anyone very exciting."

"It's early yet. Anyway, I just want to enjoy the dancing, that's if anyone asks me."

"You speak for yourself," Carol muttered, and then her eyes lit up as two tall young men appeared and sat a table not too far away. "What do you think?" she hissed, her eyes darting in their direction.

Maureen turned, to find her eyes meeting those of Greg, who looked surprised, raised an eyebrow and smiled. She smiled back.

"Hey, do you know them?"

"Only the one on the right. He's the bloke who

gave me a lift last Sunday."

Carol's glance slid over Greg with disinterest. "What about his friend! He's gorgeous!"

Maureen glanced at him. "I see what you mean!" It was true, Greg's companion was incredibly hand- some, fair and with that same heart-stopping charisma that Trevor had. She tore her eyes away, but she had to admit to a flicker of attraction.

"Eyes off," Carol said promptly. "He's mine. You bagged Trevor, you've had your turn!"

Astounded, Maureen stared at her. "I never knew you fancied Trevor!"

"Sure did, so did Elaine. Mind you, we had a lucky escape if you're anything to go by." Carol looked hopefully at her friend, hoping yet again that she'd elaborate, but Maureen just gave a quiet smile, and sipped her drink.

Greg was answering his companion's questions. "I only know her slightly," he admitted. "I gave her a lift home from church last Sunday. It was raining."

"She's certainly attractive," Sean Murphy's eyes gleamed with interest.

"Out of bounds!" ordered Greg. "Remember, I'm your superior officer."

"You're not on duty now," Sean grinned. His gaze flickered over Carol. "Her friend's a looker too, but I don't usually go for blondes."

"Well, you're going to tonight! Come on," Greg got to his feet and Sean followed him over to the table where the girls were sitting. "Okay if we join you?" Greg asked, and both girls smiled their consent. "This is a coincidence," he said to Maureen. "This is Sean, by the way."

"Hi," Carol said, smiling brightly. "I'm Carol."

"Do you come here often?" Sean said, and then looked perplexed as they all fell about laughing.

"What's the matter?" His soft Irish brogue just made it more amusing. "Where've you been living?" Carol spluttered. "That chat-up line went out years ago."

"Ah, well, you see," he leaned forward, "aren't we in Ireland always behind the times?"

Maureen felt a gurgle of laughter at his teasing. His voice washed over her like liquid honey, and she watched the attractive Irishman surreptitiously beneath her lashes. Carol, on the other hand, made no secret of his attraction for her, her eyes challenging his, blatantly angling for an invitation to dance.

Greg coughed slightly, and Sean stood up smiling down at Carol, "Would you risk a turn on the floor with someone so out of date?"

She stood up with alacrity, and Greg and Maureen watched them go on to the dance floor, where within minutes Carol was laughing up at her partner. "Is he always like that?"

"Oh, Sean's kissed the Blarney Stone all right, but don't let that light-hearted manner fool you – he's a good colleague."

Maureen looked at him. "You work together?"

"We do. We're both in the police force."

Maureen was astounded. The only other policeman she'd known had been their local constable, known in the area as Bobby Tams. As a child she'd been tremendously awed by his height and commanding air of authority, especially when he wore his black cape, and one stern look had been enough to quell even the most rebellious child! "You don't look like a policeman," she muttered and then realised it was a stupid remark.

But Greg just smiled and gazed at her for a moment. He was wondering whether to remind her about London. But then he decided against it. It might embarrass her, and whatever had driven her to that café, it wasn't happiness, so why put a downer on the evening?

"Would you like to dance?"

They moved to the dance-floor, his arm encircling

Maureen's waist. They danced well together, their bodies moving in perfect rhythm to the slow foxtrot. Greg had to restrain himself from holding her too close. He needed to take things slowly. Experience had taught him that when you weren't born at the front of the queue with regard to looks, then personality had to be the attraction. And that took time. But he already knew it was time he was willing to spend, for Maureen had aroused his interest in a way he'd almost forgotten. Not since . . . but that was a door he didn't want to open.

Maureen was just enjoying the dancing, and Greg was good, there was no doubt about that. She liked him too, liked his unusual grey eyes. Something niggled at the back of her mind about those eyes, they seemed familiar in a way . . . "So," she smiled up at him. "You guessed I wasn't from Leicester – are you?"

"Born and bred," he said promptly. "I live not far from you, in Oadby."

"It wasn't such hardship for you to run me home, then," she teased.

"It wasn't any hardship at all."

He gazed down into her eyes, and at the expression in them Maureen looked away. He was nice, really nice, but she didn't feel any quiver of excitement. Now Sean – she glanced over Greg's shoulder, where the laughing Irishman was twirling Carol around – he was really dishy! Both couples eventually left the dance-floor, Maureen glowing with exhilaration. She'd always loved dancing, the movement and music elevated her mood. Feeling hot, she sat down gratefully.

"Right, girls, how about a drink?" Sean smiled down at them both.

"Lemon and lime, please?" Maureen glanced at Carol. "Twice."

"Cheap round," he laughed, and went off to buy the drinks.

Carol turned to watch him, while Greg leaned forward to offer Maureen a cigarette. She shook her head.

"No vices, then?"

"Not her," Carol said. She took one from the proffered packet. "Now me, I just can't seem to give them up."

For a few moments there was silence, as Greg and Carol relaxed with their smokes, while Maureen was content to watch the dancing.

"'Tis like a morgue at this table, without me," Sean joked when he returned.

Carol laughed, her eyes alight. It was obvious to

Maureen that her friend was smitten, and she couldn't blame her. Sean was not only handsome, but seemed to have a warm, fun-loving personality too. Unlike Trevor, despite his looks, she thought bitterly, then pushed the memory from her mind.

"Has he told you what they do for a living?" she said to Carol.

"Yeah," she said. "Can't imagine either of them as a PC49 though!"

Greg smiled. "I can't offer you that treat. We're CID."

"Detectives! I am impressed. We'd better watch our step, Maureen."

"He's the one to worry about," Sean said. "Fresh from the Met only six months ago."

Maureen looked at Greg with renewed interest, and then her lips began to curve in a smile he found utterly delightful. "You're not an Inspector, are you?" When Greg shook his head, she laughed. "I was just thinking – Inspector Barlow, like in Z Cars!" He grinned, and she added, "I bet you get sick of that joke."

"At times."

"My dad met Stratford Johns once – you know, the actor who plays him?" Maureen said. "His car had broken down, and Dad was passing so he gave him a push. He said he was really friendly."

"Is that your claim to fame?" grinned Sean. "Haven't I stood at a bar next to Joseph Locke?"

"Who?" Carol said.

Maureen nudged her. "He's an Irish tenor, my mum loves him."

"Not exactly your Beatle, then? Now if one of us had met Paul . . ." Carol's eyes went all dreamy.

"Ah, you'd be cradle-snatching," Sean chaffed.

"Oh, yes, and how old do you think I am?"

"The perfect age," he murmured, sliding his arm around her chair. "I like a touch of sophistication."

Catching Maureen's eye, Greg stood up and they went back to the dance floor. "Those two seem to be getting on well," she said. "Have you known him long?"

"About six months, ever since I moved back to Leicester." Greg smiled down at her, his eyes intent on hers. The band began to play 'Living Doll,' and as the vocalist belted the number, they began to twist, trying to outdo each other with exaggerated movements.

"He's no Cliff Richard," she gasped.

"No, but he's not bad, either." Greg managed to keep perfect balance as he went down to the floor, while Maureen laughed down at him. He *is* nice, she thought for the second time, and when the music stopped, said, "I never imagined a policeman doing such things as dancing and having fun. Daft, isn't it?"

He smiled at her. "Oh, '*scratch us and we bleed*', you know. We're just human like everyone else, only doing a job which can sometimes create a barrier."

Maureen thought about that, liking Greg's insight, and then Sean and Carol were joining them and the two couples moved off to a Frank Ifield hit, 'Wayward Wind'. Greg sang softly and Maureen joked, "Can you yodel like him, as well?"

"Would you like a demonstration?"

Greg opened his mouth wide, and she said hastily, "No, no, I was only joking!" She looked up at him with suspicion, and seeing the corners of his mouth twitch, accused, "You were just winding me up. And there I thought you were going to deafen the whole ballroom."

"Ah," he whispered, suddenly drawing her closer, "now you'll never know." His lips rested against her hair, his arm encircling her firmly, securely, protectively. Maureen relaxed into the embrace, somewhat surprised to find how happy she felt in the intimacy.

And that was how the evening progressed, the small group splitting into couples. Out of politeness,

Greg danced sometimes with Carol, and Maureen with Sean, whose banter and soft Irish lilt flowed over her head like music. A dangerous combination, she thought, with film-star looks as well. The term brought Trevor to mind again, and she felt a sense of disquiet, then mentally scolded herself. You can't go through life mistrusting every man who's good-looking, she thought. You might as well distrust all beautiful women.

Carol, waltzing by in Greg's arms, couldn't help glancing over to the other couple. She'd fallen for Sean in a big way, and felt a stab of anxiety tinged with jealousy as she watched him expertly steer Maureen around the ballroom. But then she reassured herself. There had always been an agreement between herself, Elaine and Maureen, that they didn't poach each other's boyfriends. For a second her mind clouded at the memory, as it often did when she thought of her lost childhood friend, and then she shrugged the memory away. Life was for the living. She smiled up at Greg. "You and Maureen seem to be getting on well."

"I could say the same about you and Sean," he countered.

Carol laughed. "I see, you're not giving anything away."

447

He looked down at her. "Have you known her long?"

"All my life," she said promptly. "We grew up together."

"You're from the Potteries, too?"

"Sure am," she said.

"Then what brought you to Leicester?"

Carol told him about her mother moving to be near her sister. "Then Auntie Elsie went and died on us," she said sadly, "but by then, we'd got settled, and decided to stay."

By the end of the evening, it was decided. Greg and Sean were both off duty the following day, and the plan was that a walk in Bradgate Park would be an ideal way of spending Sunday.

"We'll pick you both up after lunch," Greg promised. "Although maybe I'll see you at church?" He raised an eyebrow in question, smiling at Maureen.

"What a holy lot you are!" Carol grinned. "I suppose you go as well, do you, Sean?"

He grinned back. "If I can get out of bed early enough."

* * *

They were lucky with the weather, and it was in spring sunshine that the two girls watched Greg draw up in his Ford Anglia.

448

"What's so special about this Bradgate Park then?" Maureen asked as Greg drove expertly through the centre of Leicester, and headed out towards the Charnwood Forest. "I mean, Carol's told me there are wild deer there, but can you actually see them?"

"You usually can, if you know where to look," Greg said. "Sometimes you can see a small herd, sometimes just an odd one – they're shy creatures really."

"There's peacocks too, at the ruins," Carol said.

"Ruins?"

"The ruins of Lady Jane Grey's home, the fifteen-year-old queen who was beheaded," Greg said.

"Oh, I've always felt so sorry for her – she was pushed into the marriage from what I've read, by her ambitious parents."

"Maureen's a great reader," Carol explained.

Sean turned round and grinned. "Do I take it you're not?"

"Not me," Carol laughed. "I'm too busy living."

"Ah, a girl after me own heart!"

Carol looked pleased, while Maureen remained silent. She liked Greg, she really did, but as she sat in the back of the car, looking at the two young men, the comparison in their looks was stark. But then, she told herself, life is about learning through experience, and you should know better than anyone, that looks aren't everything. Her logic however, didn't prevent her casting an envious glance at Carol as, once they got out of the car, she instantly paired up with Sean.

Walking behind the other couple, Maureen and Greg walked side by side, Greg explaining something of the history of the beautiful, wild park, which covered over 850 acres. "It was bequeathed to the people of Leicester earlier this century by Charles Bennion, a local benefactor."

She looked over the expanse of moorland, and bracken-covered hills, listening intently while they walked.

"It's beautiful," she said, "and vast. I can't imagine one person owning all this."

"Not bad for your back garden," he said. "They certainly knew how to live."

"It didn't do *her* much good, did it though," Maureen said. "Lady Jane Grey, I mean." She stood for a moment, looking over the vista, trying to imagine herself as the tragic young queen. How many days was it she ruled? Nine. And this would have been the background against which she grew up. She must have walked and perhaps ridden on horseback, over the very ground under her feet.

With a feeling of sadness, Maureen recalled how all through history, highly born women had been used as pawns to further their family's political ambitions. All the riches in the world weren't worth the loss of your personal freedom.

Greg was looking down at her, entranced by the fleeting expressions passing across her oval face. With her jet-black hair blowing gently in the cool breeze and those unusual green eyes, she was the most attractive girl he'd ever seen. Suddenly he was assailed by self-doubt. Was he just storing up disillusionment? Would a girl like Maureen be content with an ordinary-looking man like himself? But then he mentally shrugged. He didn't care – he only knew that stupidly, impulsively, he had already fallen in love. In fact, he could trace the attraction back to that first time he'd seen her, when the memory of her face had lingered, elusive yet familiar. There was still that mystery to clear up, for the professional side of him couldn't forget the bewilderment and despair of the bedraggled girl at Euston, nor the danger that had threatened her.

Looking ahead Greg saw that Sean and Carol had left the main path and were climbing up towards one of the small craggy outcrops. He glanced behind him and saw that people were beginning to throng through the gates, eager for an afternoon walk. "Shall we get away from the crowds?" he suggested. "See if we can spot some deer?"

Maureen nodded, and as they turned Greg held out his hand and she took it, liking the feel of his cool skin, the firm way in which he guided her over the rough hillocks. Again she thought, I really do like him. And that was how they continued to walk, hand in hand, talking softly, taking pleasure in the crisp clean air, enjoying the views. Then Greg paused as they passed a walled spinney. "Ssh," he whispered, and stood behind her, his hands resting lightly on her shoulders, as between a cluster of trees she saw them. Three fallow deer, light underneath and with brown speckled backs, their heads dipping gracefully as they nuzzled the grass. One looked up and Maureen was near enough to see its soft brown eyes gaze at them curiously, before they began to move away.

"They're wonderful," she breathed, and for a moment leaned back against Greg, feeling the warmth of his body. For a few moments, she rested there, and Greg's arms moved down to her waist and he held her close. When she felt his lips move over her hair, something stirred inside her – a longing for physical closeness, for affection – it was, after all, ages since she'd experienced any form of intimacy. Just to be held like this filled her with reassurance, with pleasure. And again she thought, I really like him. Instinctively, fluidly, she turned into his embrace and, in the isolation of the grassy clearing, Greg kissed her. His lips were cold, as were her own, but that didn't hide the warmth and tenderness of his feelings. To her delight and surprise, Maureen felt an answering warmth of her own, and when their kiss ended she didn't draw away, content and happy to remain in his arms, her head against his shoulder. Then she looked up at him and they smiled, before linking hands again and continuing up the narrow path. In the distance they could see two figures waving, and Greg said, "There's Sean and Carol," and this time, Maureen didn't feel a pang of envy. Perhaps I've had enough of glamour, she thought, I just know that I'm more than happy to be holding Greg's hand.

When they joined the others, it was to find them tussling, Carol giggling at something Sean was whispering in her ear, and for a moment Maureen felt years older than them both. Will it ever come again, she thought, that carefree light-hearted sensation? Or did you carry around forever the weight of your past traumas? Fleetingly she thought of Frank, of his serious outlook on life, and wondered what horrors he'd seen during his active service. Although he often reminisced about his life in the Forces, he'd never told them any details about the actual fighting, and for the first time Maureen thought she understood why. Some memories were best buried – like the ugliness of Elaine's death. Then Greg gave her hand a squeeze and smiled down at her, his grey eyes querying as though he'd sensed her change of mood, and she smiled back. "They're like a pair of kids," she whispered, and he laughed.

"He doesn't believe me," Carol said, her eyes alight with merriment. She looked at Greg. "I've been telling him what they say about these ancient oak-trees."

"Oh, you mean the local legend that when Lady Jane Grey was beheaded in 1554, the oaks of Bradgate were also 'beheaded'?" He grinned. "See how good at history I am? But it's true, Sean. And remember the estate was huge in those days. There's even an area near here called Copt Oak. Get it – 'copt' which would have come from 'cropped'?"

Maureen laughed. "I should think to an Irishman, that legend is nothing compared with yours."

"Ah," he said with mock seriousness, "sure they aren't legends – they're all true!"

The wind was turning colder, and eventually they made their way back to the carpark. As the other two went ahead, Greg asked Maureen if she was on the phone.

She shook her head. "No, but you can ring me at work, if you like. We're not really supposed to have private calls, but you can pretend you're a customer."

"I see," he protested. "You're trying to entice me into a life of crime, is that it?"

She laughed, and then as their eyes met again, she thought. I've changed my mind, he *is* attractive, to me anyway.

CHAPTER THIRTY-FIVE

Sandra, who Maureen wrote to regularly, soon noticed how frequently the word 'Greg' began to appear in her letters. Maureen wrote to Frank and Beryl too, but her letters to her sister were more chatty and informative. So it was to Sandra that the family turned for news of this intriguing new development in Maureen's life.

"A policeman, eh?" Vera barked one Sunday afternoon. "Well, I hope he hasn't got big feet!"

"Don't be coarse, our Vera," Nellie rebuked. "She gets worse," she said to Beryl, "not fit for decent company sometimes."

"Rubbish. Beryl might never have worked on a potbank, but she's bound to have heard that one!" Vera looked miffed.

"Maybe, but it's one thing on the factory floor,

and another in your own front room!"

Beryl listened to them bicker with a tolerant smile. She only hoped that Maureen had learned that character was more important than looks.

"What do you think about it, Beryl?" Nellie asked.

"Well," she said slowly, "she didn't mention this Greg until she'd known him a couple of months, but now Sandra says they seem to be seeing each other all the time. I can't say I feel comfortable about her going out with someone else, not when she's still legally married."

Nellie shook her head. "She's young, Beryl. You can't expect her to sit in every night. But I wish we knew went wrong with her and Trevor," she complained.

"It's no good looking at me, I haven't a clue!" Beryl began to busy herself with collecting up the cups. "Anyone for more tea, or needn't I ask!"

Getting up, Beryl took the tray into the kitchen and put the kettle on. All this time, and still Maureen had never said a word. There was Trevor, living in that new house, the house that Maureen had worked hard to help buy and furnish, and where was her girl? Sleeping in a poky back room and working in a strange city. It was a funny life, Beryl thought crossly, as she rinsed out the cups and saucers and dried them. Who would have thought any of this would happen? You brought your children up and naturally expected them to live close by, to be able to pop in and see them regularly, and now weeks went by without seeing Maureen. She didn't always have Saturday off, but sometimes she would come home, travelling by train, and that was lovely, because she stayed overnight. Beryl paused as she recalled how pleased Frank had been when, on these visits, Maureen offered to go to Mass with him. But his policy had been that it was best not to make an issue of it.

"There's no need to say anything," he told her. "You'd just embarrass the girl. Nothing would please me more than if she came back to the Church, but I want her to do so for the right reasons – not because of any pressure from us. And there's no need to keep talking about the divorce either – she'll bring the subject up herself if she wants to."

Beryl had bristled at the time, but in her heart she knew her husband was right. But when they travelled by car to visit her in Leicester, it had to be a day-trip, for there was nowhere for them to stay. Once she'd suggested that they book into a small hotel, but Frank had thought she was mad.

"It'd cost a fortune," he'd complained, but Beryl

suspected his reaction had more to do with his reluctance to sleep in any bed but his own. That was why they always went on day trips in the summer, rather than take proper holidays.

"Did you say John was thinking of buying a car?" Vera asked, when she returned.

"Yes," Beryl said, cutting them both another piece of Nellie's fruitcake. "They'd be able to go and see Maureen then, and take the children. Speaking of which, when are you two coming again?"

Vera looked at Nellie, who looked discomforted. "I don't know, love. I did enjoy it last time, but we both felt so tired when we got home. It's a long way at our age."

"I suppose you're right." Beryl looked at them both, reluctantly accepting that they weren't getting any younger. But, thank God, there was nothing much wrong with their health apart from a bit of arthritis, and in Nellie's case, a weak chest.

* * *

Maureen continued to see Greg regularly over the summer months, and whenever he wasn't on duty, they spent every minute they could together. Carol too, was immersed in a relationship with Sean, and would jokingly refer to the two young men as 'our bobby dazzlers'. Sometimes they would team up as a foursome and go dancing, or out for a drink, but most of the time each couple preferred to spend time alone.

Freda was taking a keen interest in it all. She was a great believer in observing the interaction between couples, and naturally her main concern was for her own daughter. Carol was obviously mad about Sean, and Freda couldn't blame her – he really was a devastatingly attractive young man. He had a highly developed sense of fun too, which Carol shared, and as the weeks turned into months, slowly Freda began to relax. Too much charm, she'd always thought, could hide insincerity, but although she'd been wary and distrustful at first, she realised that beneath it all Sean was a realistic and intelligent young man. Could it be that Carol had met the right man at last? That would solve everything, as Vincent was beginning to talk about marriage.

"She's a grown woman, Freda," he'd said when she told him she worried about Carol. "She's got to let go of your apron strings at some time."

That's not the point, Freda thought. It's my letting go of that sense of responsibility, which weighs particularly heavy when you've had to carry it alone. Now, if Carol was engaged, and I could see her making a future for herself, then I could go ahead with a clear conscience.

* * *

Sarah Barlow, whose keenly observant eyes had watched her son's elevated mood since the spring, was becoming restless. "When am I going to meet this girl?" she said, not for the first time.

Greg sighed. How could he explain that he sensed Maureen wasn't ready yet for a serious commitment. And bringing her home to meet his mother wasn't a good idea, not yet. Ever conscious of Sarah's precarious health, Greg never forgot for a moment the consultant's parting words, when she'd been discharged from hospital.

"With proper care your mother can look forward to many more years," he'd told him. "But any distress or trauma could have serious consequences – she needs to be kept on an even keel."

And Greg was careful. He said little about his job at home, making light of his work, implying that his was mainly a desk job. Sarah allowed him the illusion of thinking that she believed him. She was well aware of her medical condition and had managed to develop a mental discipline which allowed her to blank out worrying thoughts. She wasn't ready to die yet – her ambition was to hold at least one grandchild in her arms before then, which was one reason she was keen to see Greg settle down.

Greg's concern was that if he brought Maureen home, and Sarah became fond of her, came to look on her as a future daughter-in-law, then it would upset her deeply if the relationship didn't work out. He remembered only too well how his mother had wept when he and Anne had split up.

So now, he just teased her, saying, "I've got to let her get used to my ugly mug before I expose her to yours!"

"Oh, go on with you!" She gave him a playful push, but as she watched him go, her brow creased in concern. It was three years since he and Anne had broken up – only a month before the day they'd been due to get married. It had been a terrible time, coming as it did just after his father's death. At the time, Sarah hadn't understood why Anne, a quiet, friendly girl of whom she'd grown fond, had changed her mind. She'd said it was because of Greg's unsocial working hours – with a father in the fire brigade she'd seen how disruptive it was to family life. As Greg had been a policeman when she'd met him, Sarah was scornful of the excuse, and still hadn't forgiven her for hurting her son so much. Her scepticism had been justified, as within three weeks Anne became openly involved with someone else. Now, after immersing himself in his work for so long, Greg had a new spring to his step, joy in his eyes again, and Sarah was intensely curious about the young woman who had wrought such a change. But, she thought with a sigh, I'll just have to be patient.

Of his feelings for Maureen, Greg had no doubts. He was in love with her – what did they call it, 'head over heels' in love. Hardly a description for a steady detective, he thought wryly. He'd never felt like this before about anyone, not even Anne. And he wanted to marry the girl he laughingly called 'his Potteries lass'. Not that he'd proposed yet, or even told Maureen how much he loved her. Greg's nature was a cautious one, and he was well aware that the initial attraction between them hadn't been mutual. He didn't want to put any pressure on her; this relationship was too important for that.

Maureen, however, knew exactly how Greg felt about her. It showed in his every movement, the way his eyes would light up when he saw her, the restrained passion she sensed in him when he held her in his arms. Her own emotions were much more complex. *Was she* in love with Greg? She knew she relished the ease she felt in his company – he wasn't moody like Trevor, she didn't feel that she had to impress or take care not to upset him. When he held her in his arms she returned his kisses with warmth and when, as was increasingly happening, his love-making became more passionate, she found her own response equalled his. They would sit entwined in his car, or, on an evening when Freda and Carol were out, on the sofa in the front room. Then they would play records and dance slowly to the music, her arms around Greg's neck, his around her waist, usually just content to be close, but lately she'd sensed a new intensity in him.

He'd spoken fondly of his parents, of his concern for his widowed mother and one evening as they were sitting quietly together, had told her what had happened with Anne.

"We were due to get married, and then a month before the wedding she told me she'd changed her mind. Couldn't face my unsociable hours, but of course that was just an excuse. She'd met someone else, it was as simple as that."

The pain in his voice as he described how devastated he'd been had touched Maureen deeply, making her realise just how much she cared for this man. And caring for him as deeply as she did, she was worried that she might lose him. For she had made an unbelievably stupid blunder.

Now, as the weeks passed, Maureen would lie

awake in her narrow, single bed, staring at the ceiling, bitterly regretting her foolishness in not being honest with Greg from the beginning. She didn't know why she'd held back. And as the days turned into weeks and then months, it had become more and more difficult. Once, she'd nearly told him – that had been the night he'd told her about Anne, but somehow the moment had passed, and now, Maureen was afraid. Afraid of his reaction, knowing that she'd misled him. And the fact that he was a Catholic made it even worse. There were many sins, and lying was one of them. The fact that her own was a 'a sin of omission' was no excuse.

For how would Greg – a man who prided himself on his integrity – react when he found out that the girl with whom he'd shared laughter and tenderness, the girl he'd held in his arms and kissed so passionately, had not only been a married woman but was still not free?

CHAPTER THIRTY-SIX

Maureen's deception was also causing Carol concern. "If you haven't told him by the time I get back from Ireland, I will!" she threatened.

The two girls were sitting in the front room, their favourite magazines scattered on the coffee table, sharing a box of chocolates, and Maureen, taking the glass of sherry that Carol offered, knew that the other girl meant what she said.

Unlike Maureen, Carol had no doubts about *her* feelings. She wanted to marry Sean, she was crazy about him, and although as yet he hadn't proposed – after all it was only a few months – she knew the fact that he was taking her over to meet his family was highly significant.

"I've been telling you for ages about it," she said with bitterness. Carol had struggled with her own conscience on many occasions, her loyalty to Maureen warring with her desire not to deceive Sean. He and Greg were not only loyal colleagues, they were good friends. Why, Sean even went sometimes to have Sunday lunch with Greg's mother. He was bound to think badly of her, would think she'd been a willing partner to the deception.

"I simply don't understand you!" she went on in exasperation. "I still don't know why you didn't tell him that first Sunday when we went to Bradgate Park!" She shook her head slowly. "It's just not like you, Maureen – it amounts to telling lies, you know."

"I know." Nothing Carol could say could make Maureen feel any worse. "I suppose I never saw it as being a long-term thing, you know, at first," she tried to explain in despair. "And then when I realised I was falling for him . . ." and as she said the words, Maureen realised that it was true. She *did* love Greg, she didn't know why she'd been trying to deny it to herself. "It's no excuse, but I suppose I was afraid he'd lose interest," she said lamely. "I thought the fact that I'd been married would put him off." She looked with misery at Carol. "And now I've let it get this far! It's getting serious between us."

Carol leaned forward. "If he loves you, he'll

understand. Lots of men marry women who've been married before."

"Widows, maybe."

Carol hesitated and then said. "Look, you've never said why you left Trevor —" She held up a hand. "Don't look like that, I know it's your business and no-one else's. But it wasn't as though you had an affair or anything," she looked quickly at Maureen to see her shake her head, "so why do you feel so ashamed about it?"

"It's a terrible thing, to desert your husband." The words were said in a flat tone, and Carol was disconcerted to see the shame in Maureen's eyes.

"No, it isn't — times have changed," Carol said staunchly. "Twenty, or thirty, years ago, maybe. But not now."

Maureen looked at her in despair. "It isn't only that, Carol. It's more complicated."

Carol frowned. "I'm not with you."

"Even if Greg forgives me for not telling him straightaway, my being divorced — and I will be in two years — is going to spoil everything! He's a Catholic, Carol, and he'll want to get married in a Catholic church."

Carol stared at her. "You mean . . ."

Maureen said quietly. "No priest will marry a

couple where one of them has been divorced."

"Bloody hell! You have got yourself a problem!" Carol sat back on the sofa, staring at the other girl. "You are an idiot," she said. "You've really made a rod for your own back."

"You don't have to tell me," Maureen said bitterly. "I think I must have been on the back row when brains were given out."

"Poor Greg," Carol said softly. "I feel really sorry for him – what a shock!"

"Don't rub it in. I feel terrible about it. I should never have gone out with him in the first place," Maureen said. "I should have found myself an atheist."

"You can't choose who you fall in love with."

"Maybe not, but you can use a bit of common sense!" Maureen drew up her legs and held a cushion against herself for comfort. She couldn't avoid it any longer – Greg was going to have to be told.

CHAPTER THIRTY-SEVEN

As Greg drew up outside the door of the Farmers' house, three days later, he was looking forward to a trip to the cinema to see the James Bond film, *Dr No*. He'd missed the showing of it the previous year, and was hoping it would take his mind off a particularly seedy case he was working on. The evidence was enough to make anyone despair of human behaviour, but Greg was determined to keep his faith in the finer aspects of human nature. Good would always triumph over evil in the end – he had to believe that. Eager to see Maureen again, he gave a quick knock on the front door, and waited impatiently for her to answer.

"Mmn," he said, as he stepped inside the narrow hall and held her close. "You smell nice!"

Maureen returned his kiss and then turned away,

going into the sitting-room.

Greg followed. "Are you ready?" He glanced at his watch. "There's bound to be a queue."

Maureen swallowed. Her mouth and throat were dry with anxiety. She'd woken up at five that morning, and as the early morning sunlight filtered through the unlined curtains, had tossed and turned, desperately trying to find the right words. But there weren't any – no amount of sensitivity was going to mask the enormity of her deception. What had made her do it? Why on earth hadn't she been straight with Greg from the beginning? Even now she couldn't understand how she'd allowed all this time to drag on. She'd tried to make excuses for herself, reasoning that she *was* free in a way: after all she and Trevor were separated. But it was no use, nothing could make her feel any less guilty. And now that she'd nerved herself to tell him the truth, she needed desperately to get it over with.

She turned to face him. "Do you mind if we stay in, instead?"

He looked at her with concern. "Aren't you feeling well?"

"No, it's not that. I want to talk to you."

Greg, his trained perceptions finely tuned, heard the strain in her voice and was instantly wary.

"What's wrong?" Maureen didn't answer. Instead she went to sit a distance away from him on an armchair.

Puzzled, Greg sat on the sofa facing her, and waited. "This sounds ominous," he said, trying to keep his voice light.

Maureen looked at him, and at the stricken look in her eyes he felt as though a light had gone out in his world. He'd been fooling himself to believe that she felt as he did, that they were meant to spend the rest of their life together. And yet Greg could have sworn that she loved him. Surely he couldn't have misjudged their relationship so badly? And then came the memory of Anne, and ice closed around his heart.

"I just want to say that I'm really sorry, Greg. I don't know why I did it!"

"Did what? Maureen, what's the matter?"

"You're going to hate me," she said and her eyes, full of misery, met his.

"I'll be the judge of that," he said quietly. "Come on, tell me. Let's get it over with." Greg thought he knew exactly what she was going to say. Oh, Maureen would be gentle, kind even, and she was obviously distressed by her decision. But she was going to tell him it was over, and he didn't know if he was going to be able to bear it.

"I haven't been truthful with you, Greg." Maureen looked at him with despair. "There's something I should have told you, right at the beginning. Only I never thought it would get serious between us – not like it has."

Greg stared at her, a flicker of hope in his mind. Could it be that he was mistaken? Was it that at last, after all these months, Maureen had nerved herself to tell him about her past? What was behind that scene at Euston? But what could she have done which was so terrible that she expected him to hate her? His policeman's mind immediately wondered whether she'd been in trouble with the law, but then he dismissed the thought as quickly as it had come. Not Maureen – he'd stake his reputation on it. He waited for her to continue. Whatever she was going to tell him it was obviously taking all her courage.

"As a Catholic, you'll know what I mean by a 'sin of omission'," she said, attempting a weak smile. "It's not when you actually do something wrong, it's when you fail to do something right. Am I correct?"

"Perfectly," he said.

She took a deep breath. "I should have told you this, Greg, that first night at the Palais, or at least the following day when we went to Bradgate Park, and you first kissed me." Opening her handbag, Maureen took out her wedding ring, and turned silently to him. She held out her left hand, and unsteadily slid the plain gold band on to the third finger.

"I don't think of myself as married," she said, almost in a whisper, "and I'll be divorced in another two years. But I've deceived you, Greg. I'm not free."

Stunned, at first he could only stare at the wedding ring on her finger and then he lifted his eyes to her face to see both shame and embarrassment. Married? How could she be married? He just couldn't take it in. As the silence grew, Maureen's emotions, so desperately kept under control, threatened to overwhelm her. She got up, muttering in a strangled voice, "Excuse me," and rushed out of the room.

Confessing her deception to Greg had been even worse than she'd imagined, and leaning against the banisters in the hall, she struggled to stop herself from weeping, but it was hopeless - the tears came anyway. Greg sat motionless once she'd left the room. Married! The word wouldn't go away, he couldn't seem to think past it. Never had he imagined that this might be her secret, that there might be a husband somewhere. How could she not tell him? How could she let him go on, all these months, believing her to be one person, when in fact she was another? And then he thought, what would I have done if she *had* told me? Attracted as strongly as I was – would I have carried on seeing her? And to that question he hadn't an answer; after all so much depended on the circumstances of the divorce. Stunned by what she'd just told him, he got up and began to pace the room, still trying to make sense of it all. And the basic question remained – why hadn't she told him?

Eventually, Maureen returned. "Why?" he asked, his eyes full of pain. "Why keep it a secret?"

"I didn't," she said miserably. "At least not intentionally. It's just that I never expected to . . . what I mean is, when we first met, I thought it was going to be a casual friendship. I don't go around, Greg, telling everyone I meet about . . ."

"About who, Maureen? Are you going to tell me his name? Or is that a mystery, too?"

She flinched at the anger in his voice and looked away. "Trevor."

"Trevor. And where is Trevor now?"

She shrugged. "At home, I suppose, in Stoke-on-Trent. I haven't seen or heard from him for a year."

"How long were you married?"

"Four years."

He stared at her – four years? The words twisted in his gut. How could he have spent all these months with this girl, feeling so close to her, thinking he knew her? Four years was a huge chunk of anyone's life.

"I don't know," Maureen agonised, almost in tears, "I don't know why I didn't tell you – I can't explain it – not even to myself. Time just seemed to go on and then, because I'd delayed, it got harder and harder, until it became a mountain."

Greg leaned back on the sofa, closing his eyes, as he tried to marshal his thoughts into some form of order. Forget your personal involvement, he told himself, you can't reason through emotion. He needed to get to the truth, to find out what had been going on in Maureen's life, the history behind the scene at Euston. And then there was the fact she was going to be divorced. On what grounds?

But first of all, there was one question he wanted to ask, and he made it direct.

"What made you decide – gave you the courage – to tell me now?"

Maureen said simply, "Because I love you."

Despite himself, Greg's heart filled with joy. But then, just as swiftly, his mind overruled it. There were too many unanswered questions. He looked at her, and Maureen's eyes met his, silently pleading for understanding, but Greg kept his expression impassive.

"So," he said, "if you love me, are you going to tell me all about it? The whole truth, Maureen, please."

She looked down, unable to meet his eyes. What was she going to do? How could she explain why she'd – and she winced inwardly at the term – deserted her husband? Was she now to going to break the promise she'd made to Trevor as well? The promise on the basis of which he'd agreed to set her free, to divorce her?

Miserably, she sat in silence, until Greg could stand it no longer.

"What is it?" he said. "Have you done something so terrible you can't tell me? Did he have an affair? Did you?"

Maureen shook her head. "No, nothing like that."

"What then? You obviously got married very young . . ."

"Eighteen. We got married before Trevor went to do his National Service. He'd been deferred before, to qualify as a chartered accountant."

"And what happened?"

"He was posted abroad – to Germany, not long

after the wedding. He was away for two years, and when he came back . . ." She faltered, unsure how to continue.

Greg, whose interrogatory skills were legendary in the force, probed further. "Had he changed after living in another country, become a different person from the one you knew before?"

She thought about that, and answered honestly, "Not really."

Greg thought about the domestic violence cases he dealt with, and hoping desperately that her answer would be negative, said, "Trevor didn't knock you about, did he?"

Shocked, she said, "Oh, no. Never."

"Did he drink? Was that the problem?"

She shook her head.

Greg looked at her and, despite his misgivings, ached to hold her close, tell it didn't matter, that he loved her. He hated to see her in such distress, although he couldn't understand her indecision. It wasn't like Maureen, at least the Maureen he knew. But then, he asked himself wryly, did he really know her at all?

"We aren't getting anywhere, Maureen," he said at last. "You don't seem to want to tell me, so I'll ask you straight out. On what grounds are you going to be divorced?"

She looked at him, and said in a flat tone, "My desertion."

Greg looked at her with disquiet. So, she had left him. And he'd bet anything that was the day he'd seen her at Euston. Now if her husband wasn't violent, unfaithful or an alcoholic, what on earth had driven her to take such desperate action?

"Was it money?" he said. "Had you got yourself in debt?"

Suddenly, Maureen knew she couldn't let this go on. She gazed at Greg, seeing the strength in his face, thinking of his steadfastness, his integrity, and knew without doubt that he was a man she could trust with her confidence. And in that moment, Maureen realised how deeply she loved him. Her future was at stake, their future was at stake, and she knew that if they were to have a life together, it needed to be founded on truth.

Greg, watching her closely, saw with relief the doubt and uncertainty in her eyes fade away, and when she straightened her back, and moved slightly in her chair to face him, he knew there would be no more evasion.

"It's all right, Greg," she said. "You don't have to keep questioning me, and no, it was nothing to do with money." She held out her hands helplessly. "I just don't know where to begin."

"Try the beginning." He sat back on the sofa, crossed his legs, and tried to look calm and relaxed. But underneath he was far from it, as relief warred with apprehension of what he was about to hear.

"I was seventeen when I met him," Maureen said. "And he was twenty-two. We got married a year later before he went to do his National Service. My parents were against it, they thought I was too young, but I wouldn't listen. I was too infatuated with his film-star looks. He was incredibly good-looking, still is, I suppose." Her lips twisted. "It's true what they say – you shouldn't judge a book by its cover. It went wrong right from the start." She paused, colour rising in her cheeks at the thought of what she had to describe. "Let's just say I spent most of our wedding night in tears." Seeing the muscles in Greg's face tighten, she added quickly, "It wasn't that he was violent or anything. He just . . . I was a virgin, Greg, he knew that. But he showed me no tenderness, no love. It was cold, brutal, and all over in seconds. I was so hurt, so bitterly disappointed." She saw the anger in Greg's eyes, and forced herself to continue. "He never touched me for the rest of the honeymoon. Then he went away to Germany for

480

sixteen months. But when he came back, nothing had changed. In all the time we were married, I can count on one hand the number of times . . . I began to wonder if it was me, if I wasn't attractive enough." Tears of humiliation pricked at her eyes, and she brushed them away. "It was only when I told him I wanted a baby, that the truth came out. We had this huge row and he told me that he found sex degrading – 'like animals,' was the phrase he used."

Greg, appalled, could only stare at her. What sort of man had she married, for God's sake?

"I felt so humiliated," Maureen's voice was almost a whisper. "Then," she looked up at him, her eyes full of distress, "he told me that side of our marriage was over, and any baby I had would certainly not be his. Those words killed any love I ever had for him. I was twenty-three, Greg. I felt as though I'd been given a prison sentence."

The only words that entered Greg's mind were: the cruel bastard! "What happened then?" he asked quietly. Seeing the pain in her eyes, he hated putting her through this, but he needed to know everything.

She told him of her gradual decline into depression, how she'd lived in a 'twilight world'. "I was just going through the outward motions of living," she said. "But inside I was dead, feeling nothing. Then,

one morning, something must have snapped." She
went on to explain how she'd caught a train
standing at the platform at Stoke Station, how she'd
sat in despair and confusion in the café on Euston
Station. "It was only when I heard someone ask
where they could catch a train to Leicester, that I
thought about Carol. Even now," she said, "some of
it is blurred."

Greg leaned forward. "How much?" he asked
gently. "Do you remember the woman who came and
sat at your table, told you about her bed and breakfast place?"

"Yes," she said slowly, "I do." Then her eyes
widened. "How do you know that?"

Greg, his eyes holding her gaze, repeated in a
stern tone the words he'd used that afternoon.

*"Don't ever accept hospitality offered you by a
stranger, particularly on a railway station."*

Maureen put a hand to her mouth as she remembered a pair of steely grey eyes boring into her, the
man in a raincoat, the man whose image until now
had remained fuzzy.

"It was you!" she gasped.

He nodded. "When I first saw you in church, I
knew I'd seen you somewhere before, and then
that day when you got caught in the rain, and your

hair . . ."

"Looked like rat's tails – you remembered!"

"Something like that," and for the first time that evening, he smiled. And the fact that he could smile took him by surprise. Because the story he'd just heard was one of mental cruelty. His instinctive reaction was one of compassion but, still raw from the shock of finding out she was married, he reined in his emotions.

"I can't believe it. I can't believe I didn't recognise you!"

"The mind, particularly when it's troubled, can play strange tricks." Greg looked down at his hands, and for a moment there was silence.

"*No-one knows*, Greg. I promised Trevor I wouldn't tell anyone the real reason why I left, the reason I wanted a divorce. It was the only way I could get him to agree to it. And," she looked at him sadly, "I thought I owed him that loyalty, at least. It's been really hard though. I know my family have been hurt, they can't understand why I'm being so secretive."

"I can imagine. But you've told me."

"Yes." Her voice was low yet there was a wealth of meaning in that one word.

It conveyed so much, and Greg turned his head

away, not wanting her to see how it had moved him.

"You'll probably need time to think about it all, Greg. I know that if our positions were reversed, that's what I'd want. Look – I'll make you a coffee before you go."

Maureen stood up, knowing that if she stayed another minute in the room, she would be in tears again. Even so, she spooned coffee into cups with blurred eyes and had to lean against the sink unit for a moment in an effort to pull herself together. The whole evening had been a tremendous strain. Not only the confession that she was married, but having to sit with Greg facing her, while she tried to explain, make him understand, the reason she'd left her husband. Maureen had found it incredibly difficult to talk about Trevor in such intimate detail. She still felt a sense of betrayal, and was miserably aware that her conscience would trouble her for some time. But, she'd had no choice.

Greg, once Maureen had left the room, buried his head in his hands. There was just so much to take in, and although if he'd been working his brain would have been able to disseminate the facts, to see clearly what had to be done, this situation was entirely different. Aware that his judgement was clouded by emotion, Greg knew that Maureen's suggestion about needing time made sense.

"Thanks," he said as, when she returned, he took the cup of coffee from her. "And thank you for telling me."

"It wasn't easy," she said.

"No."

They drank their coffee in silence, and then Greg got up.

Maureen stood up at the same time, realising that he was leaving. Was he going so soon – without a word? Leaving her up in the air?

Her consternation showed on her face, and seeing it Greg put out a hand and touched her hair. "I know we need to talk more about this," he said, "but if you could just be patient? You were right – I do need time."

Maureen gazed up at him and he kissed her briefly. "I'll be in touch."

A few seconds later, he was gone.

CHAPTER THIRTY-EIGHT

On the following Sunday afternoon, Maureen walked disconsolately in the August sunshine across Victoria Park. Over the past week, each day had been one of anxiety as she'd tried to concentrate on her work, only to tense each time the phone rang. But since what she thought of as ' that night', Greg hadn't made contact. And, to her bitter disappointment, neither had he been at Holy Cross that morning, although that wasn't unusual.

But it wasn't only the situation with Greg that was lowering Maureen's spirits. Increasingly, she was becoming restless about her job. She liked dealing with the general public, liked the girls she worked with and the store, but she was becoming bored, knew she needed something more demanding. But as always, she was only too aware that her lack of qualifications held her back. Acutely conscious of Bernard's five hundred pounds sitting in the Trustees Savings Bank, Maureen was beginning to feel increasingly ashamed of her childish phobia about taking exams. She missed her family too, missed seeing Sandra and the children, watching them grow up. Oh, you're just a bit homesick, she scolded herself and squaring her shoulders, increased her ambling pace to a brisker walk. Carol was due back from Ireland in a couple of hours – hearing about that would take her mind of things.

But Carol's first words were: "Did you tell him?"

Maureen nodded. "Yes, I did. Do you want a cup of tea, you must be shattered."

Carol threw herself on the sofa and kicked off her shoes. "I am. But it was absolutely fabulous. Still, I can tell you all about that later. What did he say?"

Maureen paused before going into the kitchen. "I don't know. What I mean is – he didn't actually say anything – just that he needed time."

Carol propped a cushion behind her head, leaned back and closed her eyes. Of course the bloke needed time! So did she – time to tell Sean, because she knew it was vital that Sean heard the story from herself, and for that she needed to see him before

Greg did! Men might discuss their problems in the same way that women did. Carol wasn't sure, but she couldn't afford to take the chance. As she stretched her feet, thankful that she hadn't suffered seasickness on the ferry from Holyhead, she yawned. It had been a long and tiring journey, but she wouldn't have missed it for anything. Sean's parents lived in Dublin, and she'd loved the capital city, with its vibrancy and history. He'd taken her to see the Book of Kells, they'd walked hand in hand through Stephen's Green, drank Guinness in bars where she'd become misty-eyed at the Irish music and ballads – even now the words of 'The Fields of Athenry', lingered in her mind. Sean's parents had been so warm and welcoming – they'd liked her, she was sure of it. With a happy smile on her lips, she looked up as Maureen returned with a plate of sandwiches and coffee.

"Mmn. Cheese and pickle, my favourite." She bit into one eagerly. "Go on," she urged, as she chewed her first mouthful. "Tell me about it, then."

"It was awful," Maureen said. "But I've only got myself to blame. There's nothing to tell really. He just listened – he didn't lose his temper or anything."

"But you don't know what the fall-out will be?"

Maureen shook her head. "It's only been three

days." She looked at the other girl, and gave a despairing shrug. "Whatever it is, I'll have to cope with it." Then, with an effort she smiled and said, "Enough about me, tell me all about Ireland."

* * *

Sarah Barlow was well aware that her son was wrestling with a problem. Always, from a small boy, his brow would crease into a frown when something troubled him, and now that frown was permanently there. Even when he joined her to watch *Armchair Theatre*, which they both loved, his expression didn't change. So, she waited, all the time watching him covertly. When one week merged into two, and he spent more and more time at home, she decided it was time to do a bit of probing.

"Hold this for me, will you?" she said one evening, handing him a skein of wool.

Greg dutifully complied and with the pale blue wool looped over his hands stretched his arms wide so his mother could wind it into a ball. If only the villains could see me now, he thought with a wry smile. Talk about Barlow, the scourge of the criminal fraternity!

"Are you not seeing Maureen any more?" she asked, keeping her eyes on her task.

Greg said quietly, "Not at the moment."

489

"Oh?"

The tentative question hung in the air between them, until Greg said with awkwardness, "It's just that I've had some thinking to do."

Sarah looked up at him, catching him unawares and saw the pain in his eyes. "I'm always here, you know," she said gently, "if you think talking about it would help."

Greg gazed at her for a moment. They had always been close, but much as he valued his mother's sound common sense, it seemed rather pathetic for a man of his age to burden her with his problems. Yet, his mind was on a treadmill, with the thoughts circling unceasingly.

Almost as if she'd read his thoughts, Sarah said, "I'm not made of glass, you know. Sometimes, just putting a problem into words, talking about it, can make you see things more clearly. Thinking too much can get you bogged down, so that you can't see the wood for the trees."

Greg remained silent for few moments, his hands moving automatically in swaying rhythm until Sarah finished winding her wool. There was certainly no-one else he could talk to about such a personal matter. Although of course, he wouldn't betray Maureen's confidence, not even to his mother.

Greg hesitated, "Maureen told me something," he said, "the last time I saw her, and I'm still trying to come to terms with it."

Sarah's immediate reaction was one of anger. Was it going to happen again? Was this to be another repetition of the Anne episode? "I'd thought," she said, "that things might have been getting serious between you."

Greg nodded. "They were – are." He looked at her. "I just wanted to be sure of her feelings before I brought her to meet you." Looking down at his hands he said, "I didn't want another Anne episode. I know how much that upset you."

"And are you?" Sarah asked. "Sure of her feelings?"

He nodded, and she saw his expression soften. "Yes, I am."

It's not that, then, Sarah thought, relief flooding through her. She waited patiently, watching Greg search for the right words.

"She told me she was married," he said at last.

Sarah stared at him. Married? All this time, he'd been going out with a married woman? Profoundly shocked, her first instinct was to tell Greg not to have anything more to do with the girl, but she managed to suppress the angry words. Greg needed a listening ear, not recriminations.

"I don't understand," she said. "I thought she was living with Carol and her mother."

"She is." Greg looked at her. "She left her husband a year ago."

"Is she legally separated?"

He shook his head. "No. Trevor – that's his name – is divorcing her for desertion. It will be another couple of years before that can happen."

Sarah felt dumbfounded. "And she never told you? All this time?"

"No, not a word. Maureen says she never thought our relationship would develop the way it has." He glanced at her wryly. "After all, I suppose I'm not the sort of bloke you fall for at first sight. And then it just became too difficult."

"So Carol must have known . . . and she never told Sean either?"

"If she did, he's never mentioned it."

Sarah thought. "I think he would have done," she said finally. "It's too serious a matter for him to keep it to himself."

They both sat in silence for a few minutes, then Sarah asked, "How long was she married?"

"Four years, but he was away for the first two, doing his National Service."

"Did she tell you what went wrong? Why she left him?"

Greg didn't answer immediately. This was the difficult one. Eventually he said, "She did, Mum, but I can't tell you. Maureen told me in strict confidence – not even her own parents know."

Perplexed, Sarah gazed at her son. Similar questions to those Greg had asked Maureen hovered on her lips, but she recognised it was not her place to interrogate him. If he was respecting the girl's confidence then she admired him for it. But she did want to ask Greg one question at least.

"Do you understand?" she said. "Why she left him? Do you think she did the right thing? It takes a lot of courage for a woman to walk out on her husband." A sudden thought struck her. "There weren't any children, were there?" she said with anxiety.

Greg shook his head. If only you knew why, he thought. Then he considered his mother's question. Did he think Maureen had been right to leave, to abandon her marriage? Greg had encountered most vagaries of human nature in his career and, although he'd found it a harsh education, experience had taught him that men and women came in many guises, had different weaknesses and perversions. He'd come to the conclusion that Trevor was to be

493

pitied, rather than despised. There was obviously a
deep psychological flaw in his character. But no man
had the right to inflict a celibate, childless life on a
woman. That made a mockery of the very marriage
vows he'd taken.

"Yes," he said finally. "I think she was right."

"Is it that she kept it from you, all this time?"

Greg gave a slight shrug. "It was at first, but I
think I've come to terms with that. What's bothering me is – where do I go from here?" He looked
directly at his mother. "I love Maureen, and before
all this happened, I'd begun to hope we'd spend the
rest of our lives together." He spread his hands in a
gesture of despair. "All this complicates things."

Sarah, her brow creased with concern, said,
"You're thinking of marriage?"

He nodded. "But you know how the Church views
divorce."

"Have you spoken to her since she told you?"

Greg got up and began to pace the room. "That's
just the point. I haven't. I feel it wouldn't be fair to
go on seeing her – not until I've come to a decision."

Sarah felt helpless. It would have been so much
easier to advise him if she'd met the girl. As it was
she found it impossible to judge the situation. But
she knew one thing – Maureen must be going

through hell at the moment, not having heard anything from him. That was just like Greg. Even as a child he'd taken things seriously, had displayed almost an adult sense of responsibility.

"But why," she asked him, "do you feel you have to come to an *immediate* decision? Sometimes, Greg, it's better to let things take their natural course. And you're being unfair not contacting Maureen."

Startled, Greg said, "Do you think so?"

"Of course. Put yourself in her shoes. She drops a bombshell like this, and then you disappear for nearly two weeks! Tell me, what does your gut instinct tell you to do?"

"I want to see her."

"Then go on seeing her. Get to know her better, meet her family. For heaven's sake, you only met her earlier this year – it's far too soon to think of marriage, anyway."

"You and Dad met and married within six months," he pointed out.

"Maybe. But we didn't have complications. Take it slowly, Greg. Time will sort out what's the best thing to do." Her eyes were thoughtful as they rested on her son. "And I think I'd better meet her, don't you?"

* * *

To Maureen, the days and nights seemed endless as, filled with alternating hope and despair, she waited to hear from Greg. How could she ever have envied Carol, even been fleetingly attracted to the good looks of Sean? Maureen knew that her love for Greg was deeper and more lasting than her feelings for Trevor had ever been. The thought that he might end their relationship was unbearable, and what made the waiting worse was that she knew she would only have herself to blame.

Although she thought miserably, if she'd told him that first night at the Palais, then he would probably never have asked her out in the first place!

The morning he rang was a busy one at work. She had no opportunity to sense his mood and, conscious of a queue at the enquiry window, there was only time to agree to see him that night. How she got through the rest of the day without making mistakes, she didn't know, but as always with figures Maureen could work on automatic pilot. It was fortunate, because her mind was in constant turmoil, and by evening she had a splitting headache.

And so it was that when she opened the door to Greg's sharp knock, her face was extremely pale and strained. With her eyes full of apprehension she could only stare at him in silence, half afraid, yet longing for him to speak, and when he did, it was just one sentence: "Let's just see how it goes."

CHAPTER THIRTY-NINE

Several days later, Beryl returned from a shopping trip one Saturday, so upset that Frank had to stop listening to the football commentary.

"I just couldn't believe it," she told him. "To cut me, like that! Face to face we were, outside Woolworth's!" Her face was flushed with anger as she told him. "I went to speak – in fact I half smiled, but Henry just looked right through me, and as for Norah, well, her face looked more like a sour prune than ever!"

Frank frowned. There was no need for that sort of behaviour!

Beryl continued, "The next thing I knew, they'd walked right past me! I mean, as if it's our fault Maureen left their precious son!"

"Well, don't let it upset you," he told her. "If they

498

want to be like that, let them. It's no skin off our nose."

She looked at him with indignation. "You might say that, but it didn't happen to you!" She stopped pacing around and sat down. "Do you know, it's a horrible experience. It shook me up, I don't mind telling you."

As he visualised the humiliating scene, Frank felt a slow anger. How dare the Mountfords treat his wife like that!

"I wish I'd been with you," he muttered.

Beryl shrugged and marched into the kitchen, still seething. She'd never liked them, the stuck-up pair! As for Trevor, she didn't care if she never saw him again! The trouble he's caused in this family, she thought bitterly. If it wasn't for him – and she had no doubt that he was at fault – their Maureen would be living close by, perhaps married with young children. They'd be able to have nice family get-togethers, instead of having to drive fifty miles before they could see her! Trevor Mountford had a lot to answer for, Beryl thought grimly, as she began to unpack her shopping.

But on Monday, a letter arrived from her younger daughter that swept all thoughts of the slight out of Beryl's mind.

"Go on, then, what does she say?" Frank said, hearing her exclaim.

"She's coming over," Beryl said, and looked up at him, full of excitement. "Greg's bringing her in the car! Listen . . .

'Leicester are playing Stoke on the 7th September, and Greg's going to be off duty, so he'll be giving me a lift. I thought perhaps he and Dad could go to the match together. We should get there just before dinnertime, if that's all right, probably about half past eleven . . .'

"Well, well," Frank said, "that *is* a turn-up for the book." He smiled at Beryl. "It'll be a new experience watching Stoke play, with the opposition next to me."

"Oh, never mind the football! The important thing is that we'll be able to have a look at him!" Beryl glanced down at the letter. "She says they'll be going back the same day – I'll have to let our Sandra know, so she can bring the children over."

"The poor bloke won't know what's hit him," Frank grinned.

Beryl laughed. It was true that little Sue, who was now at nursery school, was a constant chatterbox, while Stevie was a boisterous toddler. "All we'll need is for Mum and Vera to come round."

Frank was alarmed. "Hey, you can't do that, the

bloke's going to feel swamped. You're reading too much into this – it's not as if this is anything serious. She's still married, don't forget.'

"I can hardly not tell them she's coming," Beryl pointed out.

Frank sighed. She was right, of course, but Greg was going to feel as if he was on parade! And as for Vera, he shuddered to think what gems she was likely to come out with.

* * *

"Wasn't it lucky you managed to change your duty?" Maureen said, fiddling in the glove compartment for a map. "Not that I need a map," she told him. "Dad says just stick to the A50."

"In answer to your question, luck didn't come into it," he grinned. "It was all down to my forward planning."

"I bet Mum's already rushing about!" Maureen smiled at the image. "Fussing over what to give you for lunch, plumping up the cushions, dusting the furniture."

Greg laughed. "She sounds like my mother. She wants to meet you, by the way."

Maureen felt a warm glow. She'd always wondered why Greg had never taken her home – after all, his mother only lived a couple of miles away. He'd told her that Sarah had a heart condition, so she'd assumed that perhaps she wasn't well enough for visitors. The fact he was suggesting it now, after her confession, was tremendously reassuring, although Maureen was painfully aware she could take nothing for granted.

As they drove along, travelling through Ashby-de-la-Zouch, and waiting at the traffic-lights to cross the river at Burton-on-Trent, she sat watching the scenery, content just to be with him. She knew what he was trying to achieve, and in a way she welcomed the lighter, more casual element in their relationship. Her life had been so full of problems the last few years, it would be good to have a carefree period.

Greg was enjoying the trip. It was the first time he'd driven any distance with Maureen at his side, and the atmosphere in the car was relaxed and in a strange way, intimate. As they approached their destination he became fascinated by the pottery factories lining each side of the main road, while Maureen explained how six linked towns made up the area known worldwide as 'The Potteries'.

"There's a tremendous tradition here," she said. "Most families have a member working on the potbanks, as they're called. We're a bit unusual, because we've no-one working there at the moment, although Gran used to be a lithographer, and Aunt Vera used to work in the clay end."

To Greg, the whole area seemed very industrial, although Maureen told him that it was surrounded by beautiful countryside.

"Turn left just ahead," she instructed, "and then the second right." Within minutes they were pulling up outside the house.

Beryl, who'd been flitting between kitchen and parlour window, saw them arrive, and hurriedly removed her apron.

"They're here!" she shouted, and Frank laid aside his pipe and got up. Beryl was already opening the door and going out on to the pavement, to hug Maureen before stepping back, eager for her first glimpse of Greg. He came round the back of the car and held out his hand, "How do you, Mrs Matthews."

He smiled, but already Maureen was drawing him away to go and meet Frank. "Is the kettle on, Mum?" she called over her shoulder. "We're parched."

Beryl followed the couple indoors, closing the door behind her with satisfaction. Well, he wasn't that much to look at, quite ordinary really, but already she'd gained an impression of strength, of integrity, and that was just what her daughter needed. At least this time, Maureen hadn't been bedazzled by glamour!

Frank came forward, hand outstretched. "Glad to meet you, Greg," his eyes twinkled, "or should I call you Sergeant?"

"Detective-Sergeant, Dad," Maureen said with pride.

Greg laughed. "No, Greg will be fine, Mr Matthews."

"Call me Frank."

"And it's Beryl," she said, as she came in. "Right, sit yourselves down, tea won't be a minute."

Greg sat on the small sofa and looked around the almost unnaturally tidy parlour, guessing that it wasn't used on a daily basis. There was a china cabinet at the side of him, displaying delicate ornaments of china flowers, and several famous Royal Doulton figures. He noticed a Beswick china horse and foal, the same design he'd bought as a silver wedding present for his parents.

"Good journey?" Frank said.

"Fine. It was quite interesting really, particularly coming through Longton and Fenton. I haven't been to the Potteries before."

"Aye. Well, it's not changed much, although we're beginning to lose the old pottery kilns."

"It's a pity that," Maureen said. "They were so much a part of the landscape."

"Yes, but folks won't miss the dust!" Frank said.

"You can say that again," Beryl said, as she brought in a tray of tea and biscuits. "Help yourselves to milk and sugar."

Maureen got up. "I'll just . . ." She went through the kitchen to the scullery and out of the back door to the outside toilet. It was odd, but when she was growing up, she'd taken such things for granted. Now, such a way of life seemed positively antiquated – even Freda's modest home had modern facilities. If only her parents owned their own house, she thought, they might have been eligible for an improvement grant from the council. Washing her hands in the kitchen sink, the aroma of home cooking made her mouth water and, going back into the parlour, she said, "I see you've been busy, Mum."

"Well, we can't expect Greg to go off to the match without a hot meal inside him!"

"What are we having?" Maureen took a biscuit and drank her tea gratefully.

"Lamb chops, I hope that's all right?" Beryl turned anxiously to Greg.

"Lovely," he assured her.

"All I usually get on a Saturday is egg and chips!"

Frank grinned.

"Yes, you look hard done to," Beryl said tartly, bristling that he'd implied she'd gone to a lot of trouble. Not that she hadn't. She'd made an apple-pie, the table was set with the best cloth, the cutlery polished, paper serviettes in place. At tea-time, Nellie was bringing her fruitcake – a larger one than usual, and Sandra, who had now learned to drive, was bringing the children plus a sherry trifle, at four o'clock. When Greg returned from the match, he would be facing the full family forum! Never mind what Frank thinks, Beryl thought. He's blinding himself to the truth about this relationship. A mother always knows!

Fortunately, when she told them of the afternoon's plans, Greg didn't look too discomforted. In fact Beryl intercepted amused glances being exchanged between the young couple, and began to relax. Covertly she watched her daughter's 'young man', pleased to see him enjoying her cooking, and she remained quiet, listening to Greg's answers to Frank's questions about his job in the police force. She and Maureen would have plenty of time to chat later. The only time Beryl grew impatient was when the subject of football came up, and she shot Frank an exasperated glance. The two men could discuss that all afternoon, they needed to use the short time they had to find out more about Greg's personal life!

"Maureen tells me your mother's not in good health, Greg," she said, interjecting.

"No, I'm afraid not," he said. "Unfortunately, she has a serious heart condition." As he smiled at her, Beryl suddenly realised why Maureen found him attractive. "That's why I transferred from the Met, " he continued, "so I can keep an eye on her, make sure she doesn't do too much."

Beryl nodded with approval. She looked at the Westminster chimes clock on the mantelpiece. "I'd better make you a cup of tea before you go. Frank likes to get there early."

"I do," Frank said, "and I want to call in the tobacconists." He turned to Greg. "It's not much out of the way, and you'll be able to walk through the town."

"Such as it is," Beryl said. "Remember, he's used to London and Leicester."

"But Mum," Maureen was defensive, "you can never compare Stoke-on-Trent to other cities. Everything's split up into the six towns."

"And that makes it unique," Greg smiled. "In any case, it's the people who make an area."

"And the folk in the Potteries are the salt of the

earth," Beryl said staunchly. "You won't find harder workers anywhere in the country!"

"I'll echo that," Frank said.

"Do you want me to make you a flask of tea?" Beryl looked at Greg. "Frank usually gets Bovril at the ground at half-time, but . . ."

"No, Beryl, don't trouble. Bovril will suit me fine." Greg looked enquiringly at Maureen, who told him where the toilet was. As soon as he'd gone out of the back door, she turned eagerly to her parents.

"Well?" she demanded. "What do you think?"

Frank reached for his coat. "Ask me after I've spent more time with him." Beryl hastily whispered, "I like him – but we can talk later."

Greg, returning, guessed he'd been the subject of conversation, and hid a smile – this was only the beginning. According to Maureen, her Aunt Vera was a right battleaxe! But it would be good to meet the rest of the family. Frank and Beryl had given him a warm welcome and he'd liked them immediately. It was a relief too, to see that Maureen came from a close family unit. Greg had seen too many criminals scarred by childhood insecurity, not to appreciate the advantage of good parents.

CHAPTER FORTY

The two men left for the match, and as they walked along the main road into Stoke, Frank pointed out the Royal Minton factory on the right.

"Mum's got a piece of Minton," Greg said. "It's got a gold-edged red border with a Constable print in the centre."

"She likes china, does she?"

"Very much."

"You'll have to bring her over, take her to one of the factory shops," Frank suggested.

Greg was about to reply when Frank, suddenly taking a sharp intake of breath, said abruptly, "Do me a favour! Walk on ahead, mingle with the other supporters – I'll meet you just inside Woolworth's."

Hearing the urgency in the other man's voice,

Greg, used to reacting quickly, moved away from Frank, at first falling into step with a man in front, then after passing him, crossed over the road, to where he could see Woolworth's a short distance ahead.

Frank slowed his own steps as his son-in-law approached. Why, Frank groaned inwardly, why after all this time, do I have to go and bump into him today, of all days!

Trevor didn't see him at first, and then Frank saw his eyes narrow as recognition dawned.

"Hello, Trevor." Frank stood squarely before him, and Trevor came to a halt.

"Hello, Frank."

"It's been a long time." Frank's gaze swiftly searched the road ahead. There was no sign of Greg.

"Nearly two years," Trevor said stiffly. "How's Beryl?"

"She's fine. And yourself?"

"I can't grumble." Trevor hesitated, and looked down, fiddling with his library books. "How's Maureen?"

"Fine, so far as I know. Enjoying her job in Leicester." Frank kept his tone brisk, upbeat.

"Is she still living at Carol's?"

"Oh yes. She'd have let you have her new address

otherwise. After all, it will only be another year before the solicitors can get on with it. Better for both of you."

"I expect you're right." Trevor's voice was terse.

"Oh," Frank said, "there is just one matter. Tell Henry that if ever he and Norah cut my wife again, they'll have me to deal with. It's not our fault that things didn't work out between you and Maureen. We don't blame them, and they shouldn't blame us." He saw colour rise in Trevor's face, and suddenly realised he and Beryl had no way of knowing what sort of lies he'd told his parents. For a split second, anger tempted him to carry the matter further, and then he calmed down. What was the point? The less they had to do with the Mountford family the better.

"I'd better be off," he said. "Don't want to miss the kick-off." Frank held out his hand, deciding that civility was his best policy. "I wish you all the best, Trevor."

"Thank you, Frank. You too."

Greg, who had slipped into a shop doorway, saw the two men shake hands. He'd had a good view from where he'd stood, and soon guessed that the fair-haired young man talking to Frank must be Maureen's husband. That would explain the cloak and dagger stuff. Greg wasn't sure that he liked 'standing in the shadows', but could understand Frank's reluctance to have the two men meet. He tried, despite the distance, to gain an impression of the man Maureen had married, and assessing his polo neck sweater, camel scarf, and charcoal grey overcoat, guessed that appearances mattered a lot to him. Was that why he'd married Maureen? Certainly, an attractive young wife would have enhanced his promotion prospects. From his vantage point, Greg could see what Maureen meant when she'd described her feelings for Trevor as infatuation. What young, impressionable young girl wouldn't have fallen for him, particularly one with her head full of Hollywood glamour? Having actually seen his striking good looks, Greg felt even more conscious of his shortcomings in that department, and looked down with a wry grimace at his well-worn duffle coat, before going to stand inside the entrance of Woolworth's.

Frank joined him and with embarrassment began to apologise, but Greg held up a hand. "No need, Frank," he said. "I know who it was, and I understand perfectly."

A man after my own heart, Frank thought with relief, as they went to the tobacconists. Talks good sense, and economical with his words. He bought his

St Bruno, and then they walked among the crowds to the football ground.

"I can't wait to see Stanley Matthews in action," Greg said. "He's been a hero of mine for years."

"There's no-one to touch him — just look out for number seven," Frank said. "I remember when he rejoined the Club in 1961, after fourteen years away at Blackpool. They had the BBC Sportsview cameras at his first home match against Huddersfield, and there were traffic jams everywhere. We won, 3-1," he added with pride.

"Well, you won't win today," Greg chaffed, and it was with an easy camaraderie between them that they turned into the turnstile at the Boothen End of the Victoria Ground.

* * *

"Right, thank goodness that's done!" Maureen hung up the tea towel over the handle of the oven door to dry. "How can four people make so much washing-up? Come on, let's go and sit in the front room."

Beryl waited until they were settled, then said, "Right, now you can tell me how you are."

"I'm absolutely fine, Mum, honestly. Anyway, before I say anything else, have you thought about getting on to the landlord about having this place modernised? It's ridiculous in this day and age, not

513

having a bathroom or inside toilet!"

Beryl shrugged. "I know some of the people who've bought their house are putting one in, but I don't think we'd stand much chance."

"Perhaps you should think about taking out a mortgage yourselves. You'd get it at a cheap price as sitting tenants. It would be an investment."

Beryl gazed at her daughter, envying her youth and enthusiasm – as if she and Frank wanted to saddle themselves with a debt at their time of life! But following on that thought came another. Maybe there was something in what Maureen said. "I'll see what your Dad thinks," she promised.

"And you really like Greg? Honestly?" Maureen looked anxiously at her mother.

Beryl laughed. "I've already told you what I think. And your dad will be sizing him up this afternoon, believe me!" She frowned, fiddling with the charms on her bracelet. "Mind you, he's a bit uneasy about you getting involved with anyone – not while you're still married."

Maureen avoided her mother's gaze. "It's not serious. We just enjoy each other's company, that's all."

"I don't want you getting hurt again, that's all. What about Trevor – do you still have any feelings for *him?*" Beryl was wary of asking too many questions; it was a rare moment when Maureen confided in anyone, even her own mother.

"I don't feel anything, not in that way. To be honest, I wouldn't care if I never saw him again!"

Beryl, hearing the bitterness in her daughter's voice, longed to ask yet again what had made her leave her husband, but then thought, why spoil the day? If she wants to tell me, she will.

And so she waited, but Maureen simply looked at the clock. "Gosh, I'd better tidy myself up for the onslaught."

Ten minutes later, a beaming Sandra came through the door, ushering an excited Sue and tearful Stevie. "He just tripped up as he got out of the car," she explained. "He could fall over his own feet, this one. How are you, pet?"

Maureen went into her sister's affectionate hug, surprised to find tears coming to her eyes. How she missed everyone – Mum, Dad, Sandra, the children, even Gran and Aunt Vera. At that moment Leicester seemed a hundred miles away, and she couldn't imagine why she'd ever gone away from her roots. Suddenly, Maureen realised that if she hadn't met Greg, she would probably have been thinking about returning, finding another more responsible job, perhaps even looking into furthering her education.

She was fond of Freda and more than fond of Carol, but it wasn't the same as having her own family around her.

"Just look at that!" Sandra said, looking at the mid-thigh length of Maureen's skirt. "Trust you to be able to get away with one that short!"

Beryl, who'd always been proud of the affection between her two girls, smiled with happiness and hugged her grandchildren. "Hello, my poppets! My, don't you both look smart!"

"That little pink cardie you knitted for Sue really suits her," Sandra said. "Hang on, I'll just fetch the trifle from the car."

Maureen was staring in astonishment at the two small children. "I can't believe how much they've grown!"

Sandra came back with a covered glass dish. "I'll just pop it in the fridge."

Beryl went to open the fridge door for her. The gleaming white appliance was still a controversial luxury, but even Frank had to admit that frozen peas tasted almost as good as the fresh ones. Oh, she thought happily, this is almost like Christmas – having every one together.

* * *

It was a draw – Stoke City 3, Leicester City 3, and the two men were full of the match as they walked home. Greg listened as Frank enthused about the goals. "Those two by Dennis Viollet were beauties," he said, "and with Bill Asprey scoring as well . . ."

Greg grinned, letting the older man recount the highlights. After all, it was Stoke's home match. His own thoughts were more of the social tea party awaiting him.

The moment the two men opened the front door and came into the parlour, all heads turned. Nellie and Vera were seated on the sofa, Sandra in one armchair, Maureen in the other, while the two children were crayoning in a colouring book on the hearthrug. Sue and Stevie scrambled up, expectation shining on their faces. Frank, with an indulgent smile on his face, put a hand in his pocket and gave them their customary lollipop. "Thank you, Grandad," they chorused, while Greg stood just inside the door, his eyes seeking those of Maureen. They smiled, an affectionate easy smile, and Nellie's sharp eyes both saw and approved.

"Come on in, then, let's have a look at you," barked Vera.

Greg moved forward, stood before her and, with an inscrutable expression, gave an official salute.

"Reporting for inspection, Ma'am."

Everyone watched her gimlet eyes sweep over him. "I see you were on the back row when they gave out looks! All the better if you ask me!" She darted a meaningful glance at Maureen.

"Our Vera, don't be so rude," Nellie chided. She looked up at Greg, who looked even taller in the small room, and he held out his hand.

"You must be Maureen's gran! I'm so pleased to meet you."

"And how did you know she's the grandmother and not me?" demanded Vera.

Frank hid a grin, Beryl looked the other way, and Maureen, seeing Greg's embarrassment, began to laugh.

Vera shot Maureen a sharp glance, and then, seeing the joke, said, "All right, you don't need to tell me!"

"You're unique, Aunt Vera, that's why," Maureen said. "Don't ever change!"

Vera sniffed, but Maureen could tell she was pleased.

Beryl got up. "Come on then, tea's all ready."

Later, Maureen watched Greg playing with the children. He'd told them he was a policeman and was teaching them to bend their legs at the knees and say, "Evening, all!" to squeals of merriment. He'd make a wonderful father, she thought suddenly, and seeing her family relaxed and happy in his company, she knew without doubt that this was the man she wanted to spend the rest of her life with.

When it was time for Sandra to take the over-excited children home, she managed to say in hushed tones to Maureen, "He's lovely – but don't rush into anything – remember last time."

Maureen whispered back, "There's no chance of that, not with the divorce and everything."

Eventually, Maureen and Greg, after yet another cup of tea, decided it was time they went too.

Just before they left, Beryl pressed two brown-paper bags into Maureen's hands.

"There's a dozen oatcakes for Freda, fresh this morning, tell her, and half a dozen for Greg's mother." At Greg's enquiring look, Beryl laughed. "Maureen will tell you what to do with them."

And so, in a light-hearted mood, they drove back to Leicester, at first chatting about the events of the day, then travelling in companionable silence listening to the radio. Greg had decided not to mention that he'd seen Trevor – this day belonged to the present, he wanted no intrusion from past problems.

Maureen was tired but content. The visit had been a huge success, and as she gazed out of the window and lights began to appear in houses lining the road, she wondered just what the future would hold. Greg loved her, she was sure of that, but both he and his mother were Catholics, and the issue of her divorce would be a huge obstacle. But then she shrugged away the problem. It was foolish to let her mind run ahead. So far, Greg had never mentioned marriage, and until he did there was no point in thinking about it.

CHAPTER FORTY-ONE

Maureen and Greg continued to see each other as often as possible, although both avoided any mention of the future. Living for the moment, they danced at the Palais, and to the big band sound at the De Montfort Hall. When she sat enthralled at the glamour and sophistication of such stars as Sean Connery in *Goldfinger*, Maureen would sit nestled in Greg's encircling arm, and wonder how she could ever have been so immature as to confuse the celluloid screen with real life. They teased each other over their clumsiness with chopsticks when they went to a Chinese restaurant, and whenever possible on Sundays, wrapped up against the early morning chill and drove to Bradgate. There, they would tramp over the bracken, delighting in glimpses of the herds of deer, and would return to join Sarah for a late breakfast of grilled bacon, sausages, mushrooms and tomatoes.

Sarah, whose every sense had been on the alert when Greg first brought his girlfriend home, had liked Maureen immediately. The girl who stood by Greg's side, her eyes wide with anxiety, her tension betraying her nervousness, was, in a strange way, one she recognised. Sarah couldn't explain it, but she felt as though a piece of a jigsaw had slotted into place, and as she grew to know Maureen better, she knew that she couldn't have chosen a better prospective daughter-in-law. But still the obstacles loomed large, and every week Sarah would stand before the statue of the Sacred Heart, and light a candle, praying that a way would be found.

At Christmas, Maureen went home to find Beryl concerned about Frank.

"He took it very badly, President Kennedy being assassinated. Everyone had such high hopes of him," she told Maureen. "Seeing you will cheer him up no end."

Greg spent whatever time he wasn't on duty with Sarah. But the New Year was theirs and together with Sean and Carol they joined the noisy crowds in the Town Hall Square in the centre of Leicester to celebrate. In the midst of the exuberance, at the birth of 1964, Maureen and Greg stood for a moment wrapped in each other's arms, their faces cold, their hearts full of warmth and love. And then everyone was shouting "Happy New Year!" and Maureen found herself not only hugging her friends, but in the atmosphere of general euphoria, even strangers.

But as time passed, they were both finding it increasingly difficult to restrain their lovemaking. Either one or the other would draw back: Greg, constrained by his conscience – after all Maureen was still married to another man; Maureen, sorely tempted to go 'all the way', didn't dare to risk getting pregnant. The thought of making another drastic mistake was not to be borne. She and Carol sometimes talked about the new 'permissive society' which was emerging, hardly able to believe the changing climate of sexual freedom, but it seemed far removed from their own culture.

"Now if we lived in swinging London, it would be a different matter," Carol joked, but Maureen had her doubts. Their upbringing was too ingrained for them suddenly to become promiscuous.

"It's all the fault of this Pill," Freda declared. "No good will come of it, you mark my words. I'm not religious, but there's a right way to live and a wrong way to live. And changing partners like bed-sheets isn't one of them!"

And so, Greg and Maureen carried on 'courting,' as Nellie would call it, and gradually winter gave way to spring. It was on a day when the daffodils were coming into bloom, and the trees tinting with green again, that Carol burst into the sitting-room, her eyes shining with excitement.

"You'll never guess what's happened." She paused dramatically. "Sean's proposed!"

Freda put a hand to her mouth, while Maureen jumped up and threw her arms around her friend. "That's brilliant!" She drew back. "You did say yes, didn't you?"

"What do you think?" Carol laughed. "And – wait for it – he wants to get married as soon as possible! The wedding's going to be in Ireland – he wants us to get married in his parish church." She grinned at Maureen. "You never know, I might end up as one of your lot. You're expected to be chief bridesmaid, or perhaps I should say, matron of honour!"

She turned to Freda. "That's all right, isn't it, Mum? Only it's not as if we have any strong religious views or anything."

Freda, who'd remained silent, reassured her. "Of

course it is." Then she frowned. "Aren't you rushing things a bit?"

"Not at all. It's been over a year, now," Carol pointed out, "and Sean's heard of a furnished flat that's going. We're going to see it tomorrow, after we've chosen an engagement ring!"

Unexpectedly, Freda felt her eyes sting with tears. For a moment she forgot that this was what she'd hoped, that Carol would be happily settled, that her own relationship with Vincent would be free of obstacles. For so many years, Carol had been all Freda had lived, worked, and planned for; it hurt that she would now take second place in her life. But then she looked at Carol's glowing face and reminded herself that her daughter was nearly twenty-five, a young woman more than ready for marriage and motherhood. And thinking of the prospect of grandchildren, little ones to hold and cuddle, she got up and went to open the cupboard where they kept the wineglasses.

"I think this calls for a drink!" She turned to Carol. "And where's Sean? Why didn't he come and ask my permission?"

Carol giggled. "He wanted to, but I told him that didn't apply once you were over twenty-one. Anyway, it's old-fashioned – no-one does that sort of thing any more."

That's the trouble with youth these days, Freda thought, as she poured out glasses of sherry. They want to throw out all the old traditions.

"We'd planned to tell you together," Carol explained, "but then his duty changed, and, well," she smiled happily at them, "I couldn't keep it to myself!"

Maureen laughed. "I think you'd have exploded like a bottle of pop!"

"Exactly. You don't mind, do you, Mum?"

"No, of course not." Freda said. "You know how much I like Sean – I'm thrilled to bits for the pair of you." And, she told herself, as she listened to the two girls discussing the wedding, at least now I have Vincent.

* * *

It was a lovely summer's day for Carol and Sean's wedding at a Dublin church. Maureen, dressed in a pale blue, ballerina-length dress, surrounded by four excited small bridesmaids, their faces glowing beneath their garlands of fresh flowers, watched as the couple made their vows. Once the ceremony was over, and the register signed, the bridal procession returned down the aisle where, in a pew near the front, Greg stood. As she passed, Maureen's eyes met his, and for a split unguarded second, she saw the anguish in his eyes. Stricken; she lowered her gaze, trying to bury her worries among the noise of the partying that followed. But Greg's expression remained with her, and she knew that things couldn't go on as they were. If only . . . the thought was constantly with her – if only she'd met Greg first, if only she'd realised the difference between infatuation and real love, *if only* she hadn't married Trevor.

Greg had been struggling for months with his conscience, knowing how much he loved Maureen, certain that his life lay with her, but always the problem of her divorce lay like a heavy mantle on his shoulders. He was desperate to ask her to marry him, was grateful that she never raised the subject, never made him feel pressured. But the dilemma was always there, a barrier between them. If he married Maureen, he would not be able to take his vows before God – they would have to be married in a Register Office. And that, for a man of Greg's beliefs, was an almost insurmountable obstacle. For as far as the Church was concerned, he and Maureen would be 'living in sin'; their marriage would not be valid and he would be unable to receive the Sacraments.

Sarah, wearing a peach crêpe-de-chine dress and jacket, stood by his side. To Greg's uneasiness, she had insisted she was well enough for the journey, although even as she enjoyed the ceremony, she sensed and understood his torment. But while longing to see her son happy, she had to accept that the decision was a matter for Greg's conscience, and his alone.

Maureen, during the months they had spent together, had tried simply to enjoy the fact that they were in love. But the uncertainty about their future was increasingly on her mind. Her fear, one that was beginning to surface ever more frequently, was that she might lose him. And what would she do then? Her whole situation at the moment seemed so unsettled. She was becoming tired of not having her own space, of sleeping in the cramped boxroom, which also housed some of Freda and Carol's belongings. She missed having her own home terribly. She'd loved the new house she'd shared with Trevor – had found enormous pleasure in furnishing it, and at times she would lie awake, indulging in nostalgia as her thoughts wandered through each freshly decorated room. But it had been her decision to leave, and bitter though it was, she had to accept the penalty. And lately she'd had another cause for anxiety. Sean was already living in the furnished flat in Leicester, and once the honeymoon was over, Carol would be joining him. Maureen knew that she needed to move on. It was obvious that Freda and Vincent were going to make their life together and, although Freda was kindness itself, Maureen had no wish to impose her presence on a newly married couple.

Now, as she watched Carol moving with ease among her new relatives at the reception, Maureen couldn't help a pang of envy. What did the next few months hold for her? A cheap bedsit? Remaining in a job which she found less and less stimulating? If it wasn't for Greg, Maureen knew she'd have no hesitation in moving back to Stoke-on-Trent. At least there she would be with her own family.

"Whew!" Greg rejoined her. "I thought I was fit, until I had to dance an Irish jig!" He nodded across to where Sarah was talking to one of Sean's aunts, and grinned. "Pity your Aunt Vera isn't here, she'd have met her match in Auntie Kathleen."

Maureen smiled. "Why?"

Greg leaned closer and whispered, "She's just told me in a loud voice, that Sean's cousin – you know, the priest who married them – wet his pants when he took his first test at school! Not only that, but he

529

was standing right next to her when she said it."

Maureen burst into laughter. "Can you imagine being in the same room with the pair of them!"

But after Greg had gone to get some more drinks, Maureen became thoughtful. She looked over at the priest, a tall, sandy-haired man in his thirties. She recalled his confidence on the altar, his obvious high-standing among his parishioners. He'd overcome his early trauma, so why couldn't she? All these years she'd imagined she was unique in her fear of examinations; now she admitted with self-honesty that she'd used the travesty of her eleven-plus as an excuse, a crutch.

Suddenly, she felt ashamed of her weakness and, when Greg returned, she said, "I've decided something. I'm going to enrol at the Adult Education Centre – you know, the one in Wellington Street? Perhaps I'll do 'O' Level English Language. And if I manage to pass that, I'll do English Literature as well."

"That's fantastic, I'm proud of you!" In his delight, Greg hugged her, and a passing cousin teased, "Sure it'll be your turn next," before chasing after a toddler. They just smiled and then Greg returned to the previous subject. "I'll tell you something else. I read in the paper that Harold Wilson is talking of creating an Open University. The idea is that people who missed out in the ordinary way can study for a degree at home." As Maureen's eyes lit up, he added, "It'll probably take years to come into effect, but you could be working towards it."

"That would be perfect," she said. "I'm determined to conquer this silly phobia, Greg – it's holding me back. I've got the money to pay for a course as well!"

Startled, he glanced at her.

"Remind me," she said softly, "when we get back, to tell you about Bernard."

Freda, with Vincent at her side, found her emotions a mixture of happiness, pride and – to her shame – jealousy, as she watched her daughter being enfolded into the warmth of the large Irish family. However, she knew she had to learn to share her daughter and, when Vincent quietly took her hand, she realised how lucky she was to have found such love twice in her life. As she watched Maureen and Greg circle the small dance floor, she could only hope that things would work out them too.

And then Carol and Sean were leaving for their honeymoon in Kinsale, and in the bustle and excitement all problems were momentarily forgotten. Except for Maureen and Greg, standing a little apart, their hands entwined, feeling like onlookers on a scene which would never be theirs.

CHAPTER FORTY-TWO

"Do you think there'll be any problem with the divorce?" Sandra, who'd recently sprained her ankle, winced as she rested it on a footstool. It was the Potteries' Wakes holiday, and John had taken the children to the annual Pat Collins Fair in Hanley. Sandra was making the most of a rare chance to chat to her parents without interruptions.

Frank shook his head. "I shouldn't think so. It's all cut and dried. Maureen walked out and Trevor's suing for desertion – it's as simple as that."

"Soon gone, though, hasn't it? The three years, I mean," Sandra said, taking another Eccles cake from the plate Beryl held out to her. "I'm amazed Trevor ever agreed to a divorce in the first place. It must have been an awful blow to his pride, and he's certainly got plenty of that!"

Beryl sipped her tea. "A lot more went on in that marriage than we'll ever know – I've always said it. It still worries me, even now."

"Well, she's got a different bloke in Greg," Frank said. "I know which of the two of them I'd want behind me in the trenches, I can tell you that!"

"You didn't fight in the trenches, Dad. That was the First World War," Sandra said, finishing off the last crumbs of her cake.

"It's just an expression, love."

"And I know what you mean!" Beryl got up to take out some of the used crockery. "I think we all agree that Greg's the right man for her, but can it lead to anything? That's what I want to know. She's been through enough without another disappointment."

"I can't tell you that," Frank said. "There's no getting away from it – Catholics and divorce don't mix. Everyone knows it! I don't think anyone can forecast what the outcome will be."

Sandra's eyes clouded. "Nothing ever seems to go right for our Maureen."

"Well, I've tried to talk to her about it," Beryl said tartly, "but you know what she's like."

"Never changes, does she?" Sandra smiled. "Still

doesn't communicate, bless her."

"Not like your Aunt Vera. Do you know what Nellie told me the other day . . ." and Beryl launched into a description of Vera's latest public gaffe.

* * *

Maureen, to her surprise, was finding that as the date of her divorce grew nearer, instead of the simple relief she'd expected to feel, her emotions were more complicated – remembering the first time she'd seen Trevor in the ballroom at Trentham Gardens and how excited she'd been when they began to go out together. How had it all gone so terribly wrong? She was still convinced that his cold, undemonstrative upbringing was in some way to blame. There was no affection in that household; she'd never received even a hug from either Norah or Henry – was it any wonder their son was incapable of physical warmth? She wondered what Trevor had told them – probably some story putting all the blame on her. It just seemed so sad that someone you'd loved, or thought you did, could pass out of your life so completely. She and Greg had never talked about her first marriage, not since the night she'd told him the truth. Greg had said that as far as he was concerned, that part of her life was in the past, and Maureen had no wish to raise what was still a painful subject.

It was on the first Sunday after the Decree Absolute that they drove to one of the area's beauty spots. The day was warm and sunny as they strolled along the towpath at Foxton Locks, the scene tranquil with patches of shade where trees dipped their branches down to the water. Stopping occasionally to admire the brightly painted narrow-boats, they walked with their hands linked, not talking a lot, just content to enjoy the fresh air.

Eventually, Greg looked down at Maureen. "So," he said, "it's all over."

"Yes." For a few seconds, she remained silent. "You know, I blame myself in a way, for how things turned out."

"How do you mean?"

"I should never have married him, Greg. I should have realised how cold he was, that day he bullied me into getting married in his church and not mine."

Greg frowned. "What was wrong with your church?"

Maureen looked up at him in puzzlement. "It was Roman Catholic."

Greg halted so abruptly that she almost stumbled.

He released her hand and swung round to face her.

"You mean you didn't get married in a Catholic church?"

Bewildered, Maureen said, "You know I didn't, I told you . . . I must have." They stood aside to let a man walking his lurcher go past, and she repeated, "I *must* have told you!"

"You didn't! Maureen, for God's sake, have you any idea what you've put me through?" Greg slowly shook his head. "I can't believe it! All these months!"

"I can't see how it matters," Maureen said in confusion.

"Matters, of course it bloody matters! You're a Catholic, for God's sake, you must know it matters!"

"But I don't!" she protested. "And I *am* a Catholic – well, sort of. I was brought up one, but to be truthful I was never that much into it. I only went to Mass to please Dad."

"So, that's something else I'm finding out about you," he snapped. Maureen, aware that their raised voices were attracting attention, retorted, "Do you think we could go back to the car? If we're going to have a row, I'd rather it was in private."

"Suits me!" Greg's voice was curt and, immediately turning, he began with quick angry strides to walk back along the towpath. Maureen could only follow, struggling in bewilderment to keep up with him, until at last they reached the refuge of the car. Even then, Greg didn't speak, revving up the engine almost before she was seated, and a few minutes later they were out on the main road, and heading back towards Leicester.

"Where are we going?"

"Somewhere quiet."

Maureen gazed out of the window, upset and oblivious to the beauty of the summer leafiness of the trees, the clear blue of the sky. Perhaps it had been a mistake not to mention her past, and how it could affect them, but it's not all my fault, she thought with resentment. *He'd* been the one who'd said, 'Let's see how it goes'. And to Maureen that had meant no pressure, no discussing the future.

Greg's anger, quick to rise, was already being replaced by euphoria. But how on earth had this situation developed? He was a man who was trained to look for clues, and here he'd been going through hell, when the answer was there for the asking! At last he came to the turning he sought, and after a few hundred yards along a quiet country lane, he saw an entrance to a farm gate, and parked the car.

Immediately he turned to face her and, seeing the

misery in her eyes, was struck with remorse. "I'm sorry, sweetheart, I didn't mean to shout at you. Look, start at the beginning, and tell me what happened."

So Maureen told him of Trevor's objection to the Church's teaching on birth control, his refusal to accept what he saw as interference in his life. How he'd given her an ultimatum – to get married in his church, or not at all. "It all sounded so reasonable, the way he put it," she said, "and I didn't have your strong faith, Greg."

Perplexed, he said, "But I've seen you several times at Holy Cross, and you often mention going to Mass. It never occurred to me you'd get married outside the Church."

"I never *used* to go. After I got married I just lapsed. But I told you how ill and depressed I was when I first came to Leicester. The first time I walked down New Walk, I went and sat in Holy Cross – it was so quiet and peaceful. Then gradually," she shrugged, "you know what they say, once a Catholic always a Catholic."

Greg put his arm around her shoulder and drew her to him. "What you don't seem to understand," he said, his voice husky with relief, "is that this means you can get married in a Catholic Church!"

539

"No, I can't," she protested in bewilderment. "I'm divorced!"

"Legally, yes, but not in the eyes of the Church."

Maureen frowned, not understanding.

"Listen. You were a baptised Catholic – right?"

She nodded.

"So, because you didn't have a Catholic wedding, the church wouldn't consider your marriage to be valid. That's the whole point. Certainly your divorce dissolves the legal aspect of your marriage, but from the Catholic point of view, you were never married in the first place."

"Are you certain about this?"

"Absolutely."

"Well, *I* didn't know! And I'm positive that Dad doesn't, nor our Sandra. But then, we don't know anyone else who's been divorced. I suppose unless you're in a position where you have to go into it . . ."

"It's like technicalities of the British judicial system," Greg said. "There's lots of things people don't realise. But did you never think of checking it out with a priest? Not even when you came back to the Church?"

She shook her head. "It never occurred to me."

"Then I don't suppose you've been receiving the Sacraments either?"

Again, she shook her head.

"But once you'd left Trevor, you were no longer 'living in sin', so to speak," Greg explained. "That would mean that after going to Confession, you were free to go back to them."

Maureen stared at him. "I didn't realise, I had no idea!" She was beginning to feel foolish – after all, she prided herself on her general knowledge. And all this time, she'd been sitting in the pew watching others go up to the altar for Communion!

"I'm really sorry, Greg," she said, "about not telling you, I mean. I'm always being told I keep things to myself too much!"

"I suppose I have to take my share of the blame," Greg admitted. "We never discussed it, did we?" He smiled down at her. "Perhaps we can both learn a lesson. After all, we don't want to start our marriage with a communication problem."

Stunned, at first Maureen could hardly take it in. Marriage! He'd said marriage! She swung round to face him and, seeing the joy in her eyes, Greg had no doubt of his answer.

"Do I take it . . . I mean, is this is a proposal?"

Greg looked rueful. "Not quite the romantic one I'd have planned, but yes I suppose it is." He looked down at her, his eyes suddenly serious. "You are going to say yes, aren't you?"

She smiled, her answer shining in her eyes. "You know I am."

"I should hope so." He gazed down into her upturned face. "I wonder if you can possibly have any idea how much I love you? It's been hell these past months, wanting you the way I do and having to hold back. I honestly don't think I could have let you go! Not even if it *had* meant giving up the Church!"

Maureen looked up at him, tracing the outline of his lips with her finger.

"You would have done that? For me?"

Greg nodded, and then they were in each other's arms, with none of the insecurity which had been such a large part of their relationship. Their love had never been in doubt, but now they could look to the future, secure in the knowledge that they would be spending it together. It was several minutes before they reluctantly drew apart.

Glancing at his watch, Greg started up the engine.

"Come on," he said. "Let's go and get this sorted once and for all. I'm going to take you to see my parish priest."

Maureen glanced at him in alarm. "You mean you

aren't sure? About what you just told me?"

"I'm sure! I just want you to hear it from him. And," he smiled at her, "I want him to meet the love of my life."

CHAPTER FORTY-THREE

"This is how it all began," Maureen murmured in contentment. She was standing with her back to Greg, his arms wrapped around her to keep in the warmth in the cold early morning air. They were in Bradgate Park, enjoying the solitude and sense of space, and had stopped on that same hillside to watch a group of deer grazing a short distance away.

"I remember," Greg smiled. "That was the first time I kissed you."

"And now look at the trouble I'm in." Maureen took his hand and placed it gently on her rounded abdomen.

Greg kissed the top of her dark hair. "The sort of trouble I'd like a lot of."

"You're insatiable," she laughed.

"I've told you, this is only the first – I want a football team!" He looked down at her. "Are you happy, Mrs Barlow?"

"Deliriously," Maureen replied, as turning they began to retrace their steps. She brought his hand up to her lips and kissed it gently. "I love you, father of my child."

"Any time I can oblige," he grinned, "just let me know. Mind you, I do find it an ordeal . . ." He broke off, horrified that he could be so tactless. The last thing he wanted to do was to bring back unhappy memories of Trevor!

But Maureen just laughed. She was far too secure in their relationship to let such slips of the tongue bother her. "Yes, I've noticed!"

Their wedding, held in the small Catholic church near Oakvale, had been a quiet one, but their honeymoon, spent in an expensive hotel in Scarborough, had been as romantic as even Maureen could have wished. This time on her wedding night there had been no trepidation, no nervousness. With lovemaking full of passion, tenderness and laughter, any lingering ghosts had been laid to rest forever. Afterwards Maureen had moved into Greg's child-hood home, where Sarah generously vacated her double bedroom for the young couple. The arrangement was only temporary, but although Maureen had become fond of her gentle mother-in-law, she was already becoming restless, longing for her own house, wanting to be settled before their baby was born.

Greg glanced down at his wife, and tweaked the bobble on her red woolly hat. Smiling, she turned to face him, then seeing the serious expression on his face paused, wondered what he was going to say.

"How would you like to move back to your roots, to the Potteries?"

The unexpected direct question made her gaze at him in astonishment. Then with a swift intake of breath, she said, "Greg, that would be wonderful! But how on earth . . ?"

"I could always ask for a transfer," he told her.

"And you'd to that – for me?"

"I'd do anything to make you happy." Greg smiled down into her shining eyes. "I was thinking that if Mum sold her house – she'd be much better with a small bungalow – we could take out a mortgage and buy a place of our own, very close to her. What do you think?"

"Would she do that?"

"She'll want to be near her first grandchild, I've no worries on that score," he said.

Their hands linked, they began to walk on, slowly

this time, as Maureen tried to absorb the implications of Greg's plan. She would be near to her family – her children would be able to play with Sue and Stevie. She just couldn't believe how lucky she was to have met someone like Greg. It was said that everyone deserved a second chance, and she knew she would always be grateful for hers. The very first time Greg saw her, he'd been concerned for her welfare . . .

"How about if we call the baby 'Euston'? You know, after the railway station where we first met," she teased. At Greg's outraged expression, she began to laugh and she was still smiling minutes later when they began to drive home.

THE END